I0681022

Water from Stone

ALSO BY KATHERINE MARIACA-SULLIVAN:

The Stages of Grace - a Novel
coming November 2013

The Complication of Sisters:
Collected Stories & Drawings

When a Loved One Dies: The Complete Guide to
Preparing a Dignified & Meaningful Goodbye

Author! Author! Write, Publish & Market
a Buzz-Creating How-To Book

Author! Author! Use Book Promos & Discounts
to Create BUZZ for Your Book

Author! Author! Format Your Word Document for the Kindle

Ruby Jane - Is She REALLY a Pain?
(with Heather Maurice-Stirnweis)

Water from Stone

Katherine Mariaca-Sullivan

Please note that the author has taken some liberties with mad cow disease, or bovine spongiform encephalopathy (BSE). Because people are not cows, they cannot actually get mad cow disease. Instead, they can develop a similar disease called variant Creutzfeldt-Jakob disease, or vCJD. vCJD is a rare degenerative disease that is always fatal in humans. It is thought that it can be caused by eating beef products containing infected nervous system tissue. Any misinformation about mad cow disease presented in this book (such as it being transferable to humans through drinking infected blood) is included solely for story purposes.

ISBN: 978-0-9892514-9-5 (mobi)

ISBN: 978-0-9892514-8-8 (Paperback)

Published by **Madaket Lane Publishers.**

To my mother, Elizabeth. You taught me to dream big and to follow through. I will always be grateful that I won the parental lottery with you.

To my son, Derek. You are my joy and my pride,
and I feel forever blessed to
be able to witness your journey.

And, finally, to my husband, Tim.
You, always you.

Prologue

Mar.

Lizzie shifts, sending the water bed rolling, and Mar's body flows around her daughter's so that the two remain molded together. The five-year-old has not slept well these past months and has become increasingly withdrawn as interest in her legal case has swelled into obsession. Even now, over the gentle burble of aquarium pumps, the swish of the ceiling fan, and the *crick-crick-crick* of the overweight hamster's wheel, Mar hears the ebb and flow of the reporters who have taken up positions on the front lawn and dammed the street.

She smooths a wisp of Lizzie's white-blond hair from her face and tucks it behind her seashell ear. Though, spooning her from behind, Mar can only see the downy curve of Lizzie's right cheek and the scalloped tip of her eyebrow, she imagines how the little girl's troubled dreams must be playing across her face. She has studied Lizzie, at sleep, at play, in deep concentration. She has sketched her and drawn her and painted her hundreds, if not thousands, of times these past four-plus years. She knows how Lizzie's skin flushes a dappled pink when she dances and how, caught in a fib, her eyes turn down and to the left while the right side of her mouth, the exact color of a conch shell's inner curve, quirks upward. Mar knows how the late afternoon sun plays shadow games with Lizzie's thick lashes and how there is one thin line of new-leaf green that teases from the otherwise cerulean blue of her left eye.

The room is hot. In summer Mar keeps the bedroom windows open but ever since a photographer set up a ladder in the street and aimed his camera at Lizzie's window, she has kept the windows shut and the blinds drawn. The ceiling fan, newly installed, tosses the over-warm air about but does nothing to relieve the stifling heat. Sweat trickles between her breasts but Mar does not let go of her daughter. She cannot let her go.

On the dresser, the thick violet goo of the lava lamp globs and falls, forms and rises and, watching it, Mar wishes she'd never bought it because it makes her think of deep-sea mud roiling and spewing on thermal vents. Of pale, blind creatures scrabbling along the ocean floor gobbling up the bits of flesh that have fallen, sometimes for miles, from the razor mouths of the large fish above. A band of panic tightens around her chest and she has to force herself to suck in steadying lungfuls of air. She should have put Lizzie down for her nap in her own bedroom down the hall. Not here. Not inside the coral reef world that she'd painted on her daughter's walls. In the purple haze light, fish dart from rock to coral and hover above the bed. The moray eel's jaws gnash and snap and the once-playful dolphins that look into the room from the east wall grin savagely at her. Mar only realizes that she is moaning when Lizzie begins to moan too. She shuts her eyes against the onslaught and tempers her breathing to Lizzie's. In, out, they breathe together. In, out. Skimming her fingertips across the little girl's forehead and down between her eyes, Mar gentles the frown she'd known would be there until Lizzie's features are once again untroubled.

How many more days will we have? Fourteen? Seven? One? Will they take Lizzie away today? Every time her attorney explains the process to her, Mar's mind shuts down, refuses to consider the possibility that she might lose her daughter forever.

A car door slams. Mar hears the surge of reporters as they rush whoever has arrived. She holds her breath. In his cage, the hamster stops running. Mar glances up at the wide aquarium headboard she made for the bed. Mr. Shrimp and the lobster are about, deceived, no doubt, by the murky light of the room. A clown fish, Nemo or Moby or Fudge, burrows in an anemone. The pirate chest fills with pumped air. There. There. There. It is full, and opens. Bubbled pearls of air rise to the surface. The front door slams. *Crick-crick-crick*, the hamster runs. Mar breathes.

She tries to distract herself with the *what if?* game. *What if we had run?* It would have been so easy to pack up Lizzie and the dog and point her car south. *What if they had made it to Mexico?* She imagines handing their documents off to a border guard who waves them silently through. After all, no one smuggles someone *into* Mexico. *What if we were now living on a beach somewhere in Central America?* No one who knows Mar would ever look for her near the ocean. *What if Jack Westfield had never found them?* She swallows the bile that rises hotly to her throat. This is where the game ends. Where it always ends. Jack Westfield had found them.

Lizzie draws her knees up and Mar once again flows to accommodate and envelop her. "Mama," Lizzie's voice is a velvet sigh and Mar wraps her arms around her tucked body.

"I'm here, baby. *Shhhhhhh...*"

Awash in the sensations of Lizzie, it is difficult for Mar to imagine a force strong enough to insert itself between her and her daughter and wrench them apart. Still, she knows that there are such forces alive in the world. They have visited her before.

Mar tells herself to pay attention, to drink in every detail, the little hums and sighs of Lizzie asleep, the accordion rise and fall of her shoulder, how her knobbed back curls perfectly to Mar's stomach and warms her. She forces herself to take note. Years from now, when all that she might have left are these memories, she'll need details. She runs her hand down

Lizzie's body, pausing to memorize. She rounds Lizzie's shoulder, her stomach and hip. She measures the length of the girl's thigh bone against her own forearm and examines the box-like structure of her knee. She admires the seal-pelt down on Lizzie's legs and the bones of her small feet. Separating each toe, Mar slips her finger in and out of the hollows and runs a fingertip over the moon sliver curves of her toenails. *Who will clip your nails? Who will paint them?* Mar palms the hard knob of Lizzie's heel, testing, and then traces Lizzie's body back up.

I am losing you, Mar thinks. She lifts Lizzie's hair from the back of her neck and nuzzles her daughter's damp skin. She inhales, desperate, and again, separating and identifying the smells. Sunshine and syrup and oatmeal. She presses her nose to her daughter's scalp. Baby shampoo. Sweat. Playdoh. Mar is drowning. *I am drowning.*

"Mar? Honey?" Don Bloom parts the pearl bead curtain in Lizzie's doorway and steps into the room. Mar freezes. The waterfall clack of the beads slows. "Mar?"

Mar's teeth clench and the frown between her brows deepens. She shakes her head, once, and follows Lizzie's arm to the tight "v" of her elbow and then trickles her fingers to her tiny wrist. Lizzie's hand is balled inside Boosie, one-time Mar's blanket and now Lizzie's. She works her fingers under the fabric until her hand enfolds her daughter's.

"Mar, it's time to go."

She wills her father away. Doesn't he understand what she is doing? But the bed tilts under Don's weight and she slips down the back of the wave he has created. Mar anchors her right arm around Lizzie and stretches her left hand out to grip the far side of the bed.

"Sorry." Don shifts again, putting more of his weight on the bed frame. The mattress tide reverses direction and Mar holds on as she and Lizzie crest each swell until, finally, the rocking stops.

Don clears his throat. He is a quiet, deliberate man and he has not spoken much these past weeks, but Mar, who spent her childhood patiently crouched beside him in the marshes and tide pools of the Keys waiting for the wildlife he would sketch to appear, does not need her father to speak to know his thoughts. Now she wishes he would say nothing as, really, there is nothing to say.

"I know you're awake, and I know what you're feeling."

Mar shakes her head.

"I know, Sweet Pea, I know. But we can't keep the judge waiting."

Mar snorts. Judge McClaine is the same judge she once called "a bigoted, heaping helping of horse droppings" and, while she immediately caught herself and added, "that's off the record," the reporter she'd been unloading on had found the comment too quotable to pass up. That her daughter's future is now in McClaine's hands terrifies Mar. Her voice catches. "Daddy, no."

Don shifts again and Mar prays that he is leaving. Instead, he settles and Mar is aware once again of the *tick-tick-tick* of time passing. To drown out the noise inside her head, she sings into Lizzie's hair, a song she invented long before she was aware of its implications, long before she recognized that she'd claimed Lizzie as her own. "Mama's baby, little baby, Mama's sweet baby girl..."

One

Jack.

"They dropped the six-year-old Lanski kid in a vat of blood." Jack Westfield had been in the shower when Elena's call came through.

"But that's not the worst of it," she added.

"Two minutes," Jack said, punched off and tossed the phone onto the bathroom counter.

Now, with the phone pinched between his shoulder and ear, Jack pulls on the suit pants Lindsey had laid out for him. "Tell me," he says when Elena answers.

Elena Martinez is Jack's assistant. She was with him the six-years he worked in the D.A.'s office and she came over with him when he moved to Weisman, Tannenbaum and Carruthers seven years ago. If she says it's bad, it is.

He glances at the bedside clock and curses himself for hitting the snooze button. He'd returned home from the office after midnight and then had spent more hours honing his opening arguments to the absolute essentials so that the gruesome truth they revealed could not be disputed. Sometime around three, he'd fallen into a troubled sleep. Right before the bloody air had gone off. Again.

"There was a message on the machine when I got in this

morning."

"*Mmff,*" Jack says around the plastic clips the dry cleaner put in the collar and cuffs of his shirt. As he pushes his arm through the shirt sleeve, the starch melts against the slick of sweat on his skin. Fine. He'll change at the office before heading to court.

"He's gone AWOL."

"What?" This stops Jack, dead. "Krillov?"

"Lanski."

Jack drops to the side of the bed. Lanski is his slam-dunk witness against Grigorly Krillov, the latest, sickest of the crime virtuosos to have spilled like garbage onto U.S. shores since the breakup of the Soviet Union. He'd sauntered away from his criminal trial after every last one of the D.A.'s witnesses had come down with a terminal case of amnesia. Now this, the civil trial, what Lindsey calls his "O.J. case," is the only way of getting any justice for the families of Krillov's victims. Without Lanski, Jack's entire case is screwed.

"Doesn't that asshole know he's under subpoena?"

"He skipped town. Took his whole family and got out of Dodge. Said he'd rather spend his life on the run than end up hamburger in his own butcher shop."

"He was good yesterday. I talked to him."

"They took his kid, Jack. Stole his little girl right off the school playground."

"We had guards on the family."

"Gone." Pause. "But that's not the worst of it."

"Tell me." Jack knots his shoes and stands. His watch and cufflinks are on the dresser.

"No, no, she's OK. Well, as can be expected."

"They got her back?"

"Oh, yeah. That was the point."

As Jack straps on his watch, he looks around the room for his pager. Because cell phones are not allowed in the courtroom, he has been carrying an old-fashioned pager. With Lindsey just weeks away from giving birth to their first child, he can't risk being out of touch. He returns to the bathroom.

Maybe he left the pager on the counter.

"They covered her in blood. Dropped the poor thing in from head to toe."

"Ah, Christ." Jack thinks he knows where this is going. Krillov, known by the nickname Gosha on the streets, is one messed-up psycho with a talent for inventiveness and persuasion that goes light years beyond the run-of-the-mill bullet to the brain or shattered kneecaps.

"They dumped her in front of the house. Just threw her out of the car and kept on going."

"And the guards at the house?"

"Didn't see a thing."

Jack grabs his suit coat and tie and moves past the nursery to his home office. His notes are strewn across the antique mahogany desk Lindsey gave him as a graduation present. He gathers them up and stuffs them into a folder.

"Lanski and his wife rushed her to the hospital, they didn't know whose blood it was. By the time they got there, she was puking, throwing up even more of the stuff."

"What'd Krillov do? Make her eat glass or something?"

"No, blood. Cow's blood."

"Fuck." This stops him.

"I'm telling you," Elena continues as if she cannot get the words out fast enough. "They poured it down her throat, probably used a funnel. Poor little thing spit up volumes."

Jack shudders. Christ, he'd run, too. "How is she?" he asks.

"In shock. What can you expect?"

"Yeah." These guys aren't brain surgeons. As messages go, this one is pretty damn clear. "Have they tested it?" Jack's battered leather briefcase is on the credenza behind the desk. He flips it open and shoves the file inside.

"They're doing it now. Lanski grabbed the kid as soon as he knew she was OK and took off, but Thompson caught the case. He asked for the blood to be tested."

At least there is that. If the blood is tainted, if it came from an infected cow, then this would be a new case of attempted murder the D.A. can bring against Krillov. Now if they can just find Lanski. Jack looks at the time. 6:48. He is seriously late.

"Look, Elena, call Sy," he says, referring to the P.I. they regularly hire. "Tell him to track down Lanski. I'm on my way."

***

Lindsey drags the heavy, limp hair back from her forehead, lifts it up and waves at the back of her neck, desperately trying to dry the sweat that has accumulated there so quickly. August in New York.

Perhaps on another day it wouldn't bother her so much, but she is nine months pregnant and the central air in their building has failed. Again. Ceiling fans, floor fans, freaking hand-held flap-them-in-your-face fans can't come close to keeping up with the trickle of sweat that drip, drip, drips down her spine, pools at her lower back and slyly tries for access farther south. Her cotton maternity panties have soaked up about as much moisture as they can handle and gravity will soon cause the overflow to course down her legs and intensify the heat rash that flourishes between her chafing thighs.

She twists the foot-long wheat-blond cascade into a knot. The weight of it, when she lets go, is enough to make her scream, "*Nooooooo-arghhhh*!" Lindsey grabs the pizza shears they keep in the knife rack and begins sawing at her hair.

***

Jack flips his good-luck tie around his neck, his eyes raking every surface in the office one last time. It isn't here. Perfect. He'll ask Lindsey. She probably already has the pager clipped to his keys so he can't forget it. That, of course, will solve only one of his problems. He still has to swing by the office, grab the copy of the Lanski tape telling Jack why he is taking off. With it, the judge just might give Jack an extension until Sy can track the guy down. Jack pushes through the swinging door to the kitchen and freezes. "Holy shit! What'd you do?"

Lindsey flings the scissors across the room and covers her mouth with both hands. Eyes wide, she begins to wail.

He catches her just as her legs begin to buckle and lowers

her into a chair. "It's OK, Lindsey, it's going to be OK. *Shhh...*"

Jack's heart pounds. Seeing her like that, the crazed look in her eyes, the scissors in her hand, Jesus, after the last miscarriage. He shuts that thought down, hard. Leaving her, he tries to open the window. It is swollen in its frame and won't budge. Struggling with it, banging it doesn't help. It only starts him sweating again. He mutters under his breath and grabs a handful of paper towels, soaks them, and brings them back to her. Kneeling, he wipes the tears from her flushed cheeks, cools her neck. "There, babe, it's going to be OK."

"But, my hair, Jack. Oh, god, I cut it all off. It's just so hot, and then the window wouldn't open and I wanted to make you breakfast and I didn't have a rubber band and I couldn't stand it."

"*Shhh*, breathe." Jack strokes her back until Lindsey's cries settle to hiccups and her breathing slows to normal. As he kisses her slick forehead, he is fully aware of the *tick, tick, tick* of the clock on the wall behind him and has to consciously unclench his jaw. Judge Gordon is going to skewer him if he is late. New York, used to mob bosses and gang warfare, had been riveted by the criminal case. But that had failed. Now, three years later, the civil trial for "The Mad Cow Murders," as they'd been dubbed, has turned even the most blasé New Yorker manic. Not only Jack's, but the judge's entire professional future is on the line. He calculates the time it will take him to get to the courthouse. If he bypasses the office and takes a cab instead of the subway, he should make it with just minutes to spare. Elena will have to send the tape over, and maybe she can find his pager, too. Maybe he left it at the office.

Jack leans back and blots Lindsey's forehead. "Honey? You know, it looks kind of cool. A Meg Ryan kind of thing. You know, choppy, but sexy." The eyes that rise to meet his test for honesty. He smiles. "Really."

Jack's hands skim her face, her neck, round her swollen breasts and come to rest on the sides of her belly. The heel of a very small foot kicks out at him and they both smile.

"I'm done, get me outta here," Jack says. "There, you see?

Even she wants to come out and see her beautiful mama."

"More like she doesn't want to be inside a crazy woman any longer."

Jack puts his mouth to Lindsey's belly. "Mia? Don't talk about your mother like that. She may be crazy, but she's my best hope of getting laid any time soon."

"Jesus, Jack!" But she is laughing.

Leaning in, Jack catches her bottom lip between his teeth. "*Mmmmm*, Meg, yummy."

"Yummy you." Her hands grip his wide shoulders and then suddenly she is pushing at him, heaving herself upwards. "Jack! You're going to be late!"

Jack follows her eyes to the clock and swears. "I'm sorry, I've really got to go." Taking her face between his hands, he kisses her again, his eyes searching hers. "You OK?"

Lindsey ruffles what is left of her hair. "I really did it this time, didn't I?"

"You really did," he says. "But you still look gorgeous. Maybe just go to the salon and get it cleaned up, make it look like you meant it."

"Yeah, right." But she smiles.

"Do you want to go out to your parents'? I'm sure their air's working. I can have the car brought around for you."

"No. They're coming into the city for lunch with me and Naomi. I'll just lie down for awhile and maybe the air'll come back on."

"Lindsey..."

"I'm fine."

"OK. Call me if..."

"I feel anything," she finishes.

"I love you." Even with all the crap with the trial, she can center him with a look. As soon as this trial is over, he'll take her, take them, on a vacation. Take his family on vacation.

"I love you, too, Counselor. Now go."

Jack grabs his jacket and briefcase and is on his cell phone when the front door slams shut behind him.

***

Several hours later, Lindsey wakes with an image from her dream tugging at her, trying to pull her back into its grip, even as her conscious mind yells at her to wake up. She focuses on the clock, which is way over on the other side of the bed, and groans. It is late and she'll have to hurry to meet her best friend, Naomi, and her parents, but the thought of shoveling her swollen feet into shoes makes her want to cry. That the restaurant is sure to have air conditioning makes dressing seem worth it. Just.

"A-one, a-two, a-three, OK, let's go." She prods herself into a sitting position, takes a deep breath, and then heaves upward, belly first, until she is standing. As the weight of her pregnancy shifts and lowers onto her hips, Lindsey reaches behind her back and braces herself. Everything in place, she waddles to the bathroom.

The first pain comes as she bend-squats to shave her right leg, but she dismisses the cramp as a Braxton-Hicks "fake" contraction brought on by bending over. Ten minutes later, as she rinses the suds from what is left of her hair, another sharp pain hits. She digs her knuckles into her lower back and prays that this is not another sciatic attack.

It isn't until the fifth contraction that it occurs to Lindsey that she might be going into labor.

As she dials the number for Jack's pager, Lindsey's fingers shake. In all their preparation, they hadn't seriously considered the possibility that the baby would come early. When directed to enter a text message, she enters the number "32339," for "Daddy," her message that the baby is on its way. She then dials her doctor's number and is directed to voice mail. Lindsey is just getting to her feet when another contraction tightens over her stomach and wraps around her back. "*Ohhhh* boy, ok, OK, OK," she huffs as the band around her middle begins to loosen. This is a lot more painful than she imagined and Lindsey realizes she might not be able to wait for Jack to call her back.

"Hello? Jack?" Lindsey answers her cell phone, relieved.

"No, it's me, Dr. Harding. What's up?"

"I think it's time."

"Did your water break?"

"Not yet, but I'm having contractions pretty regularly. They're about ten minutes apart."

"For how long?"

"I think for more than an hour. I didn't realize it at first."

"It could be a false alarm, but how about if we meet at the hospital just in case? I'll wait for you at the Admitting Office."

Lindsey looks at the clock. She is near tears. She dials Jack's number again and adds "911" to the message. Next, she calls his office, only to be informed that Elena is out to lunch. Lindsey leaves her a voice mail asking her to get in touch with Jack to let him know she is leaving for the hospital.

After another contraction eases, Lindsey shoulders her overnight bag and takes one last look at the apartment. The next time they come home, they'll have Mia with them. The front door shuts behind Lindsey as she is punching the speed dial number for her mother's cell phone. She never notices the low rumble coming from between the cushions of the sofa, never realizes that Jack's pager is vibrating.

***

"Thanks, Robert," Lindsey can barely find the energy to thank the doorman as she shuffles into the oppressive heat. The traffic, which is always a bear in their upper Manhattan neighborhood, has taken on a strident edge as drivers battle for space on the bottle-necked avenue, their amped-up rage apparent in the cacophony of horns and screeching tires.

"Any time, Mrs. Westfield," Robert calls over the noise. He flicks the switch on the cab call light. "Where are you going?"

Shaking her head, Lindsey says, "I'll take the car." For the past several months and for the foreseeable future, Jack has had a car and driver on call for Lindsey. "Where's Joseph? He's not in the lobby."

"He's not back yet."

Lindsey wilts against the side of the building. "But where is he? He's supposed to be here." Her voice sounds slow and distant, even to her own ears. Lindsey closes her eyes and concentrates on taking long, deep breaths.

"Your husband took the car this morning. He said Joseph would come right back, but he hasn't."

"Oh, god."

"Mrs. Westfield? Should I call an ambulance?"

A new contraction clamps down across the mound of Lindsey's belly. Her bag drops as she jackknifes forward and it is only Robert's quick catch that keeps her from crashing to the pavement. *"Ah, ah, ah,"* she gasps against the red polyester jacket of his uniform. The pain is unbelievable. It isn't supposed to be like this. Where is Jack? He promised he'd be with her.

She begins to cry hot, noisy tears. He promised.

There is a concrete bench next to the building's entrance and Robert lowers her onto it. The bench has soaked up a full morning's worth of intense heat. Lindsey jerks up off it and feels something in her back shift. "Oh, oh, oh my god!" she cries, her sciatic nerve screaming.

"Oh, jeez, are you OK? Is there anything I can do?"

"Oh, Jesus,"

"Mrs. Westfield, aw hell, tell me what to do."

"I pinched a nerve," she gasps. "I can't move."

"OK, OK. Look, stay here. I'm gonna call an ambulance."

"Yes." Huff, huff. "Please."

With its horn blaring, a cab cuts across three lanes of traffic and pulls to the curb in front of the building. Robert has his cell phone out and waves the driver away, but Lindsey sees this as the quickest way to the hospital and an epidural.

"No, no, Robert. Help me, help me up. I'll take the cab." She takes a deep breath and slowly straightens, every inch upward agony. Though Robert braces her and supports her weight, sweat pours from her scalp, burns her armpits and overwhelms her panties. She leans fully on Robert and begins the long shuffle to the car.

The cabby is leaning across the front seat. "She having baby? No, no, no, I no want her have baby in my car." Turning around, he slams into gear just as another cab noses itself in front of his car to let off its passengers. Robert yanks the back door open.

"She's not gonna have the kid in your car. You're gonna get her to the hospital and she's gonna have it there." He tosses some bills through the front window.

Lindsey concentrates on moving her bulk through the door. When she is finally settled, her head drops back in fatigue. She watches through half-slit eyes as Robert pushes her overnight bag through the window. "You can't forget this," he says. She could not care less.

"Mrs. Westfield, are you comfortable?"

Get the hell out of here, she thinks. *Go*. She nods to Robert.

"Listen, none of that crazy driving, OK?" Robert says and slaps the roof of the car.

The cabby shrugs and pulls out into traffic. "OK, lady, what hospital?"

The hospital is in mid-town, not that far as the crow flies but, in the middle of lunch-hour traffic, quite a ride. With every bump, every slowing down and picking up of speed, Lindsey's lower back screams. She reaches out to brace herself and finds the cabby's eyes watching her in the rearview mirror. Whimpering, she shakes her head. *Why the hell isn't he watching where we're going?* Whether concerned for her or concerned for his cab, Lindsey can't tell and really doesn't care. About four blocks into the ride, a new contraction envelops her. On top of the pain from the pinched nerve, it is more than she can bear. A scream tears from her lips as her body arches off the seat.

The cabby turns around and stares at her through the Plexiglas that separates them. "No, no, no baby. No baby here," he says and then, facing forward, settles into the seat and guns the engine. The car shoots through a red light, barely misses a garbage truck, a few pedestrians and another cab as they weave in and out of the havoc they create.

Lindsey clutches at the armrest and digs her feet into the floor but, regardless, she slides across the vinyl-covered seat and bangs into the opposite door. The pain is continuous and she can't tell where the contractions leave off and the pain of the pinched nerve begins. She cries forcefully and tries to hang on. The cabby continues to barrel through traffic, picking up speed rather than slowing down as they approach each intersection. His eyes shift to find hers in the rear view mirror and the level of his voice rises to meet hers. "No, no, no baby! No baby!" is his mantra. "Slow down, slow down, slow down," is hers, but it is more in her mind than on her lips, as her mouth is busy screaming.

"Ay, ay, ay ay ay!" They shoot through another intersection. They are closing in on the hospital and the cabby stomps the accelerator. "Hold on lady, no baby, we're there, we're there." They swerve around a meter maid's cart and just miss a man in the middle of a crosswalk. The man jumps back and flips them the bird. As Lindsey watches in horror, the cabby pushes out the window, his own finger raised, and he yells back, "You stupid, you stupid!"

"Watch out!" Lindsey screams.

The driver swivels forward, but it is too late to stop. He spins the wheel to the left. They narrowly avoid a front-end impact with a cement truck. He slams on the brakes. Rather than stopping, the car begins a long, graceful slide into the intersection. They pass a bus disgorging its passengers, miss a stretch limo that speeds up to make the light, and, just as it seems the car will come to a safe stop halfway down the block from where it began its pilot-less adventure, another car, speeding in from the opposite direction, clips the cab's front bumper, but enough, just enough, to send the car spinning violently and uncontrollably off into a new direction. Screaming, the cabby throws his arms up into the air.

Lindsey's water ruptures as she is propelled into the Plexiglas partition that separates the front seat from the back.

Two

Jack.

Jack squares his shoulders and steps back into the courtroom. The judge delayed the start of the trial for an hour while they waited for Elena to arrive with the Lanski tape. And then Judge Gordon called both attorneys into his chambers to hear the tape and to argue about what to do. Krillov's attorney, of course, wanted a mistrial. Jack wanted a delay. The judge listened to both arguments and told the attorneys to return in two hours while he considered.

Jack takes his place at the Plaintiff's table and sits. His second chair, Leonard Duncan, leans in. "Well?"

"He said..."

"All rise for the Honorable Judge Gordon," the bailiff calls from the front of the courtroom.

Jack barely listens as the judge repeats his decision. They will have just twenty-four hours to find Lanski. If Jack can't produce him, the judge will declare a mistrial. This is about the worst news Jack can imagine. Sure, Judge Gordon threw him a bone, but there is little chance of finding Lanski in such a short time. And even if he does find him, Jack will have to convince Lanski to come to court and face the man who terrorized his child. The gallery, which is filled to capacity with reporters and the families of the wronged, erupts in pandemonium at the judge's news.

"Jackson?" the voice is tentative, as is the hand on his arm. It is the moment Jack has dreaded, having to face a client whose case is going to hell. He is too honest to paste a fake smile on his face, but nor does he want this woman to worry. Well, to worry even more.

Jack turns to her. Mrs. Sergeyevich was the first to sue Krillov. Her only son, Pasha, had done something to really piss off the man. A year after Pasha emigrated to the States, Krillov followed him, found him and punished him. Not content to simply torture the guy and kill him quickly, Krillov had forced him to drink gallons of tainted cow's blood. For the next couple of years, Mrs. Sergeyevich had cared for her son while prions turned his brain to mush. "I've nothing left to live for," she'd enunciated each word carefully at their first meeting.

In her polished low heels, she is barely five feet tall, more than a foot shorter than Jack. He takes her hands in his and bends so that she does not have to look up so far. "It's not great news," he says. "But it will be OK."

She studies his face for a long moment. In her faded eyes, Jack sees pain, but behind that, resolution. "You will make it good?"

Jack nods. "I will make it good."

It takes a long while for the courtroom to clear. Several more clients want to talk to Jack and, though he feels the mounting pressure of time slipping away, he reassures them. When they are gone, he drops back into his chair at the Plaintiff's table and looks over the boxes of files that Leonard has packed up. "We good to go?"

"Yeah. Amy's coming up and Joe's with her," Leonard says, referring to two of their trial assistants. "If you want to head back to the office, we'll take care of the files."

Jack senses the man before he looks up. Krillov. He ignores the manicured hand that Krillov has stretched out to him.

"Well," Krillov says. "So be it."

Krillov's eyes are the color of concrete and just as dull. As Jack returns their stare, the hairs on the back of his neck rise and his lip twitches with the primitive urge to bare his teeth. As if sensing his effect, Krillov smiles. It is not a reassuring look. He gestures to the boxes of files. "Such an idealistic man," Krillov says. "You Americans place so much value on idealism."

"What do you want, Krillov?"

"What do I want? Well, for one thing, I want to extend my condolences to your client as I doubt I will be seeing him any time soon. Such a pity when children are forced to play at adult games."

Behind Jack, Leonard drops a box of files and Jack shifts instinctively to block him from launching across the table. He meets Krillov's stare. "We'll see you tomorrow," Jack says and begins lifting the boxes to the table.

But Krillov won't leave. He watches Jack stack another box and then says, "Yes, tomorrow. But for today, let me be the first to congratulate you on the birth of your child."

The box in Jack's hands thumps to the table. "What did you say?"

"I see you have not yet heard the good news." Krillov's teeth are perfectly white, perfectly straight. He has a movie star's smile, yet on him the effect is all wrong. "Your wife left for the hospital hours ago."

Jack's hands grip the handles of the banker's box. He knows Krillov is fucking with him, but he does not want the man to even mention Lindsey.

"And here I thought it was a happy event," Krillov says. "Good day, Counselor."

***

As the gate swings behind Krillov, Jack digs through his briefcase for his cell phone. "Come on, come on, come on," he says while he waits for it to boot up. "Leonard, get Elena on your phone. Come on, Lindsey, pick up."

Jack lets the call go into voice mail and then tries her

number again. She doesn't answer but, beside him, Leonard is talking to Elena. Jack snaps his phone shut and grabs Leonard's. "Here, call Sy," he says, tossing Leonard his phone. "He's in the contact list. Lainie? Talk to me."

"I just got back from lunch and there's a message here to get hold of you. She left for the hospital more than an hour ago."

Jack closes his eyes and he inhales deeply, mentally shifting through all that needs to happen in too short a time. "OK, look," he begins.

***

Jack slips through the back corridors of the courthouse, leaving Leonard to talk to the reporters who will be waiting for a statement, and hopes he can find a cab on the side street.

The humidity sucker-punches him as he pushes through the courthouse doors. Sweat gathers at his temples and under his arms. He scans the traffic but doesn't see a cab. At the curb, he shrugs out of his suit coat and jogs toward the next avenue, arm raised.

"Mr. Westfield." Jack turns at the sound of his name. "Over here."

Joseph, the driver he hired for Lindsey, is standing alongside the Town Car on the opposite side of the street. Jack's first thought is that Lindsey must have sent the car for him after she was dropped off at the hospital. Thankful, he weaves through the stalled traffic to the car. "She make it to the hospital OK?" he asks.

Joseph has the back door open for Jack. He shakes his head. "Who? What?"

"My wife, didn't you take her to the hospital?"

"No, I've been waiting here. For you."

"But you're supposed to be available for my wife. You're not supposed to be here."

"You didn't tell me," Joseph says. "You just said to bring you here. I thought I was supposed to wait for you."

Jack tries to remember if he told the man to go or to wait.

He'd been on the phone with Lainie and Sy the entire ride to the courthouse. He knows he intended to send Joseph right back to the apartment building, but he can't remember if he'd actually said the words. Now he realizes that not only hadn't he been with Lindsey for the ride to the hospital, as he'd promised her he'd be, but she'd had to find her own way there. "Get me to the hospital," he says as he throws his briefcase and jacket across the seat. "I don't care if you have to drive on the sidewalk, just get me there quickly."

***

Jack reaches under the glass partition and disconnects the receptionist's phone.

"What the hell?" she says.

"I've been waiting ten minutes. I'm looking for my wife."

The receptionist, a meaty blonde with a hairlip scar, punches at her phone. "And you're gonna be waiting a lot longer," she says.

Jack entered the hospital through the general admissions door. There, he'd been redirected to the Emergency Room. Tension tightens his chest. "Look, I'm just trying to find my wife. Lindsey Westfield? She's having a baby."

But the receptionist waves at him to be quiet as she takes another phone call.

"Jack!"

Jack turns. Naomi, Lindsey's best friend, waves to him across the crowded waiting room. Above the din of Emergency Room drama, he hears the punctuated clack-clack of her heels as she hurries to him. "Oh, Jesus, Jack," Naomi says. The fear in her bottle-green eyes is contagious.

Jack grips her arms and holds her away from him. "Naomi? Where's Lindsey? What's going on?"

"There's been an accident," she says. "Lindsey, she's hurt."

Hurt can mean so many things. "What? How?"

"Mr. Westfield?"

Jack turns at the sound of his name. A nurse, in full surgical scrubs, including a cap and mask, holds one side of the double swinging doors open. Her uniform is spotted with blood. He looks back at Naomi, uncomprehending, but her skin has lost all color and she is shaking her head, no.

"Is there a Mr. Westfield here?" the nurse calls. "Jack Westfield?"

The Emergency Room is filled with sick and injured people. Jack steps over the feet of a slumbering man whose splayed legs block the aisle between rows of hard plastic chairs. "I'm Jack Westfield," he says. "Do you know where my wife is?

"Please follow me." The nurse turns as soon as Jack reaches her and hurries down a wide corridor. Jack and Naomi take off after her.

"Wait!" Jack lunges and grabs the nurse's arm, stopping her. "What's going on? Where's my wife?" He tightens his grip and holds her in place, forcing her to look at him.

"She's in the operating room. Please, sir, Dr. Harding wants to speak with you." She pulls her arm free and hurries away. Around another corner, they come to E.O.R. #4. The nurse pushes the door open with her shoulder and calls, "He's here."

Jack pushes past the nurse into the scrub room. On the other side of the glass partition, a mob of scrubs-clad bodies surround an operating table. Jack freezes. "Lindsey," he says. The nurse tugs at his arm, but Jack feels the draw of his wife. He pushes through the double swinging doors into the operating room. His voice is strangled as he calls again, "Lindsey?"

"Get him the hell out of here," a voice barks and Jack feels himself being pulled away.

"Please, let me see her," he begs. He stumbles backward as he is pulled out to the corridor.

"You can't go in there," the nurse says and blocks the doors. "Please. The doctor will be right out."

Short of knocking her over, Jack is forced to wait. He paces. *What could have gone wrong?* He rounds on the nurse. "Look, just tell me, what was the accident? What happened?"

"There was a car crash." She shakes her head. "That's all

I know."

"Ah, Christ." He knows instantly that this, whatever this is, is his fault. Naomi reaches for him, but Jack pushes her away. "I took the car," he tells her. "I took the fucking car."

"Jack."

He turns. Dr. Harding is pulling the mask from her face. Her scrubs, too, have blood on them. Jack wonders whose blood it is.

"Sara, what's going on? How's Lindsey?"

Dr. Harding, a long-time friend of the family, reaches up and captures Jack's arms in her strong hands. "Jack," she insists, her eyes searching for his. "Listen, you can't fall apart right now. I need your undivided attention. Can you give it to me?"

The urgency in her voice sobers him. He inhales deeply and nods.

"Lindsey was in a car accident. It was pretty bad and when she arrived here, she was unconscious. We think there's hemorrhaging somewhere in her brain, but we can't know where until we can do a scan."

"So? What's the problem? Do it!" His eyes search her face.

"What about the baby?" Naomi asks. "How's the baby?"

Sara's eyes never leave Jack's. "The baby's in severe distress and I need to do an immediate C-section, or she could die." Her voice gentles, "The problem is, that we can't do both at once. The baby can't wait for the brain scan, and the scan can't wait for the baby."

The horror of her words unravels in his mind. "What are you saying?"

"You're her Health Care Surrogate. We need you to direct us."

Jack shakes his head, trying to deny what he thinks she is saying. "Are you kidding me?" he manages.

"I'm sorry, Jack, but that's what she indicated on her health care directive. If she somehow becomes incapacitated, she wanted you to make all medical decisions for her."

He flashes back to the trust they'd set up when they'd

first gotten married, the Health Care Directives they'd signed appointing each other as surrogate. A copy of that form would be in Lindsey's pre-admittance package in the maternity ward. His body goes cold, his focus narrowing to one simple truth. "I need Lindsey," he says.

Sara's eyes probe his and then her grip on his arms loosens. She appears disappointed, but nods, once, and turns to leave.

"Wait!" Naomi stops her. "What do you suggest? What do you think is best? You're her doctor."

"No, no." Jack pushes Sara toward the doors. "Go!"

"Dammit, Jack, think! Lindsey'll never forgive you if you let anything happen to that baby! Sara, tell him."

Dr. Harding's voice drops, "Jack, I think I can save the baby. If I go back there right now."

"And Lindsey?" Naomi says. "Please, can you save Lindsey?"

"I don't know." But Sara is shaking her head, no. "Jack?"

Pain grips his chest as her message reaches him.

"Jack?" Sara snaps. "I'm sorry, but I need an answer."

He turns to Naomi but she is shaking her head and he knows that she, too, understands Sara's underlying message. "I can't, Jack. I'm sorry."

"Jack, I have to go back in there. Now."

I want eight kids, Lindsey once told him. We'll have two, and then we'll adopt six more. That's a lot of kids, Jack had replied. Well, I've got a lot of love, she'd said, and after that Jack had accepted that they'd have eight kids. "Save her baby," he says. "Lindsey wants her baby."

***

Jack and Naomi are not alone in the small waiting room off of the Emergency Operating Rooms. A young couple waits for their son to have a Lego removed from his nose. A woman and her four adult children and their spouses wait for word of her husband. Jack understands that they are the taxi driver's family, but they know as little about the accident as he does, so he ignores them as he paces. He looks up when his name is called. Lindsey's parents, Amanda and Stan, hurry through the waiting room doors. He takes a deep breath and moves to them.

"Jack?" Amanda reaches for him and Jack gathers Lindsey's mother in a hug. She is shaking.

"She's a fighter," Jack whispers into Amanda's hair. "She's a fighter."

***

Later, a nurse, looking exhausted and tense, pushes into the room. "Mr. Westfield?" she calls.

"Yes?" Jack rushes to her, with Amanda, Stan and Naomi on his heels.

"Dr. Harding asked me to tell you that the baby is stable. You have a daughter, Mr. Westfield."

"What about my wife? How's Lindsey?"

"Why isn't Sara here?" Amanda asks. "Why isn't she telling us?"

"After Dr. Harding closed up the section, Dr. Gahuri, the surgeon, asked her to stay and assist. There was some mild hemorrhaging during the delivery and he wanted her nearby."

"But the baby's fine? My granddaughter is fine?"

"She is. She weighs 6 pounds, eight ounces and is 19 inches long. Her lungs are clear, everything's fine."

"Where is she now?" Stan's voice, usually so mellow, is edged with fear.

"She's been sent up to the neo-natal unit, but you won't be able to see her for several more hours. She's under observation."

Naomi, closer than a sister to Lindsey, forces her way forward. "I thought you said she's fine."

"She is, but because of the accident, Dr. Harding wants to keep an eye on her, that's all."

"And my wife?" Jack repeats, "Is she going to be all right?"

The nurse looks up at him and there is no mistaking the pity in her eyes. "They're working on her now, sir. That's all I know."

***

Five hours later, Jack is ready to tear the building from its foundations. They have received bits of news about Lindsey's progress from the nurse. Dr. Gahuri located the source of the bleeding in her brain and was going after it. The C-section began to hemorrhage and Dr. Harding opened her up again and was able to stop it. Her broken bones have been set, but the verdict is still out as to whether they can save her arm, which had been crushed in the accident. Jack hears her words and interprets their underlying message, the verdict is out as to whether it is even worth trying to save the arm of someone who will be dead soon anyway. He barely manages to keep from punching the nurse. Instead, he scarcely feels it as his fist smashes into the wall beside her head. He refuses to leave the waiting room to have the bones set.

***

Two hours and countless cups of bad coffee later, Jack is beyond exhaustion. Stress has burned through the caffeine in his system and the throbbing in his hand has spread to his shoulder. He concentrates on the pain, thinking that somehow it brings him closer to Lindsey. When the door opens and a doctor enters, Jack hurries over to him but, after a few brief words, the doctor turns to the taxi driver's family. A collective scream rises from the group and Jack knows the driver must be dead. He squeezes his damaged hand.

Some time later, the nurse returns. They are closing Lindsey up and the doctor will be out to speak with them shortly. When Amanda asks about the baby, the nurse won't meet her eyes and, while she allows that as far as she knows the baby is fine, she adds that they'll have to speak with Dr. Harding if they want to know more.

"Jack, don't," Stan's hand falls heavily onto his shoulder, keeping Jack from racing after the departing nurse and forcing more answers from her. Jack watches her disappear before pulling out of Stan's grip and returning to his pacing.

***

"Sara," Jack is the first to see the doctor. With his good hand, he takes hold of Sara's arm and searches her fatigue-bruised eyes for answers it is obvious they don't want to reveal. "How is she?"

Sara's sigh is deep. She glances around the waiting room and rakes a hand through her graying hair that has been plastered beneath a cap for the better part of ten hours. "Let's step outside," she says.

Jack's hyped up nerves, his desire for action, leave him wanting to shake her. Just spit it out, he wants to yell, but he leads her to a somewhat private alcove down the hall before demanding, "Tell me."

Sara leans against a windowsill and closes her eyes.

"Sara?" Jack prods.

Dr. Harding nods once, as if gathering strength, and then meets Jack's eyes. "In the accident," she says, her voice reluctant, "Lindsey's head was hit very hard. As you know, there was hemorrhaging. Dr. Gahuri, who is an excellent surgeon, drained the area and tried to stop it before further damage occurred. Unfortunately, quite a lot of damage had already been done. At the same time, there were problems with the delivery. Her body had been knocked around quite a bit and though we were able to save the baby, we found some internal bleeding. I had to go in a second time to stop it, and I did. Stop the bleeding. But, ah, she'd been through so much by that point and her heart went into arrest. We got her heart beating again, but she arrested two more times." Sara closes her eyes and she bites her lip.

"Is she...did she...?" Amanda's voice is a strangled whisper.

Sara looks at each of them in turn, her eyes finally returning to Jack's. "No, she's not, she hasn't. Died. Yet. But, she is dying. She's in a coma and the chances are slim to none that she'll be able to pull out of it. I don't know how much longer she'll hang on, but it won't be long."

Jack feels his knees begin to buckle and he reaches out to

grab at the wall. Tears fall unchecked down his cheeks and it costs him the last of his strength to ask, “Can you take me to her? Please?”

Sara’s look makes it obvious she has more to say, but Jack shakes his head. He doesn’t want more, he doesn’t need to hear any more of the details. He needs to be with Lindsey and that is all. Nodding, Sara pushes herself off the windowsill.

Naomi’s ragged voice stops her, “What about Mia? Is she OK? The nurse wouldn’t tell us.”

“Please,” Jack repeats. The baby can wait.

Sara holds up her hand, forcing Jack to stop. “You need to hear this,” she says.

Jack feels Lindsey’s pull. He thinks she must be scared and he needs to be with her. “Please.”

“Jack,” Sara clears her throat. “Jack,” she begins again.

Jack watches Sara square her shoulders and he thinks that somehow he should brace himself for more, though he can think of nothing more devastating than the news she has already given him.

“The baby,” Sara says, “your baby, is missing.”

Three

Mar.

They say that Sail Rock is where the hammerhead sharks live. They say it is where they go to breed. Its massive south face slopes downward, tucking in where solid meets liquid, just as a cloth sail would when billowing in a stiff breeze. The rock rises out of the water rather than simply sitting in it, solid. There. Its base, a mammoth mast that anchors the sail to the ocean floor, descends into the depths without so much as an incline to grant it grace.

It is about this pillar that the hammerheads swarm, swirling in a maelstrom of savage lust, monster bodies pushing, shoving at the scent of blood. And, just as it begins, it is over, the meal shredded, torn, devoured. Only now, there is a slight change, a heightened sensibility, maybe even a nervous excitement as goggle eyes search to and fro for the next victim, the next flesh to rip and tear from sinew, from bone. Distances are now maintained, as it would take almost nothing, a slight flick of the tail to the left or maybe to the right, almost nothing for them to turn on each other, mother against daughter, father devouring son, blood lust and greed filling their meager brains where affection and nurture might have been.

Divers go to Sail Rock. Actually pay money for the chance to watch the beasts, to suck up a few thousand pounds of compressed air, all the while pretending to themselves that they themselves look like nothing more than another piece of coral, made of something hard and inedible, not at all like something so sad, so pathetic, as flesh and blood. Wanting to believe, but not quite getting there, that they are safe, that these monsters won't turn, not on a tourist. Not on the source of livelihood for these islands. Finance, after all, rules the world. The dive must be safe or it wouldn't be allowed. Commerce would be threatened by a tourist getting hurt, the dive company would not have brought them here if it wasn't safe. Hoping that thinking it will make it so, but wanting more than anything for the dive to be over, to be in a bar somewhere, able ever after to drop a line, start a conversation with 'yeah, I dove with hammerheads, big motherfuckers, too.' This 30 minutes of water time giving you a story, marking you as somehow different, superior.

But then, you're young, you're on your honeymoon, you got the girl and now the story would be the cap of ten days of sex and sunshine. The part you can talk about. Only, she has sinus problems and the dive company won't take her, won't risk having to bail at the wrong moment. And so she sits by the pool all morning, admires how when the light hits it at just the right angle, the ring throws off thousands of sparks of light. Thinks about babies and baseball games, makes plans of how to be a great, no, a fantastic, wife, a spectacular one, a model soccer mom. Drifts off as the heat of the sun loosens every last muscle, numbs the mind. Gives in to the sensuous heat of the day. *Mmmmmmm...*

And later, when the boat comes back, she's asleep in the liquid light, unaware there's a fuss, the hotel's general manager coming to get her, to wake her up, dazed from languid hours of sleeping in the sun, to lead her away, back to her room, past all the people who are staring at her, talking about her, pointing at her, making the confusion and sudden fear in her belly grow and expand upon itself until it claws and strangles at her throat.

And then it is not she, it is you and your room is cold and dark, air-conditioning and curtains beating back the day. And there is someone else in the room, you don't know it, but he's a doctor, the hotel's on-call doctor, come with drugs, drugs you don't even know yet you're going to need, but he's there, waiting, waiting for that precise moment when your mind explodes in horror, when the silent scream that has been building in your belly finds an outlet, finds its way out your mouth, not silent now, unending.

And so you're told. The honeymoon is over. But how? But how but how but how, you ask, not comprehending. It was safe, it was supposed to be safe, they take tourists there, for god's sake. No no no, this is our honeymoon, this can't happen, not on our honeymoon. They're confused, it was someone else, someone else's husband. Someone who was unhappy, someone who has been married for too many years, someone old, the Dive Master. It was him, not my husband they chose.

But they tell you, a long monologue of backpedaling, of making excuses, of trying to redirect blame. As if blame mattered. At that moment. As if it mattered that he wasn't even the one with the bloody nose, the one who first drew their attention, the one who defined herself as a target. As if it mattered that he is a hero. In death there are no heroes, only death. And so he pushes the lady out of the way, actually believes you can punch a shark in the nose and scare it away. Or, at least, tries, maybe doesn't even think, maybe just reacts, putting his body in front of another man's wife, as he would want someone to put his body in front of his own wife's, and so to try to save her.

And they go for it. What do they care? A free meal's a free meal. And so it begins. The nudging, the pushing, the hitting the diver away from the massive coral face against which he and the woman now cringe. And the woman's husband reaches down and grasps her hair. She is now grabbing her nose, squeezing it through her mask, trying to stop the blood from seeping out and her husband is dragging her up by her hair, screw the bends, forget ascending slower than your smallest bubbles. The fucking sharks aren't watching your bubbles.

Now the diver, though, the hero, has been batted out into the open sea and in one of the passings, his hand has been scraped raw against the leather side of a hammerhead shark, causing a small amount of blood to escape, not much, but more than the one drop per billion that a shark can sense, and so, finally, as is their wont to do, call it instinct, call it nature, call it fate, one of the monsters lunges and almost casually rips off an arm, the one with a ring on its hand, the one that just that morning lay happily pinned beneath his wife's sleeping head. And so it goes, but quicker, faster and faster as more of the beasts get into it. The frenzy begins with vicious teeth gnashing, tearing and ripping until all that is left is a bit of a torso, the part that is spit out again and again as it stubbornly remains wedged inside the buoyancy compensator that remains attached to a tank. And for some god-awful reason, the b.c. doesn't fully pop, but rises, slowly, to the surface, where it is fished out by the Dive Master, a grim token of a man who once was, who just 10 minutes before had had a life.

And what, they wonder, as they stare at you and wait for answers, do you want to be done with his remains? With the small piece of chest against which you used to lay your head to hear his heart beat so furiously after making love? Covered in hair through which you used to run your fingers and which you used to clutch at in the ecstasy of release? Would you prefer a burial or a cremation?

And then, finally, you scream.

Four

Mar.

The alarm clock screams, or is it the phone? Whatever it is, the noise wraps itself nicely into Mar's nightmare. A shrill scrape of sound as she claws her way to the surface, much as a drowning woman would struggle for air. Much as she has imagined the woman with the bloody nose had struggled to the surface, yanking at her flippers, ripping them off and thrusting herself up and into the boat moments before collapsing with the bends.

And just as that woman must have gasped for breath, Mar lies in bed sucking air, her heart thumping loudly in her ears, her body soaked in sweat, her vision blurred to a dull Payne's-Gray, shot through with painful, migraine bursts of Cadmium-Red-Medium-Hue. Her stomach twists with nausea as bits of the dream gnash at her, urging her to return to its depths. *They say they say they say*, and her mind sobs back, *it's true it's true it's true*.

Mar presses her arm across swollen, tired eyes and focuses on the drone of the heater. *Tha-tha-thump, tha-tha-thump*. She draws a ragged breath and her racing heart hitches, as if changing gears, downshifting to a more reasonable speed. She draws another breath. *Tha-tha-thump*. As her mind empties of the memories, Mar gradually becomes aware of the tension about her legs, a confining, suffocating weight twining its way up her body, as if her bed has become part of the dream. She kicks out viscously, or at least tries to, but her legs are pinned in the wound-up sheet. Just like that, fury overtakes her. "No! No! No! Aaaaaargh!!!" Mar yanks at the sheets to free herself. The more frantically she struggles, the tighter the sheets seem to grab at her, until she is fighting wildly for her life. Across the bed and up on the other side, one leg trapped, sending her flying, knocking the breath out of her as she lands flat on the floor, blood erupting in her mouth as her teeth bite her tongue, cheek scraped raw when she connects with the rough carpet pile. And then she is clawing and scrambling, yanking and fighting her leg free and pushing herself up and away. And only when she is standing beside the bed, her chest heaving, the bedclothes flung across the floor, her pillow resting among the knocked-over photos on the dresser where it landed, does true clarity of thought come to her and she realizes that it was The Dream. Just The Dream again.

As she does on most Dream mornings, Mar by-passes the shower and moves down to the kitchen for caffeine. Picasso, her yellow Lab, plods after her.

Mar pushes her flower mugs aside and reaches for the Mars-Black mug she associates with The Dream, fills it with water, and nukes it. Adding two heaping teaspoons of instant coffee, she makes the usual promises to herself that tomorrow she'll quit and settle for the green tea that won't irritate the ulcers that attack her whenever The Dream starts up again.

"You done?" she calls out the back door to the dog, who appears offended that her morning romp in the snow is so short.

With her coffee in hand, Mar climbs the two flights of stairs to the third-floor attic that is her studio. When she bought the house four years before, she had picture windows put in and skylights so that the large, open space is filled with natural light. She sets the coffee down next to a plush, paint-spackled armchair and moves to the larger of her two easels.

The canvas is forty-eight inches high by sixty inches long. She began the painting several days before and is still not sure whether to keep it or to gesso over it and begin again. Up close, the landscape looks good, the dusty, adobe-colored plains with flat-top mesas in the background look realistic. The rust-colored sky screams desolate. She returns to the arm chair, curls up and stares at the painting. Her intention had been to paint a herd of wild horses racing across the foreground. Looking at it now, though, she wonders if she should just leave it as a landscape. She'll get more for the painting if she adds the horses, and she could use the money, but doing so feels more like work than pleasure. She sips her coffee and tries to dredge up a bit of enthusiasm for the project. She tells herself that she doesn't have to like it because the painting is not going to be hanging in her house. But, it will have her name on it. Mar thinks about this. *Do I care?* she asks herself. And that, of course, is her problem.

Years before, she had been a successful artist. Her paintings had sold for thousands of dollars and, by the time she'd graduated from high school, she'd had a following of collectors. Art was in her genes. The only child of a nature illustrator and a sculptress, Mar was an art prodigy. She painted under-water scenes and was often compared to Wyland, though she preferred to paint the abundant life of a coral reef while he was more famous for his paintings of whales and dolphins. That all ended with Joaquin's death while they were on their honeymoon in the Virgin Islands. Since then, she has been unable to paint the ocean, has not even owned a tube of blue paint. Now she paints mountains and deserts, wide open plains and dry washes, cowboys and Indians. And horses.

"I hate horses," she tells Picasso. The dog thumps her tail.

When she was seven, the ocean gave Joaquin to Mar. At least that is how she has always seen it. Her father, widowed when Mar was just a baby, kept her with him whenever she wasn't in school. Most days they tooled around the mangroves in their 13-foot Boston Whaler looking for wildlife to sketch.

That morning they'd been sketching birds off the Key Deer Refuge when a ramshackle wooden boat had rounded into view. No more than thirty feet long and a third as wide, the boat had a small wheelhouse aft but nothing more to cover the forty-plus people who crowded her deck. The single engine was straining and thick black smoke trailed behind it. She was listing badly to port and riding too low in the water. Don Bloom set his sketch pad down.

"Maryann," Don had said to Mar, "put your drawing away. That boat's going over."

By the time they neared the boat, it was taking on water. Panicked people were screaming and pushing each other out of the way to get to the wheelhouse. A number of people had fallen into the water and were flailing around.

"Why don't they swim?" Mar screamed to her father.

"They don't know how," he'd answered. "Honey, help them into the boat, but be careful you don't get pulled in." He set the outboard to idle. "When the boat's full, take them to shore and get back here as quick as you can, OK?"

"Where are you going?" she'd asked, fear constricting her throat.

"I gotta help them, honey." And Don dove into the water.

That day, they'd saved thirty-seven people. Five were never found. One of those they'd saved was a nine-year-old boy named Joaquin. His father, a doctor, had been prohibited by the Castro government from leaving the island and so he and his wife, sensing that life in Cuba was going to become increasingly difficult, had made the decision to escape. While most of the refugees Mar and her father had helped that day made their ways to Miami and beyond, Joaquin's family had stayed in the Keys and no one was surprised when, years later, Joaquin and Mar, as he called her, were married.

***

The phone rings, breaking through her reverie. She stretches out behind her and blindly snatches the cordless unit from its cradle, her eyes still focused on the painting.

"Hey, girl, what you up to?"

"Shirley! How are you? What's up?"

"Not much in the wider sense of the world, but things're looking up in your life."

"Why? What's going on? You're not calling me at seven in the morning to give me another sob story, are you?" she asks her best friend. "By the way, did you call about half an hour ago?"

"I sure did, honey, and yes, I am calling you about that, but it's your sweet apple pie ass that's gonna beg me for a change. Girl, you ain't got it in you to say no to this one." And Shirley, her voice saturated with glee, begins to cackle.

Mar makes a face, regretting answering the phone, and runs a hand through her hair. Her fingers become entangled in the unruly mess and she tucks the phone under her chin and tries to work the snarl free. "Don't start that Jamaican jive shit on me, please," she begs. "It's too bloody early."

Shirley's laughter grows louder, "I know, sugar, I know."

Mar gives up on her hair and reaches for her coffee instead. The woman is a nuisance. "OK," she sighs, "what've you got?"

Shirley, perhaps sensing a change in Mar's resistance, maybe a little slippage in her armor, drops the Jamaican accent and moves in for the kill. "Little girl. About four or five months. It's hard to say. She doesn't appear to be well nourished, so she could be a little older. We've had her for a couple of days down at Memorial. Otherwise healthy, though there are a couple more tests we're waiting for the results on."

"Such as?" Mar asks and immediately regrets giving Shirley an in.

"You know, the usual. AIDS, HIV, Hepatitis..." Shirley's voice trails off.

"And what are the chances of those?" Yawning, Mar rubs her tired eyes and notes that the throbbing in her left temple is easing. Just a little.

Shirley's voice drops further, "*Mmmm*, fair to middlin'. It looks like her mom was a druggie." And now, as though sensing that she's lost precious ground, she rushes on to try to make up for it, "But, you know that doesn't mean the kid's infected, or even that the mother was. It's just a precaution. The doctors think she's in good health, results pending of course."

"And the mom? Where is she?"

"Dead. The police found her a couple of days ago, arm tied off, a needle sticking out of it. A neighbor heard the kid crying and it finally occurred to him to call the police. He said he thought it was normal, babies cry and all that. Of course, he's no prize himself."

"What about relatives? Any clue?" In spite of herself, Mar's curiosity begins to get the best of her. She takes a slug of coffee, settles back into the chair and prepares to sit awhile.

"None that we can find. The people in her building are not your Joe-Good-Citizens, all eager to help. What we've gathered is that she and her daughter have been there a couple of months. They came from California – following a band, or something. Anyway, that's the story. She had a job in a local head shop. They let her bring the baby to work, said she was an angel, never cried or anything."

"So what are we looking at? Short term? Long term? What?"

Shirley pauses long enough that Mar, all the way across town, feels herself being weighed and knows that Shirley has to be thinking about Max and wondering whether Mar Delgado is stable enough to handle another child. Mar presses the phone into her stomach and smacks her head with her palm. One time, two times, three times, clonk, clonk, clonk, when will it end? Shirley has a right to doubt her, but still. She puts the phone back to her ear and bites her lip, determined not to speak.

"Mar, I'm sorry, I really don't know. The mother was a drifter and we don't have much on her. We haven't found any I.D., nothing I'd vouch for anyway, and she pretty much kept to herself. We think the head shop was paying her under the table and, if so, there won't be any Social Security numbers we can follow up on. She's been in town at least four months, though, and everyone I've spoken with so far says she was a great mother. Except for the little drug problem, that is."

"But, time-wise, what kind of commitment are you looking for?"

"I'm open, I just don't know. We could find a relative in a week, a month. It could take years, who knows? You've been there before, you know how this works."

"Yeah, I know," Mar's voice is filled with misery. She knows the emptiness of losing someone and she doesn't think her heart can take another blow.

"Honey, we're not asking that you become a mother to this kid," Shirley seems to intuit her thoughts. "We just need to find a temporary home for her until we can sort things out. It probably won't take too long and, in any case, I wouldn't put you in that kind of position."

"Yeah, I know," Mar sighs. "Alright, look, can I have some time to think about this?"

"I need an answer today. Preferably this morning. Otherwise, I've got to find another foster home for her."

"Yeah, OK. Look, let me drink my coffee, take a shower, think about it." She pauses as a plausible excuse occurs to her. "Listen, I don't even have a crib or anything..."

"That's not the issue. You know that."

"Yeah, yeah, I know. BUT...."

"Yeah, but. Just call me, alright? Say by eleven?"

Mar glances at the wall clock and calculates how long she can put off making the decision. "By noon. I promise."

"OK, baby, I'm counting on you. So is this little girl."

"You know what, Shirl? You can kiss my butt." Mar clicks off the phone. The painting, she decides, is awful. Horses will help. But it is not figuring out what to do with the painting that makes her smile. It's the thought of having a baby in the house. Mar tries to temper her enthusiasm, to keep it from becoming so big that it envelops her and eats her alive. Like it had with Max.

Five

Jack.

The jangle of the phone reaches through the fog. Strange. It hasn't rung in days. Jack pulls his gaze back from the window. "Yes, Robert?"

"There's a Mr. Colomanos here to see you, sir," the doorman says.

"Oh." Jack's eyes move to his watch and he notes that the morning has, in fact, long passed. "Thanks. Please let him up."

Sy Colomanos is somewhere in his fifties. Fit, but for the slight paunch, he wears his sparse hair just short of balding, no sweeping it over the top and gluing it down with spray for Sy. He wouldn't put up with that kind of shit and that is just one of the many things that Jack has always respected about the man. But now he reaches out tiredly and takes Sy's outstretched hand. "Sy. Thanks for coming." Jack leads the private investigator to the living room and watches as Sy takes in the charts and whiteboards that cover the walls. "Take a seat," he says, waving at the sofa. "Get comfortable." The manners, ingrained since childhood, are rusty on his tongue. "Uh, do you want anything to drink? Coffee maybe?"

"Nah, thanks, I'm OK. How you doin', Jack?"

How is he doing? Jack bites off a laugh. Now there's a

question. His eyes return to the window, as if the answer lies somewhere along the dreary skyline. There is a weight about the city in February. The invigorating crispness of the cold just doesn't do well in Manhattan, where the deep ravines created by block after block of tall buildings cause the wind to build upon itself as it tunnels through without escape. A gentle breeze can whip into a shearing knife in the winter streets. Lindsey had liked the cold, had liked the rawness of it. She'd pile on clothes and drag him out for a walk, her cheeks turning a brilliant red, her laughter egging him on, the two of them feeling like they were the only people left in the world.

"Jack?"

Sy's voice brings Jack back to the present. He rubs at the raw skin of his eyelids and then looks up at his old friend. "Sorry. I was just thinking about how Lindsey liked winter..." His voice chokes on her name, catches as he tries to hide behind a forced cough. "Fuck," he finishes, and takes a deep breath.

Sy nods and Jack knows he understands. Sy would know. Early in their relationship, Lindsey had taken a liking to the solid detective, had taken to calling him when Jack was too wrapped up in work to come home, too busy with a case to give her the attention she deserved. "He's so lonely," she'd once told him. "He's all tough on the outside, but inside he's a marshmallow." Jack doesn't know about the marshmallow part, but he can buy the bit about Sy being lonely. Leaping ahead twenty years, the same length of time that Sy has been a widower, will he be the guy that some lonely wife calls to walk with her when her husband is too busy to pay her any attention? To try out a new restaurant, take in a movie? The crushing weight of every second wasted bears down on him and Jack swears again.

Sy's eyes find his. "You want me to look for the baby?" he asks.

Jack pushes out of the chair he'd settled into. It is like that lately, up, down, up, down. Nothing makes sense anymore. Not sitting, not standing, not eating. Some people, when confronted by disaster, rise to the occasion, actually make something positive out of it. Not Jack. The double blow of losing Lindsey and then Mia is just too crushing for him to handle. He spends a lot of days lost in the fog. "I can't believe it's been six months," he says. "Lindsey'd kill me if she knew."

"Yeah, well, the cops've been following up on it pretty strong. It's not like no one's been looking." But though Sy is an adroit liar, Jack hears the emptiness in his words. People go missing all the time in New York, hundreds at a time. The cops have more than enough to handle.

"Thanks, Sy, but that's crap. Look at this city." Jack waves at the view, at the endless expanse of concrete, steel and glass. "There's drama going on all over the place and the cops can't keep up with it. At first, with the FBI staying at the house, waiting for a ransom call, we thought it'd be over in a day or two, a week at the most. But the call never came." He shakes his head, remembering. "They left, took all their equipment and just left. Said if this was a kidnapping for ransom, the call would've come within the week. They waited three weeks and then couldn't 'justify' it any more. We thought that with the reward and all..." his voice trails off, taking the failure personally. Amanda had hired the Merritt Agency to find the baby and they'd all thought they'd be enough, what with the cops and the FBI and all. But there hadn't been any new leads in months. It was like the woman who had taken Mia had fallen off the face of the earth. No one knew where she'd come from or where she might go. She could be anywhere. She could be dead. She and the baby could be dead. Jack lets his head fall so that his forehead hits the window. He can't allow his mind go there or he'll go crazy. His voice is muffled when he speaks. "I've got a list for you," he says. "It's not much and it's probably mostly crap anyway. The FBI just about creamed over it, though, thought they could tie the kidnapping to someone I've pissed off, a revenge kind of thing."

"You think that's possible?" Sy's voice is filled with even amounts of doubt and disgust. "Sounds like a buncha crap to me. I mean, yeah, sure, you've taken on some bottom feeders, those skinheads, remember them? Fuck, Krillov. Those kinda people don't like you showing the world what they've been up to. Those guards diddlin' the girls in that rehab joint, but still."

"He came to my office, did I ever tell you that?"

"Krillov?"

"Just marched right in, about gave Elena a heart attack, him and his guys. Said he came to tell me how sorry he was about 'the way things turned out.' Said it's not right to take a man's kid. Can you fucking believe it? Here's the guy that would dunk a little girl in blood, that'd poison an entire family with prions, not kill them right away, mind you, but leave them alive for a couple of years, watching their kids' brains melt to goo."

"He was messing with you, Jack."

"No fucking kidding!" Jack yells. "And you know what? If I'd had a gun, I could of killed him right on the spot, just fucking killed him." He takes a deep breath. "Only, I know it's crap. He had nothing to do with taking Mia, with the accident. How could he?"

"But he had someone waiting outside your building, someone who saw Lindsey leave for the hospital."

Jack waves this away. "The woman who took Mia, she'd been working at the hospital for awhile. Krillov couldn't have had someone working in every single hospital waiting for Lindsey to go into labor."

"He could have found out who Lindsey's doctor was, found out which hospital she works out of."

"You know what all that is?" Jack gestures at the stacks of files that litter the living room, that are piled on the sofa and coffee table, that overflow the dining room table he'd dragged there and that crowd the storage boxes that lean against the walls. "Those are the files of every single case I've ever worked on. Every single one. That's about eight years of cases here and another seven years of notes from the D.A.'s. Do you know what I've been doing for the past six months while the cops've found shit? I've been going over those, page by page. And you know what I've found? Nothing! No one had the balls, or the money, or the opportunity, hell, the brains, to pull that accident off. That's just insanity! And then, to take my kid! What the hell were they thinking?" Jack sighs deeply and stuffs his hands into his pockets, his shoulders slumping. Returning to the chair, he sits heavily. "Anyway, I made the list, people who lost a case, anyone who might hold a grudge."

"Nah, there's easier ways to kidnap a kid, if that's your thing, than hanging around a hospital waiting for it to be born," Sy agrees. "That's way too Twilight Zone. Course, that's probably why it appeals to the Feds."

"You know it's Shaheen who got the case, right?" Jack asks, referring to Sy's old nemesis from when Sy was a cop and he and Shaheen had gotten into a jurisdictional pissing contest. It was a good case, a big case, one that Sy had wrapped up but that Shaheen and the Feds had taken all the credit for.

Sy returns Jack's stare calmly and then nods. "He's good," Sy says.

"But he hasn't found a thing."

Sy pushes out of the chair and moves to the row of whiteboards on the walls. On one board, Jack has drawn out a timeline of the events leading up to the kidnapping. Several others, covered in drawings and sticky notes, contain lists of leads arranged under such titles as, "Krillov," "Ransom," "Black Market," and "Random."

Jack waits for Sy, lets him think through the possibilities. Sy has a way of cutting through the b.s., of getting to the heart of the matter. Twenty-plus years working as a cop and a dozen or so as a P.I., Jack trusts Sy as no other and curses himself again for waiting so damn long to call him in.

"Listen, Jack," Sy finally says, "I've been following it, in my own way, and I think you're right. It was an opportunity kind of thing, had to've been." He taps a grainy photo of the candy striper who carried Mia out of the hospital bundled in an oversize bag. "Any case, I'm gonna need copies of the reports Amanda's been getting from that agency, whatever you've got. Can you get me that?"

Jack picks up a manila folder that is painfully thin and

tosses it to Sy.

"This is it?" Sy asks. "This is all they got in six months? What the hell kind of detectives do they hire down at that fancy place?"

"That's it," Jack apologizes. "I told you, it's garbage."

Jack watches as Sy flips through the scant reports in the file, reports that he himself has poured over countless times, has dissected and memorized until they burn in his brain even while he sleeps. More photos of the candy striper as she hurries past a security camera, copies of her stolen Social Security card, stolen I.D., finger prints not on file, questions leading to dead end after dead end.

When he reaches the end, Sy slaps the file closed. "It's a start," he says and Jack nods, his fear that it is all crap confirmed.

"Listen," Jack says, "as far as I'm concerned, the cops have given up. Shaheen's stuck on Krillov and kids being sold on the black market. Amanda's got the Merritt guys on retainer looking I don't know where. I want you to focus on that girl." He points to the photo. "She's the one who knows everything."

Sy nods and Jack leans forward, finding Sy's eyes and holding them. "And when you find her?" he says, "I don't want you to do anything. Just tell me where she is."

"Uh, Jack..."

"Just tell me where she is, Sy." Jack's voice is flat and leaves no room for argument.

"Sure, Jack," Sy says. "Sure."

Six

Mar.

Mar drives her Hunter-Green Explorer through snow-blanketed streets. Even on this Dream morning, the towering mountains of the Front Range soothe her. When she packed her bags four years before, two weeks to the day after Joaquin's funeral, and left the Florida Keys for good, she hadn't known where she'd end up. At the time, all she'd known was that the ocean called to her and mocked her, invited her to join her husband. The invitation was almost more than she could resist. She'd found Boulder, nestled into the foothills of the Rockies, no ocean or other large body of water nearby. And that had been important to her then. Still is. The sheer massiveness of the mountains at her back makes her feel strong. Back to the wall, this is where she'll make her stand. No sharks in sight.

On this morning, she makes her way to Shirley's office. Located near the University, The Center for Child Welfare is a warm and welcoming place. Prettily painted walls, soft, framed prints and fresh flowers, even in the cold month of February, soothe the senses and refresh the spirit. And everywhere there are toys and books arranged to draw out and delight even the most introverted of children.

Mar parks behind The Center's van and lets the engine

idle. She already regrets telling Shirley she'd come. If nothing else, Joaquin's death made her realize that loving another person is too dangerous, is too all-consuming. Max's death underscored that lesson. That is why she does not date, though she's had offers, why she prefers to be alone and why, a year ago, she'd asked Shirley to take her name off The Center's list of certified foster parents. Mar tilts the rear-view mirror down. Drawn, pinched features, swollen, raw cheek, tired brown eyes, ragged auburn hair escaping from the butterfly clip she'd tried to capture it with. "Is this the face of someone who should be entrusted with the care of a child?" she asks. She gives it a chance, but the mirror doesn't answer, and so she pushes it back into place and reaches for her earmuffs and gloves. Puts them on before opening the car door and making the twenty-foot dash to the front door.

The reception alcove is empty. "Shirley?" Mar calls. "Where are you?"

"In the kitchen. Come on back."

After hanging her coat, Mar follows the sound of laughter through the converted house to the kitchen. She can't help but smile at the sight of Shirley surrounded by five neighborhood children, all of whom seem to be covered in flour. Dylan, who is both Shirley's lover and a well-respected PhD in Developmental Psychology, is there as well, decked out in a frilly apron. He, too, is covered in flour and Mar freezes in the doorway, stunned by the sudden urge to paint this scene. This, she thinks, and the fingers of her right hand curl around an imaginary pencil. For a brief moment, she sees the completed piece in her mind, the muted colors of an Andrew Wyeth watercolor, setting, facial expressions and body dynamics more important than color. This is what she would paint, if she could trust herself to feel. She pushes her hands into the pockets of her jeans, smiles broadly, and steps into the kitchen.

"As you can see," Dylan says by way of greeting, "she's got us all working again." But neither he nor the children seem to mind one bit.

“So this is how you spend your free time.”

“Free time? Girl, the only thing free about my time is how much I get paid for it. Otherwise, I’m busy 24-7,” Shirley says. “How you doin’?”

At forty-three, with closely-cropped graying hair, skin the color of warm caramel on a hot afternoon and a huge dimple in her right cheek that deepens when she smiles, which is most of the time, Shirley is a very striking woman. From Jamaica, she’d made her way to the United States twenty-some years before and worked hard to put herself through university, where she’d eventually earned two doctorates – one in Psychology, with a specialization in child psychology, and the other in Business Administration. Not easy by any means, but she’d managed to do it all as a single mother. She’d been courted by child welfare agencies the country over but, somehow, she’d ended up in Boulder, which ever since has enjoyed one of the highest adoption rates and lowest child abuse rates in the country.

Mar pours a cup of coffee from the Mr. Coffee and moves to the table. Now that she is in their space, the children pay attention to her, pointing out their own decorations and trying to get her to pronounce one the prettiest. Not stupid, she *oohs* and *aahs* over each and, for her efforts, is rewarded with a cookie from each of the little chefs.

“Dylan, honey,” Shirley says, “will you watch the kids while I go talk with Mar?”

“It would be my greatest pleasure.” Dylan, holding the edge of the apron out like a ballroom dress, tips his head and curtsies. Squeals of laughter erupt from little mouths.

“Aw, Dylan, you just a big huggie-bear,” proclaims one little girl, looking up at him in adoration. The others take up the chant “huggie-bear” as Shirley and Mar make their way from the kitchen up to Shirley’s second floor office.

“What happened to you?” Shirley speaks over her shoulder. “You sure someone’s not using you as a punching bag? Your whole face is a mess.”

“Gee, thanks, and here I was thinking you liked me.”

"I love you, Mar girl, you know that, but..."

"I tripped."

"Uh-huh, you tripped."

Mar, sensing the eye-roll even though Shirley's back is to her, grits her teeth.

Shirley's office is in what was originally the house's master bedroom. Sponge-painted a cheerful pale yellow, the office, like everything else at The Center, is neat and organized. A Little Tykes yellow, blue and red picnic table occupies one corner of the spacious room and shelves offer books and art supplies. A photo arcade of smiling faces fills the credenza against the back wall, but other than a computer monitor and simple four-line telephone, the desk is bare. Except for one file. Mar settles into one of the two visitor chairs and watches as Shirley reaches for the file.

"What we've got here," Shirley begins, her voice now businesslike, "is a little girl, probably five months old. When she was found, she was undernourished and had a pretty nasty chest cold. No bruises or bumps, however, which is encouraging and hopefully means she was not physically abused. She's a quiet child and, even at such a young age, a bit wary. She startles easily and whimpers a little, but that's about it. At the hospital, she was given antibiotics and is responding well. Luckily, the cold was just that and not pneumonia." Shirley looks up at Mar. "She wouldn't have survived pneumonia."

"Where did you find her?" Mar asks.

"In a rat-infested flop-house. Just short of a shooting-gallery. We were lucky this time. When they're this young, they can't defend themselves and sometimes, especially in winter, the rats get to the kids before we do. Before tying off, the mother had sort of barricaded the baby in a box she must've used as a crib. Anyway, it kept the rats off the kid. Or maybe they had enough to eat with the mother." Shirley sighs and lowers the file. "The mother, Natalie Jones, managed to swing the hundred-dollars-a-month rent the room cost her. They'd been there at least four months. She had a job at a head shop near the University, made minimum wage. Apparently, the rest of the money she made, and anything else she could get her hands on, went to crack, heroin, you name it. According to the guy she worked for, he'd wanted to fire her because she was becoming more and more irresponsible, go figure, but the only reason he didn't was because of the baby. He was afraid of what would happen to the baby if the mother had no income. He even let her bring the baby to work. On a good note, he did say that the mother seemed to be devoted to the child, whose name is Elizabeth, by the way. She was always clean and the mother would fuss over her. He was afraid the baby wasn't getting enough to eat and would bring in milk and baby food for her."

"Is there any family?"

"Like I told you, not that we've been able to trace. According to her boss, she showed up several months ago. Her application doesn't list family and he never heard her mention anyone. The housemate either. Of course, we'll keep looking. Ideally, we'll find a warm and loving aunt or grandmother for the baby. Ideally. But, you know how often ideally works out." Shirley shakes her head and looks out the window.

Mar watches Shirley, and waits, but Shirley won't look at her. "Why'd you call me?" she finally asks. "Why didn't you take me off your list?"

Shirley turns from the window and meets Mar's gaze. "Truth?" she asks.

"Truth."

Opening the file, Shirley takes out a four-by-six inch photo and slides it across the desk. "She reminds me of you," Shirley says.

Reluctantly, Mar pulls the photo into her lap and looks down at it. The baby is covered in a hospital blanket and wears a knit cap. Fine, blonde curls spill out around the edge of the hat. Her skin is a translucent white, so pale that Mar imagines she would be able to see the girl's heart if she pulled the blanket away. Her eyes are the color of the mid-day sky over the Keys. Mar turns the photo over. "She doesn't look anything like me," she says and her voice is a whisper.

Instead of answering, Shirley pushes back from her desk and moves around to the second visitor chair. She reaches for the photo, turns it back over. Mar looks away. "But she acts like you," Shirley says. "She is sad and lost and lonely," Shirley's voice trails off.

"Like me," Mar finishes.

"Like you."

Mar looks down to the photo. Now she sees it, the frown between the infant's faint eyebrows, the ingrained acceptance in her eyes, the set of her mouth. Mar recognizes the resemblance. She has seen this look in the mirror every day for four years. "I don't think I'd be very good for her," she says.

"Try, Mar. Please."

Seven

Mar.

Mar startles awake, fear clutching at her throat. Gasping, she curls a fist to her chest, feels her heart beating a wild staccato. "*Shhhhh*," she tells herself when she realizes she is in her own bedroom. "No sharks here, no sharks, no sharks," she whispers the mantra that has calmed her on countless other nightmare nights. As she quiets and releases herself again to sleep, a wisp of a thought floats behind her eyelids, knocks on her subconscious and, when that doesn't wake her, forms itself into a long, thin spike and jabs itself straight into nerve central. Mar jerks awake. "The baby!"

She hurries to the crib that she set up in a corner of her bedroom and looks inside. Elizabeth stares straight up at her, tension pinching her little face, her perfect hands clenched into fists. "Oh, baby, I'm so sorry, sweetheart, I thought you were a shark," Mar coos as she reaches in to pick her up. "Are you OK? Do you want some milk? Are you wet? What's wrong, little girl?"

Mar loosens the blanket that swaddles Elizabeth. At the hospital, when Mar went to pick her up, the nurses told her that binding the baby would make her feel safer, more protected. Mar isn't sure they were right, but what does she know? She has only had the little girl for two days and is still too timid to step away from the regimen set by Those Who Know Better.

Once freed, Mar checks the baby's diaper. Dry. "Nope, nothing there. So, are you hungry? Do you want to try something to drink? Why don't we go try something to drink?"

Followed closely by Picasso, Mar carries Elizabeth downstairs to the kitchen and, slipping her hand around the corner until her fingers find the switch, she eases on the lights. There are three rooms in the old house that are Mar's favorites: her third-floor attic studio, the art gallery on the first floor that she carved out of the living, dining and sitting rooms, and the kitchen. Mar rarely cooks, in fact most days she has to remind herself to eat, but Joaquin had been a talented chef who specialized in Caribbean dishes and this room, so far from home, fills her with him. When she'd first come to Boulder and begun house hunting, she'd found other houses that wouldn't have required extensive remodeling. There'd even been a loft downtown that would have been perfect for her. But she'd kept coming back to this house. More specifically, to this kitchen. With weathered brick walls, "architectural salvage," her realtor had said, gleaming appliances, an expansive central island and a walk-in pantry, this would have been Joaquin's dream kitchen. She'd painted a full size picture of him wearing his chef's hat and apron, complete with the "Mar-Joaqua's" logo over his left breast, the name of the restaurant he'd been set to open after their honeymoon, and hung it directly across from the room's entrance. As the glow of the overhead lights spreads to the depths of the kitchen, Joaquin steps out to her. It is an illusion that never fails to fracture her heart.

The kitchen is cold. Mar adjusts the thermostat and moves to the counter to settle Lizzie in her bouncing chair. The cloth-covered wire frame cradles the baby much as a hammock would and was designed so that her every movement would cause the chair to gently bounce. Except, Elizabeth doesn't bounce. She barely moves. Other than her eyes, which follow Mar. "Let's just strap you in so you don't fall out," Mar tells the baby, her voice pitching unnaturally.

"Talk to her," Shirley had said when Mar called earlier, unnerved by the baby's scrutiny, panicked by her silence. "Let her get used to you. She'll loosen up."

Mar wraps the cloth safety belt across Lizzie and clips it into place. She pushes down on the head of the chair, setting it in motion, before turning to the refrigerator for a small bottle of baby formula. After ten seconds in the microwave, she shakes the bottle and tests the temperature on both wrists and then farther up her arm.

"Here you go, little girl, do you want some milk?" She tickles Elizabeth's lips with the bottle's nipple. In response, Lizzie opens her mouth and pulls just once before ejecting the nipple and firmly shutting her lips. Mar runs the backs of her fingers down Lizzie's cheek. "Can you try? Just a little?" She puts the nipple back to Lizzie's mouth, but the baby won't take it. Mar's shoulders slump as the weight of failure washes over her. Tomorrow, she'll have to talk to Shirley about finding a better home for the little girl. She is terrified that the baby will starve.

Mar unscrews the nipple and dumps the milk into the dog's bowl. "She's a pig, Lizzie. A pig. And you are not helping matters."

Picasso slurps up the milk, her tail wagging. Mar turns back to the baby. "OK, then, your diaper's dry, you're not hungry, it's two in the morning and you're wide awake. What is it you want?"

When the baby doesn't answer, Mar lifts her out of the bounce chair, turns off the heater that has just begun to warm the room, flips off the lights, and trudges back up the stairs. "Listen, kid," she says when they reach the second floor, "you're going to have to work with me on this. I'm not that great at guessing what you want and if you don't start to eat, they're going to take you away from me." She lowers the baby into the crib. Lizzie, looking wide awake, stares back at her. "I'll tell you what," Mar says, reaching again for her, "how's about you climb into bed with me for a little bit and we'll watch some TV? Would you like that? Uh-huh. OK, let's go."

Eight

Sy.

Sy adjusts the car's air conditioner to high. Even on that setting, it doesn't come close to cutting through the humidity that hangs like a wet towel over South Florida. He loosens his shirt one more button and twists his neck to each side until he hears a satisfying crack, "*Aaaah.*" For the tenth time that hour he wonders why people retire to Florida. Just one traffic jam on the turnpike south convinced him that he'll stay in New York when his time comes to give it all up.

The car in front of him moves and Sy edges up to the toll booth and rolls down his window. "How far to Homestead?"

"About another fifteen miles," the booth operator takes his money. "You here on vacation?"

"Nah, just lookin' someone up."

"New York, huh? I got me a friend in New York sounds just like you. Says it's really hot up there now. You enjoy some of our fresh air, ya hear?"

Miserable in the heat, Sy slides the window up before mumbling, "Bite me."

Forty-five minutes later, he pulls off onto the Homestead exit. *Fifteen miles, my ass,* he thinks, glancing at the odometer. *Double that, more like it.*

Homestead is a desolate place. There are still signs of the hurricane that roared through almost two decades before. At least, he imagines it was the hurricane. It could just be lousy county maintenance and no one caring enough to keep it up. Ten minutes later, he decides no one cares. Maybe it's the heat.

The house he is looking for isn't really a house. It is a double-wide trailer that is located in one of the few trailer communities that withstood Hurricane Andrew. He drives through a light just as it changes from yellow to red and turns into Sunshine Streams Mobile Estates. A guardhouse at the entrance causes him to slow down until he notices it is abandoned. He drives on.

The community is laid out in meandering lanes where lazy curves lull the mind into thinking the place is almost nice. Pretty little flower gardens pay testament to the fact that in retirement you have time to mess around in the dirt. He thinks the lawn police should do something about all the crappy little lawn thingies, though. Funky little gnomes probably coming alive at night, getting into all sorts of trouble, little woodland animals peeing on tires, making bunny love, sprouting a whole new generation of yard junk. As he looks for her number, he wonders what makes trailer people so obsessed with the shit. You never see this kind of crap in front of mansions. But at least they keep the neighborhood clean. Not like some he's seen in New York.

Sy has spent the past four months looking for the baby, tracking down every possible lead. He's pulled strings, has even met up with Shaheen from the Bureau. Nothing. Then, two days ago, a woman who once worked at the hospital where Lindsey died and Mia was kidnapped, returned to work. "I got a divorce," she told Sy. "I was lucky to get my old job back." Arlene Thomas, who worked as a cashier in the hospital's cafeteria, had been the one to tell Sy that the kidnapper had often met another girl for lunch. It took Sy another forty-eight hours to track Elie Burrows to her mother's home in Florida.

Sy finally spots the trailer he is looking for at the end of a cul-de-sac. He can see between the houses that it backs up to a little pond or a lake. Something wet. Probably primo property around here. He pulls the car over to where the grass meets the street, reaches for his ragged briefcase and heaves his large frame out of the car. The humidity makes him feel soggy and limp. *Ah, shit,* he thinks, and reaches for the handkerchief that isn't in his pocket where it's supposed to be. Frustrated, he wipes his forehead on his shirtsleeve and walks to the trailer's door.

The door is festooned with a plastic Christmas wreath and has little white lights stapled around its frame. They blink. When he touches the bell, a tinny version of "Winter Wonderland" begins to play. Sy rolls his eyes and tries to straighten his sweat-stained shirt.

The woman who opens the door looks to be in her late-seventies, maybe somewhere in the hundreds. Steel-grey roots barely hidden by umber-colored, over-processed, tightly-coiled curls. Crocodile skin tanned nut-brown by the sun. Soft, loose jowls that sway below her chins when she cocks her head to look at him. He thinks she must approve of what she sees because the smile that reveals perfectly-cast dentures in Cover Girl White goes all the way up to her faded blue eyes.

"Hello there," says the woman. "Can I help you?"

"Yes, ma'am," says Sy. "I'm looking for Mrs. Esther Burrows."

"Well, then, sir, today's your lucky day. You found me. What can I do for you?"

Sy fishes a damp business card from his shirt pocket and holds it out to her. She pushes the screen door open and reaches for it. Leaning her bulk against the screen to keep it open, she lifts the glasses that hang from a colorful paper clip chain around her neck and fits them onto her button nose. "I've got really good eyesight for far away things," she explains. "Just can't see what's close up in front of my face."

"I'm Sy Colomanos," Sy says.

"Well, so you say you are," she replies, examining the card. "Leastways that's what it says here. Oh, my, it says you're a private investigator. Now, what's that all about? And what do you want from me? Did someone die and leave me money?"

"I'm looking for someone, ma'am, and I thought you could help me." Sy opens the file he is carrying and takes out a grainy black-and-white photo of a young woman dressed as a hospital candy striper. The photo, taken by a security camera, shows the woman cradling a bulky purse. He hands the photo over to Esther Burrows.

Mrs. Burrows squints down at it. "Well now, that's not a very good photograph, is it?"

"It was taken by a security camera, ma'am."

"Yes, I can see that. *Hmmm*. She looks familiar, but I can't seem to place her." Mrs. Burrows pushes her glasses farther up her nose and squints harder, her eyes all but disappearing into the crepe-like folds surrounding them. "Why, I saw this picture on *America's Mystery Crimes*, didn't I? This girl took that baby, right? The one's mother died? That show was last month, or maybe in May, wasn't it?"

"Yes you did, ma'am. But I was wondering if you'd ever seen her before the show. We think she knew your daughter."

"Elie? This girl's a friend of Elie's?" Surprise lights her face.

"Yes, ma'am. At least we think so."

Esther Burrows looks into Sy's eyes and he can see her wondering if this conversation is going to cause her pain. Finally, sighing, she pushes the screen door open wider. "You'd best come in. And please stop calling me ma'am. I can't be much older than you."

Nine

Sy.

"Elie, my daughter, was a late child. My husband, Earl, he came back from the war in a wheelchair. The doctors said it'd be a miracle if he could ever have kids. Well, sir, a miracle happened and when I was forty-eight years old, Elie was born. Elizabeth Barrett Burrows. I named her after that poet lady. The one whose husband loved her so much? We thought Burrows was a lot like Browning, kind of sounds the same, you know? Anyway, she was a late baby and a handful from the day she was born. Can I get you more soda?"

Sy shakes his head. Even with the air conditioner rattling away in its window perch, the trailer is hot. The two ice cubes had quickly melted in the glass of Root Beer she'd insisted he take. Now it is lukewarm and watery. Even under the best of conditions, Sy can't stand the stuff. "No, thank you. You were saying?"

"Yes, well, you can imagine," Esther peers at him from under her bushy eyebrows, emphasizing her point. "Here I was, almost fifty and with a baby. Plus, a husband in a wheelchair. It wasn't easy, I can tell you that, even with Earl's army pension. We lived in Toledo then, or outside of it. I had a job at PPG, cleaning the offices. Here, let me show you."

Putting her hands on her knees, Esther pushes herself up and moves to a small book shelf filled with photo albums. Tracing a finger over the hand-printed titles on the spines, she chooses one and returns to the sofa. Opening the book, she flips through a few pages, a private smile lifting the edges of her mouth.

"Here," she says, passing the book over to Sy. "That was our house. We got it after the war. The government used to help people back then."

The single-story house in the photo is small, but neat. There is a ramp up to the front door, presumably to help the man who lost the use of his legs for his country. Standing in front of the house is a laughing young woman. Even in black and white, it is easy to see that Esther Burrows had been a beauty in her youth.

As she had, Sy flips through a few pages. As time passed, Esther smiled less and less and her beauty began to fade. Suddenly, there she is, a middle aged woman with a baby. The toll her pregnancy had taken on her body and spirit is obvious.

"Yes, sir, it was hard. I had to switch my schedule around to work nights while the baby slept so's I could take care of her during the day. Earl, he tried, but he wasn't very good at babying. More'n twenty years in the chair had drained him and he needed to take lots of naps. Elie, though, you'd take your eye off her for a second and the house might be burned down or she'd've disappeared. She did that, you know, disappeared a lot. I think it was a trial for her, too, having parents so much older than she was. We tried, but we couldn't keep up. By sixth grade, she was takin' off least once a month. She'd be gone a day or two, stay at a friend's house, not bother to tell us where. Pretty soon, the police wouldn't even come anymore, I'd filed so many missing person reports. One time, a lady from Social Services come by and Elie got scared. She behaved for a while after that. Eventually, though, her spirit was just too big for that little house. When Earl took real bad, Elie was about fifteen. I had to quit my job to take care of him. Elie couldn't stand the 'smell of sickness,' is what she called it, and took off for good. Haven't seen her since."

"Have you heard from her since then?"

Esther retrieves a cookie tin from on top of the small television, removes the lid and hands the tin to Sy. It is full of postcards. Sy glances through them. From their postmarks, he can tell that they'd arrived every few months for years. "How long has she been gone?"

"A little over eight years."

"And she's been writing all that time?" Sy glances up.

"She was real good about it at the beginning. Sent me one every now and then to let me know she was doin' OK. After Earl died, I moved down here to be near my sister. The couple that bought the house've been sending me her postcards over the years. But the last one I got was about two years ago."

Sy sifts through them until he finds the latest postmark. He flips it over. The Statue of Liberty stares back at him.

Ten

Mar.

"You're going to have to paint her awake sometime, you know."

Jumping at the sound of Diane's voice, the paintbrush flies from Mar's hand. "Jesus! Don't do that."

"I made enough noise to start a stampede," Diane says. She shakes her head and her shoulder-length gray hair brushes the collar of her denim shirt. Denim shirt over blue jeans, Diane's standard outfit, broken up today by a bright, multi-colored scarf around her neck. She moves into the studio and stands in front of Mar's canvas, tilting her head first one way and then the other, her eyes narrowing as she scrutinizes the painting. Mar picks up the brush, wipes the smudge of paint off the floorboard with her fingers and wipes her fingers on her jeans. There is nothing she can say to discourage Diane's inevitable critique, so she doesn't try.

"You really need to paint her with her eyes open," Diane finally says. Still staring at the painting, she holds a craft store bag out to Mar. "I brought you paint."

Mar takes the bag, glances inside, sees the twenty or so tubes of various shades of blue, and drops it onto the table next to the easel.

"You could say thank you," Diane says.

"Dee..."

Diane turns to Mar, her hands fisted on her hips, and though she is half a foot shorter than she is, Mar feels cowed. "Look," Diane says, "it's time." She gestures to the canvas. "This is the, what? The twentieth time you've painted Lizzie? Asleep?"

Turning away, Mar drops the brush into a jar of water and sloshes it around.

"Her eyes are blue. There's no getting around that. I saw what you did, tried to paint her eyes brown and even purple. That's not Lizzie. If you're going to paint her, awake, you've got to use blue."

"It's..."

Diane waves Mar's comment aside. "Aw, hell, I know what it is. I'm the choir and all that. Look, I think I know how to ease you back into using blue."

***

Mar had been living in Boulder for almost a month before she met her first neighbor. "I waved to an old man today," she told her father during one of their nightly phone calls. "The one in the yellow house with the green shutters? He even waved back."

"Come home, Mar," her father said. "You've got friends here. And family."

She turned from the window and surveyed the large, open room she'd had carved out of several smaller rooms on the first floor of the house. "I'm OK."

"We need you here."

Mar tucked the phone between her shoulder and ear and reached for the razor blade she'd been using to open boxes. "The paintings got here," she said.

Pulling out the forty-eight by forty-eight inch canvas, she peeled the protective paper from its face. This one was a close-up of an anemone, a *condylactis gigantea*, the Giant Caribbean Sea Anemone, rendered in acrylic paint. Clinging to a vivid orange coral, the anemone's off-white, purple-tipped tentacles wave in turquoise water. A solitary, googley-eyed red-and-white striped cleaner shrimp peers out from among the tentacles.

Mar closed her eyes. The sea-scape faded. In its place, she saw Joaquin perched on the side of the small, white boat they'd rented during their dive vacation in the Bahamas. His deep green eyes held hers through the glass of his dive mask. She grinned and lowered her mask over her eyes, settled it into place. The boat rocked gently. Mar looked past Joaquin. Turquoise water stretched to the horizon, flat as a mirror, chips of sunlight dancing off its surface. The sky overhead was cloudless. Terns glided on thermal updrafts. Mar closed her eyes and inhaled, filling her lungs, felt the heat of the sun. When she opened her eyes, Joaquin was adjusting the regulator in his mouth. He blew out and then sucked in a deep breath, his eyes crinkling in a grin. Mar lifted her regulator to her mouth, blew, inhaled. Joaquin reached out a hand. His fingernails glowed white against the deep tan of his skin. Sun-golden hair peeked out from the wrist of his wetsuit. Mar looked into his eyes, settled her hand in his, bit down on her regulator. With their free hands, they pressed their masks against their foreheads, nodded at one another and, as one, flipped backwards off the side of the boat.

"Anyway." She leaned the painting against the wall and cleared her throat. "I met a neighbor. Diane. She used to be an art teacher at the university."

"Mar?"

"Daddy? I'll call you back," she said. She hung up the phone and let gravity release her to the floor. Curled around her clenched hand, she cried.

***

"This is going to sound silly, but I want you to think about it, OK?" Taking a deep breath, Diane exhales in a bang-lifting huff. "OK, look, ever since you got here, you've been figuring out how to do cowboy art. That's all well and good, but it's not you. Mar, people want your reef paintings. I've got an email list downstairs of people who want me to tell them as soon as you get back to your sea-scapes."

Mar dries the brush on a rag and drops it bristles-up into one of her brush jars. This is not what she wants to hear. Just the thought of the ocean fills her with anxiety. She crosses the studio to check on Lizzie, who is asleep in the play-yard Mar set up for her.

"What if you still painted these western landscapes," Diane gestures at an unfinished painting on the smaller of Mar's two easels, "but you filled them with reef life?"

Mar, who had been reaching in to run her fingers over Lizzie's cheek, turns to Diane. "You're kidding, right?"

Diane shakes her head. "I'm dead serious. Think about it, a crab crawling up a butte, or a herd of seahorses racing through a canyon..."

Diane, who has been managing Mar's small gallery for the past several years, is not a crazy person. At least, that is what Mar tells herself as she waits for the older woman to smile, to do anything to indicate that she's not serious. "A crab," Mar allows the sentence to dangle.

Diane nods. "Crawling up a butte."

"Seriously?"

"Well, what the hell are you going to do?" Diane taps the canvas. "Paint a couple of horses? Maybe stick an Indian over here? Dammit, Mar, it's been done. And, I hate to say it, but by a lot of better cowboy artists than you."

Mar's face warms in embarrassment, though Diane is not saying anything she herself has not thought. She feels nothing when she sketches a horse, or a buffalo, or, god forbid, another teepee. She has vague memories of the excitement she used to feel, the energy, when she painted ocean scenes. When she'd turn up the music so loud that the air would vibrate with Dave Matthews or the percussive thumps of Maná. When Joaquin was alive.

She looks at the uninspiring, dust-colored landscape Diane indicated. She's lucky to clear a few hundred dollars on her western art and, because of that, two years before she'd had to open her gallery up to other artists when it became apparent that her own paintings wouldn't pay the bills. "It's crazy." She shakes her head.

"This whole state used to be under the ocean. It's not so crazy as all that. Paint a school of tuna swimming through a dry wash."

Against her better judgment, Mar pictures this. The fingers of her right hand begin to tap against her thigh. She closes her eyes, willing the temptation to disappear.

A small sigh sounds from the play-yard, a sign that Lizzie is beginning to wake up. Diane crosses to Mar's side. Mar bends forward, unaware that she is holding her breath. The baby's eyelashes flicker, once, twice, and then open. Cornflower blue eyes find Mar's, and Lizzie smiles and reaches for her. Mar exhales and grins back. "Hi, baby," she says and reaches for her, but Diane waves Mar away.

"I'll get her," Diane says. "You go paint some fish."

Eleven

Jack.

Jack steps off the curb, head bowed, hands clenched in the pockets of his jeans. Months ago, unable to sleep as the shock slowly settled to the dull, throbbing ache now centered deep in his chest, he'd taken to walking. The city, which had once thrilled and emboldened him, now leans in on him, threatens to smother him, to crush him beneath the weight of its indifference.

On these almost nightly excursions, Jack makes it a point to avoid the places he'd been with Lindsey. He's learned the hard way that memories, rushing at him from the darkness, catching him unaware, have the ability to suck the air from his chest and leave him gasping for breath. Where some might take comfort in memories, in routine, for him they serve more as a reminder of what could have been, what should have been, what can never be again.

He's also learned to avoid parks, schoolyards, any place children might gather. Seeing a young mother once, her long, blonde hair swinging softly as she reached in and lifted her child from its stroller, had almost done him in. He'd reached for them. Filled with a greedy need, he'd stumbled forward and reached for them. The woman, catching sight of him, pushed the baby back into the stroller and hurried away. “Don’t let her out of your sight,” Jack yelled at her retreating back. “It’s not safe! She’ll never be safe!”

Jack has even gone down to Florida. Not that he doubted Sy had mined every bit of information from Esther Burrows, but he’d had to see for himself, had had to look her in the eye and believe for himself that she wasn’t hiding anything that could help him find Mia.

***

“I’m telling you, I don’t know where Elie is,” Esther said, her ultra-whites clacking away, snapping each word off like it was spring loaded. “Besides, I already promised your friend, that detective? I already promised him I’d let him know when I hear from her.”

Jack leaned forward on the sofa, sought out her eyes. He wanted her to see him, to see the hurt and bewilderment in his own eyes, to feel the pain that washed off of him in waves. “Mrs. Burrows,” he said, “I know you’ve already talked to Sy, and I appreciate it. I’m just hoping there might be something, anything, no matter how small, that you may have remembered since he was here.”

Esther sat primly on the edge of her chair, her perfectly-ironed housedress buttoned to the top, red Keds cutting into her swollen feet. The look she gave him was not friendly. “I’m beginning to think you think my Elie might have something to do with taking your baby.”

“I don’t. Believe me. This has nothing to do with hurting your daughter. It has everything to do with finding mine.”

“She’s not that kind of girl. She’s a good person.”

“Mrs. Burrows, look, I understand that. I don’t doubt that, but if she knows anything, can point me in the right direction, I need to talk to her.”

“She wouldn’t take your baby.”

Jack sighed. He’d done nothing more than spook the woman. “Look,” he said, trying another tack. “Did Sy tell you about the reward? There’s a big reward for whoever can help me find my daughter. No questions asked. Here, I'll tell you what I'm going to do." Jack opened his wallet and pulled out a check. "I brought you a check for five thousand dollars."

"What the heck for? I didn't do anything, and I don't take charity."

"It's not charity. I'm giving it to you for expenses, in case you need to make phone calls, whatever, to try to find your daughter."

"Who am I gonna call?" she asked. "I told you, I don't know where she is."

Jack signed the check and held it out to her. "In case you think of someone, then. I want it to be there in case you need it, in case you have to go somewhere to find her, or in case Elie contacts you and she needs it. And, if you find her? If she can help? There's another fifty thousand dollars waiting for you for putting me in touch with her."

***

As part of his policy of avoidance, Jack disregards friends and family, has abandoned the Legal Aid office where he'd once so freely given his time, and has even shut himself off from The Farm, the outreach program where he'd first met his Little Brother, DeJon. He can't stand the questions and, even after everyone learned not to ask, he sees the desire to know in their eyes. Having nothing to give them leaves him emptier than before.

In the first months of walking, rage had fueled Jack's momentum. Rage at the taxi driver, at the doctors, the hospital, the candy striper. He'd funneled that anger into blame, into litigation, but when the taxi company and the hospital had fallen all over themselves to settle, he'd been left hollow. He'd craved the fight, the righteous anger of it, the focus. He hadn't needed the money. Lindsey's trust had left him with more money than he could spend in a lifetime. He'd thrown that money at the search for Mia and had opened up a trust account for her, using his own salary to keep up the apartment, to pay the bills. When his parents urged him to return to Ohio, he'd patiently explained that he needed to wait for Mia to come home. To himself, he'd admitted that more so, he needed to hang onto the belief that one day she would.

"That's quite a reward," the anchor said the first time he appeared on *The Today Show*.

"She's out there," Jack said. "Somewhere, someone knows what happened to her, who took her. I just want her home."

"Are you out of your fucking mind?" Sy had yelled at him later. "You're going to have every nut job in the world calling in now."

"The Merritt Agency's handling the calls. If they get anything, they'll pass it on to you."

"It's just, that's a shitload of money."

Jack poured himself another Scotch. "It's only money," he said.

"Couldn't you have made it a little less only money? Something reasonable?"

Jack tossed the Scotch back. "What's reasonable, Sy? I'd pay anything to have Lindsey's baby back."

Sy flopped down on to the sofa. "Well, fuck me," he'd said.

***

So while his work suffers and his personal life is beyond resuscitation, Jack concentrates his every effort on finding Mia. He's appeared so often on the morning news programs that they've given him a moniker. "We've got Desperate Dad, Jack Westfield, with us today..."

It seems impossible, but even with all the press he's received, his appearances on *America's Mystery Crimes*, the website and toll-free numbers he's set up, they haven't received one decent lead. And, of course, Sy was right. Every whacko and his mother has come crawling out of their caves, angling for the million dollar reward.

So now, as Jack's feet eat up the streets of Manhattan, as August approaches and, with it, the anniversary of Lindsey's death and Mia's kidnapping, his mind searches for new angles, new answers to the puzzle of his daughter's whereabouts.

Twelve

Mar.

A sunflower-draped trellis has been set up behind The Center, about halfway between the swing-set and the sand box. Ten rows of chairs fan out from a center aisle. Guests of all ages mingle in the glow of swaying fairy lights, with the younger ones running pell-mell from one toy to the next, the sounds of laughter pouring from little bodies.

Dylan, dressed formally in black tie and tails, fidgets noticeably. He is speaking to Kristina, Shirley's daughter. Every few minutes, his eyes dart to the back door of the house. Mar, standing at a second floor window, grins over at Shirley. "He's falling apart," she says. Lizzie has put on a lot of weight since she has been with Mar and, asleep, is heavy in Mar's arms. Leaving the window, Mar settles into a rocking chair and watches Shirley fiddle with the strand of pearls that surrounds her long neck. "Oh, lordy," Shirley says.

"You look beautiful," Mar says. "He's going to freak when he sees you. Now stand up straight so I can get the whole effect."

Shirley turns to Mar and nervously tugs at the bottom of the form-fitting silk suit coat that is paired with a floor-length buttermilk-cream-colored skirt. "Do I look fat? I look fat. I should have gotten the other dress, don't you think?" she asks for the hundredth time.

"I told you, you look beautiful. You don't look fat. Look at you, your stomach's flat as a board."

Shirley turns sideways to the mirror and lays her hand over her belly. "I feel fat. I feel like I'm ready to give birth right now. Oh, damn, what am I doing? I'm a grandmother, for god's sake!"

"Come on, Shirl," Mar laughs as she shifts Lizzie in her lap, "You're three months and you don't even show. If you hadn't already told everyone, no one'd even know you're pregnant."

"You sure?" Shirley turns to the other side.

"Yes, I am. Now, are you going to put that hat on your head or not?"

Shirley picks up a small pillbox hat, fashioned after a style made famous by Jacqueline Kennedy, and fits it on her head. "Lordy, lordy, I look stupid. What was I thinking?"

Mar's bark of laughter startles the baby who reaches up and pats Mar's cheek before dozing off again. "Hey, there," Mar coos and kisses the top of her head. "Isn't she precious?"

"Um, not to change the subject or anything, but you know we haven't found anyone, right? No family or friends." Shirley catches Mar's eyes in the mirror.

Mar laughter clogs in her throat and the spot in her intestines, where the ulcers are the worst, twists reflexively, causing her to gasp.

"In a few months, she's going to be eligible for adoption." Shirley walks over to her and lifts her chin up so that she and Mar are eye to eye. "Why don't you adopt her, honey? You know that's what you want."

Mar fumbles with the clasp on one of Lizzie's shoes. For the past five months she has been telling herself to remain emotionally unattached from Lizzie, but her heart has been ignoring her. Mar is, and has been since the day she picked the baby up at the hospital, in full maternal love. The idea of losing Lizzie has begun to cause panic attacks in Mar. "I just don't know if I can go through that again."

"Honey, what happened to Max was a fluke in the system. You tried. You did your best and the judge screwed up. Even the judge knows he screwed up. It's not going to happen again."

Max. Even now, two years after his death, the pain is raw. Shortly after settling in Boulder, Mar had met Shirley. Intrigued by Shirley's work and with the possibility of easing her own heartache through helping others, Mar had applied to become a foster parent. Max had been her second foster child after she completed the state's training program. The first, a young girl named Sandra, had been quickly reunited with her mother. Max had no parents. His mother was a prostitute. His father a passing-through black man whom no one remembered. When Max was three, his mother sold him for a week's worth of meth, which she was later robbed and killed for. The man who bought Max passed him on to another. By the time Shirley's agency caught up with him, Max required three different surgeries to put his body back together. Mar, new to foster care, had not been the ideal candidate to care for Max, but from the moment they'd met, she hadn't been able to get the broken little boy out of her mind.

"No, that won't happen again," Mar tells Shirley, the bitterness alive in her voice, but something will. Don't you see? Something's wrong with me. I don't even know how my damn dog's lasted this long."

"That's just pure superstitious nonsense." Shirley says. "But I'll tell you what isn't nonsense, what is the cold, hard truth. That is that if you don't go for it, she most definitely will be taken away from you."

"Exactly. But, I think that even if I do try, she will be. At least this way I don't get all emotionally involved."

"Jesus, Mar, look at you. Can't you see you're already emotionally involved? You're wearing matching dresses, you go to Mommy and Me, and that child's already got a college fund started! What do you think, if you don't petition to adopt her, it's going to hurt any less when they come to take her away?"

Lizzie begins to wake and Mar tucks the baby's head against her shoulder and cups her other ear. "It's just that there are tons of couples," Mar hisses, trying to keep her voice down, "a mom and a dad just like the courts like, that are looking for little girls, perfect little girls like Lizzie. I don't have a chance of getting her."

Shirley's hands fist on her hips. "Her mom was an addict, Mar. There were traces of heroin, crack, meth, god knows what else in her when she died. That makes a difference. There's a prejudice against kids born to addicts specifically because problems can show up later. Not many adoptive parents want to take that risk, even if the baby is as cute as Lizzie."

Mar's arm tightens protectively around the little girl. "She's not a crack baby. You and I both know that. She hasn't shown any signs of it. She's perfect."

"Dammit, Mar, I don't know that."

"So what should I do? If I pretend she's got problems, I'll have a better chance of getting her because no one else will want her? Is that what you're saying?"

"That's not what I'm saying."

"Tell me. What are the symptoms? I'll say it. I'll call her case worker right now."

"I said, that's not what I'm saying."

"Then, what?"

"Look, all I'm saying is that it's right there, real big, in her papers where everyone can see it – MOM WAS DRUG ADDICT. CHILD MAY EXHIBIT COGNITIVE AND BEHAVIORAL PROBLEMS. That is going to get some people's attention, for sure." Shirley adjusts her hat. "Now, come on, I'm pregnant and I've got to go get me a husband."

Thirteen

Mar.

Shirley drops into her office chair and adjusts the lumbar support cushion she's taken to using. In the past months, she's ballooned into something she claims resembles an elephant ready to repopulate an entire African herd. Groaning, she pushes back and puts her feet up on an open drawer.

"God, if you're like this now, I don't know how you're going to last another few months. You act ancient."

"Girl, I am ancient. You forget, I'm almost fifty."

Mar, who is crowded into the Little Tykes table next to Lizzie, says, "First of all, you're not 'almost fifty' and, second, I don't see Dylan complaining," Mar looks up from the crayon sketch she is making of the little girl and winks at Shirley. "The man can't keep his hands off of you. It's embarrassing."

"That man complains, I'm gonna do some voodoo hocus pocus on his ass."

"You know what some women would give to have their plumbing still working at your age?" Mar chooses a green crayon for the ribbon in Lizzie's hair. "Most of 'em are getting hot flashes, hiding the knives so they don't wake up and find themselves filleting the hubbie in his Barcalounger. Thinking 'that fat slob tells me to bring his ass one more Budweiser, or grabs my boobs again and says 'it's halftime, baby, let's do it' and there's gonna be a lot of pain and blood flowing around here.' Now think of it like that," Mar nods for emphasis, "and a little bloating doesn't feel so bad."

"Jesus, where do you come up with that shit?"

"I'm just saying, keep it all in perspective, is all." She grins. "Hey, Shirl? I'm kidding. Man, you have so lost your sense of humor!" Mar inspects the scribbled drawing that Lizzie is working on. So far, most of the coloring has taken place on the table. "Hey, there, Lizzie, that's really good! Look at that, Shirley! It almost looks like something!"

"That's great, honey," Shirley sends a smile to the little girl. "Anyway, back to reality, Mar. I've got that appointment with the Ferrins this afternoon. I have to let them know that Lizzie is available for adoption."

"No, no, Lizzie, don't eat that." Mar pushes the girl's hand away from her mouth. "Yuck."

Shirley taps a folder on her desk. "They're not going to go away. They desperately want a child and they're very good candidates."

"I know, but look at her. She's doing fine, aren't you Dizzie Lizzie? We're doing just fine. Why can't we just leave things like they are?"

"Damn it, Mar!" Shirley's hand slams down on the desk, causing both Mar and Lizzie to jump. The little girl drops her crayon and cowers at Mar's side. "Sorry, Lizzie," Shirley says, her smile more of a grimace. "Look, Mar, you're going to have to commit. Either you want Lizzie and make a formal plea for adoption, or you're going to have to give her up to someone who's willing to make that commitment."

"It's not the commitment!"

"Look, I understand your fear. What I'm having a problem with is reality. See, the world is a messed up place. And shit happens. Every day. To perfectly nice people. But if you don't take the chance, you might as well just roll over and play dead because that's certainly not living. That's just floating."

"Well, screw it, then," Mar moves over to the window and

looks out at the towering Front Range. Today, even its majesty doesn't soothe her. "Then I'm a floater, I guess."

"Mar," Shirley tries again, in a different voice, "you two are a good team. She's come a long way with you. Look at her. When you got her, she wouldn't make a sound. Now she babbles non-stop, she'll barely shut up. She's lively and happy and she trusts you. How is she going to feel if you abandon her to someone else?"

"I'm not abandoning her!"

"Yes you are. What else are you going to call it?"

"Alright then, what do you think my chances are?" Mar turns back to Shirley. "Really are? It's like you said, these other people are good candidates. There's a mom and a dad, they've got money, they do community service, probably go to church, yuck it up with the mayor, the governor. They've got a public building named after them, for god's sakes! I can't compete with that."

"Take my word for it, Mar, they're worried about Lizzie's mom taking drugs during her pregnancy."

Mar's mouth drops open and she looks over at the little girl happily scribbling away. As if sensing her attention, Lizzie looks up and grins at her. Mar's eyes fills with tears. "I told you," she whispers, "she shows no signs! Nothing, nada, not even a blip. The tests all come back negative."

"Except that her babbling is not really talking. She's making noises, yes, but she's not making words. You know Dylan says she should be talking by now. Other than that, yeah, she's great. But Mar, and this is a big but, these things can show up later."

"What are you saying?" Mar's eyes narrows. "Are you saying you'd tell them she's not OK?"

Shirley puts on her best business voice as she considers Mar across desk. "No, Mar, I'm not going to lie to them. My job is to find the best home for the children that come under my care. My recommendation to the court, should you decide to pursue adoption, would be that you can provide Elizabeth with the best home. There will be other babies and the Ferrins are on the top of the list as adoptive parents. The fact that there is concern that one day Lizzie may show developmental or behavioral problems associated with her mother's drug abuse is not debatable. That being the case, and knowing the Ferrins, I believe that they'll opt to wait. If, however, you decide not to pursue adoption, I think that it is best that Elizabeth be placed as soon as possible so that she can begin to develop bonds with her new parents. Whatever the case, though, I need an answer. Today."

Mar looks up, panicked. "Today?"

"Today."

The fight leaves her swiftly and Mar drops down on the bench next to Lizzie. "Yes, honey, you see? The Strawberry Shortcake did the trick." With a finger, she pushes a stray blonde curl back from the little girl's forehead, watching as it catches momentarily before gently slipping away. She bites her lip to try to stem the tears, but they slide down her cheeks regardless. "What am I going to do with you?" she whispers. Lizzie looks up, frightened by the sadness in Mar's voice, and launches herself into her arms.

Mar's arm tighten around Elizabeth and her heart thumps heavily. Can she do this? Would Lizzie be better off, safer even, with a mother and a father? Will life finally give Mar someone she can hold onto? She closes her eyes and inhales deeply. The smell, the sweet baby smell of Lizzie, talcum powder, baby sweat and all the good things that little girls are made of. *Rose,* she thinks, *Rose and gold and powder-puff clouds of yellow and white.* She knows then that there will never be a day that she won't fear losing Lizzie. But that, she guesses, is probably how every parent feels. She kisses Lizzie's precious neck and smiles. "I'll do it," she whispers.

"Well, hale-fucking-luyah."

Fourteen

Mar.

Mar stands in front of the open refrigerator and groans. The light. The light is going to kill her.

"Mar? Where are you?" calls a voice from the gallery.

"Ssshhhhh," Mar whispers as she closes her eyes and leans her forehead against the cold egg basket. That feels a little better actually. Maybe she can stand here all day.

"Oh, there you are! What are you doing in the fridge?"

"Shhhh, you'll wake the penguins," she mumbles.

Diane picks up the empty bottle of wine on the counter. "Hangover?"

"From hell."

"Well, then, go sit down. Let me whip you up something. How about eggs?"

Mar's stomach convulses at the thought. "I'd really have to kill you."

"OK, but sit down. I know just the thing. Christ Almighty, Bart used to tie one on every now and then. He was a big man and could drink enough to drown a cow. Now where's the Arm and Hammer?"

"Could you not move so fast?" Mar squints at her. "You're hurting my head."

Diane reaches around Mar and plucks the box of baking soda from the refrigerator door. "You'll be amazed at how quickly this helps."

Mar rolls her head back and forth and moans.

Diane reaches for a glass and fills it with water. She then measures two tablespoons of baking soda and stirs it into the water. "Ha! Drink this."

"It looks like sewage." Mar moves to the island and slips onto a counter stool. She sniffs the glass Diane hands her and makes a face.

"Drink it, it'll help. Did you take aspirin already?"

"Two. Yuck! This is disgusting."

"Drink it. Trust me. If you live through it, you'll feel a lot better."

Mar holds her nose and drinks. Today, of all days, is not a day for a hangover. She lays her head on the table and is surprised to be woken up awhile later by Diane. She smiles sheepishly. "Oops."

Diane, cradling her cup of coffee, shakes her head. "You didn't eat again last night, did you?"

Mar tries to think back. She'd bathed Lizzie and put her to bed before going up to the studio to paint. At some point, she'd wandered down to the kitchen to wrap the presents for Lizzie's birthday, a date chosen after much meditation and a Tarot card reading by her friend, Sioux, and confirmation from Dylan and Dr. Barnes that the date was in the ballpark, according to Lizzie's physical and mental development. In any case, Mar hadn't been hungry, so she had put Sade on the stereo, poured herself a glass of wine, and started to wrap. Near the end of the bottle, she'd realized that she'd probably bought too many presents. "Unh-uh."

Diane returns from the oven and places a plate heaped high with spaghetti in front of Mar. When the scent of the garlic in olive oil hits her, Mar moans. She's famished. "Oh, you are a goddess. Thank you, thank you, thank you."

"That oughta help, anyway. Oh, here, I forgot the Parmesan."

Halfway through the pasta, Mar begins to slow down. "I feel better already," she smiles around another mouthful.

"Course you do, honey. Carbs is what a hangover calls for. Soak up all that crap."

"You're here early," Mar suddenly realizes.

"I was afraid you were going to let her start opening the presents before the party."

"Um, just a couple."

"Uh-huh. A couple. You bought out the whole damn store. It'll take that little girl all day just to get through the first load."

"It's her birthday," Mar shrugs. "Besides, she's special."

"Don't I know it," Diane concedes. "Now tell me, you hear anything new on the adoption? Which way it's going?"

Mar sets her fork down carefully. The weather has not yet turned and a light wind is blowing through the aspen in the back yard. She watches the leaves flash silver-gold, silver-gold in the early morning light. She knows Diane is waiting for an answer, but she finds she can't speak. Finally, she shakes her head, no.

"I'm sorry, Mar, I shouldn't have mentioned it today. Today's for celebrating. Now, where's the little princess?"

Mar clears her throat and wipes at the tears that have appeared so quickly. "Wow, I'm sorry. I don't know what happened. This whole thing has me a little freaked."

"I know, sugar, and I probably shouldn't have mentioned it."

"No, no, it's OK. Shirley said it's going to take a few months. The social workers have been doing the background checks on me and the Ferrins, dropping in for surprise visits, the same thing as with Max." She shrugs and smiles bravely, "Eventually, they'll decide who's best for Lizzie."

Diane puts her cup down. "Don't you worry, Mar, it'll all work out. That little girl belongs with you."

"Thanks, Dee."

"It will. Now, finish your spaghetti and go get a shower. You've got paint in your hair."

"Lizzie'll be up soon."

"Eat. Finish. Take a nice hot shower. I'll take care of Lizzie. Besides, she likes my cooking a lot better than yours."

Mar smiles into her spaghetti and takes another bite.

Fifteen

Jack.

For the first time in months, Jack meets up with Mortuary John at the gym on Fifty-fourth. John, Mortuary John to his friends, owns a string of funeral homes throughout the five boroughs. Even in college he'd been obsessed with death. Not with the dying part, but with the fact that everyone must die sooner or later and, when they do, they'll need someone to bury them. After graduating from business school, he'd taken his father's simple funeral home and had expanded it into the largest chain in the tri-state area. He'd handled Lindsey's funeral, the details of which Jack still cannot remember.

"You're lookin' good there, Jacky, my man," John dumps his sports bag on the bench beside Jack's and opens his locker. "You slimmin' down?"

Jack looks down at his clothes, for the first time aware that they are hanging loosely on his wiry frame. "I've been walking," he says, and he turns away to loosen his tie, concentrating on the sounds of the locker room, men laughing, their voices bouncing off of tile walls, a toilet flushing, the door of the steam room opening and closing, its seal a soft *whumpf* almost lost to the noise.

"It's just, well, Sherri said you're too skinny and she's

worried about you, thinks you're not eating enough."

Jack closes his eyes and counts. This is exactly why he avoids his old friends. It's easier to be around strangers than with people who are always comparing him to someone he used to be, to a man he can never be again. He'd overheard one admin commenting on his "haunted eyes." Another time, a lawyer, a man he'd once considered a friend, had told a new recruit to stay out of Jack's way, that he "used to be a real good guy," whatever that meant. He knows they talk about him, he understands even. He is their worst nightmare, a man just like them who once upon a time had had everything and then had had it snatched from him in the blink of an eye. He is a reminder that no one is safe, that at any moment their own lives might be destroyed.

Without consciously telling them to, Jack's fingers begin to re-button his shirt. He does not want to be here.

"Jack, man, I'm sorry," John's voice speaks behind him, and he does sound sorry. "It's just, well, we miss you."

Jack pauses, what the hell is he going to do? This is John. Hadn't he made the decision to try? Not to be normal, but to not be the walking dead at least? He forces his fingers to work their way back down his shirt. "You ever think about how bad locker rooms smell?" he asks.

"You think this is bad, you should see where I work."

Jack feels the remark like a knee to the groin. His hands curl into his shirt and he tries to steady himself. All sounds stop as the air is sucked from the room. *This is it,* he tells himself, *just fucking kill yourself right now and get on with it.* Taking a deep breath, he makes his feet turn. John's eyes are wide, his face stricken. Jack forces himself to chuckle. "I'll bet," he says, and then, "How's Sherri? The kids?"

Relief washes over Mortuary John's face and he grins widely. "Fine, fine. Things're good. Byron's walking. Did I tell you that?"

Jack smiles, the muscles tight from disuse. "I got the e-mails."

"Sherri's pissed at you, by the way," John mentions. He

hangs his dress shirt in the locker and begins to undo his pants. “She says you’re ignoring her and you haven’t even seen your godchild in months.”

“I’m sorry.”

“Nah, shit, she’s not pissed. Not really. Concerned is more like it. She misses you.”

“I’ll come out this weekend. How’s that?”

“Good. That’s good. The kids’ll be jazzed. They’re always asking for Uncle Jack. Wonder why he don’t love them.”

“You’re shoveling it a bit too deep there, my man.”

A twinkle lights John’s eyes and Jack is relieved to see he’s relaxing. “Aw, am I?” John asks.

Jack nods. “You are.”

“But you’ll come, right? I can tell Sherri? I mean, if you don’t show, then she’ll really be pissed. You know she’s gonna cook your favorite food, clean the house, bring over all her single girlfriends.”

Jack freezes and the smile flees from his face. “You’re kidding, right?”

John looks up from searching for his deodorant. “Shit. Man, I’m sorry. It’s just...Yeah, just kidding.”

“I just don’t...”

“Nah, man, it’s OK. It was a stupid joke. It’ll be just us, family, no blind dates.”

Jack’s smile doesn’t reach his eyes. “Thanks.”

“So, you ready to burn?” John changes the subject and pulls out his racquetball racquet and goggles.

Jack looks over at his best friend since freshman year at Yale, the guy who’d greeted him that first night they’d been paired as roommates with, “Sheeit. They put the farm boy with the black boy, keep us away from their tidy-white WASP asses. Well, sir, they made a mistake, yes they did. We’re Two-J, you and me, and they can just effing bring it on!” John has two inches on him and probably a good ten pounds of it muscle. He also carries a little too much of Sherri’s good home cooking.

Jack nods at him. “You’re going down.”

Sixteen

Mar.

The party is in full swing by the time Mar and Lizzie arrive at The Center with Mar's father in tow. Cradling Lizzie against the bitter cold, she pushes the handle down with her elbow and tries to nudge the door open with her hip.

"Here, honey, let me get that," Don Bloom reaches around her and pushes the door open.

"Thanks, Dad," she hurries past his tall frame. "Let's go into the kitchen and leave the food before we drop our coats."

The kitchen is full of people and Mar makes her way into the fray, kissing cheeks, showing Lizzie off and introducing her father, "This is my dad, Don Bloom."

At the center island, Dylan, a holiday-inspired apron wrapped around his very fit middle, waves a spatula for emphasis as he recounts once again Shirley's pregnancy progress. *God, what the man does for an apron*, Mar shakes her head ruefully. *Betty Crocker'd have him on the floor in a heartbeat*. "Hey there, handsome," Mar kisses Dylan's cheek and snatches a warm fudge brownie from the cookie sheet in front of him. She holds it up to Lizzie, who takes a big bite and grins a nasty brown smile back at her. "How goes the baby making?"

"Man, Mar, it is so cool and Shirley's just, I mean, have you ever seen anyone so beautiful?"

Mar rolls her eyes. He's pathetic. "You know, Dylan, if we could only find a way to clone you, I'd have women lining up for one of their very own."

"Hell, no! Shirley's doing all the work. That kid's packing weight like a line backer. I don't know how she can even walk."

"The way I hear it, you give a mean foot massage."

"Yeah, well I am a Very Happy Man," his grin widens. "How about you? How's your Dad?" Taller than just about everyone else in the room, Dylan looks over their heads until he finds Mar's father. "Uh-oh. Norm's got him. It'll be awhile before he surfaces again."

"Are you kidding? Norm doesn't stand a chance when Dad gets started."

"You sure we shouldn't perform a rescue operation?"

"Nah. The man is surprisingly skilled at football-speak."

Bored with all the chatter, Lizzie lunges toward Dylan. He lifts her off of Mar's hip. "How's my little girl?" he kisses her cheek and begins tugging at her coat. "What's your momma thinking, Lizzie, keeping you bundled up like that? What's that about? I know, I'll bet you want some more brownie?" Dylan hands the little girl a piece of a brownie and then, grinning at Mar, turns away. "I've gotta take my best girl to meet the guests," he says and disappears into the crowd. Elizabeth is too enraptured by Dylan to notice that they have left Mar behind.

"Well, same to you, kid!" Mar calls after her. Shaking her head, she picks up the knife Dylan had been using and begins cutting the rest of the brownies.

"Hey there, girl, Merry Christmas!" Shirley whispers into her ear. "How goes the flow?"

Mar turns around and gives her friend a long hug. Stepping back, she examines the huge belly between them. "Oh my god! Are you sure you're not gonna pop tonight?"

"No can do," Shirley replies, swiping a brownie. "I got some things to do before I take a few months off. How are you? Where's your dad?" Shirley looks past Mar.

"He's here somewhere. Norman Schumacher cornered him and he might not come up for hours."

Shirley laughs and helps Mar out of her coat. "Well, that's a few hours you don't have to talk about football with him."

"No kidding," Mar grimaces and then the two women laugh.

"Come on," Shirley says, "I've got a present for you."

"No way. We said that presents would wait 'til tomorrow. I haven't even wrapped yours yet."

"I know," Shirley says, leading the way out of the kitchen, "but I want to give you this one tonight. I've been saving it long enough."

Reaching her office, Shirley steps inside and turns on the light. "Man, I am beat already. Just a few more weeks and it's over. Don't know how I'm supposed to wait. I can't imagine this thing getting any bigger."

"You are, uh, huge. You sure you didn't count the weeks wrong or something? Maybe there's twins in there?"

"You'd think, but the damn doctor says no. There, sit down, I'm just gonna waddle over here and get me a seat."

Mar settles into her favorite chair in front of Shirley's desk, the one with the view. The setting sun has cast deep Magenta shadows over the mountains. If she were painting it, she'd choose Deep-Violet and Dioxozine-Purple, with a little Process-Blue around the crags of the mountain to reflect the chill. A shiver runs up her spine as her nervous system associates those colors with the aching cold of another winter night. Even so, she likes how the colors blend together, offset by the warm golden-white glow that spills from the windows of the shadow houses across the street.

Shirley lowers herself into her own chair and sits back with a sigh. "What have you been up to? I haven't seen you lately."

Mar pulls her eyes from the view and returns to the room. She notices how pregnancy has lent a beautiful rose flush to Shirley's caramel skin and her eyes widen. "Um, Shirl?"

Sighing, Shirley opens a drawer and pushes a pad of paper

and a pencil across the desk toward Mar. Smiling gratefully, Mar begins to sketch as she picks up the conversation, "Oh, you know, the usual. Dad hasn't been here in awhile so we've been doing his thing, travelling around looking for winter-scapes and wildlife to sketch. Lizzie's been surprisingly agreeable to stomping around in the snow while Dad goes at it. Of course, I was the same at that age. Or so Dad tells me."

Shirley smiles at Mar. She's heard all the stories about how Mar used to cut school in order to accompany Don on his nature excursions. When the truant officer showed up one day, Don simply waved her away and declared that Mar was getting a better education in natural history than any school could give her.

"Anyway," Mar shrugs, "what about you?"

"No rest for the weary. Tomorrow we have Christmas for all the kids. You're coming to that. First a big breakfast, then opening the presents, and then general chaos until lunch, which is around 2:00. Football, of course, for your Dad, Dylan and whoever else wants to watch. And then, after all the kids go home, some blessed peace and quiet. Other than that, I don't have plans until Junior here shows up. Just spend some time with Kristina and the kids. They're here for another week or so and then Shawn'll take the kids home and Kris will wait for the baby with me."

"Where is she? I haven't seen her yet," Mar asks, referring to Shirley's daughter, Kristina.

"Probably upstairs with the kids. Kadeem's teething and it takes both her and Shawn to put him down. Sabrina, on the other hand, is an angel and she's probably napping. Man, I wish I could join her."

"Pretty soon, mama bear. You'll be taking naps with the baby every day."

"True. True. But, then, I'll be up all night with him, too! OK, sweetie, we gotta get back to the fiesta, but before we go, I wanted to give you this." Shirley passes an envelope across the desk to Mar.

Mar shoots a questioning look at her friend. "Just open it,"

Shirley urges.

Mar's hand begins to tremble and she sets the sketch on the desk. Whatever it is, it can only be about Lizzie. The envelope, when she picks it up, offers a faint hint of rosewater. Her eyebrows rise. "Nice. I didn't think people did that anymore." Flipping it over, Mar sees the return address. And freezes. "But then, just that one whiff would probably feed several small nations."

"They're not bad people, Mar. Rich doesn't mean bad. Now, are you going to open it, or not?"

"Yeah, yeah," Mar mutters. She removes the single sheet of vellum. The name engraved across the top reads 'Edwina Ferrin.' "You know, that is just the stupidest, ugliest name I've ever heard. What were her parents thinking?"

Shirley rolls her eyes. "Go on, Mar. It won't bite."

"Dear Ms. McGowan," Mar reads aloud, "Firstly, we'd like to thank you for the attention you have given to our case. As you know, we are very eager to adopt a child and the sooner, the better for us. We have given quite a bit of thought to the little girl, Elizabeth Jones, who is now available for adoption and, while we have found her to be an adorable child, we continue to be concerned about the affects that her birth mother's drug addiction might have on her health and well-being. Being that we will be older parents, we feel that a child with better health prospects would be a more appropriate match to us. Therefore, while we thank you for your efforts on our behalf, we would like to ask that our names be dropped as this child's potential adoptive parents and that we be considered for any other child that fits our parameters. Thank you again. Sincerely, Davis and Edwina Ferrin."

Mar scans the letter again and looks up at Shirley. "Jesus! These people are so messed up! Nothing is wrong with Lizzie!" She looks down at the letter. "They're 'concerned' about her health and well-being. Bullshit! They're concerned about themselves, how it would look if they got a kid that isn't their version of perfect."

"Hey, down girl! Chill! Don't you get it?"

"What? Get what? These people are assholes?"

"No, honey. What it means is that there's no more competition for that sweet little girl of yours. There was going to be a hearing so that the judge could determine the best home for Lizzie, with social workers and everyone involved, just like with Max. But that's not going to happen now. I spoke with the judge and it's his opinion that you're the best parent for her and that the formal adoption proceeding should progress as quickly as possible."

Mar stares at Shirley's beaming face. She searches it for the 'but' that is sure to come. A moment passes and Shirley continues to grin and then begins to nod as if to confirm her words. Mar gasps. She wants to shout for joy. She wants to dance. Instead, she does the only thing she can do. She bursts into tears.

Shirley heaves herself up and moves around the desk to pull Mar to her. "Hey there. *Shhh...shhh.* Honey, why you crying? Why you crying, Mar child?"

"Ohmygod, Shirley! I don't know. I just don't know. I just can't believe it, I don't know if I should believe it, I want to believe it but after Max and everything, I'm afraid to believe it. It was too easy..." Mar turns her neck and presses her forehead into Shirley's swollen belly. "This is just too good, too good."

"Mar, honey, believe it. I wouldn't tell you about it if it wasn't true. Lizzie's gonna be yours, with the judge's signature and everything, and there's not a damn thing anyone can do about it. Now stop your crying. Come on!"

Shirley reaches over her desk and pulls a handful of Kleenex from the box. "Here, now, dry your face. You're all red and puffy."

Mar grabs the tissues and swipes at her eyes. When she looks up at Shirley, she is beaming. "Really?" she asks, "Really, really?"

"Really, really, babe. For true."

"Well, hot damn!" Mar jumps up and, as best she can without hurting her friend, she throws her arms around Shirley. "Oh, man, Shirley, you're the best! This is the best

Christmas ever. Thank you thank you thank you. Oh my god! OK, let's go, I gotta go tell my dad."

At the door, she turns back. "When's the judge gonna sign the papers?"

"January 8th."

"OK, let's go!" And with that, Mar runs to find her daughter.

Seventeen

Jack.

Jack sits at his desk, the lights of New York blinking unseen outside the large picture window of his home office. The reflected light of the monitor turns his skin a sickly pale, darkens the hollows of his cheeks. He jots down another statistic and flags the site. It is something he wants to check against the information he'd gotten from NCMEC, the National Center for Missing and Exploited Children. Granted, Mia hardly fits into any of the statistics. Most abducted children are taken by the non-custodial parent and those who are taken by strangers are usually older than pre-school age. Still, if he is to find her, he needs all the information he can get his hands on.

The phone rings. Jack keeps clicking. He vaguely remembers a site that offers a link to an artist who does age projection pictures. Thank god one of the nurses in the neo-natal unit had taken a picture of the freshly bathed Mia Westfield. True, the photo was slightly distorted by the Plexiglas incubator in which she lay, but it is all that he has. Maybe it will be enough.

The ringing starts up again. Jack lifts the handset. "Yeah?" he mumbles.

"Jack?"

Jack glances at the I.D. "Mom?"

"Jack? Honey? Merry Christmas," her voice is tentative.

Jack glances at the monitor's clock. He's been at it for more than five hours. No wonder his stomach is rumbling. "Hey, Mom," he answers.

"Merry Christmas, honey. It's just after midnight. I thought maybe you were at a party when you didn't answer before."

He can hear the defeated hope in her voice and catches the sigh of annoyance before it escapes his lips. The guilt floods through him. Leave it to Mom. "I'm OK. I just have a lot of work."

"But, Jack, on Christmas?"

"It's important."

"Oh, well, OK, then. I just thought..."

Jack rakes a hand through his hair and counts to five. She means well. She always means well. She wants him to jump back into life, to move on. "I know. I know what you thought. And, thank you."

Her voice brightens considerably, "Did you get the packages we sent you?"

Did he? He isn't even sure. Jack rubs his eyes and smiles grimly. "Sure, Mom. Thank you."

"And?"

"And, I'm waiting to open them in the morning. Some friends are coming over," he lies, "and we're going to do it together."

"Oh, really?" she asks and Jack imagines the smile that undoubtedly spreads across her face.

He shakes his head, feeling like a good and true shit. "Really," he soothes. "For brunch."

"Well, then. That's good, honey. That's really good news. Now here's your father. Tell him. He'll be so happy to hear it. And call us, OK? After your party? Just for a minute to let us know how it went?"

"I will, Mom. I will."

"Merry Christmas, Jack. I love you."

"I love you, too. Merry Christmas."

After he says his goodbyes, Jack gently returns the phone to its cradle. Lindsey's face floats across his screen saver. He watches it fade and reassemble itself in another corner of the screen. He closes his eyes and takes a deep breath. *Merry Christmas, sweetheart*, he sends out to her. And then, with a click of the mouse, she disappears completely and is replaced by more statistics on missing children.

Eighteen

Mar.

Christmas Day dawns bright and clear. Though cold, and with a foot of snow on the ground, the day promises to be glorious. Mar's house is nice and warm when she awakes to the sounds of Elizabeth playing in her crib.

"Hey there, pumpkin, whatchya doin'?" Mar leans on the edge of the safety bar.

Startled from her game, Elizabeth looks up. Confirming that Mar really is there, awake and ready for her, Lizzie drops the toy she is holding and pulls herself up to a standing position. She laughs as she throws her arms open to Mar.

"Yes, pretty girl, time to get up. Do you know what day it is? Do you know who came here last night while you were sleeping? Santa Claus." Mar lowers Lizzie onto the changing table.

"How about if we change into your Santa suit?" she asks when she's finished fastening a dry diaper. "Or do you want your elf suit? *Hmmmm*? Should we wear the elf suit Dee gave you? What do you think?"

Lizzie claps her hands together and laughs some more. "OK, then, elf suit it is," Mar says. "Now don't move. Stay there." Mar bends to pull the elf pajamas from a drawer, one hand holding Lizzie firmly down.

"Mama," Lizzie says as Mar unsnaps the bottom of the pajamas.

"*Hmmm*?" Mar asks absently as she maneuvers the outfit over Lizzie's head.

"Mama." Lizzie repeats as her head pops through the top of the elf suit.

Mar freezes. She grabs the changing table for support. "Baby?" she whispers. "What'd you say, honey?"

"Mamamamamamamamamama," Lizzie replies, clapping her hands together.

"OHMYGOD! Mama! You said Mama! DAD! Come here!" Mar snatches Lizzie up into a fierce hug and spins her around. "You said Mama!" she laughs.

Don Bloom hurries into the room, one half of his face covered in shaving cream, the other freshly shaved.

"What's wrong, Mar?" Don asks. "Is Lizzie OK?"

Picasso, who had followed Don into the room, pushes her snout into Mar's crotch, looking for reassurance.

"No, no, Picasso, stop that," Mar laughingly pushes the dog away. She turns Lizzie to face her father. "She spoke! She finally spoke! She said Mama!"

At that, Lizzie starts her chant again, "Mamamamamama!"

"Can you believe it?" Mar grins up at her father. "It's like she knows."

Don Bloom puts his arm around his daughter and granddaughter and squeezes. "Maybe she does, honey. Maybe she just does."

Sy watches Jack standing against the window, his back to the room and he shudders, spooked. Every time he comes to see him, Jack is at the window, looking out. One time he asked him, *What're you looking at out there, Jack?* and he got no answer. The weather outside is gray. Gray on gray on tired gray. He can feel its bitter chill even from the distance of the client chair he always sits in. It is almost like the building heat doesn't reach this office, that it stops dead at the door. He isn't a superstitious man, but this window thing is beginning to creep him out.

"I should have been there with her," Jack breaks through his thoughts.

"With who? Lindsey?"

"We knew the baby was coming. I could have taken second seat, left someone else in charge of the case, consulted. I could've spent more time with her, with Lindsey, helping her buy things for the baby, decorate."

"Aw, Jack, don't go there."

Jack continues as if Sy hasn't spoken. "You know, that morning? It was almost as if I knew something was going to happen, as if I knew the baby was coming. And I went anyway.

I went to court anyway and left Lindsey alone."

"You didn't know, Jack, don't say that."

"I could have spent more time looking for my pager. If I'd just called the number, I would have found it."

Sy's stomach begins to churn, his ulcer acting up. "Jack," he tries to cut him off.

"No, really. And, you know what? There was a part of me that was almost glad I couldn't find it. Like, this thought went through my head that if I didn't have it, I wouldn't have to worry about it going off and I could concentrate on the trial. For half a second there, I thought that. And now that's going to be with me forever."

"We all get thoughts like that sometimes. You're busy, you're rushing, you got things to do and you don't want anything to knock you off schedule. It doesn't mean you don't care."

"Yeah, well, I should have found it."

"That wouldn't have made no difference."

"I'd've been there with her. When she called, I would have gotten a car and gone to pick her up. She wouldn't have needed to take a cab, to take that cab."

"You couldn't know."

"No. But I think about it all the time." Jack sighs heavily and leans closer to the window. "So what you're telling me is that there's no hope." His voice is flat.

Sy rubs at his forehead, hard, looking for the words. "No, Jack," he finally replies, his own voice tinged with fatigue, "I'm not saying there's no hope. I'm telling you there're some leads I followed up. One really good one. But, crap, maybe not good enough. The thing is, oh hell, I'm beginning to think that maybe people really can just disappear."

Beyond Jack, the first of the day's snow begins to fall. "Tell me about this girl again," he says.

Sy, looking crumpled and feeling worse, sits forward and picks up the frayed file he'd left on Jack's desk. It isn't much fatter than when Jack had first given it to him a year ago, and he really doesn't need it, he has the damn thing memorized, but he opens it up anyway, giving himself something to look at other than Jack disappearing into the gray, keeping his fingers entertained.

Sy begins to go over the highlights of the case. *Fuck, highlights, my ass.* He shakes his head and continues, even though Jack has heard it all already. A year of looking for Elie Burrows has led to a dead end. She has disappeared, kaput, is gone. It seems almost impossible to him that not one, but two, women have disappeared, the kidnapper and Burrows. Makes him feel like a helluva detective alright.

When he is finished, Sy looks up. Jack hasn't moved. "Jack? Hey, Jack?" he says.

"What? Oh, sorry." Jack moves to turn, but the hand that he's held so long to the window sticks for a moment, frozen to the hard, cold pane. Sy moves to help him, but Jack rocks his hand back and forth and finally breaks nature's hold on him. Turning, he moves heavily to his desk, giving Sy his first real good look at him.

Shock clutches at Sy's heart and he bites down hard on a curse. Not only is Jack thinner, but his eyes, with their permanent smudge of black shadow, look haunted and old. A shadow seems to lurk over his features, casting bones in high relief and hollowing out cheeks to leave the fleeting image of death.

Suddenly, Sy doubts his approach. Maybe keeping this investigation alive is stupid. Even though it isn't much of an investigation anyway, he admits to himself. Sure, the time and energy are there. In fact, Sy spends most of his time on it, taking other jobs just to keep the money coming in, but still, his main focus is this one, to the point where he wouldn't be surprised if one of the few people he can follow up with – and has so many times – takes out a restraining order against him. After all, how many times can you badger someone who doesn't know nothin' before it becomes harassment?

No, he thinks, looking at the man who sits before him, head resting against his chair back, eyes closed to the world, *no, this man needs a break. And it isn't coming from the investigation. Shit.*

"Jack," he begins, "listen. I'm talking to you as a friend. Maybe it's time to give it up. Just drop everything."

"Yeah, yeah, yeah," Jack intones, moving his chair back and forth to some inner beat. Sy had seen a woman do that once, back when he was a cop and he'd come to tell her her husband was dead. She just started to rock and, hours later, she was still at it. "Yeah," Jack comes to a dead stop and finally looks up. "That's what everyone says. It's been, what? A year and a half? Those drawings I had made up of her, the age projection ones? They don't mean shit. Three different artists, three different projections. They're less than five percent accurate on a newborn, anyway." Jack's fingers beat a stiff staccato on the desktop. "So," he continues, "you think it's time to give up."

"Naw, Jack, I'm not saying that. Hell, I don't want to give up. I don't ever want to give up. It's just, seeing you like that, like this, I don't know what to say to you. I've got one lead that might one day become something if this girl Elie ever gets in touch with her mother again, or ever gets a real job. I got feelers out all over. She gets a job, I got her through Social Security. Or maybe she gets sick and there's Medicaid, or she goes on welfare. Any one of those, and I've got her. Or the feds do, if they're still lookin', which I doubt, but you never can tell. Sometimes they stumble on to things. But anyway, shit, I've turned over every rock and then some and nothin' is adding up to nothin'. Zip."

Just then, there is a light tap on the office door and Jack's assistant pokes her head in. "Jack? Sorry to interrupt, but Mrs. Fitzgibbons is on the phone. She's been leaving messages all morning and I don't know what to tell her anymore."

"Elena? Just tell her I'm in a meeting."

"I did, Jack," Elena replies, her voice stretched thin. "But she says it's urgent, an emergency."

"Is she dying again, Elena?" Jack asks, a somewhat nasty tone in his voice that Sy has never heard before.

"Apparently so," Elena whispers back, her hands fluttering

before her as if to ward off an attack.

"So she says she wants to change her will again? That's the third time this month," Jack tells her, not even looking at her.

Sy does, though. Looks at Elena. The once proud Executive Assistant looks harried and beaten. When once Sy had known her to spar good-naturedly with her boss, she now looks a hair's breadth away from bolting. And the fact that Jack is handling a will doesn't escape his attention either, great detective that he is. Fuck. Here's this great attorney handling a fucking will. If it weren't that this is his friend, a really good guy, really, whose entire life now seems such a tragedy, Sy might be tempted to think about how far the mighty have fallen. But he doesn't, doesn't even entertain it because he himself is part of the tragedy and is falling pretty fast in his own right.

"Just tell Mrs. Fitzgibbons to keep breathing for another fucking ten minutes and I'll get back to her," Jack hisses between clenched teeth. And then, as the door to his office quickly closes, he begins to swivel again. "They're saying if I hadn't already made partner, I'd be out by now," Jack says, his voice almost conversational.

Sy sits forward in his chair. "Jack," he begins, his voice now firm, "you gotta let her go."

The swiveling stops. "Who? Let who go, Sy? Lindsey, or the baby? Or, maybe both of them? Is that what you mean? Let them both go? The only fucking thing I have left of Lindsey is that baby and I gotta let her go? Is that what you're saying?"

Sy rubs his eyes, breaking contact with Jack's fevered glare, and takes a deep breath. "Listen, Jack, I'll keep looking, for as long as you want me to. I'm just worried about you."

"Don't be. I'm fine. I'll be fine. Just find my daughter. Find Lindsey's daughter." And he swivels around in his chair, his gaze once more drawn to the stark grays of winter beyond the window.

Sy waits a few minutes, not knowing if he has been dismissed or forgotten. Either way, he finally realizes, it doesn't matter. He gets up and walks to the door, the file in hand.

Mar.

Spring bursts onto Boulder like a jack out of its box. In the space of a heartbeat, the earth moves from snow-encrusted to flower buds popping out all over, new-green grass lengthening almost before the eyes, birds chirping and chattering and swooping and flying in an endless, melodious tune. The sound of lawn mowers replaces that of snow blowers and bare-chested young men chase Frisbees down the street, ignored by lightly-clad young ladies who have already figured out that the quickest way to a man's heart is through rejection.

Mar glimpses the changes from her studio, windows flung open to the warming sun. She is on a streak, working at a pace that she has never before matched. Whether from the change in temperature, the peace that has settled like an aura about her, or excitement for the direction her life is now taking, something urges her on, makes her squirt paint directly from the tube onto the canvas, to layer it and fold it back on itself, to pull it across and through other colors, to create, to build, to exult in her own frenetic pace.

And it is good. Not only the act of painting, but the results. Since Christmas, she has turned out five finished pieces and is working on the sixth. Each is better than the previous and she knows, without having to be told, that her work is moving to a new level, a better level. That knowledge, compounded by the peace and excitement the activity brings her, and she cannot remember a time she has ever felt so good.

Lizzie spends her mornings at a small day care center down the street where she can interact with children her own age and she, too, is thriving. On days when Mar just cannot set her brushes down, Diane and Picasso pick the little girl up and bring her back to the house for lunch.

"Hey, Mar," Diane calls from the doorway.

"Uh-huh?"

"Are you busy? Can I bug you for a moment?"

"Yeah, sure, what's up? Can you hit pause on the stereo there, please? I want to hear that again."

Diane walks over and hits the pause button on the Bose system. "It's not like you haven't heard it a million times already," Diane points out. Dave Matthews is just about the only thing Mar paints to and even Diane, who really doesn't care for that kind of music, sometimes finds herself singing along.

"I know, I know, but it's these colors here. And this, see how the Magenta goes up and around and swirls into the Gold? And then out through the Purple? I mean, look there, do you see that streak? Isn't it gorgeous? I could get lost in that." Mar points at the canvas and watches as Diane scrutinizes the painting, wills her to follow the beat of the music through the paint. When Diane cocks an eyebrow and nods, Mar knows she's made her point, "OK, what's up?" she asks.

"Well, you know the card sets? We're running low and I want to know how many we should print this time. I was thinking of twenty thousand. We've got Barnes & Noble now, too, and we get a big discount on the printing if we increase that much. Besides, I've got a couple of good leads on some gift catalogs."

So far, there are six different sets to choose from, some from her older work, a couple with reproductions of her latest paintings thrown in. Diane had started marketing them two years before to small coffee houses and independent bookstores around Boulder and Denver. Within the past year, a couple of the larger chain stores have picked them up, liking Mar's quirky paintings. Recently, Barnes & Noble had come calling. Mar, unlike other artists who have assigned merchandising rights to some of their art, produces the note cards herself rather than turning them over to a publishing house. The returns are smaller, but she has complete control over quality.

She does a quick calculation in her head. "Well, yeah, that sounds about right. Will Stan give us our normal terms?" she asks, referring to the local printer they use.

"He will, even though this is a larger outlay than we've ever done. Listen, I have another idea I wanted to swing by you."

"What is it?" Mar asks, stepping back to survey the canvas. "You know, I think that it's time to introduce a new set. I should be finished with this one in a day or two. What do you think? Should we have Gustavo come shoot these?"

"I've already got him set up for next week," Diane smiles. She enjoys jumping the gun on Mar and from what she's seen of Mar's latest work, she knows that this card set will be special. "Anyway, I'm thinking we need to branch out from the cards and prints. I'm thinking about coffee mugs and t-shirts."

"T-shirts?" Mar can't hide the dismay in her voice. "Isn't that a bit, I don't know, tacky?"

"No, not at all. I'm talking high quality. Silk, limited editions. This one, what's it called?"

"*Mother & Child.*"

"OK, maybe this one on a nice white background, with a border around it and maybe a quote or just your name underneath. Maybe your signature?"

"Do you really think that'd be interesting? I mean, would people want to wear this on their boobs? I'm talking women, of course. Mostly women would get this one."

"I don't see why not. They wear Picasso paintings. I even saw some Van Gogh moccasins the other day."

"Well, yeah, but that's Picasso and Van Gogh."

"I think it would look great with jeans. It's so pretty."

"But this one," Mar waves at the painting, "is so much different than what I usually do. It doesn't even have fish."

"You have enough figurative pieces to make a set."

Mar moves over to the little studio fridge and takes out a Diet Pepsi. "Want one?" she asks before handing a can to Diane and opening one for herself, her mind already reviewing the possibilities.

"I'm also thinking about diaries, or sketch pads – hardcover books with blank pages," Diane puts in. "Stan's working out a price for me."

Mar wipes paint off the back of her left hand. As soon as the acrylic dries, she rubs it off and has a fresh, clean palette ready for more mixing. "Well, yeah, OK, if you think it's a good idea. It sounds fun, at least. Why don't you call the guys at Barnes & Noble and ask them what they think?"

"Well, actually, I called the buyer at Nordstrom's. We've already got Barnes & Noble for the card sets and they'd be a natural for stationery and the like, but I thought this could be just the right thing to clinch Nordstrom's with a limited edition of shirts. She loved the idea, by the way, wants to know if we'll be ready for Christmas. For that, they need them by September for shipping. But they'll need samples and photos to send to the stores for ordering purposes."

Mar starts laughing. "If you've got it all figured out, why are you asking me?"

"Well, basically, I'm just telling you, in a nice way. But also, kind of because you have to decide if you want to produce these yourself or outsource them. I've got some quotes on outsourcing."

"Can we do them ourselves? I mean, it's a risk. Would it be worth it?"

Diane grins, "If it flies, it'll be worth it. If not, you'll have to paint faster and sell some new ones to pay the bills."

"So," Mar grins back and reaches for a tube of paint, "let's make it fly."

Twenty-One

Jack.

Jack leans on the fence and watches the pick-up game, watches the moves of the agile young men, black, white, Latino, Asian, who feint left then right, dribble, spin and then thunder down the court before springing through the air for that half of a second of pure nirvana when the muscles and the will are stronger than gravity and all things are possible. Here, mostly, on this court, baggage is left behind, gang mentalities are checked at the gate and the occupants become again, for a few minutes or a few hours, the young boys they might have been had they been born in another time, another place.

"I thought that was you," comes a voice by his shoulder.

"Malcolm," Jack grasps the small priest's hand and squeezes warmly before being pulled into a tight embrace.

"Ha! You think you can disappear for more than a year and get away with a handshake? Not likely."

Jack's face contorts into a real smile, the first in a very long time. Malcolm, so much shorter than he, is broad and somewhat barrel-chested. His gray hair is shorn close to, for lack of a better word, a head shaped more like a block of concrete than an egg, and his nose, flattened a few too many times by the bullies of his youth who had tried, but failed, to torment him into submission, skews strangely to the left. The parts of Malcolm Brewster, now and for quite a long time Father Malcolm or even Father Mac, are a mismatch of spares left over in God's kitchen and assembled hurriedly and somewhat haphazardly when an unexpected soul had appeared and needed a form. The soul they house, however, is monumental, and the deep crinkles by the sides of his eyes show that he, if no one else, understands God's little joke.

"You're back," Malcolm nods. "That's good."

Jack looks off at the court, watches a particularly good fake out, a spin and then a spectacular steal. Stunned, the boy watches as the thief runs off with his ball and then a wide grin spreads across his face and he charges off to steal it back. "I'm here."

"Hey there, Duane!" the priest calls out to a group of spectators waiting for their time on the court.

"Yeah, Father Mac?" a tall boy, Duane, whose newly stretched limbs haven't yet learned how to accommodate forward motion, stumbles up to the fence.

"You tell DeJon, if he shows up, to come in and see me, OK?"

"Sure thing. You want me to go get him?"

"No, no, that's fine. I expect he'll show up sooner or later. Just send him my way when you see him."

"No prob."

"I don't want him seeing you suddenly," Malcolm explains after Duane has taken off. "It's probably better if I warn him first."

"Shit."

"There's nothing for it. You're a good man, Jack. He knows that. He'll understand."

"He's too young to understand."

"He loved her, too."

"I should have come around."

"Should have, should have, should have. No one made you a saint, Jack. If anyone's to blame, it's Him," he nods at the sky. "He took her when He shouldn't have and left us mortals to deal with the mess. Now come on, there's potatoes to peel and carrots to chop. We can talk while we work."

The simple act of peeling a potato does more to calm Jack's mind than any pills or therapy or the endless hours he's been spending on the racquetball court. *Schneep, schneep, schneep,* it becomes a bit of a meditation once he gets into the rhythm of it. The background noises, the other workers calling back and forth, telling a story, sharing a laugh, the hustle and bustle of the busy kitchen as a meal for the needy is prepared, turn him away from himself and ease a bit of the tension that has fused the muscles in his shoulders so tightly. Malcolm comes by several times and nods favorably at his progress or chides gently about not taking such big digs into the spuds, leaving some for the stew, but mostly leaves him alone to his contemplations.

A few hours later, the potatoes peeled, diced and dumped into the simmering pots, Malcolm shows up and invites Jack to join him on the rooftop, where it is time to feed his homing pigeons.

The weather on the rooftop is a bit brisk in the late afternoon light. Jack, raised on a farm, had grown up with the cold, had milked cows in pre-dawn snowstorms and baled hay late into bitter cold nights. The cooling wind is refreshing and he takes a seat on the rickety metal folding chair that Malcolm keeps up there and turns his face into the fading sun. From experience, he knows that Malcolm won't need his help with the birds and the birds themselves wouldn't want him anywhere near them anyway.

"They could use you again down at Legal Aid," Father Mac breaks through Jack's reverie.

Guilt washes over Jack. "I'm sorry..." he begins.

"Wait. Stop. I didn't say that to make you feel guilty, Jack. Guilt's garbage. It's unproductive."

Jack smiles. "I thought you Catholics live for guilt."

"Ha! Always the smart one! No, Jack, what I mean is you've been carrying this burden too long. It's time to put it down."

"I just think if I'd been there..."

Father Mac shoos a bird away. "You think too much," he cuts in. "Stop thinking. Act. You're a good man. Lindsey, God rest her soul, was a good woman. You were lucky to have her. For whatever reason, though, He called her home."

"I just wish I could believe that, that she's in a better place."

"Believe it. Without that," Mac waves his arm, taking in the entire world, "all this is nonsense. You've got a gift, Jack. You've got a heart and you've got smarts. Lindsey saw that and loved you for it. If you cared anything about her, you have to recognize that and be the man she'd want you to be."

"And what about Mia?"

"Ah, well then, that's a different story. She's out there, Jack. I'm sure of it. You can never stop looking, never give up. She'll come home when the time's right."

"And when will that be?" Jack hears the bitterness in his own voice and shakes his head. He'd promised himself he'd edit that out.

The little priest shrugs. "I don't know. But ask yourself this, if she were to come home today, are you the man you'd want to be? Are you ready to help her recover from whatever she may have been through?"

It is a rhetorical question and Jack knows it. No, he isn't ready.

Malcolm lets Jack stew on that for a bit while he tidies the cage. "DeJon showed up while you were in the kitchen," he finally says. "He's angry and hurt and about all what you'd expect from a thirteen year old."

Jack focuses on his hands. They are large hands, strong hands, made that way by life on a farm. They've grown soft during the years he'd concentrated on his career. Now they are cracked and calloused, strong again, from countless repetitions at the gym. This, now, is the biggest step he's taken by far to return to life. His hands are shaking. "Is he still here?"

"He's out in the yard."

"Does he want to see me?"

"Jack, that boy wants to see you more than he wants to breathe. He just doesn't know it yet."

"What do I say to him? The kid's been dumped by every adult he ever cared about. I made a commitment to him."

"You didn't dump him."

"I haven't seen him in more than a year."

"OK, so he's hurting. He's been hoping you cared enough to come find him."

"Christ, Malcolm."

The priest shrugs and shoos the birds to the other end of the cage. "These birds here? They come back because that's what they're trained to do. They come for the food, for the warm nest. I love them, but I don't for a minute think they love me. Now that boy, he loves you and he's going to know you came back because you love him. That's what's going to make it OK."

"You think?"

"You should remember something else. He loved Lindsey. He went a little nuts when she died, but eventually he got it together and, in his way, tried to help. All that time you were waiting with the FBI, thinking maybe that ransom call would come, he was out on the streets showing the picture of that woman around. The one from the security camera? He was out for days trying to find anyone who might've seen her."

Jack drops his head into his hands. "I'm a total fucking shit, aren't I?"

"Ha! Always the guilt with you. Come on, time's up. He's waited long enough."

Twenty-Two

Mar.

The ringing of the phone demands her attention. Once. Twice. Three times. But the music is playing and she is detailing a thin line with Mars Black and Mar really can't think of anyone she wants to talk to enough to stop working. After the fourth ring, it stops and she relaxes back into the line. Dave is singing and she is going with it, swaying to it, moving with it, adding her voice, which is pretty much overkill, but enjoying it anyway. Her mind just going with the music, her brush following its path.

The phone rings again. "Dammit!" she stomps her foot. At the third ring, she looks up at the wall clock and realizes Diane must be out picking up Lizzie. And then the guilt hits her, knowing that this is the third day in a row that she has missed the pick up. Knowing it is OK because that's what she and Diane have worked out, but feeling a dose of mother guilt just the same. On the fifth ring, she snatches up the phone, all of a sudden wondering if maybe Diane has gotten to the day care center and found Lizzie sick, or worse, injured. Or, even, god forbid, dead. Maybe she choked on something? Kids are always putting things in their mouths.

"Hello?" Mar gasps into the phone.

"Mar? Is that you? What's wrong?" Shirley asks, concern in her voice.

"Oh. No, nothing's wrong. Is something wrong with you?"

"No, but you sound shaken up."

"Ah, crud! No, just working and then the phone was ringing and I was thinking that maybe something happened to Lizzie. Forget it. Hey, Shirl, what's up?" Mar collapses back into her armchair and gives into the phone call.

"Nothing. Everything's cool over here. We were just wondering if you wanted to go out tonight, grab dinner and a movie?"

"What about the kids? Lizzie's getting too big to sit through a whole movie. Anyway, it'd be a little late for her."

"No, we got a babysitter. Charlene's coming over and you could bring Lizzie by. Let her and Derek spend some time together."

"What, Miracle Baby is already up for entertaining company?" Mar laughs. It seems that every time she speaks with Shirley, there is some new magnificent feat of excellence performed by Derek the Miracle Baby. Dylan is even worse.

"Nah, you know. Whatever. Stop laughing. In fact, you hardly ever shut up about Lizzie, Miss Perfect this, Miss Incredible that. Sheee-it, girl, I never heard so much nonsense as 'natural-born-artist' and 'wall-paintings' and such when all she'd done was rub her dirty diaper all over the place. I mean, come on!"

"OK, OK, I give up. What movie, which restaurant?"

"I don't know and I don't know. Dylan has a friend of his, a visiting professor, coming over and we're going out with him. I'm letting them work it out."

"Um, so is this kind of supposed to be a blind date or something? A foursome?"

"No, it's not like that," Shirley protests, because she knows that Mar is anti anything-that-resembles-a-relationship-or-reasonable-facsimile. "It's just that he's a friend, you're a friend..."

"This is not sounding good, Shirl. I'm really not ready

yet." Mar glances off at her painting, letting her disinterest in the conversation melt into interest in the canvas and the colors. From the distance, she takes in the overall effect and then zeroes in on an area that needs work, that demands her immediate, undivided attention.

"It's a movie, for Christ sakes, not a commitment. It's not like you have to sleep with him!"

"Well, thanks for that, at least."

"Listen, Mar honey, and I say this with all the love and respect I feel for you, but, you've got more walls around you than Red China. You need to start loosening up, child."

"I am loose, Shirley. I'm fine."

"I know you are, but weren't you just telling me the other day that Dr. Frank thinks you need to start dating? Take some chances?"

"Aha! So this is a blind date!"

"No, Mar, don't change the subject."

"I thought that was the subject."

"Now you're just being difficult."

Mar sighs. "I know, Shirl, I know I know I know. It's been years and it's time to move on, time to grow up. Shit happens and people deal with it all the time. I know it all. God, I'm paying my shrink enough, I should know it by now. I guess I'm just comfortable with the way things are."

"Safe."

"Hell, yeah, safe. There's a lot to be said for it."

"Babe, there's a lot to be said for love and excitement, too. For having a warm body next to you at night. For having someone else go out and get the firewood and mow the lawn. Now, I'm not being sexist here, but that's the way it is. AND, there's a lot to be said for sex! You do remember sex, don't you? If not, you should try it sometime."

"I remember sex," Mar says tiredly.

"And oral sex. You ever heard of oral sex in that cave of yours? It's when a man does this thing with his tongue and..."

"Jesus Christ, Shirley! Shut up!" But she is smiling.

"You know, as the good friend I am, I'd lend Dylan to you,

break you out of your funk, but the poor man can't get enough of me. He's like a lovesick puppy. That means you're gonna have to go out and find your own man."

The conversation is getting too long and Mar is distracted. "Look, I'm kind of in the middle of a painting and I really gotta go." Mar gets up and heads back toward the easel. The paint on the back of her hand is drying and as they say their goodbyes, Shirley's full of disappointment, Mar dips her brush in water and adds it to the glob of paint, re-working it to a usable texture. By the time the phone is back in its cradle, she has already forgotten the call.

***

Later that afternoon, after she and Lizzie have eaten and Picasso has cleaned the floor beneath the high chair, Mar puts Lizzie down for a nap and decides to take one herself. After five hours of standing in front of a canvas, grooving to a little music, being absorbed in the colors, textures and sounds, and opening herself up and turning herself inside out to her work, she is ready to drop.

Mar closes the blackout shades in her bedroom, turns on the air-conditioner, checks that the baby monitor is on, shuts the door and crawls into bed. She closes her eyes and wills herself to fall asleep. She can't. She turns over, sticks her head under the pillow, and her mind returns to the conversation with Shirley. She flips onto her back. Just half an hour, she prays, an hour, and then she'll be good to go, can spend the afternoon chasing Lizzie around the park, maybe paint some more later.

It is no use. She needs to relax. Finally, giving into the urge, she reaches out and finds the bottom drawer of her bedside dresser, pulls it open and reaches in. She had long ago abandoned the conventional penis-shaped, battery-operated vibrators for an electric back massager. Clitoral stimulation works for her and anyway, it is easier to explain if anyone ever finds it. An old back injury. I fell off a ladder, a house. A man. Besides, she isn't interested in having a relationship with the damn thing, not enough to pretend it's something it isn't.

She turns it on low and brings it under the covers to her panty-clad clitoris. Mar shuts her eyes and lets her mind drift to Joaquin, tries to picture him over her and then realizes that she is trying to picture him. She is having trouble seeing him in her mind, having trouble imagining him there, really there, with her. She takes a deep breath and tries to change the picture of this hazy figure, tries to bring it into focus.

"Dammit!" It's no use. More and more lately, she is having trouble remembering him. He is a great, wonderful memory, but he is becoming more of a memory than a reality and she isn't sure she can handle thinking about that. She isn't sure she is ready to let him go yet.

Mar switches off the vibrator and stares up into the darkness, willing the itching between her legs to go away. It stays there, a soft throbbing, a need demanding to be met.

In frustration, she finally reaches out and grabs up the bedside phone, dials it by its fluorescent light. "Hello? Shirl? It's me. Yeah, listen, what time? OK, we'll be there."

Mar hangs up the phone and lays back in the darkness. This time, when she turns on the vibrator, she gives into the fact that the man she pictures on top of her, the man she pictures entering her, is a mystery, is maybe someone from the future rather than from her past. She climaxes before her mind quiets to the pull of her body's exhaustion.

Twenty-Three

Mar

"You look horrible," Diane tells Mar over cups of coffee.

"I know. It was The Dream again. Or, at least a version of it. This time, the water came for me first, and then the sharks. I don't know."

"You haven't been having those nightmares for awhile now."

"I know, I can't figure it out. Usually, they start up when I'm stressed, but I'm not now. In fact, I feel great. I mean, things are great in the gallery, my painting's coming along, Lizzie's healthy and happy, my dad is doing fine. What else could it be?"

Diane looks past Mar at the photos of Joaquin that decorate the refrigerator. "Could it have been your date last night? Are you feeling a little guilty?"

"Oh, that," Mar laughs. "It wasn't really a date. I mean, I went out with Shirley and Dylan and one of Dylan's friends. It was really just friends, not a date. I'm getting more coffee. Want some more coffee?" Mar feels Diane's eyes on her as she fills her mug with water and heats it in the microwave. When it is ready, she nukes Diane's mug, adds instant coffee and places it in front of Diane. As she takes her place, she looks up. Diane is still looking at her, a bemused smile on her face.

"What? What's that look supposed to mean?" Mar squirms.

"You, I'm just looking at you. If it wasn't a date, how come you're blushing?"

"I'm not blushing!" Mar insists, although she can feel the burn. She begins playing with some bread crumbs that litter the granite counter top.

"You're blushing. You are. So tell me about it. What's going on? What's he like?"

Mar covers her face with her hands and rubs furiously at her eyes, trying to clear her vision, clear her mind. "OK, it was fun. We were going to go to an early dinner and then catch a movie, but we were having such a good time, we just stayed at the restaurant."

"And his name is?"

"Kevin. McDermott. Kevin McDermott."

"Irish."

"Yeah, I guess. I mean, yes. He's from back East, from Bahstun. Typical Back Bay accent – you know, pahk the cah and all that. He was nice, and funny. We laughed a lot."

"What's he do?"

"He's a visiting professor. He developed some sort of theory about adolescence and how it's changed over the years. You know, like hundreds of years ago childhood ended and adolescence started around the age of ten. And now, childhood stops way too early and adolescence continues for a much longer time – sometimes for more than a decade until people are out of college. He says that the change is so dramatic that unless society makes plans to deal with it, we're setting ourselves up for some pretty big socio-economic problems."

"I don't know if I'd think of a twenty-five year old as an adolescent."

"Well, right, I mean, he thinks that it's a whole new stage of life that we haven't had to deal with until now. Kind of a new phase between adolescence and adulthood. And because we're not dealing with it, we're kind of just dumping it all together and we're not making real provisions for it, economically speaking." Mar looked up, realizing that she is sounding a bit more enthusiastic than usual. "I mean, well, it was an interesting idea."

Diane won't let her off the hook. "So what's he do with this idea?"

"He's here for the semester and maybe the summer. He's meeting with the psych, sociology and economics departments to show them that they need to re-vamp their programs and kind of merge in some areas."

"And then?"

"Then he goes on to some other schools, Wharton, then somewhere in England. And he's on some sort of taskforce in Washington that the President wanted put together to study his ideas."

"Impressive. It sounds, though, like he spent the whole night talking about himself."

"No, not at all. Most of that I got from Dylan. I guess he consulted on some of Kevin's work and is a big fan."

Mar moves to the fridge for a Diet Pepsi. "Want one?"

"No, I'm going to stick with coffee."

"Anyway, most of the night he was trying to get me to talk about myself. It was weird. I've kind of forgotten how to have a conversation. I mean, like a personal one. You know, one that's not with you or Shirley or Lizzie? Where someone's interested in your thoughts and ideas? I felt like I was groping to even have any. I mean, it was like, Music? OK, Dave Matthews Band. Work? Painting. Hobbies? Painting. Interests? Painting. I felt pretty one dimensional."

"You're not, and I'm sure if he's as intelligent as he sounds, he figured that out pretty quickly. I guess he's your age?"

"Forty, I think."

"Marital status?"

"Never married. Shirley told me he had a live-in girlfriend who was cheating on him and when he found out, it really freaked him out."

"His looks?"

Mar grins. And blushes. And then she laughs ruefully.

"Good. Great even."

"Sean Connery's great, Mar. Anyone else can't be that good."

"Well, yeah, OK. Maybe a young Sean Connery. Rugged, you know? Crinkly around the eyes, like he laughs a lot. Outdoor skin. By the way, he's a mountain climber in his free time so I guess that's why he's in such great shape. AND, he does look like he's in great shape!"

"Arms?"

"Strong, not ape-like testosterone strong, just, *mmmmm*, strong enough."

"I like that. Legs?"

"Good! Long and cut. But again, not the gym-freak-I'm-so-hot look. Like he earned his."

"OK, he's getting better. Butt?"

"Very nice. Very, very nice."

"Face?"

"Good. Lived in. His eyes are maybe a little close together, his nose maybe a bit too big."

"It works for Richard Gere."

"Exactly. Exactly, that's what I'm thinking. You put it all together with this great smile and it works. Oh! And his eyes are blue, this gorgeous sky-blue-on-a sunny-day kind of blue."

"Mar."

"I know, I know," Mar groans. "I sound pitiful, don't I?"

"No, honey, it's good. It's good to hear you talking about a man. I take it you like him?"

Mar's eyes slide to the full scale painting of Joaquin and then quickly away. "I do," she takes a deep, shaky breath. "I really do."

Diane and Mar catch each other's eyes and begin to laugh. "Oh, hell," Diane says, regaining her breath. "He sounds good. Good for you! Now, when am I going to meet him?"

Mar looks at the clock. "Uh, in a couple of hours?" she admits. "I kind of invited him for lunch."

"Well, then," Diane moves to the refrigerator, "let's get busy."

Twenty-Four

Jack.

The Grand Ballroom of The Pierre Hotel is alive with the many voices of the well-heeled and well-connected. The thirtieth anniversary party put on by Weisman, Tannenbaum and Carruthers is a must-do for the New York social set. Guests include past clients and the politically and financially elite who will probably at some time or another become clients of the successful law firm.

From his place beside the bar, Jack stares unhappily out at the jewel-bedecked and designer-dressed crowd. It is a far cry from The Farm, as Father Malcolm calls the shelter and youth center he oversees. Truth be told, Jack would much rather be up there, peeling potatoes or out for a movie and pizza with DeJon. It had been difficult at first but DeJon is a decent kid and hasn't made Jack grovel too much for abandoning him. In fact, he is showing signs of trust again and that is a damn good thing that Jack won't screw up. For anything.

But now, he hasn't moved or spoken with anyone other than the bartender for the past twenty minutes. In fact, if his bosses hadn't insisted that he make an appearance, he wouldn't be here at all. He drains the last of the Rum & Coke and holds his glass out for a re-fill.

"I hadn't heard that you were much of a drinker," murmurs a husky female voice by his shoulder. Jack turns toward it and offers a weak, but obligatory, smile.

"Sharon, uh, Karen, right?" he asks, reaching out his hand to shake hers.

"Nope, sorry, slugger, you're not even in the ballpark," she looks at him, irony twisting her full lips into a quasi-smile. "Want to try again?"

Jack drags his free hand through his hair, shrugs his shoulders and gives up. "Ah, crap, I'm sorry, I'm just not good with names."

"Caroline. Caroline Carruthers. We met last week."

Suddenly Jack remembers. In a long dress, with her hair down around her shoulders, she only faintly resembles the more severely dressed new associate who had joined the firm the week before. The fact that she is one of the founding partner's granddaughters should have made more of an impression on him, if only to keep up with office hierarchy. "Yes, Caroline. Right. Sorry," he fumbles.

Caroline laughs, amusement dancing in her eyes. "It's OK, don't worry. Actually, it's pretty much refreshing. As you can imagine, half the associates at the firm want to tear my eyes out. The other half want to be my new best friends. They either think I'm just one more stumbling block on their way to partnership or that I'll put in a good word for them with Grandfather."

Jack looks fully at her now, startled by her candor. She is right, of course, the competition among associates is fierce. Generally, it takes between five to eight years of intense, long, billable hours, a high percentage of "wins" and little, if any, social or family life to be invited into one of the seats of power – partnership. Some never make it and they are politely asked to leave the firm or are banished to the archives to act as flunkies and researchers for those who are invited in. For a few, overachievers like Jack, like he had at one time been, that glory is achieved slightly ahead of schedule. In any case, most associates would probably feel that Caroline's ancestry makes her a shoo-in, thereby taking up one of the precious few opportunities that open each year.

"You're right. They probably hate you," he agrees amicably, noticing that the eyes they would tear out are an interesting shade of hazel, changing from green to blue to gray as they sweep over the ballroom. Noticing also the faint dusting of freckles across the bridge of her sculpted nose. And being shocked when he realizes he's noticed.

Caroline brings those eyes back to him. "I'll take a Chardonnay, in case you're asking."

"Damn! I'm sorry. I'm not doing very well here, am I?" He turns to the bartender and asks for her wine.

"You're already a partner, you don't have to impress me, even if I did have some influence with my grandfather, which I don't. At least," she smiles, "not at the firm. Thank you. And cheers."

"Cheers," Jack agrees as the rim of her glass slips between full, moist lips and his cock throbs suddenly to life after its long hibernation.

Twenty-Five

Mar.

The weeks have flown. And it seems that all her time and thoughts are wrapped up in Kevin. When he isn't actually with Mar, he makes it a point to call her. Before going to meetings or classes, he sends her silly emails and texts. She sketches cartoons, emails them back to him. Without being aware of it, something is happening. She is starting to have very real feelings for Kevin McDermott. Feelings that he is showing every sign of returning.

The problem is, what to do about them? He is pretty heavily committed for at least the next year and, while she can set her own schedule, she isn't about to fly all over the planet with a toddler, chasing after him like some demented groupie.

In fact, the whole situation is impossible, she tells herself, applying gloss over the lipstick she had just put on. She is settled, happy. She looks at her hair. As usual, loose curls have slipped free of the pins she had tried to contain them with. Frustrated, she pulls them out and shakes her hair loose. "What the hell have I gotten myself into?" she asks her reflection. Picasso stretches out beside her on the floor, chuffs companionably. Mar bends down and scratches the dog between her eyes. "Come on, fatso, be honest, how do I look?"

The dog looks up at her and twitches her eyebrows in a very good imitation of looking Mar over. She exhales sharply through her nose, closes both eyes and drops her head back onto her paws.

"That good, huh?" Mar returns to her reflection. What she sees is a woman who hasn't been laid in too many years staring back at her. Earlier, she had frantically searched through her lingerie drawer to find something half decent, if not wholly enticing. The elastic had gone on her first choice, a lacy black number that hasn't been worn in years. She'd thrown it out and scavenged around until she found the current outfit – a little red thing with matching bra. She's been wearing grocery store panties for so long she's forgotten what a g-string feels like and has to reach behind herself to pull the wedgie out of her butt crack. Throwing her shoulders back, she tries for a sultry pose and barely manages ridiculous. "Jesus Christ on a broomstick, Mar," she murmurs, "what were you thinking?" Sucking in her stomach, she turns sideways. The image doesn't get any prettier. *Face it,* she tells herself, *Barbie just does not live here.*

Mar returns to her closet and digs through the clothes there, knowing as she does that there is nothing even slightly sexy about her wardrobe. Her daily outfit consists of jeans and one of Joaquin's old undershirts. Wife beaters, Diane calls them, and urges Mar to splurge a little and spend more than three bucks on herself. Mar, for her part, can't justify spending money on decent clothes that will just end up paint-spattered and ruined.

After pushing her clothes left and right and pawing through drawers, Mar finally comes upon a bustier that she'd bought for her honeymoon. She pulls off her bra and puts the bustier on backwards, fastens all twenty-one, count them, hook-in-eye clasps and then has to yank it around so that the cups face the front. She's put on some weight. And it is good, she tries to reassure herself, doing a little hip gyration in the mirror. Oh, yeah, extra breastage in a bustier is what it is all about, Mama. Then she notices the extra waistage that seeps between her breastage and hippage. Not good. She wrestles the bustier down so that its bottom overlaps the top of her panties. Much better, even if her nipples threaten to spill forth. *Hell, what good are breasts if not to be beheld?* She tries doing the Scarlett O'Hara eyebrow thing and fails. Grabs a pair of jeans and steps into them before slipping her feet into the only pair of slingbacks she still owns. *Well?* she asks the mirror.

God, you look stupid, her reflection answers, and Mar has the good sense to agree. She grabs a blouse from a hangar and pulls it on top of her too obvious attire, tying it at the waist. "So, Picasso, will you still respect me in the morning?" she asks the sleeping dog. Picasso's only answer is to fart and roll over.

Mar regards the dog for a moment and considers euthanasia. She sighs. "OK, fuzzface, have it your way, but it's time to get Lizzie ready and head downstairs."

At the sound of her name, Lizzie looks up from the toys she is playing with. "Mama wanna play?" she asks.

"Not right now, punkin'. It's time to get you into your pj's." She picks the toddler up and swings her onto her hip. "Hey, guess what? Kevin's coming over to have dinner with us."

"Kevvy?" Lizzie asks, grinning.

"Yep, how's that sound?"

"Goooooooooood!" Lizzie purses her lips, drawing out the sound to make Mar laugh. "Casso coming too?"

"Yep, Picasso's coming, too. OK, now which pj's do you want to wear?"

"Superman!" Lizzie squeals.

"You wore Superman last night. Don't you want to be someone else tonight? How about Bunny Rabbit or your ballerina pajamas?"

"Nope! Wanna be Superman!"

"OK, then Superman it is!"

Later, they go down to the kitchen, Mar terrified at every step that she's going to trip in the stupid heels and send them flying, to begin getting things ready for dinner. After putting

Lizzie into her play-yard, Mar moves to the refrigerator and begins removing the ingredients she needs to make a salad. She sets out a variety of cheeses on a platter to give them a chance to come up to room temperature, takes out sun-dried tomatoes, Kalamata olives and crackers, uncorks a bottle of Sterling Merlot, pours herself a glass and puts a Luther Vandross CD on the stereo. Wonders for a moment if that is too obvious. Decides *screw it.*

All is going smoothly, in fact Mar is beginning to get into the music's groove, to loosen up and move a bit with it when the doorbell rings. "Oh, shit!" she jumps, her wine slopping onto the floor, where Picasso promptly slurps it up.

Suddenly, Mar realizes that she is nervous. She likes Kevin, she feels comfortable with him, in fact she feels better in his company than she has in a long time. So far, he's kissed her goodnight several times and is always affectionate, but he's let her maintain her distance and has waited for a sign from her that it is OK to advance. It is just that she feels as if this night will be different, as if they will take their fledgling relationship to a new level. She is sure she wants it, wants him. Hell, if the workouts she has been giving her vibrator are any indication, she is desperate for it. She just isn't sure she is ready for it.

Mar ducks into the gallery restroom to check her makeup. It appears wrong, all wrong. Too bright, too brassy. Stupid. *Stupid, stupid, stupid.* She grabs a washcloth and begins scrubbing at her face, then grabs toilet paper and dabs at her lipstick. It doesn't help.

The doorbell rings again and she freezes, catches the look of panic in her eyes. "Come on, Mar," she encourages herself, "you're a big girl, you're allowed to be horny." Her reflection doesn't loosen up. "Shit," she repeats and stumbles on too-high heels to open the door.

Mar.

Later, Kevin helps Mar clean up. The dinner had been a success, though, to Picasso's delight, there had been way too much of it. Lizzie, who had taken to Kevin from the beginning, thrilled at his attentions. When it was time for her to go to bed, it was Kevin who the little girl had wanted to put her down.

"You're good with her," Mar tells him when they return to the kitchen.

"She's easy to love. Besides, I grew up with all those brothers and sisters. When you come from a good Irish Catholic family, there's always little ones to help with. OK, so what else can I do?"

"I was going to have another glass of wine. Would you like one?"

"I'd love one."

Mar hands him the corkscrew and then takes down a couple of salad bowls. "I hope you like brownies?" she asks.

Kevin groans. "You're kidding, right? I'm stuffed. I don't think I could take another bite if you put a gun to my head."

Mar opens the microwave and removes the plate of brownies she has just reheated. "I've got vanilla ice cream," she croons. "And chocolate sauce."

"Do I have to?" he asks, all defenses shot.

"You do," she grins.

Kevin tops off their glasses and makes a face, "Well, if I must, I guess I'll suffer through it. My mother taught me never to insult the hostess."

"Aye, Laddie, those good Irish manners'll keep ye out of trouble, they will," Mar drawls in a heavy brogue.

They laugh companionably as Mar scoops vanilla ice cream over the brownies. It begins to melt immediately. She pours chocolate sauce over the mess and then sprinkles a handful of walnuts on top for good measure. "Come on, let's go up to the family room. You bring the wine, I've got this."

It is a cozy room, its big bay window facing the street. The original wood plank floor shines in the warmth of the floor lamp. Mar, trying to act casual, sets the bowls down on the old wood hope chest she uses as a coffee table and lights several candles. They sit on an oversize, well-lived-in sofa. Just the sort you can sink into and get lost in. Mar curls up at one end facing him. She takes a bite and moans. "Oh, god, this is so good. They make this at The Outback, that's where I copied it from. It's called Thunder from Down Under. When I was a kid, my friends used to call me Thunder Thighs because I was obsessed with the idea that my thighs were fat. I'm sure they named this dessert after me." She takes another bite, "Anyway, that's where it's all going to end up, on my thighs."

"At the risk of sounding clichéd, you don't have fat thighs." Kevin smiles at her around a bite of brownie.

"I wasn't fishing," she smiles back. "But thanks."

"I didn't think you were, but in case you were, I thought I'd set you straight. And, you're welcome."

They are quiet for a few minutes, intent on eating. Or, rather, intent on appearing that they are intent on eating as each tries to figure out where to take the conversation next.

Mar struggles with her feelings. If she were being honest with herself, she'd put the brownie down and launch herself across the couch at him. She isn't sure she is ready to be that honest, though. She isn't sure she is even reading his reactions to her correctly. She is pretty sure he likes her, no she is sure he likes her. It's just that she'd never really been in the dating game. Since the day she'd dragged him into the small Boston Whaler, Joaquin had been the only one she'd ever been interested in. And since his death, she's turned down every offer that has come her way. At what point does someone nowadays sleep with someone else? Diane told her she's waited long enough and had even left her a small basket of multi-colored, multi-flavored and multi-textured condoms next to her bed that afternoon. Deeply embarrassed, Mar had shoved them into the bedside drawer beside her vibrator and shut it firmly. Later, she had sneaked back upstairs and hidden a couple of the more normal looking ones in the family room. Not because she was planning to seduce him, she'd told herself, but because a girl has to look out for herself.

Now she casts around for something to say that won't reveal the real direction of her thoughts. "Um, I don't usually eat like this, you know," she falters.

Kevin picks it up right where she left it. "There's no way you could and look as good as you do."

Mar blushes, tongue-tied. She thinks of several different answers, tries them out in her head. "Um, I don't know what to do with that," she finally admits, focusing intently on her bowl.

"Take it. Accept it. Listen, Mar," he takes her bowl and sets it down next to his before reaching for her hands, "I don't know where this is going, either. I have some idea where you've been, from what you've told me and from what I've heard from Dylan."

"He shouldn't be talking about me," Mar says miserably.

"I don't think it was any deep, dark secret, Mar. He just let me know that you're kind of fragile and he tried to make sure I don't hurt you in any way. He cares about you a lot."

"I'm not fragile," Mar insists. "I'm just not sure where I want this to go, is all."

"How about this? How about we start with just this and you decide as we go? No hurt feelings if you want to back off at any point." He moves to her end of the sofa and lifts her chin until she is looking into his eyes. "I like you very much, Mar, and I want to get to know you more."

The first kiss, when it comes, is sweet and gentle. He probes her lips softly and, when his tongue does reach out to lick at the corners of her mouth, she panics. She backs away and grabs her glass, gulps it and swirls the wine around her mouth. "I'm sorry," she mumbles, "my teeth, there was some brownie...don't laugh."

"I'm not laughing," he laughs. "It's just that you're so precious."

"Well, that's OK, then." And she sets her glass down and lifts her lips to meet his.

This kiss sears its way all the way down to the pit of her stomach, curls around her insides and then shoots through to her toes before spiking back up to her brain, zings around there awhile and leaves her dizzy and breathless. She puts her hands on his chest and pushes back, taking in huge lungfuls of air.

"What? Are you OK? I'm sorry, did that upset you?"

"OHMYGOD!" she gasps. She shakes out her hands, as if flinging demons from her fingertips.

"Are you OK?" he asks again, lifting her chin and searching her eyes.

"No, I'm fine, that was OK, fine, really great even. I'm just, it just, it's just been such a long time and then you and I, well..."

"Mar? Mar, it's OK. Sweetheart, it's fine." Kevin puts his arms around her and pulls her close and holds her until she stops shaking and slowly, as she calms and melts, she finds her own arms lifting until she is cupping his face between her palms. Slowly, she pulls his face down to meet hers.

This time, the kiss pools in her stomach, warms her from the inside out and then finds itself tingling up and down her spine. She begins to shake again, but less violently. A moan slips from between her lips, tickles his. Tentatively at first, and then with more passion, she begins to explore his mouth with her tongue. His lips, his teeth, his tongue. Without knowing quite how, she finds herself pressed into him, her breasts filling his hands to overflowing, her legs straddling his waist. And their mouths, delving, twisting, tasting deeply of one another, forming a communion of lust and desire, move relentlessly into one another.

Mar moans as Kevin's hands find the buttons of her blouse and fumble with them. She pulls her own hands from around his neck and helps him with more nimble fingers. Somewhere in the recesses of her mind, she makes a note to herself to use zippers in the future, then just as quickly loses the thought as his warm hands slip inside the bustier, releasing her breasts.

"Oh, god, Mar, Jesus, they're so perfect, you're so perfect," Kevin moans. She feels his hardness lengthening though his pants and grinds herself into him. "No, no, no, don't start that, god, Mar, not yet, you're driving me crazy."

Mar takes his lower lip between her teeth and begins to suck on it gently while she pleasures herself against the length of him. A wet spot begins to seep through the denim of his pants. Her own panties became sodden with her need. She moans and changes her position slightly so that she is rubbing directly against him.

Suddenly, Kevin hooks his hands beneath her armpits and lifts her off of his lap. She looks at him dizzily. "Oh, god, I'm sorry..." she begins.

"Are you crazy, woman? You're about to drive me mad doing that. Now, let's get more comfortable and slow this down before I'm no longer any use to you."

Mar smiles and relaxes back onto the sofa. Any embarrassment she had felt about her body, her weight, cellulite or any other real or imagined deficiencies disappear when she looks at his face and realizes that he isn't kidding. She has turned him on, is turning him on. It is a good feeling, this being a woman a man lusts after. It is strong and powerful and damn exciting. She lifts her buttocks and wiggles a little to help him remove her jeans. Stretching her arms above her head, she smiles at him coyly. "Holy Mother of God," Kevin's voice strangles out. "You're even lovelier than I imagined."

"Your turn," Mar counters throatily. She reaches out with her foot and tugs at the top button of his pants with her toes.

"Yes, ma'am," he grins.

When he sheds his shirt, Mar delights in her first full view of his upper body. Her face flushes hotly as she imagines her nipples sliding over the hair on his chest, his muscular arms clasped around her. Her eyes move upward and she grins appreciatively. Kevin winks at her and begins to open his pants. Breaking away from his stare, she watches him free himself and experiences a moment of doubt. He is huge. Both long and wide. She swallows. "Um, not to stroke your ego or anything, but you're, um, you're quite big."

Kevin grins at her. "I guess we'll just have to make sure you're ready then, won't we?" he asks. And then he hooks his hands into her panties and pulls them off of her. After enjoying a moment of the view this presents him, he lowers his mouth to her waiting need.

Twenty-Seven

Mar.

After singing her to sleep, Kevin had covered her with the blanket, cleaned up the desert and wine dishes and let himself out. When Mar trudges down the stairs later that morning, she finds that he has also cut her a bouquet of flowers from her garden and left them for her in a water glass on the kitchen counter. Along with a note: "Good morning, Beautiful. Didn't want you to feel awkward, so I let myself out. Please don't break my heart – have dinner with me tonight."

She smiles. Waking up alone on the couch had freaked her out. Was she so lame that he'd run away rather than face her in the morning light? *Jesus, Mar, you are such a putz*, she'd told herself as she lay there, arm thrown over her eyes in an attempt to block out reality. It had taken a supreme effort to look herself in the mirror while she brushed away the morning death breath and tried to wet down the bed head that afflicts her every twenty-four hours or so.

As she woke and dressed Lizzie, part of her babbled away to the little girl while the majority of her emotions and thoughts were taken up in mentally beating the crap out of herself. *How embarrassing! I can't believe you did that. You don't sit on a man's face you hardly know. I mean, please, he's not a bloody gynecologist, he probably didn't need to get that involved in your anatomy. He's not goddamned O'Keefe! Most people can't even say vulva and labia without puking and you went and slimed yourself all over his freaking face! And the moaning. Jesus! He probably thinks you sound worse than a ten dollar whore. Fuck me! Oh, fuck me! You couldn't think of something just a little more original, Mar? And what kind of jerk screams like that? Scared the hell out of the dog. God! I hope he doesn't tell Dylan. I can never see Shirley again. This is too bloody embarrassing.*

"Well, Lizzie, guess what?" she'd told the sleepy little girl. "We're moving to Siberia."

Then she'd gotten downstairs and there were the flowers and the note. "Oh." And just like that, she forgets all her fears and the raw throbbing between her legs becomes a good thing.

Twenty-Eight

Sy.

The temperature is rising quickly as Sy trudges upstairs to his office. Already, the heady scent of paprika fills the small staircase. By 11:00, when the Indian restaurant on the first floor of the building gets into full swing, the exotic fragrances will turn cloying.

Dora, Sy's secretary, is at her desk, her ruby-red nails flying over her keyboard. She is a large, buxom woman in her late fifties. For as long as Sy's known her, close to twenty years, she's worn her hair the same way, in some sort of twisted-up, semi-beehive. Her makeup has been updated, as have her clothes, but her hair has never changed. If he had not seen it unwound himself, he'd've sworn in court that it was a prosthetic, an alien, cone-head kind of contraption that she straps on every morning. But in the years since his wife's death, he's seen the do undone on quite a few occasions. He and Dora have that kind of friendship, one where they can lean on each other and find escape in each other when they need to or when they just feel the urge. A kind of after-work-drink-and-a-tumble with lots of laughs and good times and no strings attached.

"Hey there, Dora, how's things?" Sy asks.

She turns from her computer and looks at him over her bifocals. "Good morning there yourself, Sy. All's well here, though this weather scares me. I'm hoping it's not a sign today's gonna be another fryer. Goddamned deodorant just can't keep up with it. What do you think?"

He shrugs. You can't fix it, so you live with it. "Yep, it's hot out there," he answers. "You got anything for me?"

Dora takes off her glasses, rolls her neck around. When her head is back on straight and facing him once again, she replies, "Nah, same ol', same ol'. I'm just about finished with the Ramirez notes. She's gonna come over here around 10:00 to pick 'em up."

Sy grabs his mail and heads past her. "You want lunch from downstairs, tell me, and I'll go get it."

Sy drops the mail into the tray on the edge of his desk and sits down just as the door to his office is flung open. Mrs. Ramirez, tear-stained face ravaged by grief, twisted by anger, throws herself into the office and launches all two-hundred-and-ten pounds at him. Sy barely has time to stand and brace himself before her body barrels into him.

"Ese porqueria de un hombre, ese pendejo, hijo de la gran puta!! Como me ha hecho esto? Y con esa puta? Esa crica pudrida? Comooooooooo???" her fists beat against his chest.

Sy instinctively puts his arms around her to give her less room to wind up. "Hey, stop it! Shit! Dora! Fuck! Hey, I could use some help in here!"

Dora comes into the office and puts the Ramirez file on Sy's desk. She rolls her eyes and shrugs apologetically before backing out of the office and closing the door behind herself.

Mrs. Ramirez's great sobs eventually quiet and Sy leads her to a guest chair. It is a mistake. As soon as she rounds the desk, her eyes fall on her file. With a roar, she launches herself at the papers and photos and flings them into Sy's face, sending his inbox all the way across the room. In the erupting pandemonium, he doesn't notice the postcard that sails through the air and becomes lodged between two wooden filing cabinets.

Twenty-Nine

Jack.

Jack throws his pen onto the desk. He is frustrated beyond belief. Sy's investigation is going nowhere. His own efforts have been fruitless. He'd set up a website with Mia's age projection sketches, had linked them to just about every other website about missing children, and nothing. He'd had hopes for *America's Mystery Crimes* early on, but that had only brought out the nutcases and psychics. It is tearing his guts out and he doesn't know what else to do. God knows his career is suffering for it, but he just can't seem to give a shit anymore. Of course, the higher ups in the firm have strongly suggested that he get his act together or look for other prospects, and then they'd relegated him to dredging out yet another version of miserable Mrs. Fitzgibbons' will, this time cutting out one set of grandchildren for some unpardonable offense and reinstating a distant cousin. *The old bat will live to be a hundred*, Jack thinks grimly, *and make her family suffer through every fucking single minute of it*.

Jack's head is down on his desk, eyes closed, when the door opens. He doesn't bother to look up. "I thought you'd gone already, Elena. I'll close up."

"It's not Elena, Jack."

At the sound of her voice, Jack straightens up. He has the grace to look sheepish. "Oh, hello, Caroline, I didn't realize it was you."

"Oh, it's me. I think Elena left hours ago. Along with just about everyone else."

"You're still here," Jack tells her, stating the obvious and immediately feeling like a fool.

"Yes," a smile quirks at the corner of her lips, "I'm still here. And you're still here."

"Uh, um, how can I help you?" Jack clears his throat, which has begun to constrict. "Is there something I can do for you?"

"Well, no, not really. It's just that I saw your light still on. I was on my way out, and it occurred to me to stop by and ask if you'd like to get a bite to eat somewhere."

Since the holiday party, Jack has barely seen her. She's been around the office, but the office is large, occupying four floors of a Manhattan high-rise. Jack's office is on the top of the firm's floors. Caroline, he thinks, works a couple of floors below him in civil defense, or maybe acquisitions and mergers, he really isn't sure. In any case, he doesn't feel like eating anything, much less rousing himself as decent company for this highly attractive, quick-witted woman. "I'll have to take a rain check," is what he says. "I've got to finish this draft."

"Mrs. Fitzgibbons?" she asks, arching a well-manicured eyebrow.

"Yes. Uh, how'd you know?"

"Oh, Jack, I'm sorry to tell you, but everyone knows." She looks at him, right in the eye, from across the length of his office.

It rocks him. Not that everyone in the office knows how far he's let his career fall, but that she would confront him with it. Suddenly, he is pissed. "Well, fine, but I've still got to get it finished. Goodbye," he chokes out. And turns his eyes back to the documents scattered across his desk.

Caroline doesn't move. She stands near the door watching him, no doubt aware that he is uncomfortably aware that she has not left. Perversely, he fumes, she stands there, just lets his discomfort increase. He keeps his head down, unwilling to be goaded into playing whatever infantile game she is after. When the air is all but thrumming with tension, she speaks up, her voice husky, "Jack?"

"What?" he snaps.

"Jack," she repeats, her voice demanding that he look at her. When he finally does, she continues, "Was it just my imagination, or at the holiday party did we have a, well, a moment?"

Now it is his turn to raise an eyebrow. "A moment?" he sneers. "What is this, some Victorian fucking novel? A moment?"

Caroline's composure doesn't waver. He watches, paralyzed, as she reaches out a graceful hand and pushes the door shut. Locks it. "Yes. A moment." She reaches up and flicks off the overhead light switch, leaving only Jack's desk bathed in the warm glow of a gooseneck lamp.

Caroline begins to walk slowly toward Jack's desk. "I thought," she reaches up between her breasts and unbuttons the top pearl of her blouse. "I thought," she repeats, moving to the second button, advancing on him slowly, "when we first toasted one another, when you first handed me the wine? I thought there was one slight, but irrefutable, spark of interest." And the third button, and then the next, opens, revealing a large swell of breast. "Maybe of lust?" And, as she reaches his desk, she shrugs out of the blouse, allows it to slip to the floor.

Jack is rooted to his chair. Not only does his mind not believe what his eyes are seeing, but his cock has immediately swollen so hard, he doesn't think he could get up if he even wanted to. Mutely, he watches her as she continues.

"I was thinking," Caroline says, "that I'd at least get a call from you, maybe an invitation to dinner?" She reaches between her large, ripe breasts and unclasps the bra that holds them in place. Slowly, she peels back the bra cups, allowing her breasts to drop heavily free of the lace. Her nipples, exposed to the air and the lust coming off both their bodies, immediately pucker. Jack finds he can't swallow.

"But, nothing," she continues, her voice continuing to deepen. "Not even a call. And, I'm embarrassed to admit, I did wait around hoping for one." She reaches back and undoes her skirt. As soon as she opens the zipper, it slips down around her feet. Now she stands before him wearing only a black thong bikini and thigh-high nylons in her three-inch Manolo Blahniks.

Jack feels himself strain against his zipper. He is sure he is going to ejaculate right then and there. He reaches up and loosens his tie, suddenly unable to breathe.

"Do you like what you see, Jack?" Caroline asks, stepping around the desk and coming toward him. "Isn't this better than Mrs. Fitzgibbon's ridiculous will? Would you like to touch?"

Jack can barely hear her through the roaring in his ears. His eyes are fastened on the swaying of her breasts as she comes near him. When she gets to within a foot of him, Caroline slowly bends, allowing him to watch as they change position to hang heavily from her slim body. She puts her hands on the arms of his chair and leans forward. Suddenly, her tongue is licking at his ear. She nips his earlobe, at the same time grabbing his hand and shoving it between her legs, where he can feel the wetness that soaks her panties. "Isn't this what you want, Jack?"

"Oh, Jesus," Jack gasps and, without thinking, he is pushing her back onto the desk, sending the papers of the will scattering to the floor. He rips her panties off and pushes between her legs, his tongue seeking out her wet spot, his nose taking in the private smells of her. Her hands come down and push his head deeper. Her heels find his chair and she pushes off, her back arching on the desk.

Somehow, Jack finds himself naked, his clothes heaped around his bare feet, and he is working furiously on her, testing, seeking, finding, until the moment when he can take no more, when she can take no more, and he pulls his face away and bends forward to grab her by the shoulders. Straining, he finds her and he thrusts himself deeply inside. Caroline pulls his face to hers and as he drives himself ever deeper and harder into her, she damages his lips with her teeth, tears at his back with her nails, deepening his frenzy. Finally, with a roar he muffles into her neck, he comes, filling her to overflowing. She, bucking to the end, meets him with a long, shuddering orgasm of her own.

For perhaps two minutes, they lay like that, Jack half on her, Caroline drained, with her legs now flopping on the chair. But finally, Caroline begins to laugh, at first low in her throat and then with a body-shaking whoop. Jack, unable to help himself, joins in.

Once again dressed, their wrinkled clothes pressed back neatly into place, or at least as neatly as possible, with her torn panties stuffed into Jack's pocket so they can be taken out of the office unseen, Caroline bites her lip, looking suddenly insecure. "So," she asks, "about that rain check?"

Thirty

Mar.

Mar has come to love Boulder in every season but, as summer spreads its warmth over the dizzying beauty of the mountains, she regularly experiences a surge of adrenalin that translates itself into renewed creativity and energy. This particular year is no exception. Added to that the fact that she is relaxing into the role of motherhood, her career is taking on new dimensions. The line of gift items that Diane had suggested is getting great reviews, and she is getting sex on a regular basis. This latter is a great source of amusement for Diane and Shirley.

"Girl, there is just this amazing glow all about you. He sleeping over every night?" Shirley asks as she, Mar and Diane watch several neighborhood kids play in the sandbox behind The Center. Derek is soundly asleep in his play-yard under a tree.

"Well, not every night," Mar blushes, "but enough to keep me a happy woman."

"You go, girl!"

"Don't forget the times he comes to 'visit' during the afternoons," Diane teases her.

"Are you kidding?" Shirley asks. "He's comin' over for

nooky in the afternoons? Jaysus, Mar, you makin' up for lost time, or what?"

"Hey, a girls gotta get it when the getting's good. Aaaand... the getting's really good!" Mar grins and the three women burst into laughter.

"Oh, god," Shirley says, taking a swig of her soda. "But, what're you gonna do when he leaves? He is still leaving, right? Dylan talked to him, I think yesterday or the day before, and he didn't say anything about being able to stay longer."

Both Shirley and Diane look at Mar. In the five years they've known her, they've never seen her as relaxed and happy as she has been in the past few months. Mar knows they are afraid of what Kevin's leaving will do to her.

Mar looks off at Lizzie, whose laughter floats to her from the sand box. "Yeah, he's still leaving. In a couple of weeks. Don't look at me like that. I'm OK about it. Really."

"Hmmph!" Diane snorts and Mar rolls her eyes at her.

"No, I'm serious," Mar insists. "Look. I really like him. Maybe in time, I could love him. And, yes, the sex is great. It's just that I'm not ready to fall in love. Or, he's not the right one. Whatever. I'm just enjoying it for what it is."

"Listen, Mar, I've seen you around him. You light up. There're some feelings there." Diane says.

"Well, of course there are feelings!" Mar exclaims. "I wouldn't be sleeping with him if I didn't like him. And respect him. And, yeah, I like to be around him. It feels good to be wanted by someone you like. But that's it. End, finito, drop it."

"Mar, honey? Can I ask you a question? Something you maybe should think about a little bit?" Shirl asks.

"What?"

"Honey, do you think maybe you're holding back because you're afraid of losing Kevin, too?"

"Is that you or Dr. Dylan asking?"

"We've talked about it," Shirley admits. "It makes sense."

Mar flips onto her back and looks up at the sky through the branches of the tree they are sitting under. You'd have to mix some black in with the green if you were painting the leaves from this angle. She thinks about how to answer. "OK, yes, you've got a point and I've thought about it, too. And, yes, definitely, I've been holding back. But not so much because I am afraid I am going to lose him eventually, but because I know I am. He's going places, and that's good. I want to stay here."

"But he could be based here, couldn't he?" Diane asks.

"Yeah, sure, technically he could. But that's not what he wants. He's off to England and doing work for the President. Besides, I couldn't say he's The One, anyway. You don't make those kind of life changes for a maybe." Mar rolls onto her stomach and looks off at Lizzie. "Look, yes, I don't want to lose anyone I care about again. But, really, honestly and truly, I'm OK with him going. We've had a great time together and now I know how good it feels to open up again. If it turns out we can't live without each other, he can always come back. Jeez, it's getting hot out here, don't you think? Let's go inside." And she gets up and goes to get her daughter.

"Oh, man," Shirley mutters.

"You've got that right," Diane agrees and Mar pretends she didn't hear them.

Thirty-One

Jack.

Jack and Caroline have seen each other every day since their encounter in Jack's office and the sudden "coupleness" of the whole thing is beginning to worry him. It isn't that he doesn't like her, he does, very much. It is more that, from all appearances, she is ready for a full-blown relationship, and he isn't. End of story. That being the case, Jack senses he really needs to think about what is going on, to decide to actively participate in it or to step off the ride. Even DeJon is becoming itchy with the new set up. As he and Caroline head toward the elevator in his building, Jack thinks back to his latest conversation with the boy.

"Why you hangin' wit her all the time now, Jack?" DeJon had asked.

"We're friends. I like her. And, it's 'why are you hanging with her', not 'why you hanging wit' her."

"Shit."

Jack had lined up and sent the basketball arcing through the air. "Yeah, shit. The way a man speaks says a lot about how much respect he's got for himself. Whew! Look at that!"

"Aw, fuck, Jack, don't start with that shit." DeJon caught the look Jack shot him and sighed heavily. "OK, you're right, but you the one, you're the one, that's messing around now. You're trying to change the subject. And," he enunciated clearly, "it is not working."

Jack grinned over at the kid all gawky in the oversize basketball get up Jack had bought him. He was such a piece of work. And, he was right. He had been trying to change the subject, but whether for DeJon or himself, he wasn't sure. "I like her," he'd offered again.

"Yeah, fine, she's nice and she looks good. But you're acting all goofy and stupid around her. What's up with that?"

"Women, they do that to a man."

DeJon cradled the ball to his side and looked off down the street. He cleared his throat nervously. "So, uh, are you gonna marry her or something?"

Jack froze. Is that what he'd been thinking? Their relationship was finally back on track and now DeJon was seeing Caroline as a threat to their time together? "DeJon," he began.

"Don't 'DeJon' me. I'm not a kid. I just want to know. Are you gonna marry her?"

"No. I mean, look, I've only known her about a month. I like her. She's fun, she's funny. But I'm not planning to marry again. Not now, or ever."

The kid peered at him, his eyes older than his years. "Lindsey was 'it' for you, is what you're saying."

"She was."

"Well then, OK. So this is all about the sex then, right?"

"What?"

The kid wiggled his eyebrows suggestively and took off down the court, his laughter trailing easily behind him. After a moment, Jack took off after him.

***

Jack fits the key in the lock. He has to talk with her. If she has expectations that he can't meet, it isn't fair to keep on seeing her.

"Hey, what's this?" Jack stops and stares quizzically from

the foyer of his apartment. The living room is filled with white candles of every shape and size, all lit, casting a golden glow throughout the room, reflecting warmly off of the whites of the furniture and walls. There are several discreet floral arrangements placed tastefully about the room. The stereo is softly playing Eros Ramazotti's latest.

Jack reaches for a light switch but Caroline gently takes hold of his hand and turns him to her. She leans into him and murmurs, "Happy Anniversary, sweetheart," before taking his lower lip between her teeth and sucking in. As she begins to play with his tongue, she pulls his arm around her and puts his hand on her ass, moving it up and down enough so that it is apparent that she is not wearing panties.

Aroused, Jack reaches his other hand up to her blouse and, rubbing her breast, realizes that she is also not wearing a bra. Why hadn't he noticed that before? he wonders briefly, before dragging her to him tightly, letting her feel his growing arousal.

Somewhere in his brain, a bit of Lindsey pops up, a bit of himself comes to the foreground and says, "Hello? What's this? Anniversary? How the hell did someone get into the apartment?" but by then Caroline has dropped to her knees in front of him.

"Oh, Jesus," he moans as all thought is driven from his mind.

Later, in the shower, he flinches as Caroline gently cleanses the raw wounds on his back. It is not the first time she has drawn blood while in the mindless frenzied lust of their lovemaking, but these cuts are definitely the deepest. He makes a mental note to ask her to cut her nails before she leaves scars, but is too tired to start the conversation then.

The first sign that Jack is coming back to his senses occurs when they step out of the shower and begin to dry off. As he moves to leave the warmth of the bathroom to search for clothes, Caroline gently pushes him down onto the lip of the oversized tub and tells him to wait. She slips out of the room naked, is gone for only a moment, and returns wearing one of Lindsey's bathrobes, the one he'd given her as part of their 2nd wedding anniversary gifts to one another. She holds his own matching robe up for him to slip into.

"No need to put on real clothes," she laughs deep in her throat. "I'm sure we'll be wanting to get out of these again real soon." And she pulls the ends of the belt around to tie them for him.

Once tied, she turns Jack around to face the wall-to-wall mirror, slips in front of him and pulls his arm around her. "There now," she says, "isn't that perfect?"

To Jack, it isn't perfect. In fact, it is all wrong. Suddenly, seeing Caroline there in Lindsey's bathroom, in Lindsey's robe, with his arm around her, it occurs to him that he'd let sex cloud his mind, let his cock get him into a situation he doesn't think he can handle, doesn't know how to handle, doesn't want to handle. He pulls his arm from around her and pretends to adjust his belt, taking his eyes off of the image in the mirror. "Wow, I'm beat," he says. "How about you?"

He looks up when she doesn't answer him and is stunned by the look of mortification on her face. Apparently, she can read him better than he'd thought. "Caroline," he begins.

Caroline turns from the mirror and begins to gather up her clothes. "Yeah, me too," she flashes a strained smile at him. "Let's just wrap up the food and I'll be on my way."

"Food?" he asks stupidly. They'd planned to go out for a bite after work but now he doesn't feel like it. He feels like asking her to leave and kicking back with a bottle of Scotch.

"Don't worry. It was silly. I just thought, well, forget what I thought. Anyway, it'll still be good tomorrow," she turns her back and reaches for her blouse.

Guilt floods through him and Jack wonders why he is being such an ass. She's obviously gone to a lot of trouble to make it a fun evening and, anniversary thing aside, there is no reason he should ruin it for her. "On second thought," he reaches for her and re-ties the robe she is wearing, Lindsey's robe, "let's eat. I'm starving."

Hope blooms like a flower on her cheeks and he feels all

the worse for it. “Really?” she asks.

“Really.” Jack tucks a stray hair behind her ear and tries to quiet the voice inside his head that warns him he is agreeing to more than just a meal.

Mar.

"I'm sorry, Mar, but I don't know what else to do." Kevin reaches down and tucks the sheet more closely around Mar's shoulder. "I never expected this, or I wouldn't have made any other commitments."

Kevin is due to fly east the next morning and after that, he's off to England. He'll be gone for several months. At least.

"I know," she murmurs, her hand playing absently with the hair curling on his chest. "But you'll be back to visit soon. Thanksgiving's only a few months away."

"I'm going to hate missing Lizzie's birthday."

Mar smiles sadly. How is she going to explain to her almost-two-year-old that 'Kevvy' is gone? Lizzie idolizes the man. Her first words each morning are, "Where's Kevvy?" Funny how those are usually her own first thoughts.

Mar lets her mind drift to her feelings. "You know what?" she finally says, and looks up at him so that he can see that she is serious. "I didn't expect this. I was kind of OK with the thought that my life would just go on as it had been, painting, being a mother. You opened something inside of me that was closed a long time ago and no matter what happens, if you come back, if you don't, whatever, I'm always going to be glad you were here. I had forgotten what I was missing."

"Oh, god, Mar," he groans. "I have the feeling that for a very long time I'm going to regret not trashing all my plans and staying with you."

She laughs quietly and bends to kiss him. "I'm going to regret not having this," she murmurs and climbs on top of him.

Thirty-Three

Jack.

After a vicious game of racquetball, they go to Ozszie's for a heaping platter of ribs and beer. Loose after the workout, relaxing with the beer, Jack fills his friend in on the deal with Caroline.

"Man," Mortuary John laughs, "she's got your balls in a vice, buddy, and it don't look like she's gonna let go. The lady's got plans."

"I know," Jack says miserably, "but I don't know what to do. I mean, it completely freaked me out seeing her in Lindsey's robe. And then that whole anniversary thing. I felt like a total jerk."

"I hear ya," Mortuary John shakes his head, "I don't think I'd like anyone getting into my apartment. That's kind of like *Fatal Attraction* and all that shit. Know what I mean?"

"Yeah, I do. And we're not even dating – I mean, not dating dating, like there's a commitment. She acts like we're engaged or something." He takes a swig of beer and signals the waiter to bring another round.

"If you're not dating, dude, then what are you doing?" Mortuary John picks up a rib and begins gnawing at it. He looks at Jack curiously.

"Jesus, I don't know." Jack runs a hand through his hair, tries to find intelligent words for what he thinks is going on. Tries, fails. "Hanging out, I guess." He shrugs, sheepishly.

"Listen, my friend, to you and me you might be hanging out. But, to a woman, you're dating." Mortuary John points the rib at Jack for emphasis. "Women, they got a whole different set of values, and if you're not careful, those values can ruin a man's life."

Jack thinks back to the "anniversary" night. "And then, she gave me her picture, all wrapped up like a present. You know, one of those beauty shots. I mean, she didn't say anything, but I got the impression she thinks I'm supposed to pack away all of Lindsey's photos and put hers out. I've known her a month!"

"Was that before or after you fucked again?" Mortuary John asks, taking the bottle from the waiter's hand and enjoying a long swallow.

"I didn't say we fucked again," Jack points out.

Mortuary John laughs and grabs a new rib. "Dude, you don't have to say it. What you gonna do after she set up this nice evening for you? Send her home? Nah, you gotta love her a bit, get into the groove. Man, it's like right there, waiting for you, all nice and clean and powdered fresh, just itching for you to get back inside. And I'm sure after a couple of bottles of wine, some good food, that kind of woman knows how to put a man to bed, a hot bedtime story, tuck him in, send him nighty-night with a smile on his face..."

Jack flashes on the memory of Caroline as she rode his tongue to climax. He is pretty sure he had been smiling. He groans and rubs his face. "What am I gonna do?" he asks.

"First, let me ask you something. You like this lady, right?"

"Yeah, I do. I just don't want a relationship and, apparently, she does. Do you know, she's been going to my trials for years, keeping up on me?"

"Now that's scary." Mortuary John takes a swig of his beer, wipes his mouth. "Uh-huh, that's like stalking or something."

"No, no, not like that. I mean, she was a kid, wanted to be a lawyer and started hanging around the courthouse. She caught one of my first trials. Anyway, it's kind of flattering."

"Uh-huh." John doesn't appear to be convinced.

"I mean it. Remember Sherri, in the beginning? Didn't you tell me she'd be hanging out, watching you play ball, before you ever met her?"

"Still, courthouses and all, it doesn't sound right."

"OK, but Caroline's not the kind to hang out on a basketball court. She gets off on trials. But, yeah, I really like her. I just don't know how to keep things cool when I get the feeling she's already planning the honeymoon."

Mortuary John cocks an eye at him. "Listen, Jack, I'm not getting all psychological and crap on you, but here's a little advice. Women aren't that good at just saying what they want. They kind of come at things from the side. Like she did with that whole anniversary thing and all. They're sneaky that way."

"Lindsey wasn't like that."

"Jack, honey, there ain't no one like Lindsey. She was a class act from day one without even trying. I'm sorry to tell you that, but if you want to go on, see what else is out there, you gotta accept that right from the start."

Jack sighs, nods a little.

"So, you've got this lady. She's all hot and bothered, she's had her eye on you for awhile. You like her, but you don't know if you want it to go anywhere. The thing is, you've got to understand where her head is. Man, you're still wearing your wedding ring. You're jumping her left, right and center and all the time, her head's on the ring. Like you're still married and she's just a piece on the side."

Jack looks down at his hand. It has never occurred to him to remove the band. Just the idea of it leaves him cold. "But..."

"No, man, no buts about it. On top of making her insecure, you're disrespecting her."

"That never occurred to me."

"That's OK, baby, that's OK. You'll learn. The thing is, she's just reacting. She's pushing for validation. You got to give her a little and maybe she'll stop pushing so hard."

"Shit. You're right."

"'Course I am. Ain't a woman Mortuary John couldn't handle."

"Asshole. Sherri's holding your balls so tight, I'm surprised you're not singing soprano."

"Yeah, but they're happy balls, real happy balls."

"OK, so what am I going to do?"

"There ain't nothing to do. Hey there, grab a rib, no sense in wasting good food on this. Listen. She's got you in her sights. You can take that for granted. But she thinks she's good. She doesn't know that you know, you know what I mean? So you just sit back and enjoy it. Take her out, fuck her brains out, enjoy it. You say you like her. She's smart, she's funny, she's classy, and she can screw like hell. So? You enjoy it. Then, if she doesn't get sick of you first and you find you want out, you break it off gently. Remember, she still the boss's granddaughter, so you gotta do it gently, like it's her choice, but you break it off right the very second before it looks like she's gonna be expecting a ring." He pauses a minute, licks his fingers. "A girl like that, I say you've got about five more months of truly outstanding sex."

Thirty-Four

Mar.

"No, sweetheart, no more reading. It's way past your bedtime."

"Please, Mommy?" Which came out more like "pweeze, Mommy?" because, at three, she still has that slight lisp that drives Mar crazy with love every time she hears it.

Mar bites back a smile. Lizzie has learned quickly that opening her big blue eyes at Mar and calling her "Mommy" will, more often than not, get her just about anything. Spoiled? Probably. But Lizzie is also a sweet and kind child who has a strong sense of empathy for others. "No, baby. We've already read way past your bedtime. Now lie down and go to sleep."

Lizzie cocks her head and seems to weigh the finality of her mother's words. Apparently, she decides that Mar is serious because she drops down in her crib and curls into a ball. Within minutes, she is sound asleep and Mar shakes her head, wondering again at how Fate has given her so much. Reaching into the crib to pull the blanket up over the little girl's shoulders, Mar suddenly notices that Lizzie has outgrown her bed. It takes her breath away. When had it happened? When had she grown so tall? Mar looks around the room and realizes that the entire room is too young for her daughter.

Her interests extend beyond the little lambs and bunnies Mar had painted on the walls when Lizzie had first come to her. A smile plays at her lips as she begins to envision redecorating the room.

The next morning, Diane finds Mar up in Lizzie's room, emptying her drawers, packing up her toys.

"Hey, there. What are you doing?"

"Hey, Dee. I didn't hear you come in. I don't think I put coffee on, either. Sorry. I'm going to paint the room, get some new furniture. Last night, when I was putting her to bed, the room suddenly looked too young for her. She's getting so big, I didn't even realize it."

"Do you have any idea what you're going to do in here?"

"Lizzie wants fish."

"Fish? Like One Fish, Two Fish? Something like that?"

"No. Like dolphins. She's got a thing lately about dolphins."

"Dolphins?"

Mar looks up. "Well, that's what she said she wanted."

"And how are you going to do that? Paint the dolphins?"

"I was thinking I could do a kind of underwater scene, maybe a blue carpet?"

"Underwater? Isn't that an issue with you?"

Mar falls into the glider, begins rubbing her eyes, moving back and forth. "Yeah, I spent the whole morning trying to talk her out of it. I told her we could do a princess theme, you know, castles, lots of pink, purple. But, noooooo, not Lizzie. Miss Lizzie wants dolphins."

"And, what Miss Lizzie wants, Miss Lizzie gets."

"OK. But, look, the nightmare thing has been going on too long and it's stupid. Besides, I'm over it."

"Over what? Over Joaquin? Max, Kevin? The nightmares?"

"All of it. All of them. I've moved on and I feel much better about it."

Diane leans against the door frame. "I guess if it bothers you, you can always paint over it."

Mar stands up and begins to shove toys into one of the garbage bags she's brought up for the purpose, "No, I'm serious, Diane. I've got a great life. I do what I want when I want, I've got a great kid, I'm not out flipping burgers or, god forbid, plucking chickens for a living. One day, maybe, I'll meet a great guy whose life fits with mine. Meanwhile, though, my daughter wants dolphins, she'll get dolphins. Besides, it's still spring. Every little girl should get a new room in the spring."

"Is that more of Life-According-to-Mar?"

"Damn straight."

"Okay. What can I do?"

Mar points to the night stand. "The lamp. I think we'll keep it, dress it up a bit. Can you take it into the family room?"

Diane stops in the doorway. "You know," she says, "we could drape this in pearls, maybe, something like that."

"Hot damn, you're good!" Mar's grin reaches its full wattage and Diane finally smiles as if she just might believe that Mar truly has moved on.

Thirty-Five

Jack.

They are eating in again. The Venco case, Jack's first big case in years, is a monster. It feels so good to be back in the game and, while he is pretty sure the reprieve had come directly from Jeremiah Carruthers as a favor to his granddaughter, Caroline won't admit to it and Jack doesn't push her. He is just so damn sick of wills and he knows that if he doesn't fuck it up, he'll be able to use this case as a stepping stone to rebuilding his career. Caroline, for her part, has been amazing through it all. After long hours working in family law, she's been helping him keep up with the massive amounts of paperwork the case generates. Without her, he would have drowned in it months ago. And that has been in addition to all the help she's been giving him in his quest to find Mia.

Jack hangs up the phone after placing their take-out order and decides that they deserve a glass of wine. He uncorks a bottle of Duck Horn and fills two glasses, his mind churning through the possibility of forcing Venco to the table without months of litigation. It is a long shot but, if he can pull it off, the families affected by the contamination will get the help they need while there remains a chance that medical intervention might do them any good.

Jack carries the glasses back to the living room. "Here you go. Oh," he smiles. She is curled up at the end of the sofa, asleep. He sets the glasses down and pulls a throw over her. God, she looks so young and innocent. It is a side of her he rarely gets to see. The Caroline he knows is one very determined lady. She certainly has her soft spots, but she hoards them jealously, almost protectively. He kisses her forehead.

"Don't go," Caroline mumbles when he turns to leave. "I'm awake."

Jack pushes her tousled hair back from her forehead and smiles down at her. "No, Caro, rest awhile. At least until the food gets here."

She sighs and smiles and Jack notices the deep smudges under her eyes. He probably has them himself, but on her, against her delicate features, they look dramatic, raw. "You're working too hard. You should take some time off."

She chuckles and looks up at him, her eyes a smoky gray. "My boss won't let me. He's a total prig, you know."

"Is he?"

"Oh, yes. Total. Works me like a dog and expects me to screw him on top of it."

"Terrible."

"It is. I'll probably have to call the E.E.O.C. on him."

"Will you?"

"Mm-hmm. Absolutely."

"When?"

"When? When will I call the E.E.O.C.?"

"No, when does he expect you to screw him?"

"Oh. Well, all the time."

"At work, even?"

"Oh, absolutely at work. He says it unblocks his creativity."

"You poor girl."

"Yes, well, I suffer quietly. And often."

"Maybe I should speak to him."

"No, he's not the type to listen. He uses me, abuses me and then someday he'll throw me out, find someone he wants to marry."

Jack sobers immediately. There it is again. She's been dropping hints, they've even argued about it. He isn't ready but, apparently, she thinks it is past time he asks her to marry him. Hell, maybe it is. Maybe he should have listened to John and gotten out months ago. "Caroline," he begins miserably.

"Jesus, Jack, I'm kidding. It was a joke." She comes off the couch and heads for his bedroom. "I'm going to take a shower. Call me when the food gets here."

Jack watches her go. Shit. She really deserves better.

Thirty-Six

Mar.

Mar is in the kitchen baking a cake for Diane's birthday. She put Lizzie to bed hours ago. After almost three months, Lizzie's room is finally finished. What had started out as a simple redecoration had turned into a major affair including the design and construction of custom furniture made to fit the sea castle theme, the research and detailing of the reefs and fish that adorn the walls, and painting a cartoon Lizzie gleefully riding atop a dolphin. Earlier in the day, Mar had let the little girl back into her room to see the finished product and the excitement of finally sleeping in her new bed had been too much for her. She had run in and out of the pearl cascade that drapes her doorway, laughed delightedly as the pearls had swished around her, caught in her hair, clacked together musically. Dancing around the room, she had pointed at different fish and sea creatures and asked Mar, "What's that? What's that?" The first couple of times Mar had laughed, happy that her daughter was so excited. By the third or fourth time around, though, Lizzie had begun to get cranky but had still been too wired to settle down and Mar had had enough. In the end, she had climbed into the new water bed with Lizzie and told her a story about a mermaid princess who had stolen an evil witch's rare black pearl. About the time Mar was running out of plot twists, Lizzie had finally drifted off to sleep.

"Hello?" Mar answers the phone. "Oh, hi, Dad. How are you?" Mar takes the cake out of the oven and closes the door. After setting it on the counter to cool, she takes her glass of wine to the table and curls up for a long chat with her father.

About fifteen minutes into the call, Mar pauses, "Hold on a minute, Dad, I think I hear Lizzie." She cocks her head and focuses her attention on any noises coming from upstairs. "No, nothing, sorry. She was just so excited, I wouldn't be surprised if she tried to get up again."

"She can't roll out of the bed, can she?" Don's voice sounds worried. "You used to fall out of bed all the time and I'd find you curled up on the floor in the morning."

"No, it's got a rail so she can't roll out. She can climb out, though, so I'm sure as soon as she figures that out, I won't ever be able to sleep again. Hold on, Dad, there's that noise again."

Mar walks over to the bottom of the stairs where she finds Picasso looking up worriedly. "What's up, girl?" she asks and, in answer, the dog whines. "Dad? Look, I've got to call you back. I think Lizzie's up."

"I'll hold on. You run and check."

"You sure? I'll just be..."she begins when she hears a loud crash. "Oh, shit! Lizzie?" Mar drops the phone and runs up the stairs, taking them two at a time. "Lizzie? Baby?" she calls out ahead of her.

"Mommy?" Lizzie cries. "Mooommmmmy!"

In her hurry, Mar forgets about the safety gate on the second floor landing and, in the darkened stairwell, she doesn't see it. She hits it at full sprint and goes flying over it, crashing into the wall beyond. Stunned, she lies in a tangle, wondering where the hell she is. A small whimper brings her back to the present. "Lizzie? Mommy's coming, honey. Where are you?"

Mar drags herself up. She feels lightheaded and out of breath and leans against the wall until her vision clears. Holding her spinning head, she hurries into Lizzie's room and tries to find her by the light cast by the lava lamp. “Lizzie?” she cries when she finds the little girl’s bed empty. She flips on the wall switch and looks around. Empty.

Down the hall, she finds her room and the family room also empty. Frantic, she moves into the bathroom and tears back the shower curtain. Picasso, meanwhile, has shoved through the child gate that Mar’s crash had loosened and has headed up the stairs.

“Lizzie!” Mar screams from the bathroom and is answered by a frantic bark. Rushing back into the hallway, she sees that the only direction she has failed to look is up. “Dear god, no!” she prays as she bolts up the stairs, rushed along by Picasso’s hysterical barking. “Lizzie, Lizzie, Lizzie, please, please, please.”

Mar hits the third floor at a full run and immediately goes skidding through the darkness, her feet gone from under her when they hit something liquid. She slides across the hardwood floor and slams into her easel, knocking it over and onto her, along with a five-by-six-foot canvas and the gallon can of gesso she had been using earlier to prepare it. She drops into the darkness.

“No,” Mar moans. She is being washed by an incredibly foul smelling cloth. Mar tries to turn her head away from it but it follows her relentlessly. She pushes it away only to have it begin to whine at her. “Picasso?” she mumbles and comes to as her blood runs cold. “Lizzie?” she cries more forcefully and is rewarded by loud barking from the dog.

Mar pushes the easel off of her and rolls over, her body screaming with the effort. “Where’s Lizzie, Picasso?” she asks into the darkness. “Baby, where are you?” She feels along the floor and finds the cord to the halogen floor lamp she uses when painting at night. Feeling along it, she finds the switch and pushes it on, flooding the studio with light. What she sees brings her world crashing down around her. Lizzie’s small hand peeks out from below a large utility shelf that pins her beneath it, and around it is a growing pool of blood, the blood she herself had slipped in when she had flown up the stairs.

Thirty-Seven

Jack.

"What do you want me to say, Caroline? I'm sorry, I'm incredibly sorry." Jack stops in front of the large picture window that overlooks the city. Far below, traffic is speeding along in its maniacal dance. He flinches as one set of headlights barely swerves around another. He hopes he can avoid a similar collision with Caroline. A month ago, she'd turned thirty and Jack had presented her with a box from Tiffany's. To say her eyes had lit up would have been an understatement. In fact, she had literally screamed with delight. Until she'd opened the box and seen the diamond earrings. At that point, she'd gone pale and had rushed to the bathroom. When she'd returned, she'd opened the box, thanked him quietly for the jewelry and then gone to bed, claiming a migraine.

Now, Caroline is curled up on the sofa behind him, her eyes raw from crying. They've been at it for more than an hour and remain in the same place where they'd begun – she wants to get married and he doesn't. Can't.

"Sorry? That's it? What am I supposed to do with sorry? Jack, we've been together for more than a year. What am I supposed to do with 'sorry'? I can't take sorry to bed at night."

The lawyer in Jack could have pointed out that, technically, they'd been together only eleven months, though they had known each other more than a year. Thankfully, he knows when to shut the lawyer up. "Caro..."

"No way, Jack. Don't you dare call me 'Caro' when we're fighting."

Jack rubs at the tension that has settled so heavily between his eyebrows. "Fine, Caroline," he enunciates, "I don't want to fight with you."

She comes off the sofa so quickly, her long legs flashing and then planting themselves across from him, that Jack instantly regrets his tone. "What the hell is that about? 'Fine, Caroline,' like I'm bothering you?"

"Alright, enough, I'm sorry. I don't like this any more than you do."

"But it's what you want. How can you say you don't like it when it's you who's creating it?"

"Look, Caroline, dammit, what do you want from me?"

"A commitment. Is that so goddamned difficult to understand? I'm sorry I'm not Lindsey, I'm sorry Mia is still missing, but I don't understand why that means you can't get on with your life."

Jack allows his head to hit the glass. The air-condition-chilled pane cools the hot throbbing of his skin, clears his head. How can he explain something she just doesn't get? He can't 'get on' with something he doesn't have. Yes, Lindsey is gone, he has come to terms, if not peace, with that. But his daughter, Mia, she is something he won't let go of. She is out there somewhere, he knows it, he feels it, feels her and, until he knows where she is, until he's found her and brought her home, he will not, cannot, even begin to think of starting a 'new' family.

Jack turns from the window and looks at her. "I'm sorry," he repeats, sadness filling him.

Caroline freezes. "That's it, then?" she whispers. "It's over?"

The apartment's intercom buzzes loudly, startling them both. Caroline glares at Jack, daring him to answer it. When he shrugs and begins to more toward the foyer, she swears loudly and stomps off toward the kitchen.

"Yes?" Jack asks the doorman.

"DeJon is here to see you, sir."

"DeJon?"

"Yes, sir."

"Send him up, please."

"Will do, sir. You have a good evening."

"You, too, Harry."

DeJon? That doesn't bode well. He's stayed over with Jack on numerous occasions but has never shown up unexpectedly before. Jack moves out to the landing to wait for him.

When the elevator opens, DeJon steps out, his usual swagger missing. "Hey there, DJ, what's going on?"

"Uh, Jack, hey there."

Jack takes in the scuffed duffel bag that looks ready to burst and the basketball that DeJon cradles under one of arms. "Are you OK?"

DeJon nods, his eyes sliding off to the side, refusing to meet Jack's.

"Come on, then. Let's talk inside."

DeJon sets his bag on the floor of the foyer and balances his ball on top of it, careful not to let them touch the wall. That care, while Jack appreciates the consideration, only underscores the fact that even after all these years, DeJon is not fully comfortable in Jack's home. It makes him feel like a double failure. He mutters a curse and leads DeJon into the living room. "Are you hungry?" he asks.

DeJon shakes his head.

"DJ? Hey, look at me." Jack lifts the boy's chin and catches his eye, catches the fear and sadness that have moved in and taken up residence there. "Shit. What's wrong?"

"She's gone, man." DeJon's eyes fill with tears and he wipes at them angrily.

"Your mom? She's gone?"

"Yeah, the bitch cut out last week. Took up with some new dude and cut out."

"She's been gone a week? Why didn't you tell me?"

"I thought she'd be coming back. She's never been gone for more'n a day or two before."

"Well, what the hell have you been doing? Where have you been staying?"

"At home."

"Alone?"

Finally, DeJon rolls his eyes. "I'm thirteen. In my part of the world, that makes me a man."

"You're a kid. Don't give me that street-life crap. Now tell me what happened."

"It's like I told you. She met this guy awhile back, he'd give her some of his shit now 'n then, 'n when he told her he was taking off, I guess she decided to go with him."

"And leave you? Goddammit!" DeJon's mother is no prize, but the kid is loyal and won't let Jack even talk about helping him get out. How DeJon has turned out smart and clean, Jack has no idea. He suspects it has a lot to do with Father Mac and the Big-Brother-Little-Brother relationship that he and DeJon share. He hopes so.

"I'm OK. I can take care of myself."

"Dammit, DeJon," Jack swears again, "why didn't you call me?"

"You've been busy with that big case 'n'all."

"I'm never too busy for you. You know that." But the year he'd hidden away from the world, including from DeJon, stands between them and Jack's words don't ring true. "OK, fine, so why did you finally decide to come here?"

"They kicked me out," DeJon mumbles, his eyes once again on the floor.

"What? Who kicked you out?"

"The landlord. Big, ugly white dude, carries a bat."

"The landlord kicked you out?"

"Rent's past due."

"When? When did he kick you out?"

"Coupla days ago."

"A couple of days ago? Where've you been staying?"

"Around," comes the mumbled reply.

Jack grits his teeth. He'd like to find the ugly white dude with the bat and show him a new use for it. He takes a slow breath and heads toward the kitchen. "Come on," he orders, the anger coursing through him, "let's get you something to eat and then you can put your things away."

"I'm sorry, Jack. I didn't know where else to go."

Jack turns on him. "Listen," he says, "let's get something straight here. I am incredibly pissed right now, but not at you. Never at you. OK, wait, I take that back. I'm a little pissed at you right now for not coming to me sooner. But, other than that, we're cool. Right now, though, I want to get you some food and let you get a good night's sleep. In the morning, we'll figure out the rest of it. Understand this, though," he finishes, "this is your home. For as long as you want it to be. Now, come on."

The kitchen is empty when they get there and Jack wonders what has happened to Caroline. He'll have to go find her, try to set things right with her. Shit. But first, he wants to get some food in the kid. From the way his eyes follow Jack to the refrigerator and pantry, Jack knows he has to be starving.

As Jack sets the sandwich and milk in front of DeJon, the kitchen door swings open. "So, who was...? Oh." Caroline stops in the doorway and glares at Jack.

"Something came up and DeJon's staying here for awhile," Jack tells her.

"Fine. That'll be nice," Caroline's smile is all ice. "At least you'll have company." She turns and stomps out of the room.

"Man, I'm sorry," DeJon begins.

"Cut it. It's got nothing to do with you. Eat up. I'll be right back."

Jack catches up with her at the door, where she is struggling with two over-stuffed bags. "Caroline..."

"Back off, Jack."

"Look, can't we talk about this?"

"No, Jack, we can't. Don't you see how awful this is? Don't you understand what all this, this shit, has done to me? I used to be this strong, independent person, and I just begged you to marry me! That is the most pathetic thing I've ever done."

"I'm sorry..."

"I don't care, Jack," she cuts him off. "Can't you see that I don't care that you're sorry? You're like this walking wounded man who's so caught up in feeling sorry for himself that he can't see how fantastic the world really is."

"It's not like that."

"It is, dammit, and I am such a jerk, I fell for it, did the Florence Nightingale thing, thinking I could save you. But, no, you're having too much fun drowning. Go drown, Jack."

Jack doesn't stop the door from slamming behind her. He doesn't go after her and beg her to stay. But the minute she is gone, he kicks the shit out of DeJon's basketball and smiles grimly when it knocks a hole in the plaster wall.

Thirty-Eight

Jack.

Jack pours himself a glass of Scotch while DeJon makes himself another sandwich. "She'll be back, man. Just give her a chance to cool off."

"No, she won't. And, I don't want her to."

That stops him. The kid actually pauses with the sandwich halfway to his lips. He sets it down carefully. "You don't want her to? Now why you sayin' that?"

Jack thinks about brushing him off, treating him like a kid, but he can see there is real curiosity in DeJon's eyes. He's grown up without a father and the men his mother brings home won't have taught him anything good about relationships between men and women. It is probably way past time he gets some answers to the questions that have to be brewing inside his adolescent head. "Look," he says sitting at the table and indicating the chair across from him, "I love her, she's special, but I can't give her what she wants."

"She wants to marry you."

"Right, and I've been incredibly selfish about it. I stayed with her all this time even when I knew I'd never marry her."

"Yeah, but she coulda gotten out."

"She could have," Jack agrees. "I told her a long time ago

I didn't ever want to marry again, but she didn't believe it. I guess she thought that if she loved me enough, I'd eventually change my mind."

"But you love her, though, don't you?"

"I do. She's great. It's just, look, it's me. I've always believed that when you marry someone, you give everything you've got, and then some. I'd be lying if I said I have that much left to give to her."

"But maybe she'd be good for you," the newly-minted love counselor says around a bite of his sandwich.

"She probably would," Jack smiles sadly, "but I wouldn't be very good for her."

***

A short time later, while DeJon is drying his dishes and Jack is working on his second Scotch, the phone rings. DeJon, who is closer to it, looks a question at Jack who nods.

"'Lo?" DeJon asks. "This's Jack's."

Jack has to smile, how could he not? When Lindsey had first introduced him to Father Mac and The Farm, DeJon had been a sad, quiet little kid of six. His mother, in one of her more sober moments, had arranged for him to hang out at The Farm in the afternoons. Jack, growing up in rural America, had seen poverty, had known the depression in people's eyes when the banks foreclosed on their farm loans. He'd seen kids go hungry and seen his parents take more than one family in crisis in, help them sort things out. But this, the filthy, angry desperation on the streets of New York's slums, had depressed the hell out of him. DeJon had been that rare jewel in the mix. A smart, funny kid once you got past the barriers, he'd stolen Jack's heart right from the start.

Now DeJon holds out the phone. "It's for you," he says.

Jack chuckles, "What? You were expecting calls already?"

"Naw," DJ starts before he realizes Jack is kidding him. He smiles sheepishly and hands over the phone. "Some white dude."

"Hello?" Jack sets aside the disappointment that it isn't

Caroline and answers.

"Jack? Jack Westfield?"

"Yes? How can I help you?"

"Mr. Westfield, this is Special Agent Mike Shaheen. We met several years ago, when your daughter disappeared."

Jack's grip tightens on the phone. "Did you find her?" he finally forces out. "Is she OK?"

"Um, I'm sorry, sir. I should have sent someone to see you..."

"Is she OK?"

"She's, well, we don't know if it is her. We'll be doing DNA testing..."

"I asked you if she's OK, Special Agent," Jack snaps. "Could we start there, please?"

The FBI Agent's voice suddenly becomes muffled as if he's covered the receiver with his hand.

"Agent Shaheen?"

"Yeah, I'm here," his voice comes back. "I'm sorry. Listen, Mr. Westfield, I'm sorry, I know this is sort of sudden, but we need to ask you for a blood sample."

"Goddammit!" Jack shouts, all pretence of civility gone, "IS SHE OK?"

"Sir," Shaheen continues calmly from the other end. "I'm sorry. Look. We have a little girl here. There's only a possibility that she's your daughter, which is why we need to get a sample from you."

"Shaheen? I get that. You need a sample, you'll get it. Now tell me, is she OK?"

"She's in a bad way."

***

Fifteen minutes later, Jack is stuffing an overnight bag with a change of clothes and his and Lindsey's medical records that he'd taken from their home office. Mortuary John and Sherri, who had, thankfully, been in the city to catch a show, are coming over to pick up DeJon. He will stay with them until Jack returns from out west.

"Why can't I go with you, Jack?" the boy asks.

"I told you already. I take you out of state, your mom can say I kidnapped you."

"She wouldn't do that."

"DJ..."

"Yeah, OK, fine. Can I help you with anything, though?"

"No. Yeah. Go to my office. In one of the drawers, I have an address book. It's navy leather. Find it, can you?"

Jack flips through his cell phone contacts and chooses an airline. He hits send and waits for the reservations office to pick up.

DeJon is coming out of the office when the front door of the apartment slams open and a very pissed Caroline stomps inside. DeJon freezes, staring at her.

"I got to my bloody apartment and didn't have my wallet or my keys," she says as she strides past DeJon into the kitchen. "I left my goddamned briefcase here."

Jack moves to follow her but stops when a reservations agent answers. "Yes, hello?" he replies.

When Caroline returns from the kitchen, briefcase in hand, DeJon still hasn't moved. "Don't bother to tell Jack I was here," she storms past him, obviously not seeing Jack across the room. At the door, she stops and looks back at the boy. "What? What's wrong?"

"It's Mia," DeJon manages. "They found her."

Caroline reaches out to the wall for support. "Where? When?"

"I don't know. Jack said out west. He's trying to get on a plane."

"Is she OK? Are they sure it's her?"

DeJon shakes his head. "I don't think so. The FBI guy just wants Jack's DNA but Jack made him tell him where she is and he's going out there."

"Shit. OK, look," Caroline says, "call the doorman and tell him to tell my cab to wait. We'll be down in a minute. Where's Jack?"

"There," DeJon points at Jack who waves weakly at

Caroline.

"No, I'm here," Jack says into the phone.

Caroline starts to take off in his direction. "Wait a minute," she pauses, "what about you?" she asks DeJon.

"Mortuary John's coming to get me."

She nods, "Good, that makes sense."

"But I wanna go."

"You can't, DeJon. He doesn't have custody of you."

"But..."

"I'm sorry, no buts. Believe me, I do family law, and that would be a big mess."

Dejected, DeJon moves to the sofa and sits, his eyes on Jack, who is speaking urgently into the phone.

"What? OK, look, this really is an emergency. What if I have the FBI call you? Can you get me on the flight? No, no, not standby. I need to be on that plane."

"Jack," Caroline says.

"Just a minute. No, not you," he says into the phone. "Yes, OK, I'll wait. What are you doing here?" he asks Caroline.

"My briefcase, I forgot it. Look, forget the airlines. We'll take Grandfather's jet."

Jack's eyes search hers. This isn't the time to argue. "You sure?" he asks.

"I'll call him. I'm sure it's fine. One of the pilots is always on standby, so it'll be faster than waiting for a commercial flight."

Jack is in motion before her words are all out. The adrenaline that courses through his body blurs his movements as he grabs his bag and heads toward the door. "DeJon," he barks, "you'll be OK until John gets here, won't you?"

"I'm cool," he nods. "Here, here's your book," he continues, handing Jack his address book. "You be good, Jack. Give me a call, OK?"

Jack pauses and then turns to DeJon to give him a hug. "Thanks," he answers the concern in the boy's eyes and voice. "I'll call you as soon as I know anything."

Thirty-Nine

Jack.

The private jet certainly makes things easier, but the trip is pure hell nonetheless. Once airborne, Jack, unable to sit, paces up and down the aisle feeling like the proverbial caged animal snapping at everything in his path. It can't have come to this, he reasons. Life can't be so damn cruel to hand him back his daughter as she lays dying in a hospital. No fucking way.

"Jack," Caroline tries again, "Are you sure I can't get you something to drink? A scotch? It really will help."

"No, nothing," he continues pacing.

"Tell me something," she says to his retreating back, "you've been snapping at me from the moment we got into the cab. Is it me in particular, or don't you care who you fight with?"

"Goddammit, Caroline, this isn't about you."

Caroline finally picks up her book and Jack feels relief that he won't be expected to have a conversation. He turns and walks back to the front of the plane.

***

Shaheen hadn't wanted him to come, but he had had

the decency to send a car when it was obvious Jack wasn't backing down. As they speed through the city on the way to the hospital, Jack lets his head fall back. He closes his eyes and begins to pray, to pray to Lindsey to take care of their little girl.

Shaheen meets them at the entrance of the hospital, no doubt alerted by their driver. "Mr. Westfield, Special Agent Shaheen. I'm sorry we have to meet up again under these circumstances."

"Good evening, Special Agent, I'm Caroline Carruthers," Caroline holds out her hand when it is obvious Jack is in no shape to make introductions. "Where is she?"

"Mia," Jack corrects.

"We're not sure of that yet, Mr. Westfield. Everything we have is circumstantial at this point, which is why we wanted to get your DNA before having you come out here."

"You said she's dying, Shaheen. I don't think we can wait for the DNA."

"OK, fair enough. Her blood type is a definite match, though, AB-negative, which is common to only about 1% of the population."

"That's still about 3 million people," Caroline says doubtfully.

"Of course. I know that," Shaheen says. "It's not just that, though. For several years, we've been tracking a ring of kidnappers who take babies and very young children and sell them to people who don't want to wait for the normal adoption process to work. It's incredibly lucrative work, with each kid pulling in a hundred, two hundred thousand. They were working in the New York area when your daughter was kidnapped. In fact, it was her abduction that first put us on to them. Usually, they'd buy the babies from women who didn't want them and then re-sell them. We've even tracked back to a few women who are in it for the business. They allow themselves to get knocked up with the intent of selling the kid when it's born. There's a whole black market breeding program out there."

"That's sick."

"It is. But, like I said, it was cases like Mia's that put us on to them. In a few instances, a baby'd been promised and a deposit had been made when the mother either backed out, disappeared, or the baby died before coming to term. In a few of those cases, the middlemen had snatched a baby as a replacement. That's what we think happened in your case, Mr. Westfield. We've got the people who brought her to the hospital in custody while we check out their stories."

Jack, silent through this exchange, feels his stomach turn over. "Can you take me to her now?" he whispers. "Please?"

Shaheen looks at him and says, "You realize," he said, "that there is still a possibility this isn't your daughter?"

"Please?" Jack repeats.

"But..."

"Special Agent Shaheen," Caroline cuts in, "in addition to being a close, personal friend of Mr. Westfield's, I am also his attorney. I assure you that if it turns out that this isn't his daughter, he won't find you or the agency at fault. If, however, it is Mia Westfield up there in the ICU and she dies before her father gets the chance to see her..." She leaves the rest of her threat unspoken, sure that Shaheen understands.

Shaheen, for his part, seems about to protest further and then thinks better of it. "Follow me," he instructs, and turns on his heels.

Forty

Mar.

The water is rising, she can feel it, even though it is for now a ways from the coast, washing back from the sand with every slow, heavy wave. She stands glued to the window, watching it move in, and then out again, drawing back on itself for a few beats and then pushing forward, not violently, not this time, but ponderously, inevitably.

She wonders if she should get out, if the water will make it up to her this time, or if she has time to get out of the building, flee down six flights of stairs and out to the street, go inland a few miles. But she watches the water nervously instead. Something tells her that if she runs, it will lash out angrily and rush after her, boil her up in a suffocating froth of sea foam and water, crush her beneath its weight.

And so, she watches.

Out and in...out and in...back and forth...Soon, too soon, the water has consumed the beach, just covered it up and reclaimed it for its own. It is working its way across the back patio where she used to play as a child. Where she thinks she used to play. Where she and her friends would meet after school to play volleyball or hopscotch. To flirt with the boys who would come to visit.

The patio is under water now and the water is climbing up the side of the building. She presses her face to the glass and glances to the right. Yes, the whole city is under water. It doesn't really matter, though. She knows this is for her, knows it is coming for her, knows the rest of the city is empty, just there to give her something to think about, something to tease her mind away from the water that is coming for her.

Belatedly, she thinks to check the apartment for open windows. No sense in inviting it in. She pushes a window in the living room closed, locks it and then hurries from room to room checking the other windows, fighting the ones whose metal arms are frozen open from too much time beside the sea. Struggles to pull them in, to latch them. By the time she is satisfied she has done all she can, on this floor at least, the water has climbed to the fourth floor.

Anxiously, she looks down into it. She can see that it is still pulling back and forth, can feel it in the groaning and straining of the building around her. Its movements are not so apparent now, though, as the new shoreline is behind her somewhere, somewhere off in the city of ghosts.

She senses movement off in one of the rooms. It is the cat. Must be the cat. But then she remembers, the cat is dead. Had died years ago when it fell from the balcony, lived long enough to drag its smashed body into the bushes before dying alone and afraid, in pain. She wonders now if the cat has somehow come back, just like all the others have gone. Really, though, she is too tired to go find out, feels she should be watching the water. Someone should. And it is just her now.

"Snowy," she calls softly. Then again, "Snoooooowyy," but she doesn't really think the cat will come out.

As the water creeps up the fifth floor, she can look down into it. The color is not friendly, not at all like she thinks of the sea. It is green and dark and murky and she is sure she can hear it whispering. Like the sound of a thousand insect voices, whispering from the depths. *Stop it!* she tells herself, it's water, just water. But the just-water just keeps on coming.

Now the water is at the bottom of the floor-to-ceiling

windows on her floor, on the sixth floor. If she could step out onto the ledge, her feet and calves would be under water. She can almost feel the rigid cold of it on her skin, can feel it creeping up her legs, invading her most private places. But, no, it is still outside and for now the windows are holding. Straining, but holding.

Inch-by-inch, the water climbs up the window. It had seemed to move so quickly before, but now that it is in her space, she feels time moving excruciatingly slow. *Just get it over with!* her nerves scream. *Just fucking get it over with!* She barely resists the urge to squat and look through the water that is now waist high.

The windows are bulging in from the pressure. She puts her hand out and touches the glass. It is cool to the touch. She notices a drip coming in through a seam in the metal frame, watches it turn into a thin stream. She reaches out and tastes it. Salt. Heavy with salt. The taste gags her. It is the taste of death.

She tries to spit, but her mouth is too dry and she longs for a nice cool drink. If she will just leave the sixth floor and go up to the seventh, to the top floor of the apartment, she can get a glass of water from the kitchen. The water will crash through soon anyway, where she is standing. She looks back at the stairs.

Suddenly, she sees movement out of the corner of her eye. The water has reached her eye level. She drags her eyes back to the window, dreading what she will see.

Swirling greens and grays are out there. Muck, kicked up from the land that the sea is swallowing, blurs her view, makes mushrooming clouds in the water, here and then swish, gone, sucked away by a current, leaving more green as far as her eyes can see. She turns to the stairs now, determined to get to the seventh floor. Maybe the sea will recede, maybe she can be saved.

She turns, takes several steps and puts her right foot on the bottom step, looks back. Oh, GOD! NO! She is frozen in place, her heart beating wildly. They have come, the sharks have come. Without realizing it, she has fallen to the floor. Panicked, she reaches out and grabs the railing, drags herself up a step, looks back, looks at those cold, dead eyes of the graceful creatures outside her window as they do a slow dance of death, around and around, swirling the water, faster and faster as they sense her time approaching.

She scrambles up two more steps, slipping as if the water is already underfoot, falling and catching herself, ignoring the pain of her hand snapping back, of her chin hitting the hard wood. She closes her eyes, knows what is coming and wonders how she knows, why she is so sure, but thinking if she can just keep her eyes closed, it won't happen.

Another step, and then another. Her eyes open, just a little. It is enough. The scream begins deep in her stomach, builds up as it works its way through her chest, becomes trapped in her throat as her eyes open wide in horror. There. Right outside her window, the hammerheads are casually tearing at something, ripping at someone, taking a bite and then casually dropping the body so that another can take a torturous, bloody strike at it.

And as she watches Joaquin's body being torn to shreds, she becomes aware again that the cat is back, is screaming, in fact, screaming in terror at the swirling menace that begins to rush into the room. She tears her eyes away from her husband, away from the ragged strips that are all that is left of him, from the hand with the wedding band still gleaming dully on it as it disappears into a mouth, away from the terrified eyes that burst from their sockets as his head is crushed between monstrous jaws and looks around for the cat. Too late, if she is going to save herself, she cannot go back for it. She gets her legs under her and propels herself up and into the darkness, hears the cat scream, hears the cat howl, hears the scream turn to MOOOOOOOMMMMYYY! as the hammerheads rush in for her.

Forty-One

Jack.

The Pediatric ICU is quiet but for the low hum of the machines that are keeping people alive. Jack stands outside ICU #6 and closes his eyes, trying desperately to calm his nerves, still his heart. He'd asked Caroline and Shaheen to wait down the hall for him, not wanting company at this point. Not wanting anything but for the little girl inside to be his little girl. And for her to be alright.

Jack takes a deep breath and enters the unit. His first look at the tiny form doubles him over like a sledgehammer to the gut. Most of the child's body is covered in casts, the rest either bandaged or bruised. Just as Shaheen said, she looks as if she's been crushed.

Jack stands over the child, his own breathing ragged. Most of her face is free of bandages, if you ignore the breathing tube that snakes down her throat, into her lungs. Her face looks beautiful, peaceful. The oxygen-enriched blood coursing through her has left her rosy-cheeked rather than wan and she looks almost as if she is sleeping peacefully, her golden eyelashes curled softly on downy cheeks.

He searches for signs that this is Mia, a resemblance to Lindsey or to himself. A wisp of blond hair that pokes out from the bandage around her head could be the color of Lindsey's. He touches it gently and closes his eyes, overwhelmed.

Jack pulls up the guest chair and snakes his hand through the bed's railing, his fingers seeking out the tiny hand that lays atop the sheets. As his fingertips brush the fingers that will never curl around his, he begins to weep.

Mar.

Mar wakes with a start and reflexively clutches at her head. The pounding is relentless, leaving her nauseous and weak. Lifting her head, she sees that her right arm is encased in plaster, which accounts for the fact that it weighs a ton. As she stares at it dumbly, unsure how or when the cast got there, she feels a growing sense of dread. Slowly, as her numbed brain begins to take note of her surroundings, she lifts her eyes to the room before her and lets out a shriek.

"Mar, Mar, honey, it's OK," Shirley is immediately beside her and tries to wrestle her gently back into the chair. "*Shhhhh*, honey, *shhhhh*. Dylan, baby, can you help me out here, please?"

Mar feels Dylan's strong arms encircle her waist and physically lift her off the railing she is trying to climb over. "Come on, Mar, you've got to relax. There, honey, let go of the railing, I've got you. Shit, Shirley, hit the call button, please, she needs more meds."

Shirley captures Mar's face between her hands. "Mar, stop it! Calm down right now or they'll make you leave. I mean it. Mar, can you hear me? Honey, nod, please, or say something. Do you hear me? Are you with me here?"

As Shirley's face swims into focus, Mar deflates, all the fight gone out of her. Dylan lowers her back into the bedside chair and tucks a blanket around her.

"Jesus, girl, you scared the hell out of me. Are you here? Are you OK?"

The concern in Shirley's voice finally makes its way through the fog in Mar's brain. "Shirley?" she asks.

"Yeah, honey, I'm here. Christ, you scared me."

"I couldn't get to her," Mar's voice is full of sorrow. "She was calling me and I couldn't get to her."

"I know, baby, I know. But she's alright. She's going to be alright. You've got to concentrate on you getting better, let the doctors take care of Lizzie."

"She was getting me a star, from the studio," Mar's eyes begin to overflow, "for painting her room. She had the gold stars in her hand when I found her."

Mar collapses back into tears and Shirley, unusually unhinged, looks at Dylan for help. "I'll go find the nurse," he says.

"Baby, child, *shhhhhhhh*. It's OK, honey, kids climb, it happens. What's important is she's gonna be alright."

***

The next time Mar wakes, she has a hard time opening her crusted, swollen eyes. Without thinking, she lifts her arm up to feel her face and screams in pain when something hard comes crashing down on her forehead.

"Hey, hey, don't do that. Here, just a minute, Mar, let me help you."

"Daddy?" she manages past parched lips and a mouth that tastes like a public toilet bowl.

"Hi, there, honey. Now, *shhhh*, don't wiggle. I'm going to wipe your eyes. You've got that sleep stuff caking them together."

Mar shoots straight up, knocking her father away, as the memories come flooding back. "Lizzie!" she cries.

Don Bloom steadies his daughter as the fight returns to

her. “No, Mar, she’s OK. Your little girl’s fine.”

“I’ve got to find her.” She struggles to free herself of the binding sheets. “Where is she?”

“Maryann Carla Bloom!”

Mar freezes. She hasn’t heard that intimidating voice since the last prank she’d pulled as a child. “Yes, Daddy?”

Don chuckles and pats her hand. “Mar, you’re going to hurt yourself again if you keep struggling like that. Now, if you’ll just give me a minute, I’m going to help you get ready and I’ll take you to her.”

“I’m ready now, Daddy.”

“Uh, honey, trust me on this one, OK? If you go looking like that to see her, you’ll end up scaring Lizzie more than helping her.”

“That bad, huh?”

“Well, you’ve got a mighty impressive shiner and your hair’s sticking up all around the bandages there.”

“And my breath stinks.”

“I wasn’t going to mention it.”

***

Twenty minutes later, Don Bloom rolls his daughter up to Lizzie’s floor. She’s brushed her teeth, straightened her hair and wrapped herself in the bathrobe Diane had thought to bring. While she would prefer to walk, she’d quickly found out that she’d sprained her ankle. The last time she had awoken, Don told her, she’d jumped out of the bed to find Lizzie and hadn’t realized she was still attached to an IV. Which also accounts for the bandaged left hand. In all, her father told her, she probably has more hospital-induced injuries than the ones she’d suffered in the accident at home.

“Are you sure you’re feeling OK?” he asks as he rolls her down the hallway toward Lizzie’s room.

Mar nods tersely. “I’m fine.”

“Because that Demerol’s still in your system.”

“I’m OK.” Apparently, she’d forgotten to tell the admitting nurses about her sensitivity to Demerol and had spent the first hours of her hospital stay fighting hallucinations. No wonder she is exhausted.

Much to Mar's frustration, Don parks the wheelchair several feet from the door to Lizzie's room. He says he wants to peek inside first. As soon as he steps out of sight, she tries to roll the wheels forward, but her damaged hands aren't up to the task. She finds, though, that if she jerks her body back and forth in the chair, she can cause it to roll forward a little bit at a time.

"Mar? What in god's name are you doing?" Diane asks from the doorway.

Mar looks up, startled. "Diane. Hello," she manages. And then, inexplicably, her eyes begin to overflow with tears.

"Oh, Mar, honey," Diane reaches down and wraps Mar in an awkward hug. "You do get yourself into the worst kind of fixes."

"It's a talent I have."

Diane looks into Mar's eyes."How are you feeling?"

"I'm fine, tired. Scared, angry, upset. Is she OK?"

"Honey, she's fine. She's banged up some, understandably so, and she's got a broken leg. Well, frankly, she looks a mess, but the doctors say she'll be fine. She's a strong little girl."

"But she lost so much blood..." the memory of the spreading pool of blood sends icy slivers of fear tearing through her body.

"Blood?"

"I stepped in it, it was everywhere, and when I got the shelf off her, it was all over her. I thought she was dead," Mar's voice is ragged with emotion.

"Honey, Mar, look at me. That was paint."

"Paint?"

"For the heart."

"Heart?"

"That Lizzie was painting for you. When you didn't come back to the phone, your dad called 911 and then called me. I found the poster Lizzie was painting."

"But, how did she...?"

Diane shakes her head and sighs deeply. "I don't know.

All I can tell you is she takes after her mama. That little girl is you inside and out. That being said, I'm afraid this is only the beginning. Now, do you want to go see her?"

Diane rolls Mar's chair right up to the bed. Mar has to bite her lip to keep from crying out. Her little girl is bruised, badly bruised, from the heavy shelf filled with paints falling on top of her. Her tiny leg is encased in plaster and her skin is a tired green. Mar reaches her bandaged hand through the rails of the bed and brushes Lizzie's tiny fingers.

"Mama?" Lizzie whispers hoarsely, her eyes flickering but not opening.

"I'm here, baby."

"Hokay," Lizzie sighs and, as Mar watches, her tense body relaxes into sleep.

Mar lays her forehead on the side of the bed and begins to pray.

Forty-Three

Jack.

The funeral is a circus, with the curious and the media jostling for best viewing positions. Jack's family and Lindsey's had flown in earlier in the week when there had still been a chance the child was Mia. They'd stayed on afterwards, like Jack unable to say goodbye to the little girl they'd never known. When the time came, they accompanied the small casket out to the cemetery where hired guards kept the press at bay.

The little girl's name had been Cassidy Renfro. At least, that is what her "adoptive parents" had called her. She'd been raised by a wealthy family. After all, who else could have paid her hefty purchase price? The girl's parents were in custody, the father in jail for beating her black and blue, and eventually to death, the mother locked away in a psychiatric hospital, having suffered a psychotic break when she'd walked in on her husband punishing the little girl with his massive fists.

The story, pieced together over the past week, is sad and stupid, a testament to the evils and idiocies of the human heart and ego. The father, sterile, had been unable to father a child, but had refused to allow his wife to be artificially inseminated. The mother, somewhat fragile to begin with, had wanted nothing more than a child of her own. Finally, giving in to his wife's pressure, he had one day shown up with a perfect little girl. The baby, who the couple had told everyone they'd adopted from Russia, seemed at first to fulfill the mother's needs. In fact, by all accounts, they had been a very happy family. For awhile.

Over time, the stress of maintaining the charade began to eat at the woman. She'd started to see spies everywhere, began to imagine the police breaking into their house in the middle of the night to take the little girl back to her real parents. As her paranoia progressed, she'd cloistered herself and the child in the house, refusing to go out in public where they might be seen and found out. The husband, frustrated, angry and eventually violent, began to hate going home.

It had been a small thing that had set him off the day he beat Cassidy. A downward trend in the stock market, something that reversed itself the next day, too late for the little girl. Added to his financial frustration, Renfro had tripped over one of Cassidy's toys when he'd come home from work. What had started out as a spanking had erupted into a violent bludgeoning of the worst kind the police had ever witnessed.

Even when the preliminary tests came back that Cassidy was not his biological daughter, Jack had refused to leave her side. Shaheen, as the agent in charge, had arranged for him to stay with the little girl. After all, there was no one else there for her. Her biological parents had not been found, and it was a long shot they ever would be. Shaheen was beginning to think she was one of the ones whose mother had sold her as an infant. When the time came, Jack had made all the funeral arrangements, everything from selecting the casket to choosing the prayers and hymns for the service.

By the time the actual funeral took place, word had leaked out about Jack's involvement and all the old stories of Lindsey's death and Mia's kidnapping were once again dragged out and turned into grist for the voracious mill of human consumption.

"Jack?" Caroline breaks through his reverie. They are the

only two left graveside. His mother and Amanda, both worn out by the emotional week, have returned with their husbands to the hotel. The press, kept back from the hillside grave, had long ago become bored and were sitting around, drinking coffee and joking among themselves as they wait to see if Jack does anything else noteworthy.

"Yes?" he asks quietly, his gaze on the small casket that lies at the bottom of the deep hole.

“They need to finish up,” she says, indicating the Bobcat that is waiting off to the side.

“I don’t feel her anymore,” he says, not indicating whether he means Mia or Cassidy. Over the past week, the girls have become one in Jack’s mind and he truly feels he is burying his own hopes for his little girl, if not the child herself.

“I know,” Caroline leans her head on his shoulder and waves at the bulldoze driver to continue, then stands by his side while the machine finishes the job.

Mar.

Mar takes a sip of wine and stares out over the moonscape that is her backyard. A foot of snow blankets the ground and the moon casts a tapestry of shadows across the landscape. Her father, who had arrived right after the accident and then had stayed on well past the holidays, and Lizzie are sleeping upstairs and it is just Mar, Picasso and Luther Vandross playing softly in the background.

"So, what do you think, fatso? Is it the holidays or the real thing?"

The dog looks up at her as if considering. She chuffs her answer and drops back down onto her paws.

Mar smiles. What can you expect from a dog? The landscape is pretty, though. With her own lights turned off, she can see far into her back yard, can see millions of stars in the clear mountain air.

Give it up, Mar, she tells herself. *It's time to let go*. She picks up a photo of Joaquin taken on their wedding day. He looks so strong, so confident, so happy. The man had his whole life before him. A whole life that would last just another ten days.

Mar closes her eyes and pictures him in front of her. She

can almost feel the hands he lifts to her cheeks, can almost smell the aftershave he wears. There is no mistaking the love in his eyes, or the words *I love you* on his lips. With a last kiss to her forehead, he turns away.

When she opens her eyes, the image is gone. But it had been so real, as real as the tears streaming down her cheeks. She wipes at them and kisses Joaquin's picture one more time before gently laying it on the table and picking up the other photo.

Kevin. Kevin with Lizzie happily snuggled into the baby pack he wore. Kevin with the long hiker's legs and gentle hands. The baritone voice that sent her to sleep and laughed so freely. The man Lizzie adores and Mar finally admits she loves. It has been fifteen months since he left and the long absence has convinced her of her feelings. The visits have always been too short and there have been so many moments, big and small, that she would have liked to have shared with him. A favorable art critique, Lizzie's fourth birthday, the accident. Yes, she would have liked Kevin to have been there for that.

Mar picks up the phone. It is time. Hell, it is past time.

She smiles at the *brrrrrrp* sound of the phone ringing at his hotel in Ireland. It is a happier sound than the annoyingly metallic ring of an American phone.

"Hello?" he picks up.

"Kevin? It's Mar."

"My god, Mar! What an amazing surprise!" His laughter floats across the ether and knocks her smile into full wattage.

"I'm sorry. I know it's the middle of the night for you, but I just had to talk to you."

"No, no, this is great. I've been sitting here for hours waiting until it was a decent time to call you."

"Really?"

"Yes, absolutely. It's wonderful to hear your voice. How are you?"

"Fine. Fine. Wonderful, even. I couldn't wait. There's just something I have to tell you and I didn't want to wait until morning."

"Really?" His voice, so full of hope and happiness, warms Mar's belly. There are no more doubts that this is the right thing. Asking Kevin to help her to find a way so that they can be together is definitely the right thing.

"Yes, really," she laughs.

"Well, that's great. God, you sound good, Mar. And I've got something to tell you, too, something wonderful."

Mar sucks in a deep breath. Is this it? Is he going to ask her to marry him over the phone? She catches herself before her shriek of YES! can escape her lips. "So?" she finally manages.

"No, no. You called, tell me your news first."

Mar shakes her head. Let him wait a moment longer, let the excitement build. She laughs. "Nope, caller's prerogative. It's my dime so I say you have to give it up first."

"Mar, Mar, sweet Mar." His sigh tickles her ear and, closing her eyes, she can almost see him take a deep breath before plunging in. "OK. Me first. Are you ready? Are you sitting down?"

"I am."

"Good. OK, here goes. I've given this a lot of thought and I've decided it's time to get married."

"Yes!" she screams. And then she is laughing and crying and she misses his next few words.

"Mar? Mar? What's wrong?"

The worry in his voice brings Mar back to the call. "No, nothing. Nothing at all. Oh, God, Kev, I'm just so happy. I was sitting here, waiting to call you and thinking about it and then, I just, oh, I've got to go wake my dad and tell him."

"Mar? Are you OK? You're taking this awful well. I mean, I'm glad you're happy, it means everything to me, especially considering. But, waking your dad?"

"He'll be thrilled. He'll want to know."

"Yeah, OK, but he doesn't even know me."

"But he's heard all about you. Really, don't worry. When will you be able to get back here?"

"Well, with the wedding plans and all, I think it's best if I cancel my trip. That's one of the things I wanted to tell you."

"Cancel your trip? I don't understand."

Kevin laughs softly. "I don't think Annie'd appreciate our more lenient American sensibilities. They're still a little conservative over here."

"Annie?"

"I know, I know. Short for Ann Catherine. She's one of those fourth cousins twelve times removed I told you about. Our families split off a couple of centuries ago, but these people, man, you just tell them your last name and they track you back. Anyway, I think her father'd shoot me if I told her I was going off skiing with an old girlfriend."

Mar's head is spinning. She feels sucker-punched and has a hard time finding a breath.

"Mar? Mar?"

"I'm here," she manages weakly.

"Listen, I know this is kind of sudden and I dropped it on you like that. It's just, being with you, I thought, I really believed, we could have made it. I wanted so much for us to. But, there I was thinking she's the one for me and you were still caught up in Joaquin. I guess it took me a long time to realize that you weren't going to come around. And then I met Annie. I know it's fast, but she's a great girl. Funny thing, we have so much in common and, well, it feels good. She's..."

Mar gently sets the phone down and walks stiffly to the sink. She wills her mind to be still until she gets there. Once there, however, it hits her in a rush and all the wine, the food she'd eaten at dinner, her heart and soul spew forth in great, heaving spasms. When she is empty and nothing but the acid dregs of bile are coming up, she lets herself sink to the floor where she curls into a fetal ball and begins to cry, great soul-wrenching sobs of despair. Picasso pads over and tries valiantly to lick the tears from her face.

Sy.

Sy sits at his desk. It is Tuesday, his day to review the firm's current cases. He picks up the Gorman file. What a stupid, pathetic case that has been. That poor kid, stuck with that mother, beating up on him, pushing him down the hotel's stairs so she could file an insurance claim. Sy had filed his report, along with photos, hospital reports from earlier "accidents," neighbor reports of continuous abuse, all of it. Though it wasn't really conclusive that the kid hadn't fallen down the stairs at the hotel, it showed the mother had a long history of abusing the kid and, as her lawyers had to have told her, wouldn't look good for her in court. In any case, the insurance company sent a thank you note along with payment. Makes his heart go all flippy-floppy saving them big bucks, thinking about the poor kid. Jesus.

Around noon, Dora comes in with two Styrofoam boxes of food. Lately, she's been thinking about her yearly trip to Florida to see her sister. She wants to lose some weight, fit into a nice dress when they go to the Indian casinos down there, show off a little flesh, put it out there a little before it all ends up around her ankles. She'd talked Sy into doing the Atkins thing with her. Hence, the boxed lunch from the steakhouse around the corner.

Sy takes off his reading glasses, tosses them onto the desk. "That smells good, Dora. Whatcha got?"

"New York today. In that sauce you like, the mushroom one? And some green beans. I told them not to put in too many, but we can have some. You want some soda? Water, maybe?"

"Nah," Sy replies, clearing the files off his desk. "I think I'll have more coffee. We got any left?"

"Yeah. I put on a fresh pot before I went out. I'll go get you some."

Sy is arranging the food on his desk when the door to his office crashes open.

"You-mother-fucking-son-of-a-bitch!" the broad from the insurance case screeches at him, gun raised, pointing it at him. "You fucking scumbag asshole mother fucker! They took my kid away, asshole pig, they took my kid and you're gonna pay for it."

And she shoots him. Just like that.

Sy, who had been too shocked to react to her ranting, is now doubly so as the bullet tears through his chest, slams him back into his chair. He looks up at her dumbly, his brain not yet catching up with the events, his out-of-shape body not reacting like it is supposed to.

"What, what the...?" he begins, staring at her in disbelief.

The crazy lady brings the gun back up, aims a little lower, more toward his heart. In the second that Sy gets ready to die, another screeching female tears into the office, arm raised, steak knife coming down in a mean arc, catching the bitch in the back. The gun goes off again as Mrs. Gorman goes down, the bullet whizzing by Sy's ear, snapping him out of it.

"Oh, fuck me," he says, trying to get up, get to Dora, keep her from yanking the knife out and plunging it back into the broad's body. And now that one is screaming, adding to the general chaos as Sam bursts into the office, her gun drawn.

"Dora, no!" Sam orders. "Leave it, she's down. You pull it out, you could kill her."

"Well, what the fuck you think I'm trying to do?" Dora snaps, her hand frozen on the hilt of the knife, her fat ass sitting on the woman's thighs, not letting her get up, even if she could, a knife in her back.

"Oh, hell's bells," Jonesy comes in, takes one look and turns around, hurries to Dora's desk, calls 911.

"Dora, now get off her, she's not going anywhere. Go see Sy. Sy? You OK?"

"I'm shot," he says, and falls back into his chair. "Ah, hell," he whispers as all goes black.

Forty-Six

Jack.

Mortuary John hangs his winter coat on the booth's coat rack and drops down onto the bench across from Jack. He is wearing his funeral outfit today and there is a look about him, a tightness around the eyes, that catches Jack's attention. "Tough one?" he asks.

"Fuck." John takes a deep breath and sighs, shakes his head.

Jack returns his attention to watching the people in the restaurant.

"It was a kid," Mortuary John finally speaks up. "A little girl. Some psycho shooting off guns in the street and a bullet comes in through the window, takes half her face off. She's just sitting there, playing with her dolls and, boom, half her face is gone. The other half, though? It's perfect. Beautiful. Her momma wanted an open casket, wanted to see her baby one more time, so we had to turn her head sideways, like she's sleeping. Man, I don't get this world." He wipes his eyes and takes hold of the bottle Jack pushes his way. "Thanks."

Something about the story hits Jack hard. It must have shown on his face because when Mortuary John next looks at him, he sees it there. "Aw, fuck, Jack, I'm sorry. I wasn't thinking."

Jack shakes his head. "It's OK. I've just been thinking about her a lot lately."

"I shouldn't have said anything."

"No, no, really, it's OK." He sighs and looks up at his friend. "It's just that, sometimes, when I hear something like that, it makes me wonder."

"No news, then? Nothing from the FBI or maybe that detective you hired? What's his name? Sy? You haven't heard anything from him in awhile."

"I didn't tell you? He was shot."

"No effing way!"

"Way. Thanks," Jack reaches for the beer a waitress has just put in front of him. "Some woman from a case he was working on got pissed and shot him."

"Is he OK?"

"He will be. He's recuperating."

"This is one screwed up world we live in."

"Tell me about it."

After the waitress has dropped off menus, Mortuary John picks up the conversation. "So, no news, huh?"

"No. None. Not from him or Shaheen."

"I'm sorry, man. I'm sorry."

"I know. Thanks."

Mortuary John looks him over. "So, uh, how you doing? Really?"

Jack's smile is strained as he raises his beer. "Good," he finally answers.

John leans forward onto his crossed arms and searches Jack's face. "You sure about this, my friend?"

"About Caroline?"

"Yeah about her."

Jack appreciates the concern. After all, the only time he and Caroline had gone out with John and his wife, it had been a pretty awful evening. Something about the chemistry just hadn't clicked. "I'm sure."

"She is one fine looking lady. And smart."

Jack looks off into the middle distance. "She is. And funny and kind."

"And rich. Don't forget rich. Her granddaddy owns New York. Well, at least the half Trump hasn't got his paws on yet."

Jack smiles. There is no denying that. "And rich," he agrees.

"But she's not the one."

Jack clears his throat. It still twists his heart. He takes a swallow of beer and shakes his head. "Nope."

"Man, I'm sorry."

"Yeah. Me too."

"I respect you, though, I gotta tell you that. I respect a man who can walk away from that kind of money in that kind of package because he's doing the right thing. Hell, most men'd do the wrong thing for at least a coupla years, collect the interest. Know what I'm saying?"

"She can do better."

"Goddamn, you're the only one that can say that and I know you really mean it."

Jack smiles sadly. It just is what it is and he doesn't have any more to give her. "Did I tell you I'm thinking of leaving?"

"The law firm? Her granddaddy giving you a hard time, now you dumped his granddaughter?"

"No, not that. New York."

Mortuary John looks shocked. "The city? You're thinking about leaving the city? What? Move out to the 'burbs? Man, that's slow death out there."

Jack has to laugh, it is so rare to catch MJ so completely off guard. "Not just the city. New York, the Northeast, the whole thing."

"And go where? Like to California?"

"Home."

"Oh, shit. Not that bumfuck town you grew up in? Jacky, rural America's not for you. They got cows and chickens and things out there. Corn! They got corn as far as the eye can see. Now, I ask you, what the fuck you gonna do with all that corn?"

"I'm serious. Dad's thinking about retiring. He should retire, take Mom traveling like she's always wanted."

"They can travel. You don't have to go out there so they can travel. It's not like they can't grow the corn without you there, tellin' 'em how it's done."

"Are you hungry?" Jack tries to cut him off. "Do you want to order now?"

"Hell, no! I wanna hear about you joining the Bible Belt."

Jack shrugs. "He's thinking of retiring but doesn't want to close his practice. I'm thinking of going out there and running it for him."

"Uh-huh."

"Venco is finally settled, I'm swamped at the office, but nothing that I can't step away from, hand off to someone else. If I'm going to go, now would be the time."

"So you gotta go out there, save a few more farms from foreclosure?"

"Something like that."

"Goddamn, Jack. When are you gonna get over the guilt? Lindsey, Mia, this little girl, what's her name, Cassidy? Man, you gotta let it go."

At the mention of Lindsey's name, Jack's throat begins to burn. It is an entirely psychosomatic response, he knows that. Still, it burns. He ignores it and decides he shouldn't have even brought this up. Not now. Not until he's fully made up his mind. "Anyway, it's just an idea, nothing I'm committed to at this point."

Jack can see that John wants to continue the conversation. He can see the questions in his eyes. And he appreciates MJ even more for backing down, for holding his tongue. Truth be told, Jack still feels the weight of Lindsey's death heavily on his shoulders, a weight that he will never be able to put down and that can only be relieved, if barely, by finding their daughter and bringing her safely home. He waves to the waitress to bring two more beers.

"So, how's old DJ doing?" John asks after an awkward pause.

"DeJon?" Jack finally smiles. "He's good. He likes his new school, though you won't get him to admit it."

"Kid was always too smart for that old neighborhood, though pretty soon he'll be sporting a blazer and cravat and there'll be no dealing with his uppity ass."

"He's still working up at Father Mac's twice a week."

"No one better'n Malcolm for keeping things in perspective."

"Anyway, his mom looks like she's finally going to let me adopt him. I think he's relieved. He wants some stability and he'll still get to see her."

"Unless you put him out to pasture, make him the local target practice."

Jack looks up sharply. "It's not that bad. There are black people in the Midwest."

"Picking the crops."

"Goddammit, John! I told you, it's only a possibility. Of course I'm thinking about him, too, what's good for him."

"Shit, of course you are. I'm sorry, man," he smiles sheepishly. "I'm just wondering if you're thinking about me? What'm I gonna do without you?"

And that, Jack knows, is the crux of the matter, and he appreciates John's ability to say so. "Like I said, it's not final. Just a thought."

"'Course," John brightens, "they gotta have dead people out there, too. Maybe I can open me a local office."

Forty-Seven

Sy.

The day Sy goes back to work is cold and dreary. His shoulder throbs under the weight of his winter coat. The sling gets in the way and he can't even button the damn thing up properly, his arm all tucked in underneath, the sleeve hanging like he is an amputee.

Everyone is waiting for him when he comes in, Dora, Sam, Jonesy, the three other investigators. There are flowers and balloons, all of them waiting around to greet him on his first day back. It is kind of nice, really, but after the donuts and coffee, he can tell they are ready to get on with it, get back to their own work. He is ready to move on, see what's up.

"You sure you're OK, Sy?" Dora asks when he moves to go to his office.

"Yeah, Dora, thanks. Thanks for all this, for all the time you spent in the hospital and at the apartment taking care of me. That was really good of you."

"Hey, Sy? That's what friends are for. I'm just glad they aren't gonna prosecute me. I don't know what came over me, that woman with the gun, trying to kill you. I went a little nuts." She shudders, probably remembering how it felt as the steak knife cut into the woman's back, grateful the lady is going to live, get the psychological help she needs. "But, listen, I'm still taking my vacation. In a week or two, when you're feeling better."

"That's good. Get yourself some sun, maybe win a few bucks. OK, enough of that. I gotta go see what's up. Is there anything I should know?"

"Nah, nothing. I told you all the good stuff that's going on. Everything else is on your desk, the reports, the mail that didn't seem urgent. Oh yeah, hey, listen. That rug was kind of a mess. The cleaner got most of the, you know, stains out of it, but I had to move some things around in there, cover up what they couldn't get."

Sy shrugs, "Hey, no problem, Dora. Thanks."

After bringing him the cup of coffee he can't carry, Dora closes the office door, giving Sy a little privacy his first day back. He reaches for the pile of mail. It is kind of difficult opening the envelopes, pulling the papers out. He has to finally use the letter opener that has been in his drawer for years, decades even, never been used. *Ssshhhrrrrrrk!* He likes it, though, likes the sound of it.

The mail is mostly junk, some Get Well cards, information on trade shows, sales at spy stores, that kind of thing. When he is mostly through the pile, he comes to a postcard, has a big palm tree on it, kind of dirty around the edges. *Welcome to Miami!* it says in gold, the ocean a kind of reddish color with the sinking sun behind it, bringing out the shadows. He turns it over, his heart stopping in his chest. "Dear Mr. Colomanos, Elie finally wrote me. In case you still want to talk to her, call me and I'll give you her number. Sincerely, Esther Burrows."

"Oh, shit," he gasps, looking at the post date. "Hey, Dora! Dora? Can you come in here a minute?" he yells, not bothering with the intercom thing on the phone.

The door flies open, Dora a little panicked, probably thinking he is hurt or something. "What's wrong? You OK?"

"Yeah, yeah, I'm fine. Hey, Dora, when'd this postcard come in? Do you know anything about it?"

"Oh, that," she relaxes. "Yeah, I found it when they were

taking out the carpet. It was stuck in between the file cabinets, way in the back there. Why? What's up? Is it important?"

"Shit. It's been there more'n a year. Oh, fuck me. Man, man, man. Listen, Dora, call the airlines. I gotta get the first plane down to Miami."

"Miami? You sure? You sure you're up to it?"

"Yeah, yeah, I am. I gotta be."

Forty-Eight

Sy.

Sy drives south, using his right arm to drive, everything. Grateful the damn thing has electric windows, not even pissed he has to pay extra for it, get a bigger car because he can't work the handle thing with his left arm, can't reach around far enough with his right. He is so goddamned royally pissed at himself in general, that he doesn't mind the fucking money, would've paid double, triple even, just to get the first car available.

This time the trip to Homestead takes much longer. Probably because he is so anxious to get there. Maybe because he is ready to scream, his arm hurting him so much. He'd banged it up some getting in the cab back in New York, but forgot to bring his pain pills when he'd hurried out of the office, Dora going 'why don't you just call? Wouldn't that be easier?' Not getting it, not realizing he just has to follow up on this personally. Has to see the lady in person, maybe jolt her memory, pick up the postcard from her daughter. Shit, he doesn't even know if she'll be home, if she is even alive anymore. It's been a long time, anything coulda happened.

When he finally gets there, Sunshine Streams is looking about how he remembers it, stupid little deer, come up to maybe his knee, forever grazing in someone's yard. A teddy bear, a few flamingos, pinwheels. Taiwan making a killing on this neighborhood alone.

Pulling into the cul-de-sac where she used to live, going *please please please* under his breath. Stopping the car and struggling to get out, all caught up in the seat belt. Finally getting out and noticing that the same Christmas decorations from the last time are still up, only they've multiplied, had multi-colored little offspring, a few little Santa babies, a coupla new reindeer, some strung-out chili pepper lights. Hoping it is still Esther Burrows living here, not someone else who kept old Esther's shit, added some of their own.

Sy rings the bell, same old song, only it sounds like it needs new batteries, not as fa-la-la as a coupla years ago.

The door opens and Sy's knees go week, he feels like his bladder is gonna go. "Oh, thank god!" he says seeing Esther Burrows there, right in front of him.

"Yes? Can I help you?" she asks, looking through the screen door at him. "Well, my goodness! Is that you? Aren't you that detective?"

"Sy, Sy Colomanos. Yes, it's me. I am so glad you're home."

Forty-Nine

Sy.

Sy had had to overnight in Miami and is feeling sore and dirty. By the time the small commuter plane touches down in Asheville, North Carolina, it is mid-afternoon. Elie is expecting him between 5:00 and 5:30. He pushes up the speed. With his anxiety to get there, just freaking get there, find out what happened to Lindsey's baby, he misses his exit and has to backtrack five miles, cursing all the way.

Sy glances at the notes he's jotted down. At the third BP, just before Brush Creek Middle School, he takes a right, just like Elie had told him to. Follows it around and immediately finds himself in the country. Just like that. The blacktop turns to gravel and the road starts to wind around. On his left is a mountain and, down to the right, fields.

The mile-long drive up the mountain is excruciating, every bump in the dirt and gravel road shooting knives of pain through Sy's shoulder. By the time he reaches the top, his teeth are clenched to keep the tears away.

As he gets out of the car and moves toward the front door of the single story, wood-sided home, wild barking begins behind him. He turns just as the largest goddamned dog he's ever seen comes bounding up to him, pushes its nose right into his crotch and sends him sprawling back against the car. It is the most intimate inspection of his private parts since his last prostrate exam.

“Sadie! Chico!” he hears someone yelling. “You two jes’ shet up now, y’hear?” And sure enough, right behind the big dog is a tiny little Yorkie-thing, barking up a storm, growling and otherwise threatening to tear Sy’s head off, if he’d only bend over so it can reach him.

“Sadie, Chico, now I tol’ y’all to be quiet and I spec yew ta listen. Now, git!”

The man is about six-three, must be somewhere in his sixties, early seventies, with a full head of snow-white hair combed back from his forehead and a neat little mustache to match. He wears jeans, work boots and a dress shirt rolled up to the elbows, and carries an old, battered tennis racquet in one hand. The man sticks out the biggest, roughest hand Sy has ever seen and says, “Hey, there. Yew must be that private ‘tective Elie’s bin talkin’ about. Beau Jon. Beau Jon Kincaid. Welcome, son.”

Sy’s hand is swallowed up in the giant’s paw. “Yes, hello, I’m Sy. Sy Colomanos. I’m here to see Elie.”

“Aw, well, she’s not here now. She’s off to the store but’ll be back shortly. Yew know. Heh, heh, heh. I’d’a gone down myself, but I gotta see ta mah honey bees. They’s swarmin’ today an’ pretty riled up right now. Think tha winner’s over, this heah warm weather we’ve bin havin’ ‘n’all.”

Sy can’t understand a freaking thing the guy is saying, but there sure is a lot of it. “Excuse me?”

“Well, yew bes’ come in ‘n wait. Yew want somethin’ to drink?” he asks. “Now, Sadie, I told you to GIT!”

The mammoth that has been aiming in on Sy’s crotch, slouches off, the little one yipping at its heels. “Thanks,” he says, wanting to reach down, check for damage.

“No problem,” he laughs and slaps Sy on the back. It takes every ounce of control for Sy not to scream out. “Them dogs’ll get real personal with a man if he lets ‘em.” And he turns and heads into the house, leaving Sy to wonder about that.

Shit.

"Hey there, have a seat. What kin I git yew? Yew like Moun'in Dew? Or mebe some water? Elie's got some cola in here somewheres, I think," Beau Jon says, looking through the refrigerator.

"No, no, water's just fine," Sy tells him and asks for a bathroom. He is just so thankful they have indoor plumbing, but when he lets himself out of the bathroom, the guy isn't in the kitchen. Looking around, Sy sees him out on the back deck. The guy is swatting at the air with the racquet. Hopping around, all concentrating, looking up at the sky and hitting the hell out of the air. Sy thinks about leaving, right then and there, sort of creeping out the front door, getting back to civilization. He goes out onto the deck instead, careful not to get in the target area.

"So, um, when do you think Elie'll be here?"

"Jes' a minute, son. Almos' got me one." And the old guy takes off down the stairs, racquet raised. Sy watches him, sees him turn the corner around the house, disappear. Doesn't know what to do.

The man finally comes back, his face creased in a wide grin, shaking his head. "Got me two! Two'n'one! They was fightin' or somethin' and zoooom! got 'em both!"

"Both what?" Sy asks.

"Bees! Got me two-n-one playin' thar mountain tennis! I got another racquet iffen yew wanta play."

"Uh, no, it's OK, thanks. I'm not too good at tennis."

"This here's mountain tennis, son! Yew h'ain't never played it, yew don' know what yer missin'" And then, just then, a huge, like the size of a small bird, black thing buzzes by Sy's head and whoosh!! the old guy knocks it out of the air, sends it flying to the deck. As soon as it hits, he pounces on it, whacks the shit out of it with the edge of the racquet, leaves a mess of ooze and goo.

"What the hell was that?" Sy asks, shaken up.

"Bees, I tell yer! Bees! They's borer bees, which's diffren' 'n ma honey bees. Eat the hell outta yer house iffen yew don't git 'em firs'. I jes' sets out here, enjoy my drink, play mountain tennis an' git 'em afore they kin git the house! They shoulda bin gone already but with the warm spell, yew can still git one'r two. It's a lotta fun." He nods, clicks his teeth, smiles. "Yew should try it sometime."

"Another time, maybe," Sy tells him. "Right now, I kind of want to talk Elie. Do you think she'll be back soon?"

"Aw, hell, sure she will. Jest hadda git somma those diaper things." Whack, whack, he caroms off the porch. Haw, haw, laughs at the mess on the floor. "Gotcha!"

"Right."

"Jes' sit there, she'll be back."

Sy sits there for another twenty minutes. Jethro finally brings him a drink, not the water he'd asked for, but some Southern Comfort and Mountain Dew combination that is more Comfort than Dew. Grateful, not even caring that he still has to find his way down the mountain in the dark, Sy gulps it down, tries to stay out of the way of Tennis Man.

Fifty

Sy.

The dogs put on a huge show and Sy guesses they hear a car coming up the mountain. He gets up and looks off the porch. Sure enough a SUV is pulling into the driveway. A small blonde woman carrying a bag under her arm gets out. Instead of going through the house, she goes around and climbs up the steps to where Sy waits.

"Hey there," she says, "you must be Sy. I'm Elie." She holds out her hand and smiles warmly, the light reaching up into her clear, blue eyes. He shakes her hand and finds himself smiling back.

"You want some coffee? I left some on. You must be getting cold out here."

"Yeah, coffee'd be good," he says. Even with the Comfort easing through his veins, he is beginning to freeze.

She eyes the glass Sy carries with him, "I see Beau Jon's taken care of you."

"Uh, yeah."

"Do you know where he's off to?"

"Something about bees swarming."

"Oh, hell, are they still out there?"

"That's what he said."

She hands him a mug. "I guess you didn't come up here to learn about bees though, did you?"

Sy smiles and laughs a little. "So, uh, you've been hard to find," he tells her.

"Yeah," she acknowledges, shrugging. "It took me awhile to get my act together, to settle down. I guess my mom told you? She said she did."

"Well, she told me you'd run away when you were seventeen or so. Traveled around a lot."

She laughs, rueful. "It was hard, you know? We came from this small town in Ohio. Kids hanging out at the mall, looking forward to getting old enough to work in a factory. Getting pregnant, having kids of their own. I don't know, as long as I can remember, I wanted more." She looks around and laughs. "You know, it's that old saying? Something about running away until you find yourself right back where you started from? So, here I am, in a smaller place than where I started. And, you know what? I love it. These people are great, this place is great. My husband's from around here. His family's been here forever. Beau Jon insisted that Shane – that's my husband – get a good education. That's pretty rare up here. So, Shane went off to college and then med school. We met right before I left New York. He had just finished his residency and wanted to come back here, wanted to make a difference. I came with him and finally realized that this is what's important, making a difference. Alright, I'm babbling," she catches herself. "What can I tell you?"

Sy hadn't minded listening to her. It is obvious she is smart, has a good head on her shoulders. He'd expected dippy renegade tough girl runaway dropout. But, she isn't. And her story explains why he hasn't been able to find her, not working, married with a different name, not showing up on any government records.

"I'm looking for a woman who kidnapped a baby from a hospital about four years ago in New York," he hands her the grainy photo. "A woman who works at the hospital said you were friends with the kidnapper. I'm hoping you know where she is."

"Myrna. You're talking about Myrna." Elie looks off into the falling darkness, thinking. She shakes her head. "She was a real basket case."

"Do you know where she is? Or anything that can help me find her?"

Elie shakes her head again. "No. I'm sorry. After I left New York, I never heard from her again. We weren't really close. It was more that we were both lonely."

"How'd you meet her?"

Elie thinks back. "I volunteered at the hospital. It wasn't anything, really. I mean, it didn't pay anything. They let you eat for free in the cafeteria, though. I'd had it with the whole runaway scene, the sleeping in the streets, the stealing. One day, I found myself in this church and they helped me out, gave me a place to stay, helped me find a job. Jobs were pretty hard to find when you didn't have any skills, didn't finish high school, you know? So, anyway, I volunteered at the hospital, kept the patients company, took them for their tests, delivered flowers and all that. It helped keep me off the streets, gave me some food, some dignity. Myrna was there, too. I think she started about the same time I did. Anyway, they had us doing a lot of the same things and we'd have our breaks at the same time, so a lot of the time we'd eat together. A couple of times, she came back to the dorm with me, hung out. At the end, I got a part-time job bussing tables and we went to a movie. I don't remember what it was, though." She looks off again, thinks about it. Realizes he probably doesn't care about the name of the movie and looks back at him, waiting for his next question.

"You said her name was Myrna. Do you know her last name?"

"Cross. Myrna Cross. It was a really weird thing about her name. She didn't want anyone to know it. She used this Oriental name, Sun-something-or-other. It was really strange because she wasn't Oriental or anything. I didn't really get it, but one day we were talking and she just popped out and said it. Said that her real name was Myrna Cross, but that no one could know. She said something about her father looking for her but that he was abusive? So she forged an I.D. and used a different name, something he'd never find? I think that was the story."

"The I.D. was stolen," Sy tells her.

"Oh. Well, everyone had a story. We were all running away from something, so you kind of learned not to get too much into the details. Your coffee's getting cold. Do you want some more?"

Sy looks down at his cup and realizes he's hardly touched it. His mind is on other things. He takes a sip. It is cold, but he doesn't want to stop now that he is finally getting answers. "No, thanks. This is fine. So, what happened? Why do you think she told you her name?"

"Like I said, we were lonely. She once told me I was her only friend. I guess she wanted to tell me something personal about herself, let me know I was important to her."

"What about her background? About her family? Or where she was from?"

"Look, I'm guessing here, but out west, I think. She talked about the Rockies, said she missed them. She really didn't have an accent that I can remember, so it definitely wasn't from around here! No, I remember her saying she'd like to get back to the mountains. I can't say for sure, though."

"No family? She never mentioned any family?"

"Other than her dad, not that I remember. And all she said about him was that he was abusive. No, wait, I think she said her Mom died when she was a baby. She told me once it was the worst kind of lonely there is, not having a mother."

"Oh, Jesus," Sy says.

"What? What'd I say?"

"Do you think that's why she took the baby? Because the mother was dying? Can it be that simple?"

Elie is quiet for a moment, sorting it out in her head.

"I don't know. I mean, I don't know much about the circumstances of the kidnapping. I hadn't even heard about it until a year or so ago when I got back in touch with my mom. Wasn't the mother still alive when the baby was taken?"

"She was dying. They worked on her for a long time, but there really wasn't much of a chance she'd make it."

"That just seems a little too easy, doesn't it? Oh, here's a baby whose mother is going to die, I'd better take it, be its mom?"

"Yeah, I guess," Sy agrees, dragging a hand across his scalp, thinking about it.

"It could've been the trigger, though. I mean, she was always talking about being a mother some day. I'm guessing here again, but I think her dad raped her. That kind of abusive. She told me she had an abortion once. I think it was her dad's, more from things she didn't say than from what she did. Whatever, I know that ate at her. She always talked about finding the right guy, having a baby, someone to love her." She looks up at Sy. "Yeah, maybe you're right. Maybe she just freaked, took the baby on the spur-of-the-moment kind of thing. She didn't seem like someone who'd plan a thing like that. She didn't seem evil. A little needy, maybe, but not evil or anything. You'd have to be evil to plan something like that. I'd kill anyone who tried to take Cody from me."

He looks up at her. He isn't fooled by the matter-of-fact tone of her voice. "OK, so you think she came from out west, maybe she'd go back there. Any idea where exactly?"

"Nope, none at all."

"You weren't in touch with her after you left New York?"

"No. I'd met Shane and he was leaving the city. I decided to go with him."

"Just like that?"

"I wasn't making the smartest decisions back then," Elie admits. "If anyone told me they were taking off with a guy they'd only known a week, I'd say they were crazy, but it was like that. I just knew I had to go with him. We came back here, and I lived with him for a few years before the baby came and we decided to get married. Either way, it was the smartest thing I ever did."

"You didn't tell Myrna you were leaving?"

"No. It was like, at the end, she started to get real needy, real clingy. She was always asking me where I was going, what I was doing, who I was seeing, that kind of thing. I was probably just being a bitch, but I didn't want to tell her I'd started dating this doctor. I didn't want her to start ragging on Shane. Or on me for liking him. Anyway, like I said, it wasn't for that long anyway."

"And then you left."

"And then I left."

Elie glances up at the wall clock and Sy realizes it has gotten late. "Look, um, do you mind if I call you if I think of any other questions?"

"No, not at all. I want you to find that baby. I mean, her mother's dead, but she should be with her father. It's just awful, what happened."

"Yes, it is," agrees Sy. He stands and thanks her. "I think we might finally have a chance of finding Mia."

"That's her name? Mia? That's pretty. Maybe if this one's a girl, we'll name her Mia." She pats the slight bulge of her belly. "Then again, maybe that's not such a lucky name."

Sy smiles sadly. She has a point.

Mar.

"How you doin', girlfriend?" Shirley drops down onto a deck chair beside her.

Mar smiles at her and reaches out to squeeze her hand. "Good. Great even."

"Uh-huh."

"No, I mean it." She ups the wattage of her smile. "See?"

Shirley peers into Mar's eyes and sighs. "OK," she finally says. "If it makes you feel any better, she's fat."

Mar closes her eyes and leans her head back. "Thanks, Shirl."

"No, I mean it. And she's got that funny accent thing."

"Irish. It's Irish, and men go for that kind of thing."

"Damn, that's right."

"How was he?" Mar finally ventures.

"Good. He asked about you."

Mar's eyes snap open. "You didn't tell him, did you?"

"No, friend, I didn't tell him that you really called to ask him to come home. I wanted to, though."

"It wouldn't have been right."

"I know, honey. The thing is, though, from the look in his eyes when he asked about you, I think he still might have dropped the whole wedding thing and rushed back here."

"Don't say that, Shirl," Mar whispers. "Please don't tell me that. Ever." There are tears in her eyes and she closes them again. "Just tell me he's happy. Really, really happy, OK?"

Shirley twines her long fingers through Mar's and squeezes. "He's happy, baby. He asked about you, but he's happy."

"Thanks, Shirley."

They sit in silence while Shirley watches the kids bumble around in their snow suits and Mar raises her face to the gentle March sun.

"I notice Lizzie doesn't limp anymore," Shirley finally says.

Mar smiles, "She's strong and the bone healed well. It's a good thing."

Shirley smiles as Derek falls on his padded butt and Lizzie helps him right back up. "This is all good, Mar. I'm proud of you, baby, real proud of you."

"Yeah," Mar finally grins.

"Imagine."

Mar laughs. "I do. All the time."

Fifty-Two

Sy.

Sy returns on the noon flight and goes straight to the office, doesn't even stop to change clothes. Dora is ready for him, stands up as soon as he walks in the door, a fistful of papers in her hand.

"You got it?" he says by way of greeting.

"Well, I've got something," she replies, holding back a little, not ready to celebrate anything just yet.

He looks at her, gauging her response. Wonders if it is just herself holding herself back, or maybe a bit of coyness? Has she found the girl that easily? Just a few clicks of the mouse while he'd been in the air?

"Well, come on, then," he says, heading for his office.

He opens the door, tosses his briefcase onto the desk and shrugs out of his jacket, the one arm floppy, tosses it on the back of the chair and sits. Dora comes up behind him and places the papers down on the desk. Sy goes through them quickly. And then again more slowly. Dora reads over his shoulder. When he sets them down again and swivels around in his chair to look out the window, she sits across from him.

"So, you think it's this guy? The one in prison?"

"From what you told me, it fits. He has a daughter around

Elie's age, born in Colorado. Can't get closer to the Rockies than that. Her name's Myrna Cross, just like Elie said, mother died when she was a baby. Even the father matches up. He's in prison for assaulting a little girl. It fits, Sy."

He swivels back and forth a few minutes, closes his eyes and looks inside himself, checks his own instincts, double-checks to make sure they are good. They are. "It's gotta be her," he says, coming around to face Dora. "OK, so we've got the birth certificate, mother's death certificate, father's history. But we don't have anything new on the girl?"

"No, not that I can find so far. Now that's not saying much. You said not to contact the FBI. I'm sure they could open a few databases we don't have access to, but so far, I don't have anything new on her, no juvie records I can find. Unless you can think of somewhere else I haven't looked?"

Sy picks up the papers again. "No, you done good, Dora. This is real good." He smiles up at her, sees the color creep up into her face, plans to ask her to dinner as soon as this is settled.

"But, don't you think we should call in the Feds?"

"No," Sy barks. And then shakes his head. It had just come out that way. He hadn't realized how angry it makes him. "No," he says more softly. "They didn't find crap four years ago. I'm not gonna hand this over to them now, let them bring Mia home. I owe that much to Lindsey, to bring her baby home myself."

"Sy," Dora insists.

"No, I can't. They'd tell Jack, and what if it's not her? What if this goes south? It'd open it all up for him again. I don't want him to know until I know. You know?"

She knows. "OK, Sy. We'll do it your way. You want me to book you a flight?"

"Yeah, do that. And, Dora? Thanks."

She turns at the door and looks back at him. "You're welcome. I just hope this time it works out."

"Me, too, Dora. Me, too."

Fifty-Three

Sy.

Lompoc Prison is located in Santa Barbara County in Central California. On the long flight west, and then on a regional hop into Sta. Barbara, Sy tries to sleep. His arm and shoulder are killing him, and the strain of the search is beginning to take its toll. On the other hand, he is once again medicated.

The car Sy rents comes with a built-in GPS. He tries several times to input his destination but, being technologically-challenged, can't figure the damn thing out. Finally, he goes back into the rental agency and has someone come out and set it up for him.

"You really going out to the prison?" asks the clerk, punching in the address.

"Yeah," Sy replies, meaning *shut the fuck up, what business is it of yours?*

"Cool. I've never been out that way. I do know of one kid that went there, though. Tommy Garcia? He was with the Bloods, you know? That gang down in L.A.? Yeah, he got sent up there. Killed his girlfriend in high school. She was a nice girl. Don't know what she saw in him. But, anyway, he killed her. Shot her dead. I heard she tried to break up with him.

Can you imagine that? The guy was seriously screwed up, if you ask me. Now, listen, if you screw up with these directions, she'll tell you what to do to get back on course, you know? I say 'she', because it's a woman's voice. 'Turn left at the next corner, thirty yards until you turn left', something like that. Just listen to her. She'll get you there OK. When you want to come back, you just punch in the rental agency's address here at the airport. See? Just type that address in and punch the same button. But, it was really crazy how he just walked up to her and killed her right in front of her house. I mean, in broad daylight and everything, can you believe it? Jesus. Man, I hope you're not going to see someone like Tommy up there? I mean, someone violent like that? That just freaks me out, man. I mean, like, hey, live and let live, you know what I mean?"

Sy thinks about not letting the kid live. Maybe getting himself a nice little cell up there with Tommy Garcia. Sleeping easier, knowing this total moron is finally quiet. No way in New York you'd get a car guy talking to you like this. It's like 'Fuck you' is a complete conversation. But this kid, man, this kid could talk Gandhi into some violent acts of aggression.

"Do you ever shut up?" Sy asks.

"What? Me? Oh, am I talking too much again? Sorry. My mother always told me that, and my boss here keeps telling me, but it's like, hey, it's a free world, free speech, and all that? I mean, it's not like I'm hurting anyone. Just trying to be, like, helpful, you know? And then, like, you mentioned the prison, and it's like, a coincidence, because I know someone at the same prison. Well, I don't really know him know him, you know what I mean? I mean, he went to my high school. Well, not really my high school cause, like, I only went there for one year and then my mom decided to get out of L.A. Man, that was the smartest move she ever made. Got herself a better job up here, the new school was so much better, not so much violence, you know? It's been cool. It makes a difference, you know? Being happy where you are."

While the kid is talking, he gets out of the car. Sy heaves

himself in, reaches over with his right arm to close the door, but the damn kid is bending over, hanging on to it.

"So, like I was telling you, punch in your destination and then just push that red button there and she'll change your course. It's really cool, man, can't understand how people used to use maps and all. That's like, so archaic. You know what I mean?"

Sy heaves himself to the left, reaches over and grabs the door handle, pulls it out of the kid's hands and slams it shut. It was that or maim him. As he shifts gears and screeches away, he can still hear the kid back there, yammering away. The guy has issues. Probably lucky for him he lives in the land of fruitcakes. He wouldn't last a day in New York.

It is late afternoon when Sy follows the long, seemingly abandoned road that ends at the prison's guard-towers. He pulls up to the gatehouse and says his name into the microphone. A guard waves him through, indicates where to park.

Once inside the prison, Sy goes through security screening and is made to empty his pockets, remove his shoes and go through a metal detector before being given a visitor's pass and his x-rayed shoes back. Finally, he is told to follow a guard to the administrative wing, where he has an appointment with the Warden.

"I don't have an appointment with the Warden," Sy corrects him. "I'm here to see a prisoner. Eddie Cross."

"Sorry," the guard responds, not slowing down, "I was told to take you to the Warden, and that's where I'm gonna take you."

Sy shrugs and continues walking. Besides the crisp staccato of their shoes on the concrete floor, he hears the muffled clanging of metal gates being opened and closed. The sound shrivels his balls.

"Here we are," the guard says, opening a door, letting Sy enter first. "Nancy, this guy's got an appointment with Warden," he tells the receptionist, and then turns and leaves.

Sy stands there, feeling stupid. "Uh, hi. I'm Sy, Sy

Colomanos. I, uh, think I'm in the wrong place. I was supposed to see a prisoner, but the guard back there brought me here instead."

"Good afternoon, Mr. Colomanos. The Warden's expecting you. Why don't you have a seat there and I'll just let him know you've arrived?"

She indicates a hard bench pushed up against the wall. Sy sits. He wants to call Dora and find out what the fuck is going on. He doesn't like surprises. Unfortunately, he also doesn't like cell phones and so far has resisted getting one. Now he wishes he hadn't been so stubborn.

Five minutes later, the receptionist ushers him into an office. It is a large and well-decorated space. Not comfortable, but very masculine. Obviously meant to intimidate, show who's boss. A large gun cabinet fills the wall behind the warden's desk.

Warden Sheffield stands as Sy enters. He is a large, robust man. There is no doubt that, in pure physicality, he can hold his own in a fight. "Mr. Colomanos, welcome to Lompoc," he says. "I'm Warden Sheffield."

"Sy Colomanos."

The Warden waves to a seat. "What can I do for you?"

"Well, actually, I'm not sure. I'm here to meet a prisoner. Eddie Cross. My secretary set it up."

"Yes, I heard about that."

Sy has the feeling the man is not willingly going to give out any information. "Is there some problem? Isn't the guy available?"

The Warden leans back in his chair, looks Sy over. "Just what is it you want with Cross, Mr. Colomanos?" he asks.

"He's tied to a case I'm working on. I'm hoping he can help clear some things up."

"A case? You're no longer an officer of the law, though, are you? You're a private investigator, if I'm not mistaken." His tone says he is not mistaken.

Ah, shit, Sy groans internally. This guy has a major bug up his ass, no respect for the private sector. "Yes, I am," is all Sy gives him.

"Well, Mr. Colomanos, your secretary gave us a brief explanation of what you want from Cross, but I think you should refresh my memory some."

"Is there some sort of problem here? I mean, I was under the impression I could see him."

"Curiosity, Mr. Colomanos. Simple curiosity. I like to know what my prisoners are involved in, if you see what I mean."

Aw, fuck. Sy takes a deep breath, tries to let it out quietly. *Fucking control freak. Fine.* He gives him an overview.

The Warden stops rocking when Sy finishes speaking and looks at him. Hard. Finally, he says, "Well, I'm sorry you've come all this way for nothing, Mr. Colomanos. Cross is dead."

"What!?" Sy launches upward. "Dead? What do you mean he's dead? Why didn't someone tell us? How'd he die?"

The Warden is unruffled. Probably a fucking hurricane couldn't ruffle this ice cube. "He died in an outbreak attempt. Last week."

"Ah, shit," Sy slumps back into the chair. Another dead end. *Goddammit, when am I gonna catch a break?* he thinks.

The Warden watches Sy pull himself together. "I'll tell you what, though," he says eventually. " Your secretary told a compelling story. You tell a compelling story. Normally, I'd call in the Feds. This sounds more like their business. But I don't know for sure that you're on the right trail. If you are, I think you're going to follow it to the end. So, for whatever good it'll do you, I can tell you that Cross came from Colorado. Around Fort Collins. He hadn't been back there in years, but you might pick up something on the daughter there. And, I think that's really who you're looking for."

Relief floods through Sy. The trail isn't cold after all. "Thank you," he says, "that helps a lot." Realizing the interview is over, he stands and holds out his hand.

The Warden stands, shakes it. Nods at him curtly and then sits back down. Sy lets himself out.

Sy.

Before going to bed, Sy calls Dora. “Listen, Dora,” he says after he’s woken her up and waited ‘til she is through cursing him out, “I’m not going back to New York. I’m heading outta here tomorrow morning and going to Denver. This woman headed out west somewhere. She comes from Colorado and she’s got a thing about mountains. Maybe she went home. Maybe she’s got some family or friends there that know where she went. In any case, that’s what we got. Meantime, I want you to start a search for single mothers, mothers on welfare, that kind of thing.”

“Sy, isn’t it time to call in the Feds? I mean, they’ve got more access to this kind of information...” Dora begins.

He thinks about that for a second. His initial thought is to say no, offhand. But, if Dora says it is time to call the FBI, it probably is. He rubs his hand across his balding head. Screw it. “Nope,” he says, “this is my game.”

“Yeah, OK, Sy,” she grumbles. “I’ll check records for welfare, W.I.C., whatever local programs they got out there. Maybe something’ll pop. You going out to the dad’s place?”

“Yeah, this little town, called Saliva or something. I fly into Denver and then drive out. He’s dead, but maybe someone remembers him."

"What about Joe?"

"Joe?"

"Yeah, Joe Doodle? You know, Noodle Joe?"

"Holy shit! That's right! Is that where he ended up? In Colorado?"

"Yeah, somewhere out there. Call me when you get in. I'll try to find his number when I get to the office."

"You think he's still active? Maybe he's on the force?"

"I don't know. He was pretty pissed when he left here. Just wanted to get out there and be a cowboy or something."

"Yeah, but he's maybe got some contacts, probably friends with the sheriff or something."

"Anyway, I'll get his number for you."

"You're the best, Dora."

"Yeah, fuck you, too, Sy."

Sy.

The plane touches down at Denver International Airport around three in the afternoon. Sy goes immediately to the Hertz counter and rents a car. The desk agent hands him printed instructions for the GPS. Sy hands them back, asks for a real map. The agent insists the GPS is easier, tries to give the instructions back to him. Sy loses it. "Just give me the fucking map!" Freakin' techno-nerds, taking over the world, so many of them they're even working at Hertz, probably McDonald's. Pretty soon you'll have to order online, get your burger.

It takes him several hours to get to Salida. Just getting out of Denver confuses the hell out of him. The roads don't seem to end up where they're supposed to, and the locals show no fear on the roadways. A lot like Manhattan cabbies, always zipping in and out, but these guys do it with pickup trucks. Big pickup trucks, with oversized tires and gun racks on the back. Shit, you drive around with a gun rack in the city and they'll haul your ass in, send you on a nice, long vacation. These guys're driving around with rifles in their cabs, hanging in their windows for everyone to see. And then, there are the hats. Real, true cowboy hats. Like in the movies, but these are real guys wearing them, not like some actor putting on a role, these guys – and the ladies, too – actually wear the damn things, keep them on in their cars. Probably cover a lot of bald heads. He thinks about getting himself one. Fucking New Yorkers would laugh him outta the city.

Salida itself is worth the drive. An old mining town nestled in the Fourteener Mountains, mountains in excess of 14,000 feet, it has experienced a rebirth, an influx of creative energy that has revived it and made it into a hip, funky, fun place to be. As he drives the streets, he sees too many art galleries to count, along with restaurants, bars, hotels, all the signs of a thriving economy. He pulls into the hotel courtyard and parks the car.

"Hey, Dora, it's me," he says when she answers. "I just checked in. What's going?"

"Damn it, Sy, I wondered when you'd call. Why didn't you call from the airport? Hell, why don't you have a fucking cell phone like every other civilized human being in America?" she gripes.

"Ah, Dora, I guess that's because I'm just not too civilized," he grins into the phone.

Dora is silent. Sy does not, stress, does not, tease. Ever. "Uh, you getting enough air out there, Sy? You want me to call the hospital, get you an oxygen tank or something?"

"No, no, this is great! I'm feeling great. This place is beautiful, Dora. The mountains, I've never seen anything like them."

"You're worrying me, Sy. You're gushing. You never gush. What's going on?"

"I'm telling you, nothing. Not a goddamned thing. It's just, these mountains..."

"Yeah, OK, the mountains. Uh, Sy, you wanna snap outta it a moment? Come down off those mountains, maybe pay attention?"

Fucking-A, is that jealousy creeping into her voice? Sy pulls the phone away from his head and looks at it in bewilderment. Is she freaking jealous of mountains? Sy shakes his head and laughs. Maybe he'd better pick up an oxygen tank. Or cut back on his meds.

"Listen, Nature Boy, snap outta it, will ya?" Dora says.

That gets Sy's attention and he laughs again, feeling good. "Yeah, Dora, I'm here. Whatcha got?"

"I found Joe. It wasn't too hard. Checked with the Chaffee County Sheriff's Office. By the way, you're in Chaffee County. Anyway, he's a deputy there. Been with them a coupla years. Anyway, he's gonna meet you for dinner, what, uh, let me see, uh, like seven minutes ago."

Sy glances down at his watch. He hadn't realized how late it is getting. Suddenly, he feels hungry, ravenous. His belly churns and he laughs again. "OK, so tell me where I'm supposed to be meeting him."

Sy jots it down. "OK, Dora, thanks. You've been great. You want me to call you after I talk with him, or you want to sleep some?"

"Sy, it's two flipping hours ahead of you here. I'm beat. Call me in the morning." She hangs up.

Mountains! Shit.

Fifty-Six

Sy.

The restaurant is all frontier funky, with plank walls, floors and beamed ceilings, glassy-eyed dead animal heads on the walls, a huge fireplace with a real fire burning.

"Well, hell, if it ain't Sy Colomanos," booms a voice from behind a tankard of ale. The tankard is set down and Joe "the Noodle" Doodle stands up. He is a contradiction in every term imaginable. Barely tall enough to get himself admitted to the NYPD, a runt from every physical standpoint, he owns a huge voice, a voice that belongs on a much larger, much heftier man. He speaks, and the people in the next room hear him. In addition to his squirt-like stature, he looks uncomfortably like a weasel, all beady-eyed and sharp angles. Feral teeth and slim little hands add to the image. Joe never let his looks, nor his size, stand in his way, though. One of the nicest guys you'd ever want to know, and one of the smartest. Several years ago, he'd opened a magazine and seen a spread on Colorado. Joe Doodle decided to become a cowboy.

"How ya doin', Joe?" Sy asks, realizing he is truly happy to see his old friend. And realizing there is something different about him, something off.

"I'm good, Sy. Sit, sit. You want something to drink? A

beer? Whiskey?"

"I'll have a draft, whatever he's having," he tells the waitress. "You look good, Joe. This place must agree with you."

Joe laughs, a rumble that comes from his non-existent belly. "It does. Life's great out here. Can't even imagine going back. In fact, won't ever go back. Who needs that shit when you've got Colorado?" And he laughs some more.

And then it hits Sy. There is something different about his teeth. They are huge, pearly motherfuckers. Not that little, rat-like stuff he used to have. Hell, these teeth look good enough for a toothpaste commercial. "You got teeth", Sy says, somewhat indelicately.

Joe grins, showing them off. "Yeah, finally did it. I got married. You didn't know? Well, yeah, how could you? Met this girl out here, owns herself a little ranch. Shit, little. The things a thousand acres! Anyway, it was love at first sight. She suggested it, thought it'd help with the smile. I'll tell you, man, I've been smiling ever since I met her!"

"Yeah, they look good," Sy says. "Big." And then he laughs, too. Must be the freaking air, he decides. He isn't getting enough oxygen to the brain. But something, something about the whole place just makes Sy feel good.

Sobering up, Joe brings him around to the matter at hand. "So tell me about this case you're working on. Dora – that's her name, right? Well, Dora told me a little and I did some research. Hey, she tell you I'm a Sheriff's Deputy now? Tried doing that cowboy stuff, but those horses are big! I'm telling you, they move fast, too. I leave that to the wife now, and I'm back in law. Anyway, Dora told me a little. I'll tell ya, though, nobody around here remembers that girl's father too fondly. He had a bad reputation for hurting women, that girl included. But I did track down an aunt. She's on the same rodeo circuit as my wife. Anyway, I gave her a call and told her I'd be taking you out her way tomorrow. Can you be ready around nine? It's about an hour's drive from here."

Fifty-Seven

Jack.

Jack puts his fork down and looks across the table. DeJon, usually so vocal at dinner, at breakfast, throughout the day, is silently picking at his food. "It's OK, you don't have to eat the leeks," Jack tells him.

"Nah, man, it's not the leeks. They're not so bad."

Jack nods. He'd figured as much. "What is it, then?"

"It's just weird, you know? This whole thing?"

"The adoption?"

"Yeah, man. It's like, I'm almost fifteen. Who gets adopted when they're fifteen?"

"I don't know," Jack shrugs. "Is it your age that's bothering you?"

"Naw, it's not the age so much. I don't know, Jack. It's just weird."

"Are you having second thoughts? Maybe you want to think about it some more?" Jack is due to sign the papers in the morning. DeJon's mother, somewhere in Texas, where she'd finally turned up, has signed them already. Jack has been wondering when the boy's meltdown would occur.

DeJon shakes his head and swallows hard.

The fact is, no matter how bad the woman has treated him

all these years, she is still his mother and DeJon is struggling with the fact that she signed the papers. He wants to be with him, Jack is sure of that, but he is hurting because his mother signed her kid away.

"DJ, it sucks, I know it does," Jack intuits his thoughts. "I can't tell you what's going through her mind, what happened in her life. I can't, I'm sorry. I can tell you, when I talked to her, I thought, and I still think, that she thinks this is what's best for you. 'You give my baby a chance,' is what she said."

"It's like she don't want me."

"Maybe she knows she can't keep up with you and she's letting you go so she doesn't get in your way."

"What's that supposed to mean?"

Jack sighs. Talking to a fourteen year old, so full of opinions, is hard, but talking to one about his mother is like walking in a field full of landmines. "You're smart, for one. Very smart. The school you were in just couldn't give you the challenges your mind needs. You like school now, don't you? You're always talking about how great your new one is."

"School's fine," DeJon mumbles.

"And you're safer. Traffic sucks, there certainly are drugs to be had around here, if you're looking for them, but the dealers aren't hanging out on the corners, playing target practice with each other. Every other building isn't a crack house. These are things your mom has to have been thinking of. She did what she did with her own life, but I know she wants more for you."

DeJon pushes his steak aside and begins flattening his mashed potatoes into a pancake. "But, I'm black," he mumbles.

"What?"

"I said, in case you haven't noticed, I'm black."

"I noticed."

"And you're white."

Jack bites back a smile. "Can't be helped."

"So, is this some sort of social experiment or something?"

"Is that what's bothering you? You think you're a cause for me? Like Eliza Doolittle?"

"Who?"

"Forget it," Jack shakes his head. "DeJon, listen, if you're uncomfortable with this, we don't have to go through with it. You can still live here, I'll still take care of you, make sure you get a good education, put you through college. I don't need to adopt you to do that."

"Then why? Why are you doing this?"

A million memories race through Jack's head, any single one which would have been answer enough for him. DeJon as a little kid, fiercely holding the basketball Jack had just bought him, afraid that someone would try to take it away. The same little kid crying brokenly a week later when someone had taken it from him. DeJon proudly showing Jack his first grade report card, his second grade report card, the trips with Lindsey out to the shore, taking him to his first Broadway play – that hadn't gone over too well, but still – times on the court, at Father Mac's, in arcades, taking DeJon up north to see the leaves change, taking him ice skating. "I love you," he says simply.

"Ah, shit."

Jack smiles. His own dad is forever telling Jack how much he loves him, so for him it is normal to hear it. He knows, though, that it has to be pretty uncomfortable for a kid DeJon's age to hear it. "I'd be proud to call you my son," he continues. "And I certainly think that my life's been a lot better since you came here, so my reasons are kind of selfish, too."

"I'm not gonna be your little girl," De Jon tells him.

Jack nods. "I know. And I wouldn't want you to try. The dresses, I don't think I could stand it."

"Shit. You know what I mean."

Jack sobers. He knows that they've finally gotten to the heart of the matter, DeJon doesn't want to be a substitute. "I know, and you're not. Just like Mia, if she ever comes home, wouldn't replace you."

DeJon seems to weigh the truth in Jack's words. Finally, he looks up at Jack and nods. "OK, just so we're clear."

"We're clear."

"We got any more of this gravy, Jack?"

Fifty-Eight

Sy.

At nine sharp, Sy is outside the hotel waiting for Joe, stomping around to keep his feet warm. When he drives up a few minutes later, it is in the requisite dirty pickup truck. Perched jauntily on Joe's head is the requisite cowboy hat. He laughs loudly when he sees the look Sy gives him. "You live here long enough, son," he says as Sy maneuvers in, "you take to the way of locals. Wasn't no way the locals were gonna put up with a Deputy all gussied up like a city slicker. Those words I quote from the great Big Daniel Rasmussen, my boss, the Sheriff of Chafee County. Amen."

"At least you don't have a gun rack," Sy concedes with a nod.

"Nah. That's in the wife's truck. Bloody coyotes'll bring down a calf if you don't get 'em first."

An hour or so later, Joe turns off onto a dirt road. They roll over a cattle guard that sets Sy's teeth on edge, reminding him of the pain in his shoulder, and Joe announces they've reached Myrna's aunt's ranch. "Lady's name is Trudy Mason. A real spitfire, if our phone conversation's any indication. Or maybe hearing her brother's name just pissed her off. I don't know. Just understand, she's not too fond of talking about him, and I didn't even get into the real reason you're here."

The ranch house is a one-story affair with an unpretentious, wrap-around porch. As the pickup drives up, a variety of ranch dogs run out to meet them, run beside the pickup the last few yards, barking up a storm.

"Get back, you dogs!" a voice calls out from the house. The door slams open and a rail-thin woman in denim and boots steps out. "Tango! Moon! Get outta here! Stupid dogs. You can get out," she calls to Joe and Sy. "They won't hurt you."

Joe steps right out, cuffs a few dogs fondly as he passes them on the way to the house. Sy takes it a bit more gingerly, finding the noses that shove for space in his crotch a little disconcerting. Wonders if there is something about his personal hygiene that makes dogs nuts.

"Boots! Get your nose outta there, you old pest!" the woman commands. Boots, however, doesn't choose to listen and Sy finds himself fending off about eighty pounds of excited canine as he makes his way to the porch.

"Come on in," the woman says and opens the door to let them into the house.

"Ms. Mason, I'm Deputy Doodle. This is Sy Colomanos, the one I told you about on the phone."

"You all can have a seat, I guess," she replies, waving them to worn country furniture. "I've got coffee on if you want some."

"That'll be fine," Sy tells her. "Thanks."

The thick, black brew finally in hand, the three sit looking at one another for a few minutes, taking a moment to size each other up.

"Well, I reckon you want to talk to me about my brother," Trudy eventually speaks.

"Well, not so much about your brother, but about your niece. About Myrna."

Trudy takes off her hat and drags a sun-and-work-roughened hand through her short-cropped hair. "Ah, hell, what's that girl gone and done now? Is the baby OK?"

"The baby?" Sy asks cautiously.

"The little twit went off and got herself knocked up in New York City. The daddy wouldn't have nothing to do with her or the baby so she came back here, came home to start fresh."

"Was this recent? I mean, how old's the baby?"

Trudy looks at him a moment. He can see her thinking, coming up with the questions. "Listen, Mr. Colomanos," she begins.

"Sy"

"OK, Sy, whyn't you tell me what's on your mind, why you want to know about my niece."

"Well, there's a possibility, and I mean a possibility only, that your niece got herself mixed up in something back in New York and if it is her, I've been looking for her for about four years."

"Mixed up in something? What kind of something?"

Sy shoots a look at Joe, how much to tell this woman?

Before he can answer, she speaks up, "Listen, Sy. You seem to be having some trouble wondering what to tell me. Let me tell you, I don't truck with nonsense. Ain't got no time for it, nor any interest in it. When my brother finally got caught, it was me that told the police where to find him. That sonofabitch had been hurting people and, family or no, there was no way I was gonna let him go on hurting people. If you're here to tell me my niece got herself into some kind of trouble, then you'd better tell me all of it. If I can, I'll help her. But, I'll help her through legal ways. I won't help her break the law or hurt people like her daddy did."

Sy believes her. The coffee goes cold while he lays it all out for her. She asks a few questions, he answers them. In the end, she believes it could be her niece he has been looking for.

"She was a troubled girl," Trudy tells them. "I didn't have any idea what her daddy'd been doing to her. Not until it was too late. But any idiot could see she had some serious issues. She had this little doll, a baby doll, that she carried around for years. The only thing she'd talk to. She'd have full-on conversations with that doll, but wouldn't say boo to any human being. It was down-right scary sometimes. She'd be talking to that doll, and then when you come up to her, her eyes'd go all flat and she'd fall mute. She couldn't go to school. Social Services came out a few times to check on her. We all figured she was a bit crazy, you know? And then her daddy took off and all of a sudden she started talking, like she'd been normal all along. It was the damndest thing but, hell, I was just glad she wasn't crazy anymore. It wasn't until a couple of years later that she told me about her daddy. Shortly after that, she took off and I didn't hear from her for years."

"When was the last time you did hear from her?" That from Joe.

"Oh, hell, when was it?" she muses. "I think that was the year Spark was born. Yeah, that's it. I remember her looking at the foal and commenting on how pretty he was. So, that'd make it about three, maybe four years ago."

"So, she came out here."

"Yeah. Came to 'visit', so she said, but that girl wasn't much good at visiting. I could tell it was more like to see if I had any money. Said she'd pay it off and all, but that never happened and I don't expect it too. Anyways, she showed up with her baby and, hell, she'd never had much anyway, so I gave her some. Thought it'd be the least I could do for her."

"Tell me about the baby," Sy prompts.

"Oh, she was a little thing, and quiet as a mouse. Never did make much noise. Maybe she's feeble-minded or something, but it didn't seem too natural for a baby that young to be so quiet. Not mute-like, just real quiet."

"Did Myrna tell you about her? About her father?"

"Well, now, and remember, this is what she told me and what I always believed, but she told me she'd been living in New York City and doing real well, selling flowers or something. Said she met a nice man, someone she had hopes of having a future with, but when she told him she was pregnant, he confessed to being married. He wanted her to get an abortion, but she wouldn't have anything to do with it. After the baby was born, she came back home to raise her by herself."

"She had a boyfriend? Did she tell you anything about

him? Maybe his name?" Sy has a sinking feeling in the pit of his stomach. He'd been so sure that this was the right lead, that he was finally, finally getting close. If having a boyfriend checks out, then it is more than likely that Myrna is not the kidnapper he is looking for.

"I'm sorry," she says finally. "I don't remember his name. She mentioned some high-powered man, but, personally, if you ask me, her story sounded a little off. I mean, what would a high-powered man want with Myrna? She wasn't much to look at, and not at all sociable, if you know what I mean. I kind of thought that maybe someone else was the father of the baby and she was too ashamed to admit it. Like, you know, maybe she got raped, or met up with the wrong kind of man. Anyways, I never did find out. She hasn't been back and she hasn't called."

"Do you know where she went? Where she was going?"

"She said she had a job in Boulder, working in a shop. It was one of those college shops, sell all that crap to druggie kids. I swear, I don't know where this world is going to, they let that kind of place do business. It's ruining this nation. Anyways, I tried to get her to stay here, help me work the ranch, give that baby a good home, but she wouldn't. Said she was just working in that shop until something better came along. So, she stayed a few days, I gave her some money, and she took off. We had a real nice time while she was here, though, and I've been wondering when she was gonna come back again. Do you think maybe something happened to her?"

"I don't know, ma'am," Sy says. "If it did, I'll find out and let you know. And, if it didn't, I'll let you know as soon as I find her."

"I'd appreciate that."

Sy.

Compared to the years of waiting, the rest is almost too easy. It takes Sy three days to track down the kid who had owned the head shop. He now owns a juice-and-snack bar in a local fitness club and he admits that there is a hell of a lot more money in health than there had been in drugs.

He pushes the photo Trudy had given to Sy back across the juice counter. “So, you really think Natalie stole that kid? That’s freaky,” Craig says. “But, yeah, there was something weird about her. Now that you mention it, that explains why she hardly ever answered when I said her name. You kind of had to get in her face and get her attention. Myrna. Yeah, that fits her better than Natalie. I felt sorry for her, man. It was obvious she was doing something, always looking strung out, but she kept that kid clean. Took real good care of her.”

“Why didn’t you call Social Services or something, if you thought she was doing drugs around the kid?”

Craig looks at him like he is from Mars. “Man, you just don’t get it, do you? You’re spending too much time in the clean world, all polished up. I’m talking about a whole different culture. There are kids out there, teenagers and younger, running the streets of America, homeless kids, drug addicts, kids that'll sell their bodies for a slice of bread. You think calling Social Services is gonna fix that? You gotta be kidding."

Sy's heard it all before. Always a reason for not stepping in. He feels the anger build and thinks about pounding the punk in his prissy little spandex outfit, his designer hair and perfect little teeth. He sighs. Hell, the kid is right. How was he supposed to know that turning the baby into Social Services might have brought her home four years sooner?

"Nah, you're right. There was nothing you could've done."

"Exactly my point. I did what I could. I gave her a job, paid her. Hell, half the time she was so wired, she wasn't worth having there anyway, but I liked the baby. So I kept Natalie, I mean Myrna, on, and brought in food for the baby. Probably did a helluva lot more good for her than Social Services."

"OK, I got ya. Now, you said she only worked for you for about six months. Any idea where she went after that? Where she is now?"

"Well fuck me blind!" the kid says. "You mean you don't know?" His eyes are wide as saucers.

"Know? Know what?"

"She's dead, man. OD'd about three years ago. Fried her brains out. That's when I started looking for something else to do, got outta that business."

Now it is Sy's turn to look incredulous. Dead? He's been looking for a corpse all these years? Well, no wonder no one could find her. "You're sure about that?" he asks, just to be sure.

"Sure. The cops came down to the shop, asked me a few questions. The lady from Social Services came down a couple of times, asked me a bunch more. Did she have any family? Where was she from? All that," he waves expressively.

"What'd you tell them?"

"Hey, I might've been selling paraphernalia to druggies, but I wasn't one myself, and didn't need any hassles from the cops. I told them what I knew. Natalie didn't have any family. In fact, until you just told me, I didn't even know her real name. I thought her name was Natalie Jones. At least, that's what she told me. And, yes, OK? I did pay her under the table, and I did have a nice long talk with Uncle Sam about that. Won't be doing that ever again, no way. So, no, I didn't know her Social Security number or anything else. She just showed up one day, looking for a job and she had this baby to take care of and I felt sorry for her. End of story."

"But she said she didn't have any family?"

"That's what she said, man, and I didn't press."

"What happened to the baby?"

"Lizzie? I don't know. That lady from Social Services or the Kid's Network, or whatever that place is, came and took her away. I heard she wasn't doing too good. Natalie, I mean Myrna'd, been dead for awhile before someone came and the kid had been in there all alone with the body, nothing to eat or drink. It was pretty messed up, let me tell you."

Yeah, it is pretty messed up. Sy rubs his eyes, feeling a headache coming on. Something to compete with the pain in his arm that doesn't seem to be going away any.

"So, Social Services took the kid."

"Yeah, yeah. I checked a couple of times, called them just to see how Lizzie was doing. They put her in foster care and eventually she got adopted by some local artist lady. I thought that was good, it all worked out, then."

Sy gives him a look.

"Well, yeah, but that was before I met you. Before I knew the kid was stolen in the first place." Craig pauses, shifts gears, "So, what're you gonna do?"

"I'm going to find the kid. See if it's really the one I'm looking for."

"Of course," Craig allows, "it'll be really fucked up for the artist lady. She thinks she's the kid's mom."

Sy hadn't thought of that. Now he does and he realizes the kid is probably right. It is going to be a major fuckfest all around.

Sy.

Sy takes the rest of the afternoon off. Finds himself a table at Mickey D's and has a strategy meeting with himself. Dora is still harping about going to the Feds, though now that he is so close, she isn't yammering quite as much. Still, they could come in and wrap this thing up by sundown. They'd be able to just go down to Social Services and get the records from around the time Myrna'd died. Hell, by tomorrow, the kid could be on a plane home.

But he doesn't get up to call the Feds. He takes another bite of cholesterol and waits for the pieces to settle in his mind.

He could go to Social Services, find out what agency deals with foster care up here, maybe ask them. But what are they going to do? Probably deny deny deny, make him get a court order to see their records. Maybe call in the FBI themselves. They'd have to, if there was a kidnapping involved. And what if this wasn't the baby? A lot of people would be hurt by this. Not to mention the artist lady who's been raising the kid as her own all these years. Yeah, that could screw you up. Like that case a few years ago, the mom putting the kid up for adoption without the dad's consent. Then the adoptive parents raising the kid for years until the courts made them give the kid to the biological dad. He remembers the news on that one. Heartbreak all around. Mostly for the kid. The kid was too young to understand why it couldn't be with Mom and Dad anymore, why it had to go live with a stranger.

Sy makes a decision and calls for opposition. There is none. Meeting concluded, he gets up and heads back to his hotel for a drink. Tomorrow will be soon enough to start looking for the artist lady.

A nice-looking woman looks up as Sy pushes the gallery's door open. She seems to look him up and down and he feels like an ass. Under his winter coat he wears a denim shirt, jeans and cowboy boots.

"Can I help you?" she asks pleasantly. When he meets her eyes, her smile broadens.

"Uh, yeah, I guess so. Is it OK if I just look around?" He asks, wondering if there's some sort of gallery protocol he should be following.

"Of course, go right ahead. Do you know Mar's work?"

"Well, no, I'm afraid not."

"Would you like me to tell you about her? Or maybe you'd prefer to look around first?"

"No. I mean, yes. I think I'll look around first."

The woman smiles at him and returns to her desk.

Sy nervously jams his hands in his pockets, afraid to touch anything. She'd picked up right away on the fact that he doesn't know a damn thing about art. Maybe he'll say he is looking for something for his wife and she appreciates art. Something special for her birthday or something.

He continues to meander through the gallery, going a lot

more slowly than he had planned. Hell, even he can tell it is good. A little weird with all those bright colors and not at all like what he is used to seeing, realistic stuff. But, it is good. Not that whole crappy, modern stuff that looks like a kindergartner on acid had done it, throwing the paint all around, stomping on it, gluing weird stuff to it and calling it art. These paintings make you feel something just looking at them.

He glances around. There are a lot of women artists in Boulder. Most do Native American kind of art, or flighty kinds of stuff with angels and apples and a lot of weird things all mixed together, shit he wouldn't want to look at day-in-and-day-out. Hell, shit he didn't want to look at even the first time around. So far, though, he hadn't found any artists with a daughter around Mia's age. Mar Delgado is one of the last on the list.

After wandering around the gallery, he finally makes it to the woman's desk. She smiles at him and asks him if he'd like to sit down, if she can get him a cup of coffee, or maybe a soft drink?

He finds himself sitting and accepting a Diet Pepsi, watches her as she sits in a chair near him, crosses her legs. Sees there isn't a ring on her finger. Listens to himself telling her he is looking for something special for his sister whose birthday is coming up.

"So, you've never heard of Mar? Do you know much about art, Mr...?"

"Colomanos. Sy Colomanos. Sy," he fumbles, reaching out his hand.

"Well, Sy, nice to meet you. I'm Diane Carmichael. Diane." And she puts her small hand into his big one and for some strange reason, he doesn't want to let go.

He looks at her and sees a faint blush creep up her neck. What is going on? When she pulls her hand from his, he feels the urge to reach for it, to hold it again.

Diane fumbles with her own glass of soda and clears her throat. "Um, yes, well, so, um, you want something for your sister?"

"My sister?" Sy asks, still caught in her eyes. They are alive, shining. He notices the crinkles around them and likes that they make him think of laughter. Warm bread and laughter.

"Yes. You said you were looking for something for your sister."

"Oh, yeah, my sister," Sy says. "It's her birthday soon and she likes art, so I thought..." Sy knows he sounds like a fool, a babbling parrot, but he is having trouble forming a distinct, coherent thought. What the hell is happening to him?

"Well, that's so nice of you!" Diane grins. "Do you know what she likes? There are so many different kinds and styles and, with a lot of people, you either love it or hate it."

"This kind. She likes this kind," Sy says, waving toward the walls.

Diane looks at him curiously. "This kind. I see," she says, though clearly she doesn't. "OK, then, Sy. How about if we walk around together and I'll tell you a little about the paintings, about Mar and the other artists whose work we show, about what the paintings mean to them. Then you can tell me which, if any, appeal to you for your sister. What's her name?"

"My sister? Dora. Her name's Dora." And Sy mentally kicks himself. Hard. Dora'd be pissed if she ever finds out he is calling her his sister.

"OK, then. You can tell me if you think Dora would like any of them."

As she takes him around the gallery, Sy feels himself falling more and more under her spell. She is tiny, only about chest-high and he bets that, even with his bum arm, he could lift her up, easy. Her voice is warm and friendly and he likes watching the changes come over her features as she explains the meaning of the different paintings. It is everything Sy can do to remain somewhat focused on what she is saying and not reach out to touch her.

"And this one is one of Mar's favorites, one of mine, too. It's called *Mother & Child*. As you can see, it's a lot different from her normal subject matter. Maybe that's why a lot of collectors have asked to buy it, sort of like Picasso's blue period which is all so different than his later work. Anyway, she always comes up with some excuse or other why she can't. I guess it's because it's the first painting she did of herself and her daughter."

That snaps Sy back to attention. "Her daughter?" he asks, his voice cracking.

Diane smiles warmly. "She has a daughter, the cutest little thing you ever saw. Her name's Lizzie. Just the light of Mar's life."

"Lizzie."

Diane looks at him quizzically. "Is something wrong? You've gone pale."

"Low blood sugar. I didn't realize how late it is. Um, do you think, I mean, would you like to have lunch with me? Can you leave?" Sy cannot believe the shit that is coming out of his own mouth. What the hell is he doing?

A grin spreads across Diane's face. "I'd love to. Let me just leave a note for Mar. She's taken Lizzie to the museum. I can put the sign on the front door. Why don't you have a seat while I take care of it?"

Sy can't sit. He stands in front of *Mother & Child*. Purples, pinks, white and gold. An interplay of light and color. A woman's face in the upper left corner, a baby's face in the lower right, both looking out from the canvas. The mother's eyes filled with what? Fear? Uncertainty? The child looking directly at you. A glimpse of the mother's hand cradling the baby. He can't tell what is going on. The mother is either passing the kid off or snatching it back. Something is going on.

"Mar painted that one when her daughter first came to her. Lizzie's adopted, you see. In any case, she was so afraid of losing her to another couple, or of maybe some family member coming forward to claim her. It was a pretty upsetting time for her. You can see it in the eyes. As much as I love this particular piece, I'd think Mar would want to sell it, it has some difficult memories for her. Well, shall we go?"

Mar.

Diane sits on the floor with Lizzie. They are playing some sort of card game that Diane had given up trying to understand twenty minutes ago. Lizzie keeps changing the rules, or making up new ones, or just following her whims. Mar is painting, taking advantage of the last usable rays of the sun. “So, what you’re telling me,” Mar muses as she bends her head critically and then applies a wisp of a Pthalo-Blue line to the Crimson Red-Medium Hue one already there, “is that you like this guy. A lot.”

“I didn’t say ‘a lot’,” Diane dissents.

“OK, so you didn’t say it, but that’s what you mean,” she looks up and grins at Diane.

“Well, yes.”

“I winned!” Lizzie shrieks, throwing the cards up in the air.

“You won, honey, won! I swear, though, I’ve never met a little girl who can win so much as you, Lizzie.”

“Wanna play again?” the little girl asks.

“Sure, sweetheart, I’ll play again.” Diane looks up at Mar and rolls her eyes.

“OK, but let’s play another way,” Lizzie says, and she begins to randomly put out cards. "You do this, Dee-Dee, when I give you a card." She shows Diane how to put her cards in a pile. Diane shrugs and follows directions.

"So when are you going to see him again?"

Diane blushes. "We're having dinner tonight," she admits.

"Tonight! Wow, lady, you sure do work fast!"

"For an old fart," Diane puts in.

"Hell, no. For anyone! So what are you doing here? Shouldn't you be home getting all dolled up?"

"I'm not getting all dolled up. He'll either like me the way I am, or he can go screw himself."

Mar smiles. Grabs a clean brush and dabs some more Yellow-Orange-Azo from the back of her hand.

"Besides," Diane continues, "he wants to meet you."

"Me? What for?"

"Well, first of all, because he likes your paintings, but mostly because you and Lizzie were about all we talked about at lunch."

Mar looks up.

"Don't give me that look! You're about all I ever talk about. You're as close to family as I've got. Now wait a minute, Lizzie, why'd you do that? You said I was supposed to put it in that pile."

"That was before. Now you put it in this pile!" The child's eyes threaten Diane to disagree.

"Oh. Well, then. I guess it goes in this pile. No, really, Mar, he was fascinated by your story."

"I don't have a story. I have a life. Besides, I don't know how comfortable I am with you talking about me to a stranger." She adds more Ultramarine-Blue, liking the way it complements a swath of Transparent-Red-Iron-Oxide nearby.

"First of all, Mar, he's a potential buyer, so of course he wants to know about you. And, second, I know you like your privacy. I didn't tell him anything that's not in your bio, or that hasn't been written up somewhere."

Mar puts down her brush and begins to rub dried paint off her hands. "OK, look, what time's Prince Charming coming to get you?" she asks, giving in.

"At seven," Diane smiles.

"Then let's go downstairs. I could use a glass of wine before I'm put on display."

Sixty-Three

Sy.

At seven o'clock sharp, Sy rings the doorbell to Mar's home and gallery. He is nervous as hell and is wondering what the fuck he is doing here in his too-tight boots, holding a bouquet of grocery store flowers, his heart jumping around in his chest. He is having a hard time convincing himself Diane is as special as she'd seemed at lunch when the door swings open.

"Hi. You must be Sy."

"And you're Mar." Jesus, it is kind of surreal. Here is that face in the painting, even down to the pointy, little chin, slanted eyes. Yeah, she'd got herself good, only now she is relaxed and grinning.

"The one, the only. Come on in. Diane'll be out in a minute but, if you're up to it, you can follow me to the kitchen and join me in a glass of wine." She looks at his Marlboro Man outfit. "Or beer, if you're more of a beer guy."

Sy grimaces. He is still wearing his new clothes. His feet have swelled up so much in his new boots that he hadn't been able to pull the damn things off. Probably'd have to amputate them off. "Uh, actually, wine would be great. Thanks."

As he limps after her through the dimly-lit gallery, he feels, rather than sees, the faces in the *Mother & Child* painting staring at him, weighing him, finding him lacking. He'd spent a good hour that afternoon telling himself he is an asshole, getting involved with someone on an investigation. Especially this one because, when it comes down to it, how the hell do you tell someone you're the guy who's gonna take away their kid – or their grandkid, which is how Diane acts about Lizzie – fuck up their life?

"I have a bottle of Merlot open," Mar calls over her shoulder, "but there's just about every color, kind, flavor, whatever, in the wine cooler. What's your choice?"

"Merlot'd be great," he says and follows her into one of the largest kitchens he's ever been in. He lets out a low whistle of appreciation as he takes it all in, knowing he doesn't know a damn thing about what most of the gadgets are about, but appreciating that they look so purposeful. He glances over at the bay windows and almost has a heart attack on the spot. Sitting in the corner, her hands and face covered with ketchup, is Lindsey. A small Lindsey, of course, but Lindsey. He wants to weep.

"OK, sugar," Mar says, heading back to her daughter, "thanks for waiting. You can have your hot dog back now." She takes a plate from the counter and lays it back in front of her little girl. "Lizzie, say hi to Sy. He's a friend of Dee-Dee's. Sy, meet my daughter, Lizzie."

"Hi, Sy! Mama, that's a rhythm."

"A rhyme, little smarty. You're right. It rhymes." She turns to Sy, "Have a seat while I get the wine. She's mostly over the stage of throwing food, so you should be safe." At this, Lizzie giggles and makes to toss a few slices of hot dog in Sy's direction. A stern "Lizzie" puts an end to that, but the giggles continue.

"Hi, there, Lizzie. I've heard a lot about you."

"I'm four. Do you want some hot dog?" she asks, offering him a ketchup-covered fistful.

"Uh, no, thank you. But you go ahead. It looks good."

"I like hot dog," she says and grins, her little white teeth shining through the ketchup mess. She pops another slice into her mouth and chews noisily.

"Diane should be down in a few minutes," Mar says as she takes a glass down from a cabinet and clinks it on the counter. "She's just gone upstairs to tidy up."

Sy is still staring at the Mini Me Lindsey. He is having a difficult time breathing as the enormity of the moment dawns on him.

"Here you go," Mar tells him, placing a glass of Merlot in front of him. "Cheers."

"Cheers," Sy agrees.

Sixty-Four

Jack.

When the call comes, Jack is totally unprepared for it. He can think of no way to deal with the possibility – and Sy had pointed out that it is still only a possibility – that his daughter is alive and well, is a happy little girl living in Colorado. He has imagined so many horrible deaths for her, has wondered which day he'd wake up to the news that her remains have been found in some shallow grave. He has imagined so many horrible lives for her, starving out a living in a grungy trailer park with abusive captors, forced into prostitution at an early age by drug-crazed pedophiles, sold into slavery in the Middle East. Never had he thought that she could be happy and healthy. And now, as he sits at his desk in Manhattan, looking out over the skyscrapers, he wonders about that.

Jack moves to his favorite spot by the windows and looks out over New York. It is snowing again, mean wet flakes falling heavily from a steel gray sky. Mia would be four and a half now. He tries to picture John's kids at four-and-a-half, picture how tall they'd been, and can't. Would she be in school? Taking dance classes? Would she be like Lindsey, a tomboy? Preferring to climb trees than play with dolls? Would she run outside at the first sign of snow, stay there until her lips are blue and she is dragged, arguing, inside? He's lost so much, missed so much, time he will never get back. Time he can never get back.

Jack is lost in a river of doubt, the skin around his eyes burning and throbbing, when Elena sticks her head in the office. "Jack? Your flight leaves in four hours and your friend, John, is on the phone."

Jack.

By the time the plane lands in Denver and he retrieves his bag, Jack is a little rocky. Three scotches and too much adrenaline haven't made for a good mix. He falls asleep as soon as he buckles himself into the rental car Sy drives.

"You, my friend, need some food. Hell, I could use some carbs, myself. Let's go," Sy pulls into the parking of a fast food restaurant.

As they get out of the car, Jack stops and looks at Sy. "What the hell? You're wearing cowboy boots."

Sy grins sheepishly. "I don't know," he says. "It's something about the place."

"But, boots?"

"I know."

When they are seated, Jack stares glumly down at his burgers. "I feel like crap," he says.

"Yeah, well, eat then. It's not gourmet, but there's no hangover cholesterol can't kill."

"Yeah, thanks, Sy."

They eat in silence, Sy waiting for Jack's attention, Jack waiting for his stomach to settle. "You know, after all this time, I'm kind of at a loss about this," Jack finally admits.

"No wonder there. This is a helluva thing. I'm still in shock myself."

"OK, so tell me again about how you found her."

As they eat their burgers and fries, Sy retells the story, adding more details than those he'd given Jack on the phone.

"So what do we do now?" Jack finally asks.

"Like I told you, this might not be her. From everything I've got, I'd say it is, but the big question is, how're we gonna prove it? I mean, what if it's not her? I've been here more than a week. I've been around these people. They're nice people, some of the nicest people I've ever met. I don't think we can just announce this is your kid and you're taking her. I mean, it's gonna kill this woman, Mar. I think, before you say anything, we gotta be sure."

"Did you go to Child Welfare, Social Services, whatever, pull the records?"

"Nah, I was gonna do it. Then, I got to thinking that what if they tip this woman off and she runs with the kid? Anyways, I'm glad I didn't. Turns out the lady that runs the agency here is Mar's best friend. She'd'a told her for sure."

"It's going to come out pretty soon anyway."

"Course it is, and then we're gonna need proof."

"What, like DNA testing?"

"Well, yeah, sure, eventually. But first, why don't you come out, meet them, see what you think? Maybe you'll look at it different, tell me I'm way off-base."

"But why don't we just do DNA now and get it over with? I've waited a long time for this, Sy."

"And you can wait a little longer. Look, Jack, you can't just go in and fuck up these people's lives like that. What if you get this mother all crazy and everything, and it's not her?"

"What if it is her? Don't I have some rights?"

"Jack, all I'm saying is, go out, meet these people, see the girl, get a feel for it. Hell, talk to the mother and hear the story yourself about how she adopted this kid. Then, if you think I'm on the right track, we take it to the next level."

Mar.

"You're not having lunch with Sy? That's the first time this week," Mar teases. She plops down into one of the chairs in the gallery. Picasso heaves down at her feet and spreads out like a frog. "You're fat, dog. We have got to put this tub on a diet. Yes, you," she says, when Picasso gives her a hurt look.

"His nephew's coming in from New York and he had to pick him up. And the dog's fat because Lizzie keeps feeding her. Haven't you noticed that she's not dropping food out of clumsiness, she's doing it on purpose?"

"Yeah, I saw. This morning a whole pancake disappeared, syrup and all. I turned around for just a second and when I turned back, gone. At first I thought Lizzie had eaten it, but there she was, grinning, and there was El Tubbo Lardo under the table, smacking her lips."

Diane smiles. "You should take her running. It'd do you both good."

"I know, I know. But honestly? I'd rather eat dirt. Anyway, what's up down here?"

"Things are going well. Very well, actually. I'm seriously thinking we should look into more space soon, though." Several months ago, Mar had decided to expand the gallery to include the works of potters, sculptors, metal and glass workers and other assorted artists from around the country. The gallery is becoming the in place for interior designers to bring their clients and their current location is too small for the volume they are doing.

"I hate that," Mar says. "Who's stupid idea was it to expand anyway?"

"Yours."

"Well then, fire me. It was a stupid idea." She likes having her studio, home and the gallery all in one building and doesn't want the hassle of having to drive somewhere to see her paintings or to meet with Diane.

"We could keep the majority of your paintings here and open another location for the rest."

"No, no, no, that wasn't the point. Besides, I want to get more artists involved anyway, and for that, we'll need more space. It's just that it's been so cozy here and I hate change."

"Well, you know what they say, change is good. Besides, you can have a studio at the new gallery, too. You spend too much time in this house anyway."

"Don't give me that look."

"I will give it to you. Mar, you have got to get out more. Hell, you haven't gone on a date in months."

"Just because you're in love, doesn't mean we all have to run around like love-sick fools."

"I am not in love. People my age don't fall in love," Diane says primly.

"Oh, bullshit. I can spot it a mile away. It's all I ever hear anymore. 'Sy this' and 'Sy that'. In just a week, you're totally head over heels."

"Well, when it hits, it hits. But, back to you..."

"Unh-uh. You're not getting away that easy. Come on, fess up. Have you done the dirty deed yet?"

"Why, Miss Mar, I did not raise you to talk to me that way."

"You did!"

Diane blushes and Mar lets out a whoop of laughter. "You slept with him! My god, Diane, what if he has AIDS or something?"

"Don't get all prudish on me, young woman. At my age, we don't waste time anymore. But, for clarification, we have not slept together. Yet."

"Yet. Wow!" Mar grins. "So, when does Wonderboy get back?"

Diane checks her watch. "He should be here soon. He said he's going to stop by on the way to the hotel. His nephew's a fan and wants to see the gallery."

"A fan? From New York? That's a reach."

"Now stop it right there. You are too famous. A fan from New York isn't a big thing."

"What's he in town for?"

"I don't know. Business of some sort. He's a lawyer, I think. I don't know, maybe it's pleasure."

Mar puts her hands on her thighs and pushes up. "OK, enough slacking. I've got to get back upstairs, just wanted to check on you. Come on, Fats Galore, time to move." The dog only snarfs and closes her eyes again. "Fine, have it your way. Some loyal companion you are."

"You'll come down when Sy gets here? Meet his nephew?"

"For you, darling, anything." And with that, Mar blows her a kiss and heads back to the studio.

Sixty-Seven

Jack.

After meeting Diane, Jack had spent a good fifteen minutes in the gallery. Even with his limited knowledge, he can tell that Mar Delgado is the real thing. She paints sea scapes, or sea life, that is. Some of the sea life lives under the ocean, while others live in dusty canyons and deserts. It is strange, but arresting. Without understanding why or how, Jack acknowledges that her quirkiness works. When he gets to *Mother & Child*, his stomach lurches so strongly he has to take a deep breath to keep from tossing his lunch all over Diane's desk.

"How much is it?" he asks Diane, his voice cracking with emotion.

Diane smiles quietly. "I'm sorry, but I don't think that one's for sale."

He looks at her, dismayed, "Why not?"

"It's one of Mar's favorites. Quite a few people have made offers for it over the years, but she always makes up excuses why she can't part with it. I could ask, but I'm sure her answer will be the same. If you'd like a reproduction, I can find out if anyone is willing to sell one."

"Why? Can't you print more?"

"No, not the giclees. Mar only does thirty of each and

they were all sold years ago. It's a remarkable painting, and it's something a lot of parents, especially, can relate to, the needing to let go of your child, but the desperate urge to keep it close. Of course, Mar's story is a little different. Do you have children?" she asks.

"Uh, no. No, I don't, but I guess you don't need to be a parent to feel its pull," Jack answers lamely. He glances at Sy, who shrugs. They'd agreed to present Jack as his nephew, a bachelor attorney from New York, in case Mar remembers all the press from when the baby had been kidnapped and puts it all together. Sy had introduced him using his mother's maiden name. Hence, he is now Jack Rollins.

"Yes, that's true," Diane agrees. "In any case, I'll ask Mar, but I wouldn't get your hopes up. If you decide to look into a reproduction, it'll most likely take a couple of days to track one down. Of course, there are prints available..." she lets her voice trail off.

"Uh, no, no thank you," Jack replies, looking up at the painting. "There's something very compelling about this one. I'd really like the original."

Diane laughs gently, as if he's told a joke. "Well," she changes the subject, "Mar doesn't seem to be answering upstairs, but she did say she'd like to say hello to you, Sy, when you got here, so I guess we can go up."

Diane precedes them into the studio. Stepping aside, she allows Jack his first glimpse of Mar. In New York, where the artists he's met, or even heard of, are so much about attitude, style and image, it surprises him that she looks so normal – at least from the back. She is smallish, at least compared to Caroline, and is tucked into a pair of form-fitting, hip-hugging jeans and a man's undershirt. And she is dancing, actually dancing, to the music, splashing paint here and there on a large canvas positioned on an enormous easel. He smiles unconsciously.

"Uh, Mar?" Diane calls, competing with the sound of the music. "Mar?"

When Mar doesn't answer, Diane walks over to the stereo

and hits the mute button.

"Oh, shit!" Mar jumps, the brush sailing out of her hand. "Crap! You scared the hell out of me!"

"I'm sorry, but you didn't hear me shouting at you," Diane tells her.

"Sorry, I was just..." her voice trails off as she notices Sy and Jack. "Wow," she blurts out and then blushes furiously. "Oh, god, I'm sorry, uh, that just came out." She begins to look around for her brush, obviously embarrassed.

Jack laughs out loud. She is not at all what he'd imagined when Sy had said "foster mom." He'd thought large as a bus stop, faded muumuus and cigarette-stained fingers. Not this, not this woman with the paint streaks in her unruly auburn hair and a body that stretches at the fabric of a man's imagination. "I'm sorry if we surprised you," he holds out his hand. "I'm Jack, Sy's, uh, nephew. Diane thought it'd be OK if we came up."

"No, no, that's OK. I was just, uh, painting and you startled me, that's all," she holds out her own hand and Jack is completely unprepared for the jolt that shoots up his arm at her touch.

Mar snatches her hand back. "Static," she supplies lamely, shaking off its effects.

Jack looks down at his hand, wondering what had just happened.

"Oh, gosh, I'm sorry," Mar stammers and snatches his hand, turns it over and shows him the paint she's smeared all over his palm. "Let me get you a towel to wipe it off."

"It's OK." Jack takes the paper towel she offers him and begins rubbing at the paint, his fingers still tingling.

"I'm sorry, I just don't think when I'm painting. I kind of get messy." She holds up her hands, the backs of which are covered in paint swatches.

"I guess I deserve it after barging in on you while you're working."

Mar smiles, "I'll have to put a sign up – Caution, Artist at Work, Enter at Your Own Risk."

“Who’d have thought artists are dangerous to society?” Jack says and mentally kicks himself at the triteness of the comment.

“Oh, hi, Sy,” Mar turns away. “I’m sorry, I didn’t notice you there. How are you?”

“Good. Listen, I’m sorry, we didn’t mean to interrupt you. It’s just that Jack wanted to meet you.”

“I like your work,” Jack puts in. “Diane said that *Mother & Child* isn’t available, though.”

“Oh, well, that, unh-uh.” She waves vaguely and then changes the subject. “So! How do you like Colorado?”

“I haven’t seen much of it yet.”

“Right. Of course not.”

“Listen, Mar, we’ve got to go get Jack checked into the hotel and everything,” Sy says. “But how’d you like to join us for dinner?”

“But, um, don’t you guys want to catch up?” she asks Sy, but her eyes are on Jack.

“No, not at all,” Jack jumps in. “We’d love to have dinner with you and Diane.”

Mar picks up her cell phone, flips it over and looks at the time.

As if reading her mind, Sy suggests, “Why don’t you bring Lizzie? We can go early.”

Mar smiles up at him. “OK, if you’re sure you two don’t want to be alone, then we’d love to.”

“Great,” Jack says. “That’ll be great.”

Sixty-Eight

Jack.

Jack stares across the table at Mar. Her head is bent close to Lizzie's and she is examining a crayon drawing the little girl has done. "That's a beautiful flower, honey. I like the house, too. Shall we show Jack? Here, Jack, look." She passes the paper across the table to him.

Jack really has no point of comparison for a four-year-old's art. As far as he can tell, though, there's a house and a flower. He looks up and smiles. "It's beautiful, Lizzie."

"It's for you. It's a flower and a house for you," the little girl tells him matter-of-factly, her sweet little girl's voice warming his heart. "I can draw you a dog, too, if you want."

"I'd love it. Thank you."

"Pays stay mean or lemony good?"

"Payne's Grey," Mar smiles at Lizzie and then explains to Jack, "Colors. She's asking if you want a mean, old, ugly dog – in Payne's Grey – or a happy dog in yellow."

"Oh."

"She feels colors."

As this seems to make perfect sense to Mar, Jack turns back to Lizzie. "A happy, lemony dog would be great," he says.

Lizzie screws up her face in disgust. "Pains stay are funner."

"Oh, OK. Then how about a mean dog, instead?"

Lizzie sets the gray crayon down with a drawn out sigh and reaches for the yellow. "That's OK," she says, "some people are scared of mean dogs."

As Lizzie returns to her drawing, Mar takes a sip of her wine, a smile curving at her lips. "She likes you."

"She's beautiful."

Mar ruffles Lizzie's hair and grins. "She is, isn't she? And smart. Aren't you, pumpkin?"

"I can count to a bazillion," Lizzie tells Jack. "Wanna hear me? One, two, three, four, five, six, seven, eight, nine, ten, cetera, cetera, a bazillion!"

As if he is outside of his own body, Jack sees himself laughing, sees the little girl grinning across the table at him, the dimple in her right cheek deepening as her smile spreads across tiny white teeth. And, as he watches, a woman's head bends into the scene as she leans in to kiss the little girl's cheek. As the woman straightens up, her blond hair parting from her face, he catches his breath, watches as Lindsey looks across at him, pride gleaming in her eyes. He sees his own hand lift to stroke her cheek, his lips murmur I *love you, I've missed you.*

"Jack? Jack?" her smile is replaced by concern and concern by fear as she pulls back from him.

"Jack!" Sy's voice cuts through the fog and in an instant Jack is back in his own body and Lindsey's face melts into Mar Delgado's. A sharp pain punches through Jack's chest and he pushes away from the table and staggers to his feet.

"Jack, are you alright?" Sy moves to Jack's side.

"Air. I need air," Jack gasps, pushing Sy away in his hurry to get outside.

Jack.

Jack sits in the dark. He'd fucked up. He never should have gone through with it this way. Christ. He should have taken a few more days to figure out how to handle this better, called Shaheen and let him handle it. What was he thinking, rushing out here. For what? To look at some little girl and say, 'yeah, she's mine, thanks for taking care of her all these years, but we've got to go now?'

But that's what it comes down to, isn't it? At some point, after the DNA tests are done, he'll have to take her, get on a plane and go home. Will she think of it as home? He doubts it. That little girl's world is all about Mommy, about Mar. And vice-versa. No way is she going to want to leave the only mother she's ever known.

FUCK! He throws his empty tumbler across the room. The satisfying shattering of glass doesn't come. Instead, the glass rolls off the bed and thunks impotently onto the floor.

Jack puts his head in his hands and tries to think. He should never have come here, should never have met them, seen them together as a family. As a lawyer, he should have known that. You make your clients keep their distance, keep it as clean as possible. You send the lawyers in to do the dirty work, mess up people's lives. If he'd been smart about it, he'd've hired a local attorney to get the court order for the tests, waited it out in New York, and then flown in just to pick up Lizzie. Mia.

He laughs at himself in the dark. Yeah. That's clean. That's easy. For him. What about Lizzie? He can't even think of her as Mia anymore. What about Mar? His thoughts return to the look of horror on her face as he'd reached for her in the restaurant. Jack gets up to fix himself another drink.

Twenty minutes later, Jack isn't surprised when there is a knock on his door. In fact, he is glad for the respite from his own mad thoughts. He opens it and lets Sy in.

"How're you feeling?" Sy asks. "I been calling, but your phone's shut off and the room phone's been busy."

"I took it off the hook. I needed some time alone."

Sy takes the beer Jack offers him and sits on the suite's sofa. "It's her, isn't it?"

Jack picks up his drink and sighs heavily, "Yeah, it's her."

"So why are you so depressed?"

"Because I get it. I get what you said about it not being so easy as coming in and picking up my daughter. I mean, if she'd still been with the kidnapper, hell yeah, with guns blazing. But Mar? This is going to kill her."

"Uh-huh."

Jack gets up and starts pacing. "Help me out here, Sy. I'm at a major fucking loss. What am I going to say to her? Lizzie? That woman you've been calling Mommy all these years? Well, she isn't really your mommy after all, so let's go home." He shakes his head.

"You don't think Mar'd move to New York? Isn't that an option?"

Jack shakes his head, "No, I think she'd do it. From what I saw tonight, I think she'd walk on water for Lizzie."

"So?"

"So all these years I'm thinking when we find her, she'll come home and she'll be as happy to be with me as I am with her. Only now, I see that's not going to happen. I take her home and she's going to hate me."

Jack drops into a chair across from Sy, but the nervous energy can't keep him there. He pops back up and resumes pacing. "And what about Mar? How do you think she's going to react?"

"She's gonna lose it."

"Exactly. And she's going to get lawyers and she's going to fight me every step of the way. No way is she giving up Lizzie without a fight."

"But, shit, Jack, she's not stupid. You gotta talk to her."

"I don't know. Don't you see? The whole problem with this is that I'm too close and it's all too fucked up. I spent four years wanting to find that woman, Myrna? Natalie? Whatever. I spent four years wanting to find her and rip her fucking head off. Now I'm here and this mom person, this really nice lady who has no fucking idea I'm her worst goddamned nightmare, is sitting at home with my daughter not knowing her whole world's about to blow apart."

"Yeah, I get that."

"Fuck you, Sy."

"No, I mean, that's what I've been tellin' you."

Jack rounds on him. "You know what? This is bullshit. This is all bullshit. That little girl? She's my daughter. Mine. I'm sorry for Mar Delgado, but Mia is my daughter, and I really think the biggest fucking problem with this whole thing is that I'm here trying to figure out a way to be nice and I'm the one who was wronged. I'm the one whose wife was killed. I'm the one whose daughter was kidnapped. I'm the one who's had to live with nightmares every fucking night for the past four years, and now I'm gonna be the bad guy. How's that for justice?"

"Jack..."

"No, Sy. No fucking way. That's it. I'm going home. I'm getting a lawyer and I'm going home. Ms. Delgado'll just have to deal with it. I did."

"So now she's Ms. Delgado."

"Back off, Sy."

"Just see her, for Christ's sake."

"No."

"Just give her a chance. Maybe you can work things out."

"No."

"Jack, come on. What can it hurt? Just talk to the lady."

"No, Sy. No."

"Please? Come on. What can it hurt? Maybe you guys can work it out together."

"I don't think so."

"So it won't hurt to try, will it? She's your daughter, right? You can always get a lawyer later."

Jack smacks his hand on the window. If anything, he feels worse now than he had in the past four years. All that time, Mia'd been only a dream. Now she is a gorgeous little girl named Lizzie. He takes a deep breath and lets it out. "Fine. Fine. I'll talk to her."

Mar.

"No."

"Mar."

"Don't 'Mar' me, Diane. I said no and I mean no. The guy's a creep."

"He had jet lag, he was sick."

"You're damn right he was sick. Sicko is more like it. Did you see the way he was staring at Lizzie all night? And then how he touched me? That was sick."

"Come on, Mar. Before that, you thought he was a really nice guy. I mean, what was that yesterday when you shook his hand? You were interested in him."

"I wasn't."

"You were. You said so. You said you think he's gorgeous and funny."

"That was before I knew he was a creep."

"Honey, please."

Mar throws some Payne's Grey onto the canvas and instantly regrets it. "Christ," she mutters, and begins scraping it off before it has a chance to dry.

"Mar," Diane's voice turns pleading.

"I'm not listening."

"Please."

"That's not fair."

"I never ask for anything."

"Shit!" Mar stamps her foot and slams the palette knife onto her worktable. "This is so not fair."

"I know, but..."

"Stop it! Fine, we'll go, but if that freak so much as looks at me weird or does anything to Lizzie, we are so out of there."

Diane nods, "I hear you."

"I mean it. I'm only doing this for you."

"Thank you, sweetheart."

Mar glares at her, realizing she's been played. "Shit!" she repeats and stomps down the stairs to change for a day of sightseeing.

Seventy-One

Mar.

Lizzie fell asleep on the drive home. Contrary to Mar's expectations, it had turned out to be a fun day that had included lunch, sightseeing and then dinner. Jack had been on his best behavior and Mar had slowly warmed to him, had been touched by how easily Lizzie had taken to him.

When they pull into Mar's driveway, it is the most natural thing in the world for Jack to offer to carry her from the car. "Be careful to bend your knees. It's the weirdest thing, but when she's asleep, she weighs so much more. There, now, jump her up. She'll put her legs around you."

And she does. Instinctively, Lizzie wraps her little legs around Jack's waist and buries her face in his neck.

Mar, turning from closing the car door, has to catch her breath. Something about the sight of Jack holding Lizzie causes her world to shift a few degrees. She blinks, and it is gone. She'll have time to think about it later, figure out what she was seeing.

Mar leads the way through the curtain of pearls and turns on the lava lamp before asking Jack to put the little girl on the bed. He does so and laughs gently when the water bed begins to rock her.

"Won't she wake up?" he asks as the waves rise and fall.

"No. When she's out, she's out." Mar smiles. She'd been wrong about him. Today he'd been wonderful. Kind and attentive. She offers him a seat in the gliding chair while she gets Lizzie ready for bed.

"Wow," Jack says looking around the room. "This is pretty incredible."

Mar straightens, pajamas in hand and looks around the room. The undulating light from the lava lamp makes the room come alive, lends life to the sea creatures painted on the four walls and the ceiling. "I really didn't want to paint it. At the time, I kind of had a phobia about the ocean."

"Really? It all looks so real."

"It's what I used to paint. My husband died in a diving accident," Mar begins as she undresses Lizzie. "Well, anyway, for awhile after that, I didn't want to paint the ocean. This," she waves her arm to indicate the room, "kind of put me back on track."

"It's beautiful. I really like Lizzie on the back of that dolphin."

Mar turns her head and smiles at the image. "That's my favorite, too. I can't believe how much she's grown since then, though. I don't know what I'll do if she ever wants to change this room. I'll have to take that wall down and find a way to frame it."

"I can't imagine anyone ever wanting to change this room. It has to be the coolest kid's room ever."

Mar tugs Lizzie's pajama bottoms up and then pulls the covers up over her. Reaching for Boosie, she tucks the blanket in next to Lizzie, who instinctively reaches for it. After tucking a stray hair behind Lizzie's perfect seashell ear, Mar bends to kiss her daughter. "Dream well," she whispers.

She straightens and turns to Jack, "Coffee? A glass of wine?" she asks. And then, "Are you OK?"

In the murky light, Jack looks spooked, but then the goo in the lava lamp shifts and Mar sees that it was only a trick of light.

Jack pushes up out of the glider. "All good," he says and smiles.

Mar is again struck by his good looks. When he smiles like that, a thrill runs up her spine and buzzes around inside of her. She stares at him, enraptured. There is something so familiar about him, so compelling, that she can't take her eyes off of him. "I'm sorry I'm staring," she says as soon as she realizes that she has indeed been staring at him. "You remind me of someone."

"Who?" Jack asks.

"I don't know," she says. "I've been trying to figure it out, but I don't have a clue." Finally, she pulls her eyes away from him and heads through the pearl curtain. "Anyway, would you like a glass of wine? Or maybe some coffee?"

"I really should be going."

Mar laughs. "Got a blowtorch? That's what it's going to take to peel Sy away from Diane,"she says, referring to the other couple who'd headed over to Diane's house.

"Well then, sure," he says, "a glass of wine would be great."

Mar reaches in and turns on the kitchen lights. As the lights come up and Joaquin steps out to greet them, Jack lets out a sound of surprise. "Sorry," she says, "I should have warned you."

"Is that your husband?" Jack asks.

"Yes," Mar says softly. "That's Joaquin."

"He was a chef?" Jack asks.

"Yeah," Mar nods. "He was going to open a restaurant in the Keys, in Florida, when..." her voice trails off. "Anyway," she continues, "he was killed and he never did get to open that restaurant."

Jack's eyes find hers. "I'm sorry, Mar."

She nods. "Me, too." She lets out a large sigh and then turns back to the kitchen. "I've got Pinot Noir, Merlot, Cabernet, Chardonnay, any preference?"

Jack whistles softly. "Wow."

Mar turns to find him taking in the kitchen. "I know, it's great, isn't it? The guy I bought it from thought of himself as a kind of Emeril. Bam!" She shakes her head ruefully, "Not much 'Bamming!' going on since I got it. Oh! That didn't come out right, did it?"

Jack laughs, "No, I think it came out just fine."

"Sorry. It's a thing I do, open mouth, insert foot. So, to definitely change the subject, what would you like? I think I've also got a Zinfandel and possibly a Pinot Grigio. Your choice."

"Impressive."

"It comes with the territory. The previous owner was also a wine fanatic and he left that huge cooler. It looks stupid empty, so I keep it filled. Look, he has a pantry just for the reds." She opens a door. "Well, there you are, Goofball. I was getting worried."

Picasso stretches and shakes herself off. Catching sight of Jack, she moves to him and sticks her nose deep in his crotch. "Picasso, no! God, I'm sorry, she has no shame." Mar grabs the dog by the collar and pulls her back. "Now, sit! Be nice." The dog sits for a second and then runs to the back door and sits again. "OK, that's better. Out you go." Mar opens the door and Picasso takes off. "I'm sorry," she repeats. "Do you have a dog?"

"No, not in the city. I always had dogs growing up, though."

"Oh. Well, I can't imagine not having one. When Lizzie gets a little bigger, we might get another one. We've certainly got the space. Now what have you decided? How about a Merlot? I've got this Blackstone from Napa that's delicious."

"Sounds great. Would you like me to open it?"

"Sure, the opener's over behind you. No, to the left. There." She brings two glasses over to the island and allows him to pour. "We can take these upstairs to the family room or, if you prefer, out onto the porch. The fire pit out there keeps it pretty warm and I have a couple of Adirondack chairs that are real cozy."

"Then the porch it is. What about Lizzie, though? Will she be OK?"

"She's fine. I'll just take this," Mar shows him the baby monitor she has in her pocket and leads him to the back door.

Seventy-Two

Mar.

The fire catches quickly and puts out enough heat to keep them warm. Jack settles into a chair and Mar hands him a heavy down blanket to tuck around himself.

"My god, I've never seen so many stars before," Jack says.

"That's Lizzie's star," Mar points out.

"That's the North Star."

"I know, but it's also Lizzie's star. She wanted one and that's the one we chose for her. Whenever we come out here at night, she wants to find her star."

"She's beautiful."

"Isn't she? I still can't believe how lucky I am."

"She's adopted?"

"Yeah," Mar smiles proudly as she tells him how it had all happened.

"She's lucky to have you."

Mar laughs, "No, I'm lucky to have her. I had no clue what I was doing, but she was patient enough until we got it right."

They are companionably silent for a time, sipping their wine and watching the heavens. "Oh, look," Mar points out a shooting star. "Make a wish."

"I'd forgotten what a real nighttime sky looks like. New

York insulates you and you forget that there is the rest of the world beyond its borders."

"I don't know how you live there," Mar says. "It's too busy, too loud, too impersonal for me."

"You're right," Jack agrees after a moment. "I guess I don't think about it anymore, but when I first got there, I hated it."

"How'd you end up there?"

"I was recruited for a job out of law school. And, my best friend lives there. He was always telling me how much I'd love it." Jack shrugs, "I guess I believed him."

"Where's home for you?"

"Ohio. I grew up on a farm there."

"You grew up on a farm? You don't seem farmer-ish."

"Oh, I can probably still milk a cow and plow a field."

"It's funny how you see someone in one setting and think you know all about them," Mar wraps her arms around her legs and lays her head on her knees. "I'm not from here. Growing up, I would never have imagined I'd end up here. Or anywhere, really, other than the Keys."

"A Florida girl."

"Well, the Keys. The rest of the state is something else."

"Will you ever go back?"

Mar uncurls herself and reaches for her wine. "I don't know. A few years ago I'd have said that I'd never go back, but my dad is getting on. He says he wants to move here, to be near me and Lizzie, but I can't imagine him anywhere but the Keys. I know he would move here, but he'd be miserable."

Mar picks up the bottle and tops off their glasses. "There," she says, pointing, "another shooting star."

Jack nods and toasts the star.

After a while, Mar says, "I know you don't know me, but is everything OK?"

Jack pulls his eyes from the sky and looks at her. "What do you mean?"

"Upstairs, earlier, you seemed upset. Is there something I can do?"

Jack shakes his head, no, and his eyes break away from

hers.

"I'm a real good listener. If you want to talk."

"No. Thanks, but I'm fine. Anyway, I should go find Sy." But he doesn't get up.

"I was married," Jack finally says. "My wife wanted, no, we wanted, children so badly and Lizzie, she reminds me of her. That dimple, her hair."

Mar sits quietly so as not to distract him. When he finally speaks again, his voice is raw. "She died. She was killed. In an accident. In a car accident. It's still..." he shakes his head.

"I know," Mar smiles sadly. "I know. I'm sorry"

They sit in silence then, watching the fire spark, sipping their wine, their thoughts all their own, but Mar is aware of a connection of sorts that runs like a current between them.

Jack turns to look at Mar. "Sy told me. About your husband."

"Did he now?" Mar asks, but she doesn't feel her usual bitterness. "Diane must have told him. It's a story, you know? I mean, it's unusual, probably pretty interesting if it didn't happen to you."

"I'm sorry. I shouldn't have brought it up."

"No, it's OK." She shifts in her chair so she is turned to him. "It's strange, you know? People hear about it and all of a sudden I'm the woman whose husband got eaten by sharks on their honeymoon. It's almost like I'm not me anymore. I'm this person to be pitied and talked about."

Jack nods, "As if the tragedy defines you."

"Exactly," Mar smiles. "Exactly. See? You understand."

They fall back into silence, enjoying the stars, the occasional meteor speeding across the heavens, the warmth of the fire.

"He also told me about Max," Jack tells her.

"Max?"

"God, here I go again. I'm sorry. I just, Sy said. No, I'm sorry. I didn't think."

Mar's fingernails dig into her palms. She takes a deep breath and lets it out slowly.

"I'm sorry," he repeats. "Again."

"It's one of those nights, isn't it?" Mar whispers. "Like at camp? When you're young and you share your deepest, darkest secrets with these people in your tent because in the moment it seems like the night will go on forever and you have to get it off your chest."

"You don't have to say anything."

"No, I mean, it's like that. You spill your guts thinking these people understand me and we'll be best friends forever and then the next morning you hate yourself and you spend the next two weeks avoiding them and being petrified they'll tell everyone your secrets."

"It's not like that. I just...Anyway, Sy shouldn't have said anything."

"No. Diane shouldn't have said anything."

"Then Sy shouldn't have. And I shouldn't have."

Suddenly, Mar begins to laugh. It is a soft laugh, a sad laugh, but it is a laugh just the same. "Do you know? It really is OK. I think I'd like to talk about Max tonight. And if? In the morning? If you run around and tell everyone? That'll be OK, too. I think it's time to let him go."

"Mar, I'm sorry."

"No. I mean it. But first? First, more wine."

Seventy-Three

Jack.

What am I doing here? Jack asks himself as Mar disappears into the house. He pulls out his phone and looks at it, wills Sy to call him, to give him an excuse to break away. He is supposed to be talking to her, to let her know who he really is, what is really happening, not this, not getting to know her, not getting to like her.

"I hope you liked that wine," Mar says, shutting the back door softly behind her. "I brought another bottle."

"It's great," Jack tells her.

"Good, here," she hands him the corkscrew, " you open while I go grab some cheese and crackers."

As Jack uncorks the wine, he tries to think of a way to broach the subject to Mar. His mind is blank.

Mar returns and places a plate of cheese, crackers, meats and olives on the small table in front of their chairs. When she is tucked once again into her blanket, she holds out her glass to him.

"To Max," she smiles.

"To Max," Jack agrees, enjoying how the light flickers across her features.

"He's how I first became a foster mother," Mar begins,

turning toward Jack. “He was really cute, funny cute. He had these huge, brown eyes and long, long lashes. Women would kill for those lashes. Anyway, when he came to me, he was this skinny little thing, just a little kid. I don’t know why I did it, I was pretty much a basket case myself, and new to Boulder and all. I’d met Shirley, I told you, she’s the one who runs the children’s center? Anyway, I’d met her in a supermarket and she invited me over for coffee. Before I knew it, I was spending more and more time there, just playing with the kids, helping out.” Mar closes her eyes, a smile on her lips, and Jack can almost see it in his own head.

“So one day I’m there and Shirley asks me if I’d ever thought of being a foster parent. I told her I never had. Hell, I didn’t think I was much good at taking care of myself and my dog, much less a kid. I mean, what do you even say to a kid? Especially a kid who’s been through whatever to make them a foster kid? But, I started to think about it. I mean, a lot of these kids had been abused or neglected and just needed a safe place to be, you know? Just to be. So what if I fed them pizza three times a day, or let them play in the mud? It’s not like that was going to hurt them.”

Mar’s voice trails off and Jack finds himself wanting to bend down and kiss her, to taste the memory that is playing in her soft smile.

“Anyway,” Mar picks up the story, “I applied, went through the whole investigation thing, came out ‘clean’ and, before I knew it, Shirley was calling me about this little girl, Sandra. Her mother had been caught shoplifting and got a thirty day sentence. Sandra was great. She was terrified because, who was I? But I just treated it like an adventure, an extended sleep-over. Anyway, her mom was out on good behavior in two weeks and Sandra went home. Well, that was easy, I thought. I can do this. And then Shirley called me. About Max.”

Her voice drops to a whisper and Jack finds himself moving in closer. “He was beautiful. I mean, maybe not physically gorgeous, I don’t mean that, though he was cute as hell. I mean, his bearing. Here’s this little kid, his world’s all messed up. He'd been abused, kicked around, punched, beaten. Starved. His mother was a druggie, a real winner. She whored around, stole, whatever. Once, she was taken to jail and 'forgot' to tell anyone she had a kid at home. Left him there by himself for three weeks. He was just four-years-old, drinking out of the toilet, eating whatever he could find in the kitchen, ketchup, that kind of thing, being real quiet so he wouldn't get caught, get in trouble. That was the first time he went into foster care. When the mother got out, she did rehab and got him back. About a month later, the boyfriend showed up again and beats the crap out of her because she doesn't have any drugs for him. They come up with this idea that they can sell Max for drug money. And, they do. They sell him to some guy who rapes him for a week until he needs money and so he sells Max to another abuser. And so it goes, at least another couple of times, until finally someone leaves him outside an emergency room. Max spent time in the hospital and then went to Shirley's for placement. And she called me. I got there and there's this little kid, sitting there so straight, refusing to look up at me, but holding himself there so quiet. I'm trying not to cry and grab him into my arms, and he's just trying to be composed, scared out of his little mind.

"I took him home, and it was so amazing. At first, he was just so good, yes ma'am, no ma'am, not daring to ask for anything, afraid to do anything that would draw attention to himself. I'd take him for ice cream and he'd only eat a few bites, like he was afraid he'd get in trouble for wanting something. Or, we'd go to a movie and all the other kids would be laughing like crazy and he'd just stare at the screen, not letting himself enjoy it. After a couple of months, I was feeling like such a failure. I was ready to call Shirley and tell her to find him another home, someone who could get through to him, and I'm sitting on the floor of my studio, crying my eyes out. I thought he was in bed, when suddenly I feel this little hand patting me on the back and saying, '*shhhhh, it's alright Mar, it's gonna be OK.*'"

Mar looks up at Jack, her eyes pooled with unshed tears.

"Can you believe it? This little kid trying to comfort me, after all he'd been through? I just lost it, grabbed him, and hugged him, and cried, and told him how much I loved him, and how scared I was I wasn't taking good care of him. And pretty soon, while I'm rocking him and holding him, he puts his arms around my neck and tells me he loves me. This beautiful little boy loved me."

As the tears begin to flow, Mar's words quicken, as if she has to get the rest of the story out before she loses her nerve. "By that time, Max's mother was dead. She'd been killed by her pimp, not that she'd ever have gotten custody of him again. I talked to Shirley about adopting him, and had started on the process, and then one day, Shirley called me. There was an aunt that no one had been able to find before. Suddenly, she shows up and wants him. But she's got no real job, lives in a dump, had problems with drugs in the past. It was obvious she just saw him as a meal ticket, but she's blood, so it has to go before a judge.

"We get there, and I'm so sure it's going to go well for Max and me. I make a good living, the social worker was on my side, Max was doing so well with me. But, do you know what that fucking judge did? He decided that since Max was black, living with me could 'confuse his racial self-image.' Can you believe it? He gave Max to that freak because we had different skin colors? The day they took him away, he was traumatized, he wouldn't let me go, and this nasty woman comes and drags him off of me, actually slaps him on the head and tells him to stop sniveling while she's dragging him down to her beat-up car. And the social worker's there, telling me that I can't do anything but file an appeal."

Mar sits up, tears flowing down her face, her eyes glazed, seeing a different time and space. "A week later, he was dead. She'd locked him in a closet while she 'entertained' some pusher. After he left, she passed out with a lit crack pipe in her hands. It lit a bunch of trash on the floor, started a fire. Somehow, she got out, but she was too fucked up to tell the firemen about the little kid in the closet. He burned to death because our skin was different colors."

Jack gathers her in his arms and rocks Mar until her tears finally ease. What else can he do? As he holds her and listens to the sounds of her sorrow, he pushes the damp hair from her forehead, gently kisses her eyes, tastes the salt of her tears, smells the scents of Mar. And hates himself for it, even as he can't help himself.

Mar.

Mar leaves her curtains open and they undress one another by moonlight. This is not the rushed madness she felt with Kevin, or the sweet inevitability of Joaquin. This coming together feels almost hallowed, as if, finally, two halves are coming together as one.

Jack.

Jack turns to the soft noise, opens his eyes and startles. A face, a very small face, is inches from his own and is scrutinizing him intently. “Lizzie,” he whispers.

“Hello,” she says.

Jack glances over at Mar. She is sound asleep, head buried under a pillow, her arms flung above her head. He turns back to Lizzie. “Uh, hello,” he whispers.

“Are you gonna get up now?” she asks. “I’m hungry.”

“Uh, sure,” he says. He has no idea where his clothes are or how he is going to manage to get into them. He looks around her and down at the floor. Thank god. His clothes are there. “Um, why don’t you go downstairs and I’ll meet you in the kitchen?” he suggests.

“I’m not allowed to go down by myself.”

“Right.” Jack reaches down and grabs his boxers. He pulls them under the covers and fumbles them on.

“What are you doing?” Lizzie asks.

“Nothing,” Jack says and then, because he can think of no other way, he points to his shirt and asks her to hand it to him.

“Picasso has to pee,” Lizzie informs him as he sits up and pulls the shirt over his head.

"Do you have to pee?" Jack asks her.

Lizzie considers this a moment and then says, "OK. I'll be right back."

As soon as she is out of the door, Jack swings out of bed and grabs his pants off the floor. He pulls them on in record time and is just slipping on his shoes when he hears the toilet down the hall flush. He meets Lizzie in the hallway.

"Did you wash your hands?" he asks.

"Yep. They're still wet. See?" she slips one hand into his and pulls him toward the stairs.

When they enter the kitchen, Lizzie points to the painting of Joaquin. "That's my daddy," she tells him. "He's dead."

"I'm sorry," Jack says.

Lizzie shrugs. "It's OK. I didn't know him. Do you know how to make pancakes? I like pancakes."

***

Twenty minutes later, just as Jack eases the first pancake from the pan, Mar walks into the kitchen.

"Mommy!" Lizzie yells. "Jack's making me pancakes."

"She was hungry," Jack tells Mar.

"Thank you," Mar says, clearly embarrassed. "I didn't hear her get up."

Mar is wearing gray fleece pajama bottoms, an oversize t-shirt and slippers. Somehow, it works for her. "I'm sorry," Jack says. "I meant to be gone..."

"No, that's OK," she answers, though it is clear that it is not, that she wishes Lizzie hadn't found him in her bed.

"Now that you're up," Jack tells her, "I should go."

"No, stay. Really," she emphasizes. "Have breakfast with us."

Seventy-Six

Jack.

"What do you mean you didn't talk to her? Isn't that why I left you alone with her last night?"

"Don't start, Sy. I tried. It just wasn't the right moment." Jack looks around the room wondering what else there was to pack.

"Moment? Of course it wasn't the right moment. There isn't a good time for that conversation. You just gotta do it."

"No. I don't. What I've got to do is get back to New York and hire an attorney."

"Jack..."

Jack points a shoe at Sy. "Don't you get it?" he asks. "The longer I'm around her, the more I get sucked into her sad, sorry life. Look, I'm sorry. She's a nice lady. For her sake, I wish this wasn't happening. But it is. It is and I want my daughter back and I'm going to get my daughter back. End of story. Besides, in case you've forgotten, I've got to tell Shaheen about this."

"No, you don't. This isn't part of his investigation."

"Yes. I do. We still don't know if that Myrna lady was working alone or if she was part of the ring of kidnappers he's been looking for."

"Ah, come on. The lady was a fruitcake. She did it on her

own."

"OK, I think so, too, but Shaheen's still got to look into it."

"Can't you just drop it? Man."

"No, I can't. I could be disbarred for withholding evidence in a federal investigation. Besides the fact that this could help Shaheen find other kids and bring them home."

"How, if Lizzie's not a part of that?"

"Because Shaheen's been spending time wrapping her up with the other cases and, if she doesn't belong there, she's muddying up his information."

There is a knock on the door and Jack shoots a questioning look to Sy who shrugs. "Can you get that?" Jack asks and goes into the bathroom to gather his shaving kit.

"Hey there, you got a present," Sy tells him, handing Jack a large, flat package.

A slow burning begins in Jack's stomach and spreads quickly. "No. No, no, no. I don't want it."

"Open it. What is it?"

Jack takes the package and peels back a corner of the heavy wrapping paper. "Shit."

"Holy crap! Is that what I think it is?"

"Yeah, it is."

"You musta made a big impression on her."

"I can't take this. Here, give it back to her."

"Me? No way."

"I'm on the way to the airport."

"You want to run away, fine. But I'm not giving that back."

"Crap. I don't need this."

"There's a card. What's it say?"

Jack hadn't noticed the card taped to the front of the package. He pulls it out and opens it. "Thanks for the campfire chat. You taught me that letting go can be a good thing, and now I think it's time I let go of what this painting represents for me. It's time for happier thoughts. Mar"

"What's it say?"

Jack rubs at the headache that is quickly forming behind his eyes. "It says I'm going back to New York."

Seventy-Seven

Mar.

"You gave him your painting? You gave him *Mother & Child*? Mar, what were you thinking? You just met him."

Mar smiles. "It's OK, Dee. It was the right thing to do."

"Listen, I'll get Sy to get the painting back."

"No. I want Jack to have it."

"Mar, look, I have a list, a long list, of people who wanted to buy that painting."

Mar takes a sip of her coffee and smiles. "Nope. That one was never for sale."

"But why?"

"Because."

"Because?"

"Because, Diane, that painting was all about fear. Last night I realized I don't have anything to fear anymore." She laughs. "Come on, Dee, sit down, drink your coffee. It's a good thing."

"A good thing."

"Yep. A real good thing."

"Oh, my god! You slept with him!"

"Did too," Mar grins.

"You just met him!"

"Yep."

"Mar!"

"It's the new me, Dee. I'm going for it. There's something about him that just feels right. It's like I've known him forever."

"He lives in New York, Mar."

"I know."

"So?"

"Diane, what did you tell me about Kevin? You told me to go for it, to take a chance. I didn't, and look what happened. This feeling, this attraction to Jack is strong. Really, really strong and I'm not going to sit on the sidelines anymore. If it doesn't work, if we only have a few great days together, fine. But, I'm going for it. Whatever it turns out to be."

Diane drops to a seat across from her. "Wow."

"It's OK, Dee."

"OK, then, tell me this. Was it good?"

Mar thinks back to the night before, to the way their bodies had seemed to melt together, how Jack had caressed her in all the right places and how his urgency matched her own. Her eyes sparkle brightly as her face lights with a grin, "The best, Dee. The best."

Seventy-Eight

Jack.

"Tell me you didn't just do that."

Jack ends the call. "She'll know how to handle this."

"Jack, you never mix your personal life with business."

Jack closes his eyes and wills the car to go faster. Sy has been harping at him non-stop on the long ride to the airport. "Caroline's a family attorney. She'll know how to handle this. Besides, it was over between us a long time ago."

"Fucking hell," Sy grumbles. "It was bad enough, the situation. Now it is royally screwed. Can't get any worse."

"It's done, Sy."

"How about if I tell her?" Sy asks. "Let me explain it to Mar, clear the air."

"No!" Jack's response is harsher than he'd intended. "No," he begins again. "When the time is right, I'll talk to her. I screwed up by coming out here in the first place and I need to straighten it out."

"So, you'll call her?"

"I'll call her."

"Shit. Mar's gonna bloody freak."

"It's not personal," Jack says

"With Mar? About Lizzie? It's all personal."

***

Grabbing his bag from the carousel, Jack strides into the frigid New York cold to look for his driver. A man is waiting for him, waving a sign with his name printed on it. Jack waves back and heads in his direction. Just then, a flash goes off in his face. And then another, and another. Jack covers his eyes. "What the hell!?"

"Mr. Westfield, Darren Fry, *New York Post*, how is your daughter? How is Mia?"

"What? Who the hell are you? Get that camera out of my face!"

"Darren Fry, *New York Post*. I heard you're coming back from Colorado, that you found your daughter. How is she? Where is she? Are you bringing her home?"

"Listen, I don't know who the hell you are, or where you get your information, but I don't need this. Now, leave me alone!"

It is all happening so fast, Jack doesn't have time to wonder or to think. He looks around, hoping to spot his real driver and make a getaway.

"Have you told Lindsey's parents yet? Does your family know?"

"Leave me alone!" Jack pushes past the reporter and photographer and through the crowd that has gathered around, watching him. He gets to the curb and spots the driver standing in front of the limo. Jack pulls the door open and slams it behind himself before the driver has the chance to react. "Get me the hell out of here!" he yells.

Seventy-Nine

Jack.

With shaking fingers, Jack dials the hotel in Colorado and asks for Sy's room. "Come on, come on, come on," he intones, but the phone just rings and rings. Finally, an answering machine kicks in to ask if he wants to leave a message. "Shit, shit, shit."

It is dark in New York, but, on a long shot, he dials Sy's office and catches Dora just as she is leaving.

"A cell phone? Sy? You gotta be kidding. The man uses an abacus. What's this all about anyway?" And so, he gives her the brief version.

"Holy crapola, Sy's gonna be pissed. He's gonna be there when that woman goes nuts. He'll be lucky if she doesn't kill him."

"Yeah, I know. Listen, does he ever call in?"

"Sometimes, but not on any regular basis. There's something weird going on out there. First, it's the mountains is all he wants to talk about, and lately he hardly calls at all. Is something going on out there, Jack?"

Jack can hear the jealousy in her voice and suspects she thinks of Sy as more than her boss. No way is he getting involved in that mess. "He's stressed. He's been waiting to hear what I'm going to do," he evades.

"Yeah, but what's he still doing over there? Can't he wait here?"

"I guess he decided to stay there in case we were going to ask for DNA testing." It sounds lame even to his own ears.

"I don't know, Jack. He could do that by phone. Besides, it'd be the FBI that would take over in that case."

"Yeah, well, listen, Dora," he changes the subject, "I really need to get in touch with him before a reporter finds Mar. If he calls the office, can you please ask him to call me on my cell phone, no matter what?"

"Can do. But are you sure there's not something else..." she begins.

"I'm sorry, Dora, I've got to make some other calls. I'll talk to you later." He hangs up, already exhausted.

Jack looks at his watch. Diane will still be at the gallery. He takes a deep breath and dials, afraid Mar will answer, wanting her to answer.

"Mar Delgado Gallery, how may I help you?" Diane answers.

"Diane! Thank god. It's Jack."

"Jack! Where are you?"

"I'm in New York. Listen, is Mar there? I really need to talk to her."

"No. She and Lizzie went out with some friends. Why'd you go back to New York? Mar was expecting you all day."

"It's, look, something came up. Can you ask her to call me? No matter what time she gets in?"

"OK, but..."

"Thanks, Diane. I've got to go." Jack ends the call and looks out the window. Sy was right. He shouldn't have called Caroline.

Jack.

Jack sets the glass down on the counter and heads for the front door.

"Hey, DeJon, how have you been?" Caroline asks as he holds the door open for her.

"Good. Things're good."

"I'm glad. Is Jack here yet?"

"Yeah, but, man, is he pissed."

Caroline stops. "At me? He's mad at me?"

"For calling the press."

Jack stops at the foyer entranceway. "Caroline..." he begins.

She holds up her hand. "No, Jack, stop there. DeJon told me you think I called the press. No way. I didn't."

"Well if you didn't, who the hell did?"

"I don't know, but it could have been anyone. It's the talk of the office."

"How the hell do they know?"

"Oh, please, Jack. It's gossip. It happens."

Jack rubs his hand down his face and nods. "I'm sorry. I shouldn't have thought..."

"It's OK. I understand."

"Christ." He turns away from her and heads back to the kitchen. There, he pours a shot into the glass and looks at her, frustrated. "What am I going to do?"

"For starters," Caroline smiles warmly, "you can say hello nicely and pour me a glass of wine."

Jack laughs. It is good to see her. "Hello, Caroline."

"Hello, Jack. I'm glad you called me."

"Thanks for coming."

Caroline takes a sip of the wine he hands her. "You're welcome. You know that, Jack."

"I know." He lets out a long sigh, dreading the question but having to ask it anyway, "So, what do you think?"

"About Mia? I think you should decorate her room. She'll be home within a month."

Mar.

Mar forces herself to look in the mirror. “You are a total, bloody idiot, Mar Delgado,” she tells herself. Images of opening her heart to Jack, of telling him about Joaquin and Max and even Kevin, come to her and she feels the crippling embarrassment begin to return. Worse, she’d slept with him. God, he must think she’s a slut. “No,” she says and shakes her head for emphasis. “Get over it.”

She’d given him the painting. What an idiot. The man listens to her and she hands him a valuable painting. Next thing, he’s on a plane and doesn’t even bother to call. He probably has a girlfriend. Or a wife. She sighs and bites her lip. Yesterday, she’d paced the floor, waited for his call, finally gone out with Shirley just to put an end to the waiting. No way is she going to do that again today. No way. “Lizzie, honey, come on, time to go to school,” she calls out. Today, she’ll keep busy.

Her first stop after dropping Lizzie off at school is to look over the retail space Diane has been harping about. She can see it, can imagine the walls covered with paintings, the lights spotlighting the sculptures. An hour later, she walks out with a binding two-year contract and a blueprint. Later that week, she'll meet with the contractor to lay out the gallery's design.

Next, she drives out to her favorite bookstore and spends another couple of hours looking at art books, filling her soul with the great Masters, with architectural splendors that give her a great deal of graphic inspiration. She avoids the gift aisle where card sets of *Mother & Child* will just piss her off, ruin the day.

After choosing several books for Lizzie, Mar heads to Pearl Street, the outdoor walking mall in the heart of Boulder, where she eats a delicious lunch and enjoys the sight of the mountains rising up around her, reminding her to be strong. At a shoe store, she forces herself to buy a pair of strappy heels and promises herself she'll find occasion to wear them soon. And, finally, with just enough time left before she'll have to pick up Lizzie, she finds herself at the art store, where she buys paper she doesn't need, new brushes, tries eighteen colors on the back of her hand before settling on nine of them, and wanders through the aisles, dreaming of all the beautiful things that can begin there.

Mar is pleasantly tired as she makes her way home. And quite a bit poorer. She'd written the deposit checks for the rent and for the contractor from her personal checkbook and she is reminding herself to tell Diane to make the account adjustments, when she pulls into her street and her heart stops. News vans are parked up and down the street, a crowd gathered in front of her door, and policemen are busy directing traffic around the mess.

"Lizzie!" Mar slams on the brakes, dimly aware that she can't get closer. She opens the door and, slipping on a patch of ice, goes down, hard. Getting up, she begins running, fear tearing at her mind, clutching at her throat. She doesn't notice that she hasn't put the car in park, that the Explorer is slowly, but steadily, making its way toward a patrol car. She doesn't notice that the mob, sensing her, turns and begins its own marathon to reach her first.

Finally, blocked by the human wall, engulfed, her forward progress halted, Mar begins to cry, "Lizzie, let me through,

Lizzie, my daughter, let me through."

Through the roar of her terror, she doesn't hear the voices that shout at her, doesn't understand their cries. Doesn't register the questions, "Why did you kidnap the Westfield baby?" "When are they taking her away?" "What did Mr. Westfield tell you when he was here?"

Eighty-Two

Mar.

Mar's hands are shaking as she faces off with Sy. She picks up a glass from the counter top and begins to fiddle with it simply to give her hands something to do. Dylan, bless him, has taken a very frightened and upset Lizzie upstairs and is keeping her entertained. Keeping her away from Mar whose own emotions are flying out of control. Diane, unable to face Sy without tearing into him again, is upstairs in Mar's studio trying to book a flight for Don Bloom. Shirley, the only calm one of the bunch, is sitting quietly at the kitchen table taking notes, but even she is pale and jumpy.

"I'm sorry, Mar," Sy tells her for the thousandth time. "It's not how you were supposed to find out."

"I couldn't give a rat's ass how I was 'supposed to find out', Sy. The fact of the matter is that you lied to me. To us. You came out here, pretended to be my, our, friend, and all along you've been scheming how to take my daughter away from me? Do you know how fucking sick that makes me? Goddammit, I let you into my house! I let you bring your 'nephew' into my house!" The glass sails through the air and crashes into the refrigerator. Both Sy and Shirley jump.

"Mar, honey," Shirley murmurs.

“I let you into my house,” Mar repeats, hot tears of frustration beginning to roll down her cheeks. “Into my house,” she says yet again and slowly slips down to the floor where she curls around herself and begins rocking. “Oh, god, oh god, oh god.”

“Mar...” Sy moves to her.

“No,” Shirley tells him, gently pushing him aside to get to her friend. “Go, Sy. Just go.”

***

Later that night, Mar wakes up, her arm clutching Lizzie fiercely to her side. “Daddy?” she whispers.

“*Shhh*, honey, I’m here,” Don tells her. “Go back to sleep.”

“They want to take my baby away,” Mar says into the darkness. “They want to take Lizzie away.”

Eighty-Three

Sy.

It is late afternoon by the time the elevator opens at Jack's floor of Weisman, Tannenbaum and Carruthers and Sy steps out. Elena sends him down to Caroline's office, a floor below Jack's, and tells him that Jack will be down as soon as he wraps up a conference call.

Now Sy is sitting across from Caroline while she pours through his files. Occasionally, she looks up, asks a question, jots something down, goes back to her reading. It is pissing Sy off.

Caroline marks a paragraph with her finger and looks up. "So, you never actually interviewed the people from Children's Services?" she asks.

"No, I told you," he gestures to the file, "it's all there."

"And you didn't contact the FBI?"

"Shit, what is it with you? Didn't you hear a word I've been saying?"

"I'm just pointing out that you were out there, what? A week, ten days, after you found Mia..."

Sy cuts her off. "Her name's Lizzie."

Caroline continues as if he hadn't spoken, "A week after you found Mia and you didn't follow up with any government agency."

"There was no need."

"No need? Sy, let me be bottom line with you. A crime was committed four years ago. It's an open case, meaning the government is still very much interested in solving it. Now, it appears you solved it, and I use 'appears' very loosely because, until Shaheen puts his stamp on it, it's still open. Got it?"

"I got it, but what's going on now doesn't have a goddamned thing with what went on back then."

"So you say."

"Yeah, so I fucking say. These are good people who're just as fucking hurt by all this as Jack."

"Not even close."

"Yeah, whatever. I just don't understand why this can't be resolved between Jack and Mar."

"Mar? Don't you think you're a little too close to this, Sy? And that maybe you dragged Jack in and now he's too close?"

"Jesus F-ing Christ! These're people! Don't you get that? They're just people. You talk to them, you work things out." Sy gets up and starts to pace, anything to keep from smacking some sense into her. "You lawyers," he continues, "you lawyers, you can't even talk to people, it's all gotta be motion this, motion that. You forget there're people involved."

"This is why we have lawyers, Sy. For people like you who can't separate the emotion from the facts, from the law. Do you think your precious Mar is going to sit by and let Jack take his child? No. She's going to do everything in her power to turn this around and, if she can't turn it around, to stall, to drag it out, to make Jack suffer even more than he has. She's not going to sit down at a table and be reasonable, to say, 'sure, I understand, take her.'"

"Well, she's got some points."

"See? That's where you and I differ, Sy. I don't think she's got any points. I've been going through case law and, guess what? Though there's not much, the law says she doesn't have any points either. None. And if you want to help Jack, you'd better remember that."

Sy stops in the middle of the office and stares at her, frustration and anger raging in his belly. He knows she is right, hell, hadn't he been the one to run all over the country, to find Lizzie in the first place? Still, it is personal to him, she's got that right. "Fuck!" he swears and kicks a chair.

"What's going on?" Jack asks from the doorway.

Caroline shakes her head and waves at Sy. "Talk to him, Jack. He's got his boundaries confused."

Eighty-Four

Mar.

"I'm sorry, Mar. Really, I am."

Mar stares at Stacey Lindquist, the attorney Shirley had recommended. She hears the words, but their meaning does not compute. "But," she counters helplessly, "the adoption was legal. Everything about it was legal. I have the papers."

Stacey takes off her reading glasses and sets them on the table. "I know, but the adoption was based upon the assumption that Lizzie was free to be adopted."

"But that's not my fault! She was free. Everyone thought she was free."

"It doesn't work that way. The court, to the best of its ability, determined that she was free, that she had no living relatives and that adoption would be best for her. All this, though," she waves at the files on her desk, "no one could have foreseen this."

"But, they should have!"

"Mar, honey, calm down," Don Bloom reaches for her hand and squeezes it.

"You're right. They should have. But they didn't and, from what I can see from the files, there was no reason to believe Lizzie was not that woman's child."

"So what you're saying is that I'll lose her."

"Mar," Stacey sighs heavily. "What do you want? Do you want the bottom line? Or do you want the one where I pretty it up for you?"

"I want the facts. I want the worst case scenario so I can work it from there."

"Worst case scenario? OK, yes, you certainly could lose her. She was kidnapped and there are no provisions for keeping a kidnapped child from being returned to its parents once it's found. Unless, of course, there are extenuating circumstances. Unfortunately, I can't find any in this case."

"What would an extenuating circumstance be?"

"Usually, in kidnapping cases, the kidnapper is a parent or another family member. Occasionally, the court has given full custody of the child to one parent and almost always for good reason. Meaning the other parent was abusive or criminal or just plain off the deep end. In very rare circumstances, the court gave the child to the wrong parent, and the one who took off with the child was able to show that the child had been in danger while living with the custodial parent. Again, though, the courts still don't look lightly on the non-custodial parent taking off with the child. Regardless of the reasons, that person still has broken a few federal laws. But, Mar, remember, that isn't the case here."

Mar's face is pale as she tries to listen past the migraine that pounds in her head. Her heart hurts in her chest and her eyes and nose are raw from crying. She clasps her hands together to keep them from shaking and asks again, "So, I'm going to lose her, aren't I?"

"Mar, what we just spoke about is the worst case scenario. All things being equal, the most likely outcome would be for the courts to return Lizzie to her father. There are, however, a few things to keep in mind. First, though, I want you to know that it's a long shot. You have to understand that."

Mar nods and whispers, "I know."

"OK, look, courts nowadays are very careful about doing the right thing by the child, and that's key, 'by the child.'

I'm sorry to say it, but in high-profile cases like this one, the pressure to get it right is even stronger. As far as Lizzie is concerned, you're her only parent. She doesn't know Jack Westfield from Adam. And, from what I can tell, you've been a good parent to her. I think it's incumbent on us to show that having Lizzie remain with you, as her only known parent, is in her own best interests."

"Is that possible?"

"Anything's possible. It's slim, but it really is our best bet. If that doesn't seem to be going our way, we ask for joint custody, with Lizzie living with you but Mr. Westfield having full access to her."

Mar nods, "That could work. How do we do it?"

"Research." Stacey begins to tick off the list on her fingers, "First, we pull up every single piece of supporting evidence that shows that removing a child from its parent at such a young age can be traumatic. Second, we have Lizzie evaluated and find child psychologists who are qualified to testify on your behalf. Third, we interview every single person that you and Lizzie know who will support that you have been a caring, loving parent. Fourth, we research adoptive rights laws. They've become stronger over the years. We need them to be very strong now. Fifth, we use the media."

"The media? But, why?"

"Mar, this is already a high profile case. You have all the elements of a great story – the baby's mother was killed, the baby kidnapped, the grieving father, a four year search. On that side, throw in a kidnapping ring, the FBI, and a private detective. On your side, you've got a woman who has overcome a few of her own tragedies, not the least of them the one she is currently involved in. The tabloids live for this kind of thing."

"That's sick. This is my life."

"Get used to it. Better yet, learn to love it."

"How can that help?"

"Because, like it or not, the rules in our society are dictated by the media, and judges and juries are only people, too. Some of their opinions are bound to be formed by what they read, by what their family and friends read. You need to be the media's darling because, make no mistake, this case is going to polarize the nation, much like the Baby M case did in the '90's."

"What happened then?"

"A teenage mother put her newborn up for adoption without the biological father's consent. He didn't even find out he was a parent until years later and, when he did, he filed for custody. By that time, the child, a little girl, had been with her adoptive parents for almost four years."

The blood rushes from Mar's head as something pricks her memory. "What happened?" she whispers.

Stacey closes her eyes for a moment and when she opens them, she looks directly at Mar. "The biological father was given full custody."

"Oh my god," Mar cries.

"And that's why we fall back on our sixth task."

Mar's eyes are intensely focused on Stacey. "And that is?"

"We pray."

"We pray?"

"I'm sorry, but sometimes that's all we've got left."

Eighty-Five

Jack.

Special Agent Shaheen reaches across Jack's desk and shakes his hand. "Thanks for seeing me."

"Thanks for coming. Sit, please. Can I get you anything? Some coffee? A soda? Water, maybe."

"No, thanks, I'm fine."

Jack sits and pushes aside the file he'd been working on. No hardship there. His mind lately has been more on his own case than any other. "So, what'd you find out?"

"Well, first of all, the DNA checked out."

Jack nods. The final results had come in the week before, not that he'd needed them. "I know."

"And, your friend, the detective, was right. There's nothing there to tie Ms. Bloom or the local child services department to the kidnappers."

Strangely, Jack feels relief. He knows that Caroline will be deeply disappointed but, for himself, he is happy to have Mar cleared. "And? You look like there's an 'and' or a 'but' to that statement."

Shaheen allows himself a small smile. "It's a 'but.' As in, 'but, we think that Myrna Cross may have been involved.'"

"You're kidding, right? I thought she was just a flake."

"She was, there's no doubt there. Most likely, she was bribed to kidnap a child, a white, female child. Instead of turning the baby over, though, she took off with her."

"Jesus."

"The funny thing is, that may be the only reason you know where your daughter is today."

"I don't understand."

"I've been after this group for four years. They're good. They're pros and they know what they're doing. They move around a lot, disappear, show up somewhere new entirely. When the kids are that young and they drop off the radar screen, the chances of finding them are next to nothing. Chances are, if that woman had turned your daughter over to them, we'd never have found her."

"So I'm supposed to be grateful?"

"Considering the circumstances, I'd be grateful she ended up in Ms. Delgado's care."

"Jesus Christ, Shaheen."

"I'm not saying you don't get your daughter back, Mr. Westfield. Christ, I'm a father, too, and I'd move heaven and earth to get my kid back. I'm just saying you're lucky she was found and taken care of, that she didn't end up like Cassidy Renfro."

Jack turns and stares out the window. Spring has slipped into summer and for a few more days the weather in New York should be perfect. He wonders about the weather in Boulder, wonders what Mar and Lizzie are doing with their day.

As if reading his thoughts, Shaheen tells him, "Ms. Delgado handled it pretty well. The investigation. It was pretty obvious from the beginning she wasn't involved, but she was helpful."

"She's a nice lady."

"Your daughter, Lizzie? Mia?"

"Lizzie."

"Lizzie's pretty strung out. All that media attention's taking its toll on her."

Jack turns to him, puzzled, "Why are you telling me this?"

Shaheen shrugs. "I've seen a lot of things in my career, Mr.

Westfield," he says. "This one, it got to me."

"What would you do?"

Shaheen shrugs again. "What can you do? She's your child. She belongs with you."

Jack.

"Hello, Caroline," Jack greets her at the door. "Come on in. I'm having Scotch. What can I get for you?"

Caroline pauses in the foyer and looks at him critically. "You're drunk."

"Yes, but I'm a happy drunk," he grins at her. "Would you like to get happy with me?"

"Jesus, Jack, we need to talk."

"So talk, my illustrious defender of justice. I'll get happy for you, too."

"Jack."

At her tone, the goofy smile drops from Jack's face. "I'm fine, Caroline. Just enjoying an after-work drink. I'm fine. What's up?"

"Where's DeJon? Shouldn't he be home by now?"

"He's off at a movie with some friends. Can't stand to be around me lately."

Startled, Caroline asks, "Why not? What's up with that?"

"I don't know. He's pissed about something and isn't ready to talk about it."

"Jack, that's not good."

"Hell, I know it's not good. It's like talking to a wall. He comes home and locks himself in his room." He shakes his head, "I don't know what to do."

"No, Jack, I mean it's not good for the case. You've got to talk to him."

"The case? What the hell does teenage testosterone have to do with the case?"

"The press are all over this. If he's going to be pissy about anything, now is not the time."

"Jesus, Caroline."

"It's a fact, Jack," she snaps. "And you know it, too, so it's bloody unfair that you make me have to remind you."

"What's that supposed to mean?"

"It means we're under a media microscope, and the whole bloody world is worried about what is going to happen to your daughter."

"I'm worried about what's going to happen to my daughter."

"Exactly. And, like it or not, a public family fight between you and DeJon would not be helpful at this time."

"This has nothing to do with that."

"Of course it does! Right now, Mar Delgado is winning the media war. She's the Princess Di of the new millenium, the tragic heroine in everyone's eyes."

"Well, hell, Caroline, her life pretty much does suck at the moment."

"Be that as it may, that's not your concern. Your concern is to stay clean and remind everyone that you're the guy that got hurt here."

"Look, I've read the case law. There's nothing that indicates Lizzie won't be returned to me."

"Well, then, why hasn't she been already? Don't you see what they're doing, Jack? They're trying to show that Lizzie is better off with Mar. It's their only chance."

"It's not going to work."

"But, they're trying, and a public fight with DeJon right now can't help you." Caroline sighs. "Look, all I'm asking is that you talk to him, find out what's bothering him and fix it."

"Fine."

Caroline shakes her head and goes into the kitchen to pour herself a glass of wine. "Anyway, I came here to ask you to change your mind about something."

"About what? I thought we were agreed on everything."

"On the venue. I really want to bring it to New York."

Jack sobers immediately. "No. I told you. It stays in Boulder."

"But, Jack, it would be so much easier if we brought it all over here."

"Easier for us, yeah, but not for Lizzie."

"Mia."

"Lizzie. Look, I talked to Shaheen today. He was just out there and he says Lizzie's a mess."

"All the more reason to bring it here. Get her away from all the media."

"You don't think they'll follow her here?"

"Of course they will, but she'd be staying in a hotel with security to keep them away."

"No, forget it. At least there, she's got her home and her room and people she knows."

"Dammit, Jack, listen to yourself! You can't keep talking like that. You say something like that to anyone but me and the judge hears about it and you've just made their entire case for them."

Jack drops into a chair and looks at her. "I don't know. It just seems that maybe we took the wrong tack. I should've stayed out there and tried to work it out with Mar."

"Work what out? There's nothing to work out."

"Maybe we should have gone for joint custody."

"Haven't you been listening all these months? We talked to Dr. Hartford. He's the best child psychologist there is. He told you that would be the worst thing for her. She wouldn't have any stability, wouldn't form solid attachments. She needs to settle. She needs to come home and know this is her place and settle."

"She's settled now."

"Alright, Jack, you want to talk about this? Let's talk about it. Can you tell me, honestly tell me, that you're going to give her up? That you're able to just walk away from her?"

He shakes his head miserably. He can't tell her that. Just staying away from Lizzie these past few months while the whole thing is being worked out is difficult for him. Mar's attorney has proven formidable and has been able to stall and drag things out. She'd countered Jack's Boulder attorney's motions at every turn. Finally, next week, the judge is expected to rule on temporary custody. Jack has asked for weekends during the trial and he is sure to get them. And even though seeing her on weekends is more than he currently has, is more than he'd ever had, Jack knows in his heart that it won't be enough. "No," he answers.

"Exactly. I'm sorry, Jack, but that's what it finally comes down to. Either you or Mar Delgado has to have custody of that child, and she's yours, above and beyond anything Ms. Delgado ever had with her."

"You sure?"

Caroline smiles and reaches out to touch his cheek. "I'm sure."

Eighty-Seven

Mar.

Painting. That's all there is. Just painting. Gold and Magenta and Cerulean Blue. Orange and Umber and Indigo Blue. Green and Black and Aqua Blue. Raw Sienna and Black and Aegean Blue. Gray and Black and Mediterranean Blue. Black. And Blue. Ocean Blue, so blue so blue so blue....

She nervously checks outside the studio windows, licks her dry lips. The mountains are there, standing tall. Shaking her head, she returns her gaze to the painting. Creeping slowly up through her spine, and then spreading throughout her body, she feels the wrongness of it, feels it on her skin, in her skin, feels the treason of it as a physical blow. How did this happen? When did this happen?

She is becoming agitated now, anxious in her frustration to change it, to fix it, to make it right. Taking her brush, she dips it in red, shovels it from the can to the canvas, throws it on and spreads it around and around. Goes back for more. When did the paint can move so far away?

Turning back to the painting, she gasps. The colors are moving, swirling, dripping. She'd used too much paint. Too much! They aren't drying fast enough, are bleeding into each other, creating a hellish, chilling miasma of color and emotion.

She closes her eyes, willing it to dry, to stay in place. Opens her eyes slowly, peeking out between heavy lashes, praying for it to be better, but feeling the nausea begin to toss inside of her. Swallows hard as her skin turns clammy. It is still moving, the Blues with the slashes of Red, the swirls and gashes and splashes of Red.

And, it drips. Already, just in the moment it has taken her to reach for more paint, it has dripped, formed a puddle on the floor. Where had so much paint come from? It is pooling on the floor, Blue with its river of Blood, drip, drip, dripping onto her hardwood floor, forming a small rivulet that winds its way, picks its way almost, across the hardwood floor toward the glider. And, how strange, she thinks, but I've never noticed the floor slant that way before. And she thinks she'll have to clean it up, it is becoming such a mess.

But then the music starts and she is reminded she's let her mind wander, has ceased paying attention to the colors and they did not like that, not one little bit. No, she wills, please, no, no, no. Turning is difficult, almost impossible, her feet have more sense than her brain and refuse to move, refuse to turn, refuse to be. Taking her hands from her eyes, she reaches down and tugs at a leg, yanks her damn foot and makes it obey. And then the other one, the music rising, grating, scraping at her ears, saying look, look, look, ha ha ha.

And the painting is there, of course it is. And it has grown. Of course it has. If she'd only been paying attention, she'd have foreseen it. Stupid stupid stupid. Leaving a painting with a stupid stupid woman. And now the mess in the corner and the river, is that a river already? Yes it is, on the floor and she'll need a mop and rags and that goddamned music, trilling actually, she recognizes the word of it, trilling, at her. Ha ha ha ha, ha ha ha. *La la la la, la dee da,* almost like a children's song, but sung by something that is not very nice. She can tell that now. It isn't mean little children, it can't be, children can't be that mean. It is a something else. And it is coming for her. Oh, shit! The painting, she has to take care of the painting.

It is there, its so much bigger self, still swirling madly,

dripping onto the floor, but more steadily now and she can sense the clog, as if a twig is caught, oh, yes, there is the Umber, caught in the corner, holding it back. And she thinks, yes! this is my chance, while it holds.

She moves more purposefully now, with her feet back under her control and the can of gesso in her arms. The trilling is becoming more shrill, as if it knows she can win, can shut it up for good, and she takes grim pleasure in its distress, wants to rip its vocal chords out and throw them out the window, toss them at a passing shark. Car. Where did that come from? She glances uneasily out the window. Car. Toss them at a passing car, to be squashed and flattened and mangled beneath its tires, one last, long *trrrrrrriiiiiiiiiiiiiiiiiillllll* as the air is squeezed from it one. last. time.

Ha Ha Ha. Fool. Tra La La. Fool. Stupid Fool. Stupid trusting, dusting, musty. Fool.

It is deeper now. Deeper and stronger and pounding in her head. Stupid! No, No! Fool! What kind of a mother are you? Throwing your child under a car? Ha Ha Ha STUPID!

Oh, god! Oh, NO, and she is running, running, slogging, through the river, or is it a pond by now, lake, that is pouring from the painting and the window is so much farther away. No No NO, had she thrown Lizzie out the window? She'd heard a crunch, do tires crunch? She'd heard it, a sound and the weight in her arms, she'd thought it was gesso, but was it Lizzie? Her baby? Oh, god, why is her blanket in her arms and the window so far away and the stupid stupid stupid now an insidious mocking, mimicking, piercing needle threading throughout her brain, distracting her from the window, she needs to get to the window, to see Lizzie, to find her baby and she's swimming, the Umber has cracked and the rushing of the backwaters has caused rapids, has knocked her to her knees and she needs to swim, needs to swim, has to swim but her arms won't work, please please please I need my baby, my arms won't work and then boom! The first swipe is just a playful bunt really, just a playful guess who's here now, girlie?

Ha Ha Ha. Stupid. Fool.

Eighty-Eight

Mar.

She's been awake for months. The Prozac isn't working, how could it? She is on such a high dose of Prednisone because of the ulcers that have formed in her intestines and is so wired from that, that there is nothing that can calm her down. When she is very quiet and closes her eyes, she can even hear the blood rushing through her veins. Shoosh, shoosh, shoosh. Feel it under her skin, like the memory of a sunburn, raw and irritating. She calls it the heebie-jeebies, and it is driving her mad.

Mar sits in the darkened room and watches her daughter sleep. She'd taken off her watch weeks ago and has become adept at avoiding looking, or even glancing, at clocks. Still, she is aware, almost to the minute, of time passing. Sitting in the chair, watching Lizzie sleep, she's already figured she is down to about 19,563 minutes until the meeting with the judge that will determine whether Mar continues as Lizzie's mother.

The irony of it doesn't escape her, how the law feels it can turn motherhood on and off. Just like that, poof, you're a mom, bang, now you're not. She's struggled with it, cried over it, fought about it, screamed and ranted and raved and kicked and thrown things because of it, but at the end of the day, it is what it is. Someone has to make a decision, and she's lost her opportunity to have been the one to have made it. She should have run.

She knows that now. She should have taken Lizzie, Picasso and whatever money she could get her hands on and gone. Adios, bye-bye and sayonara, buddy. Now she can't go to the bathroom without the press writing about it. No way are they not going to notice if she takes off. Even with the judge's orders that forbid her from taking Lizzie out of state, she'd try it, if she thought she could pull it off. Her attorney, aware of where her thoughts are turning, tried to talk her out of it.

And that is another irony that stings. When she had been a struggling foster mother and then the new, legal mother to Lizzie, no one had cared that she was absolutely clueless about how to take care of her. They'd just handed her the baby and told her to go be a mom. Now the world is watching and critiquing, making it an armchair sport to tear her apart, comment on what she should have done, how she should have acted.

Nineteen thousand, five hundred and thirty eight. Stop it, Mar. This may be all you have.

Mar stretches out on the bed, pulls Lizzie to her and holds her close for the next seventy-eight minutes that the little girl sleeps.

Jack.

Jack, DeJon and Caroline are eating dinner at Jack's apartment. Caroline takes a sip of wine and picks up the notebook she's been referring to. "So, you've got weekends and a bonus, three afternoons a week," she says. "I wasn't sure the judge was going to come through."

Jack looks up, curious. "Why not?"

"He's the same judge that screwed up her earlier bid for adoption. I was afraid he was going to go out of his way to accommodate her this time. I'm glad to see he's not."

Jack shakes his head. "From everything we've learned, he's a fair man."

"For an old white dude," DeJon mumbles.

"And what's that supposed to mean?"

"Means he used that reverse prejudice bullshit when he didn't give that little boy to Mar Delgado."

Jack carefully sets his knife and fork on his plate. "I wasn't sure you'd even been paying attention all this time."

DeJon stares intently at his plate. "Not much you are sure of."

Jack's fist slams down on the table, startling them all. "That's it! What the hell has gotten into you?"

"Me? What's gotten into me? How about what's gotten into you? All of a sudden, you're like, 'maybe the baby should stay with her', then it's, 'no, she's gotta come to me.' Why can't you make up your goddamn mind?"

"DeJon..."

"Shit! You know what? I am so sick of this shit. All Mr. Conflicted when you can't even see what's going on in front of your fucking face. What about me? Huh, Jack? What about the kid that's been with you all these years? The dumb ass fool that looked out for you, tried to find your kid for you? The one that sat at the hospital with you and was always there, fucking waiting for you? What about that kid? You gonna give me back now that you're getting your little girl back? My momma comes calling like you're doing with that Mar Delgado woman and you're gonna give me back?"

DeJon's chest is heaving as he towers over Jack, tears glittering in his eyes. "You think it's black and white, Jack? And, you," he points at Caroline, "all hiding behind that lawyer shit. You think you got the law on your side, talking trash about that woman to the press, and you, Jack, just sit back and let it happen like it's OK 'cuz that little girl belongs to you, right? Well, then, who the hell do I belong to? You told me I belong with you because you love me and you take care of me. Well, maybe that little girl belongs with her momma."

Stunned, Jack watches DeJon run off to his room. He flinches when the door slams shut. "Don't," Caroline reaches out and puts her hand on his arm when he moves to follow. "Let him go. He's got a lot on his mind and he's got to work it out."

Jack sinks back into his chair, his emotions raw. Malcolm was right. He has a corner on the guilt market.

Mar.

Mar hangs up the phone, bewildered.

"Who was that?" Very few people have the recently-unlisted number.

"Stacey. The Sonnenheims are in Denver, and they want to see me tomorrow."

"Lindsey's parents?"

"Yeah."

"Why, whatever for?"

"I don't know, Dee. We haven't heard a thing from them, ever. I don't know why they're suddenly so interested."

"Come on, be fair. Maybe they were told to stay away. That's what Stacey said."

"I know, but why now?"

"I don't know. Are you going to see them?"

"I think so."

"What does Stacey suggest?"

"It could go either way. I can tell them to screw off, and make things even more contentious, or see them and at least find out what they want."

"Maybe they want to talk about visitation rights or something."

“For who? For them, or for me?” There is no disguising the bitterness in her voice.

“For them, Mar. You have to be strong.”

“I know, I know,” Mar says. Twelve-thousand-two-hundred-seventy-three.

Ninety-One

Jack.

Jack is late and he is running. He'd gotten out of the cab three blocks away when it was stuck in traffic. Now, as he nears The Farm, he slows to a jog and finally, as he comes up to the basketball court, to a slow walk. It is no good. The game is in full swing and DeJon is out on the court. Jack leans against the fence, feeling the failure in the pit of his stomach.

"DeJon!" Jack calls when there is a break in the game.

DeJon, slick with sweat, glances over at the fence and glares at Jack before turning his back dismissively.

"Great," Jack swears, "just great."

"You can't blame him, Jack."

"Oh, hey, Malcolm. You spying on me again?"

"Ha! Watching out for you, waiting for you, yes. Spying? No need when I can pick up the National Enquirer and read all about you."

"Very funny."

"How ya doing, Jack? Really?"

Jack watches DeJon move in for a shot and smiles when the ball swooshes into the basket. "Other than letting him down again, great."

"He was really counting on you being here."

"Salt on the wounds, huh?"

Malcolm shrugs. "It is what it is. So, what kept you?"

"The custody case. Just wrapping up some loose ends."

"Uh-huh."

"Uh-huh. What's that supposed to mean?"

Malcolm shifts his attention to the court. "You know, we started these Father-Son games six or seven years ago to encourage togetherness. Other than that first year after Lindsey died, you haven't missed one."

"I feel bad enough, Malcolm."

"You haven't missed one," the priest continues as if Jack hadn't spoken. "This is the first year DeJon officially has a father, and your being here meant something to him."

"I get it, OK? I fucked up."

"Jack, what's going on?"

"Nothing. Everything. This case. I don't know," he shakes his head. "And now, DeJon. We're not getting along."

"Do you have any idea why? Have you talked to him?"

"He won't talk to me."

"But, have you tried?"

"Of course I've tried! He just shuts me out."

"Could it be he's afraid?"

Jack looks down at Malcolm, surprised. "Afraid? Of what? There's nothing for him to be afraid of."

"What about of losing you?"

"That's ridiculous."

"Is it?"

"Of course it is."

Malcolm turns back to the game. "Is it?" he asks again.

Ninety-Two

Mar.

Stacey Lindquist meets Mar and her father in her office.

"So, did you have any trouble getting past the hordes?" Stacey asks, referring to the news media who are camped out on Mar's front lawn.

"The usual. Everyone's looking for a new angle. I was offered $10,000.00 to pose with Darrell and Cindy Matthews, that couple that lost Baby M. This week's *People*'s rehashing that whole thing. And the adoption rights people came by again. They've got that rally staged for next week and want me to speak at it."

"Letterman's people called again. They'll fit you in any day this week or next, though they'd rather do a piece this week and then a follow-up after the ruling."

Mar scratches her arms, the heebie-jeebies are flowing. "What am I supposed to say, Stace?"

"It helps by bringing awareness."

"If this were a normal adoption situation, I'd say yes, in a heart beat. If the parents had put Lizzie up and I adopted her, and now they want her back like that dad in the baby Veronica case, hell yeah, bring it on, I'd be out there screaming from the roof tops. But they didn't put her up, and what am I going to say? You know, inside, I feel like if the tables were turned, I, me now, should give her back. I understand their, his, right to her. And that's so messed up, because it doesn't help me and, if I'm on TV, and someone asks me what's the right thing to do, and I say, legally? To give her back, but, emotionally? For Lizzie's sake? To leave her with me, where she's settled. And are they going to hear the difference? No, they'll just say, well, she said she should give her back, so it's all agreed, and, boom, the judge says give her back."

Don pulls out a handkerchief and hands it to Mar.

"Mar, the judge knows that, he learned. He sees the difference. That's why this has taken so long. If it had been a purely legal issue, he'd have returned Lizzie to her biological family months ago."

"He only learned that because of Max."

"Yes, and that can go in your favor."

"But not in Max's."

"Mar, you've got to stick to current issues."

"I can't. I'm just so bitter."

"Of course you are. That's understandable. But for now, you have to focus."

"I know. I know."

"Good. So, I need you to think about Letterman."

"Whatever."

"OK, fine. We'll talk about that later. Right now, let's talk about the Sonnenheims."

"Have they told you what they want?"

"No. I say just meet them and, if at any time you don't like what they're saying or whatever it is that they want, then I'll stop the meeting."

"Fine."

"Should I wait here?" Don asks.

"No way," Mar takes his hand. "It's two on two with Stacey as referee."

Ninety-Three

Mar.

Stan and Amanda rise when the door opens. Mar looks at them warily. If she'd met them socially, she'd probably be drawn to them. They look nice enough, tanned, fit, pleasant, open faces that look as if they laugh a lot. They dress casually, too, even though Mar has learned they have bizillions of dollars.

Stan reaches out his hand, "Hello, Ms. Delgado, I'm Stan Sonnenheim, and this is my wife, Amanda."

Unconsciously, Mar wipes her sweating palm on her jeans before shaking his, and then Amanda's, hand. "Mar. Please call me Mar. And this is my father, Don Bloom."

Amanda's smile is warm and friendly. "It's nice to meet you," she says, "even though it's under such difficult circumstances."

The pleasantries accomplished, Stacey invites them all to sit before turning to the Sonnenheims. "I've told Mar the little you've told me, so I guess it's up to you to let us know why you've come all the way out here and asked to meet her."

"Well, you see," Amanda begins, "we've wanted to come out here, would have, months ago when this whole thing started, when we found out that Lizzie'd been found, but Jack's attorneys forbade it, and now that we've seen how things are going, we realized that we should have come anyway. Damn lawyers, they screw everything up."

"Amanda."

"No, Stan. I'm sorry, Ms. Lindquist, but in this case, it's true. Though I must say, you've been refreshingly restrained through the whole matter."

"Uh, thank you."

"No, I mean it," Amanda speaks earnestly. "This is a terrible situation for everyone concerned, and it should have been handled differently, delicately. Instead, it's been turned into a circus, and if you take all the adults out of the picture, I can't imagine what it's doing, or what it's going to do, to that little girl." She turns to Mar, "How is she?"

"She, um, she doesn't understand why she can't go to school, or why there are always reporters on the lawn trying to take her picture." Mar feels a tear forming and bites her lip to hold it back. "I don't know what to tell her, or how to prepare her for, uh, whatever."

"I know. It's awful."

There is an uncomfortable silence and Mar feels the minutes slipping by and kicks herself for being away from Lizzie. She has to leave. "Excuse me, but you seem like nice people, and I can understand that this is pretty crappy for you, too, but, can you please tell me why you're here?"

"Honestly? I don't know." Amanda seems surprised by her own answer. She looks at Stan.

"I don't know either, sweetheart." He picks her small hand up, squeezes it, and smiles at her gently. "It was just something you had to do."

When Amanda turns back to Mar, there are tears in her eyes. She covers her mouth with her hand, as if afraid to open up. "You see," she finally says, "we know what it is to lose a child. And, I understand you've already lost one. Max, wasn't it?"

Mar nods, not trusting herself to speak.

"Yes, well, we heard about that, so I know you know

how bad it can be, and I can imagine how terrified you are, thinking you might lose Lizzie. I don't know, I don't know why we're here. I'm just hoping that we can find a way to make this better, between us, before this all gets worse."

Mar puts her face in her hands and swallows heavily. She doesn't want empathy from these people. She is fighting for her daughter and doesn't want to feel for them. Stacey seems to pick up on Mar's distress. "Does Jack know you're here?" she asks.

"No," Stan replies. "We thought it best not to tell him. At this point."

"I see," Stacey says.

"Well, then," Mar says, "I'm sorry. I can't help you. If he was looking for a solution rather than waiting for the judge's ruling, maybe we could talk, work out what's best for Lizzie. But without him, there's really no reason to daydream, is there?" She smiles sadly and shrugs.

"Maybe we could talk to him. I'm sure he wants what's best for Lizzie."

Don says, his voice filled with anger, "I don't think so. That man has done nothing but attack my daughter from day one. Do you know that the FBI even came to investigate Mar? They talked to everyone she's ever known, tore her life apart and all but accused her of being a kidnapper!"

"Dad," Mar tries to head him off.

"And now her best friend, who, I will tell you, has done more good for the children of this area than anyone, is being investigated. It's too much. Just too much."

"Dad, please."

"No, that's OK. We agree, in fact. It has been handled badly."

"Badly! It's been in all the papers that she's a drunk! Fills her wine cabinet and they assume she's getting sloshed every night, putting Lizzie in danger!"

"Dad!"

"Please. We know. We're not here to make excuses for Jack, though he really is a good man. He really is. And, you've a right to be angry. I'd be livid. But, please, that's what I meant about attorneys messing this up. Unfortunately, Jack's attorneys haven't taken the high road on this one."

"Listen," Mar says, "I wish there was a way we could all work this out, but there's really no common ground. You see, I know Lizzie should stay with me. I know that's what's best for her. Regardless of him having fathered her, I'm the only parent she's ever known." Mar gets up. "I'm sorry for all your grief, I'm sorry about your daughter. But, Lizzie's fine and she should stay with me."

At the door, she turns back. "Um, thank you for coming, for trying."

Amanda smiles bravely through her tears. Stan just nods.

"Would you like to see her?" Mar asks suddenly. "To meet her?"

Amanda tries to speak, can't. Stan pulls her to him and speaks over her shoulder. "Could we? It would really mean a lot to us."

Mar smiles gently. "One way or the other, you're still her grandparents."

Ninety-Four

Jack.

Jack is having a particularly bad day. At breakfast, he had tried once again to get through to DeJon, to talk about what is eating at him, but he'd only been rebuffed. Again. He is been placing a call to Father Mac to ask him to intervene, to mediate, to help him find a way to reconnect, when Caroline bursts into his office.

"Great news!" she waves a stack of articles at him. "Your message is getting out."

Jack looks up from his desk. "Message? I didn't know I had one."

Caroline laughs happily. "Of course you do. The Fathers' Rights advocates love you. Congressman Neely's using your case to push for stronger acknowledgement of a father's right to custody in divorce cases."

Jack shakes his head and moves to the window. New York. Jesus. What is it about the city that holds him? That repels him? All he'd wanted was to come here, to make his mark. Well, apparently he had. But at what cost?

"Jack?"

He watches the cars so many floors below, everyone hurrying from place to place, meeting to meeting, jostling, ignoring one another. Would Lizzie even like it here? "This isn't a divorce case, Caroline."

"But it's still great press. Jack, even the bleeding hearts are finally coming around. Little Miss Delgado doesn't look so innocent anymore."

Finally interested, Jack turns from the window to face her. "Mar? What are you talking about?"

Just then, the door bursts open and Amanda sails into the room, followed slowly by Stan.

"Amanda? Stan?" Jack is stunned to see them. "What are you doing here? Is everything OK?"

"No, Jack," Amanda plants her hands on her hips, "everything is not OK."

Jack glances at Stan, who only shrugs. "Sit down, please. Let's talk. You know Caroline."

Amanda barely manages a nod. "Caroline."

"Amanda. Stan."

"Sit, please," Jack tries again.

"Thank you, no. We've just gotten off a plane and I don't feel like sitting anymore,"

"I didn't know you were going out of town. Where were you?"

"We've been to Colorado. To see Lizzie."

Jack freezes. "How is she?" he finally manages.

Caroline turns on the smaller woman. "I thought we asked you to stay away. At least until the ruling."

"You know what? We did. For months. And only out of respect for you, Jack," Amanda says pointedly.

"But, I didn't ask you..."

"Well, no surprise there, now is there?"

"There's a very good reason we asked you not to get involved."

"Wait a minute," Jack cuts her off. "Caroline, I didn't ask them not to get involved. Amanda, I never suggested you shouldn't go see her. That would just be cruel to try to keep you away."

"I did," Caroline states.

"But, why?"

"Yes, Ms. Carruthers, please do tell us why you wanted to keep us from our granddaughter."

"Jack?" Caroline turns to Jack for support.

"Amanda, please. Look, you're obviously upset. Why don't you sit down and tell me. I'm sure there's an explanation."

Stanley takes a seat but Amanda stands, hands on hips, firmly glaring at the younger woman.

"Amanda. Mandy, come sit. Please." Stan pats the chair next to him. Finally, Amanda sits.

"Caroline," Jack motions to a chair. "Now tell me, please, what's bothering you? You said you were in Colorado."

"We went out there several days ago and met with Mar. And Lizzie."

"Do you mind telling us why?" Caroline asks.

"How are they?" Jack eyes bore into Amanda's, then Stan's.

"They're terrible. How do you expect them to be?" Amanda snaps. "Mar's as sick as I've ever seen anyone and Lizzie, who I understand used to be a happy, outgoing child, is withdrawn and angry."

"Ah, Christ," Jack feels suddenly sick.

"It's not your fault," Caroline snaps. "What are you doing here?" she demands of Amanda. "Do you really think this is doing him any good?"

"Do you really think it's doing Lizzie any good? What the hell are you doing, Jack?"

"I'm just trying to bring my daughter home."

"Couldn't you have done it differently? Without the entire world watching?"

Jack scrubs at his face trying to dispel the tension. "I didn't want it to happen this way."

Caroline says, "I'm sorry, Amanda, Stan, I can understand your distress, and know that it is sometimes difficult to understand how these things work, but this has all been in Mia's best interests, after all."

"Lizzie's," Amanda, Stan and Jack say simultaneously.

"Yes, well, see, her legal name is Mia and all the documents I've been working with..." Caroline's voice trails off lamely.

"But don't you see? That's just the point! You're working with paper. Paper! We're talking about a little girl, a person, a human being with thoughts, opinions, emotions and desires."

"You can hardly think to include a child in the decision making."

"Why the hell not?" Stan asks.

"Because she's a child! The law doesn't even recognize her ability to make decisions for herself, much less her right to do so."

"Aren't you listening?" Amanda demands. "We don't care about the law! This is not, and should never have been, a legal issue!"

"I'll remind you that a crime was committed."

"Yes, but not by any of the parties currently involved."

"We don't know that for sure."

Amanda turns to Jack, "Tell me, Jack, do you think, in any way, shape or form, that Mar was involved in the kidnapping?"

"Mar? Absolutely not."

"She may have been an accessory after the fact," Caroline puts in.

"That's already been looked into, hasn't it? Legally. And there's no shred of evidence that she's anything but another victim of this whole debacle." Amanda turns back to Jack, "So, if you don't think she was involved at all, then please tell us if you think her friend, Shirley McGowan, had anything to do with it."

"The children's services lady?"

"Yes. The Director for The Center of Child Welfare out in Boulder. Do you think that she had anything to do with it? Maybe that she's the head of some kidnapping ring? Pays off mentally disturbed people to steal babies and bring them to Boulder to be placed with unsuspecting foster families? Is that what you think?"

"That's ridiculous! From everything I've seen, or can gather, she did her job in placing Lizzie, and then in supporting

Mar as the adoptive mother."

"Against that other couple that was interested? You think she did her job in recommending Mar over them?"

"Absolutely. I don't know them, but it's obvious Lizzie hasn't wanted for anything."

"I'm glad to hear you say that, Jack. But I have to wonder, then, why you've filed a lawsuit against her?"

"What?"

"Jack, please," Caroline cuts in.

"What a load of crap." Stanley gets up and walks to the window.

"I haven't filed any lawsuits, Amanda. I don't know where you heard that."

"Jack, wake up! I just can't believe you're not getting this."

"Getting what?"

"The whole picture, the chaos you're causing, destroying people's lives, walking over everybody. And for what? Have you even stopped to think about Lizzie in all this?"

"Jack," Caroline cuts in. "Please don't do this. I know you care about them, but you really need to cut this short before more damage is done."

"Damage! Lady, you're buckshot in a bra! You kill a few and leave the rest dying and bleeding, wondering what hit them and why! That's damage. That's what you're doing to all those people who only tried to do the best for Lizzie. You don't care who you hurt."

"Amanda, no one's being purposely hurt. I'm sorry you have that impression."

"Then why the hell is there a lawsuit, filed in your name, against that lady, that you're apparently not even aware of?"

"Caroline?" Jack turns to her.

"It's nothing, Jack. Just a strategic move..."

Jack goes cold. "What strategic move?"

"Well, look, we felt that the judge might look preferentially on Mar Delgado because he's the same judge who gave her last foster child back to his family. Well, you know that. So, when you wouldn't agree to try to move the decision here to

New York, and we couldn't get a different judge, well, Marion thought it would make a stronger case for you if there were doubts about the handling of the adoption."

"So you filed suit?"

"Just until this is over. Then we'll drop it."

"Jesus Christ, Caroline! You can't screw with people's lives like that!"

"I told you, it's just until this is over."

"She may lose her job! She's a lady who's worked very hard against some pretty big odds to get where she is, and she's doing a world of good out there. Now your damn 'strategy' is casting doubts about her integrity. Don't you get it?"

"No, don't you get it?" Caroline shoots back. "Jack lost his daughter and he's just trying to get her back."

"Caroline, you're going to retract that," Jack tells her. "Now."

"We'll talk about it, Jack. Later."

"No, I mean it. Now."

"I really think we should talk about this before you make any decisions."

"I don't need to talk about it. I asked you and Marion to get my daughter back, not to hurt innocent people."

"Dammit, Jack, that's how the law works."

"No it's not. It's evil," Amanda says.

"It's necessary."

"Is it? Or is it just revenge because she slept with Jack?"

"Amanda," Jack winces. "Please."

Caroline pulls herself up to her full height. "This has nothing to do with that," she spits out.

"Are you sure?"

"Jesus." Jack's head is pounding and he now regrets being up front with Caroline about his night with Mar. Full disclosure. As his attorney, he felt it was only fair that she have all the facts. She'd quit right then and there. And then walked out on him. The next day, however, she'd apologized and asked to represent him. He massages his temples. Sy had been right, you don't mix personal with business.

"What about how you've been harassing Mar?"

"We're not harassing her."

"No? That woman is so inundated with your legal crap that she can't breathe. You've demanded all her bank records, her insurance records, her gallery records. You've asked for her husband's death certificate, actually insinuated that it was too convenient that she wasn't diving with him the day he was attacked, as if she'd paid off a shark. And what about Max Turner's aunt? You dug her up, and now you're asking the courts to investigate Mar for child slavery! You don't call that harassment?"

"Child slavery?" Jack is afraid to ask, but can't help himself.

"Yes, apparently Mar tried to pay off the aunt to leave Max with her."

"That's not slavery!"

"Well, technically," Caroline says, "it's child trafficking. She tried to buy another human being."

"She tried to give that little boy a good home! That woman is a drug addict! She was just using him to get his state aid payments."

"You're investigating Mar for child trafficking?" Jack can't quite get his mind around it.

"No, Jack, technically, you are," Amanda purses her lips. "Jack, technically, you're hurting a lot of people out there."

"I didn't realize..."

"I've got to say, I'm relieved about that, at least."

Jack's head is in his hands. He can't see how this can get any worse. "Anything else?"

"Sy."

He looks up. Caroline turns away. "What about Sy?"

"He's been asked to explain how he bungled the investigation."

"What? Sy?"

"Yes, Sy. Apparently, you're making a case that if he had followed up a year earlier, when he first received that postcard, things wouldn't have progressed so far and Lizzie wouldn't be so attached to Mar. Basically, you're just a big victim, blah blah

blah and the courts should feel sorry for you. Sorry enough to take Lizzie away from the only mother she's ever known."

Jack's head is back in his hands. No wonder Sy won't return his calls. "Is there anyone else who should hate me?" he asks, his voice muffled.

"Lizzie."

"What have I done to her?"

"It's not what you've done, Jack, it's what you're about to do. Mar is the only parent she's ever known. Taking her away would be incredibly traumatic for her."

"Your saying that you think Mia, Lizzie, should stay with that woman?" the shock is apparent in Caroline's voice. "You'd have Jack give away his own daughter?"

"Yes, I think she should stay where she is. But I do think Jack should work out some sort of joint custody. Lizzie deserves both her parents and Mar is willing to work out visitation schedules, both here and in Colorado."

"Willing! What is it with you people?"

"What it is, Caroline, is that 'we people' care about Lizzie. We're convinced she's having a great upbringing, and we'd be very happy to have Mar be a part of our family."

"Oh, god, please. How dramatic."

"Caroline..."

"No, Jack, I won't be quiet. This has been going on too long. It's sick! Mia is your daughter. Yours, Jack! This is just too ludicrous to listen to."

"Jack, listen to Amanda," Stan urges.

"Jack," Amanda pleads. "Please, look at it. What kind of life would she have here? Yes, you'd give her things, but you can do that anyway. You'd be gone all day. She'd be raised by a nanny. You've seen her. You've seen what kind of mother Mar is."

"She takes her to day care. That's not very hands on," Caroline sniffs.

Amanda shakes her head. "That's really neither here nor there. What's important is that if you bring her here, she's going to be ripped away from all she's ever known. Do you know what that can do to a child that age?"

"We have a very good psychiatrist waiting to deal with her as soon as she arrives."

Amanda ignores her and continues to focus on Jack. "She doesn't need a psychiatrist, Jack. Or a nanny. Or a driver. Or maids or doormen or anyone. She needs her mother and, to her, Mar is her mother. Jack?"

He finally lifts his head from his hands. His eyes are sad. "I know, Amanda, I hear you."

Stan walks over and puts his hand on Jack's shoulder. "I'm sorry, Jack, that things have gotten to this. I'm sure it's not what any of us would have wanted. Especially Lindsey. But, it's what we've got to deal with. Do what's right, son."

Jack simply nods to let Stan know he's heard, and continues to massage his temples.

"Darling? Amanda? Are you ready?"

"Yes. Yes I am." She moves to Jack and kisses the top of his head. "Please think about it, Jack."

"I will, Amanda. Thank you."

"Caroline." Amanda nods to her and then sweeps out the door in front of her husband.

From the door, Stan says, "Caroline, I've been around quite a lot and if there's one thing I've learned, it's this, oftentimes, being legally right doesn't mean you are right. I'd urge you to think about that. Goodbye."

Caroline immediately turns on him, "Jack..."

He holds up a hand. "No, Caroline. Not now. Please, not now." The headache is crippling. "Please get some aspirin from Elena and just let me be for a little bit. Please?"

"I'm doing this for you, Jack," Caroline pauses in the doorway. "I'm trying to bring your daughter home for you."

"I know." The bitch of it is, as an attorney, she is doing the right thing, going for the jugular. Christ, all he wants, all he and Lindsey had ever wanted, was a family. Why, when it looked like he'd finally get his daughter back, is everything going to shit?

Ninety-Five

Mar.

Mar glances at the caller ID and picks up the phone, “Yes, Fred?” she asks the guard posted at her front door.

“Mar, I think you’d better come out here.”

“Is something wrong?” She cocks her head and listens. Sure enough, the press camped out on her front lawn are raising a ruckus again.

“There’s someone here to see you.”

Mar closes her eyes. The visit from the Sonnenheims had about wiped her out. She had smiled bravely through it and tried to excite a withdrawn Lizzie about the prospect of having a new set of grandparents but, really, it had cut her already bleeding heart. The way things are going, very soon the Sonnenheims will have more access to her daughter than she will. “Please don’t tell me it’s Jack’s parents.”

“No, ma’am, he says he’s his son.”

Mar.

"I'll talk to you later, Dee," Mar urges Diane out the door.

"You sure?"Diane cranes her neck to see around Mar to the boy who claims to be Jack Westfield's son.

"I'm sure. I'm fine. Just go be with Lizzie, OK? I'm fine." She all but shoves Diane out the door and shuts it firmly behind her. "Now, are you sure you wouldn't like something to eat or to drink?" she asks DeJon.

"No, ma'am," he mumbles, looking down at the floor.

"I can make you a sandwich."

"I had something on the plane," he tells her rug.

Somehow, Mar sincerely doubts that, but she figures Diane will be back in about five minutes anyway, carrying a tray of food, anything to get another look at the boy. Mar sighs and sits down. "OK, so tell me what's going on."

"There sure are a lot of reporters out there."

Mar rolls her eyes. "Tell me about it."

"Jack's gonna kill me."

She doesn't know Jack well enough to comment on that one, but she is pretty sure he'll be extremely pissed when the photos of DeJon on her doorstep hit the airways. "So, he doesn't know you're here?"

"No, ma'am."

"Call me Mar, OK? And I'll call you DeJon. That is your name, right?"

"Yes, ma'am. Mar."

"So, are you going to tell me what you're doing all the way out here? You're what? Sixteen? Seventeen? Isn't that a bit young to be flying by yourself?"

DeJon bites back a grin. "I'm fifteen," he corrects her. "Well, almost."

"Holy crap! Wow. You look a lot older than that. Jack's gonna have a conniption."

"He don't care."

Aha! So there is trouble between Jack and his adopted son. Mar is sorry for the boy, but figures Jack Westfield deserves any grief that comes his way. Alright, maybe not. But still, she is pissed off about the trashing she is getting in the press. She tucks her legs under her and drops her chin into her hand, her eyes focused on DeJon. "I'm sure that's not true," she tells him.

"All he cares about is getting back your little girl."

Mar swallows hard. She doesn't need the reminder. "Listen, DeJon, he adopted you, what? Five months ago? Six?"

"Six."

"I'm sure it's because he loves you very much."

"Nah. All he cares about is Lizzie."

"I'm sure it seems that way, with all that's going on."

"It's all he talks about."

"Is that why you're here? You're mad at him?"

"Yeah, I'm mad at him, but that's not why I'm here."

"Then why?"

DeJon squares his shoulders and looks Mar in the eye. "I came to ask you to let Jack have Lizzie."

Mar's face crumples as her eyes fill with tears. She shakes her head and takes a deep breath. "I'm sorry. You caught me by surprise."

"Naw, ma'am, I'm sorry. I don't want to hurt you any more than what's already been done."

“Wow.” Mar’s head is spinning. Already things are strange and now they’ve slipped way past the falling-down-the-rabbit-hole kind of unreal. It occurs to her that she probably should have called Stacey before letting DeJon into her home. God knows how this is going to play out.

“I know that’s not what you want to hear, but maybe you could think about it?”

Mar shakes her head. “I’m sorry, DeJon, but Lizzie’s my daughter. You don’t just give your kids away.” As soon as it is out of her mouth, Mar realizes her mistake. Wasn’t it *People* magazine that had said that is exactly what his mother had done? “Shit. I’m sorry,” she says when his shoulders drop.

DeJon shakes his head. “I just thought, well, maybe, I don’t know, it’s stupid.”

Mar moves over and sits next to him on the sofa. Physically, he is larger than she is, but the little boy in him is crying out loud and clear. She takes his hand and asks gently, “What did you think?”

“I thought maybe I could stay here and Jack could have Lizzie.”

Ninety-Seven

Jack.

Jack snatches up the phone. The police have come and gone, saying he can't file a missing person report until twenty-four hours have passed They didn't even want to put out an Amber alert because there was no reason to believe DeJon hadn't gone to a friend's house and forgotten to tell him. "This is Jack," he barks.

"Jack? It's Mar."

"Mar?"

"Mar Delgado."

Jack shakes his head. For months he'd half hoped to hear from her. Now, though, he has to find DeJon. "I know who you are, Mar, but now isn't a good time. I'm waiting for an important call."

"DeJon's here," she says softly.

"What?"

"He's here. He's fine."

Jack drops onto the sofa, his legs unable to support him. He waves a hand at Caroline, who is trying to interrupt him to find out what is happening. "What's he doing there?"

Mar sighs. "It's a long story," she says.

Ninety-Eight

Mar.

Mar wakes with a start to the sound of Lizzie's giggles. For a moment, she imagines that it has all been a horrible nightmare, that everything is normal. Shortly, however, she hears a deeper laugh and remembers. DeJon.

"So, you've met," Mar can't help smiling. This is the first time she's heard Lizzie laughing in months.

"Hi, Mommy, he's my brother."

DeJon, who is lying on the floor playing Chutes & Ladders with Lizzie, scrambles up. "I'm sorry," he says. "It kind of came out."

Mar sighs. It is all coming out, all coming undone. "That's OK. Of course she should know. You're pretty good with her."

"She's great."

"No, I mean it. Lately she's been pretty shy."

"Really?" DeJon smiles.

Poor kid, Mar thinks, *this is tearing everybody up*. "Really," she says firmly. "Now, Miss Lizzie, why don't you take your brother downstairs for some breakfast? I think I hear Grandpa down there and I'm sure I smell pancakes."

"I wanna play with him."

"Him's gonna be here for awhile, Missy, and I'm sure he's

pretty hungry, so go on down and eat and you can play some more after."

Lizzie grabs DeJon's hand and begins tugging him toward the door. As he comes abreast of her, he asks Mar, "Did you talk with Jack?"

"Yes and he's heading out here today."

"He's gonna hate me."

Even though he is taller than her by several inches, Mar has to lift his chin to bring his eyes up to hers. "Listen to me, DeJon. Jack loves you. He was frantic when I called him last night and the only thing he cares about right now is that you're safe."

"Yeah, but it was stupid coming here. I just thought I could make it better."

"Honey, you did," Mar whispers past the tears in her throat. "I think you did a fine and brave thing."

"You do?"

Mar nods. "I do. But, let me tell you something very important. If Jack whips your butt over this, I won't stop him. What you did was also very, very stupid. You put yourself in danger and scared Jack at a time when he doesn't need more stress."

"Huh," DeJon's shoulders drop as he obviously tries to work out Mar's mixed message.

Mar shakes her head. "I know. It's all mixed up for me, too."

Ninety-Nine

Jack.

The hotel room door opens and Jack looks past Mar into the hallway. "Where is he?" he asked worriedly.

"Hello, Jack," she tells him pleasantly.

Jack looks down, is hit again by how small she is. And tired. He notes the dark smudges under her eyes, the weight she can't afford to lose, but has. "I'm sorry, Mar. I just thought DeJon would be with you."

Mar looks down the hallway. "Could I maybe come in? There's at least one reporter behind me. Probably a busload."

"Of course. I'm sorry." He moves aside and gestures her into the living area of the suite, over to a sofa. "Can I get you anything? A soda? Some juice?"

Mar shakes her head. "No, nothing," she says. "Let's just talk for a few minutes and then I'll go."

Jack sits on the edge of a chair and leans toward her, his eyes unconsciously probing her, taking in the hair that won't stay in place, the paleness of her skin, her long artist's fingers that are currently shredding a tissue. When she looks up and meets his eyes, he freezes. There is fear there and sadness. He knows he'd put them there and the part of him that remembers the taste of her lips on his wants badly to take them away.

One Hundred

Mar.

Mar notices Jack's drawn features, the haunted eyes that stand out in such bold relief against his tired skin. Regardless of the threat he poses to her future, her world, a traitorous part of herself wants nothing more than to reach out and pull him close. Mar swallows.

Jack clears his throat. "About DeJon," he says.

"He's at the house. We figured that the press would follow me here and so when I leave here, he'll sneak over to Diane's and she'll bring him over. Hopefully they won't notice."

"It's been horrible for you, hasn't it?"

"It's been hell."

"I'm sorry, Mar..."

She cuts him off, "Are you going to change your mind? Let me keep Lizzie?"

Jack freezes. "No, that's not..."

Mar sits up straighter. "Fine, then let's talk about DeJon and I'll be out of here."

"Mar..."

"No, Jack. I have nothing else to say to you. Obviously, I said way too much to you already," she says bitterly, referring to the night they'd spent together.

"I didn't mean that to happen."

"Which part of it? The talking? My telling you everything about me? About my life, so that you could use it against me? My wine cabinet, Jack? My husband's death? Lizzie's accident? That worked really well for you in the press, didn't it? It made me look like an incompetent mother."

"I didn't mean that."

"Oh, you didn't mean that. Then what did you mean? You didn't mean to kiss me? To hold me? To make love with me? To make me believe something special was happening between us?"

"Jack?" Caroline stands in the doorway to one of the suite's bedrooms.

"Christ," Jack swears. "Mar? Caroline. My attorney."

Caroline nods tersely at Mar. "Mrs. Delgado."

Mar closes her eyes and counts to three. The woman is a goddess. No wonder Jack had hurried back to New York. But, she is also a bitch."Miss Carruthers, isn't it?"

"Yes, it is. Jack, I told you I didn't think this was a good idea. We should have met at the office with all attorneys present."

Mar stands up. "You know what? You're right. This wasn't a good idea. I came here because a scared kid ended up on my doorstep and I thought we could discuss him like adults. Obviously, my mistake."

"Mar, sit down. Please. Caroline, look, this is something separate. I just want to deal with it with Mar."

"No, Jack, it isn't separate. Did you see the paper today? There's a photo of DeJon on her front porch with the headlines screaming that he's moved over into her camp. Obviously, nothing is separate."

"Ignore the press."

"I'm your attorney, remember? Could you just listen to me on this one? Maybe Miss Delgado can get her attorney and we can meet later?"

Mar grimaces. "Sorry, but Mrs. Delgado isn't interested in wasting any more time with you. I've got to get home to take care of my daughter." She heads for the door.

"Jack!"

"Caroline. Mar. Goddammit! Would you both just back off?"

"Jack," Caroline hisses under her breath, "if she talks to the press about you and DeJon fighting, she could really screw this up for you. I've been telling you that for months."

Mar stops at the door and turns. "Do you know what? I came here to talk about DeJon, one parent to another. He's a troubled kid who's just trying to help."

"Mar..."

"Unlike you, Miss Carruthers," she continues as if Jack hadn't spoken, "I have no interest in talking to the press about him or anything else. My only interest was in trying to help DeJon."

"Mar, please don't go."

"Jack!"

"Caroline, please. Look, Mar, I'm sorry. I know this is a mess and I'm forever apologizing to you, but could you just stay a moment? Please? I'd really like to hear about DJ."

Mar looks back at Jack, who looks sincere, and at Caroline, who looks like she'd like to rip Mar's head off with her hundred dollar manicure. She sighs and shakes her head. "Fine," she agrees, "but anything else out of your 'attorney', and I'm out of here."

"Thank you."

"Jack."

"Caroline, please. Do you want to stay?"

Caroline grits her teeth and sits.

"Please tell me," Jack asks when both he and Mar are again seated. "Why is he here?"

"Because he loves you. He thinks you want Lizzie so much that you don't want him anymore."

"That's not true."

"He offered to exchange himself for her."

"What?"

Mar rubs her eyes. *What the hell am I doing here?* "He

seems kind of desperate to be wanted and he doesn't think you want him anymore. He thinks you only want Lizzie. Also, he heard about Max. I guess he thinks I'll be happy with a kid, any kid, and if I'd let you have who you really want, Lizzie, he could be my consolation prize."

Jack groans as he drops his head into his hands. "You're kidding, right?"

"No. I'm very serious. That boy needs some major reassurance."

"Malcolm said he was scared he was losing me."

"Who?"

"Nothing. A friend."

"Well, your friend was right. DeJon loves you so much, he thought he could get you what you wanted, even if it meant losing you."

"Jesus."

"Yeah. Look, apparently he's had it pretty rough and this whole thing is affecting him, too. Please don't be too hard on him."

Jack looks into Mar's eyes. "Thank you."

Mar nods and rises to leave. At the door, she turns once more. She can't stop herself. "For the record? I think what you're doing is bullshit."

"She's my daughter, Mar," he says quietly. "She belongs with me."

"No, Jack, no." She advances on him again. "You can talk about biology and nature all you want, and you know what? I can't fight you on that. But if you think that's what makes someone a parent, you're wrong, you're very wrong. And, you know the saddest part? The one who's paying for your mistake is Lizzie."

"Mar, I know," he begins.

"No, you don't know. You don't know anything. You don't know her favorite color, her favorite song. You don't know that she's allergic to peas. Peas, for Christ's sake! Or that she punched Grady McMillan in the nose when he teased Jilly Sanders for wearing hand-me-down clothes. You don't know that when her tummy hurts she likes to curl up with Picasso and eat soft boiled eggs with butter and toast. You think you know, you think your sperm..."

"I'm not saying..."

"But you are," she insists. "You're saying that the 30 seconds it took you to put your sperm in your wife's vagina are more important than the four years I've raised her."

"Jesus Christ." Jack pulls his hand through his hair and takes a deep breath. "As a matter of fact, I do think that was important. We wanted Lizzie. We wanted her more than anything. My wife died giving birth to her!"

"And, I'm sorry for that, for you. But I didn't have anything to do with that and I can't do anything about it now. We're talking about now. We're talking about four-year-old-Lizzie, not sperm-and-egg-Lizzie or fetus Lizzie. You're trying to make this a philosophical question, and it's not."

"Jack, I think..."

"Caroline, please," he cuts her off. "Look, Mar, I don't doubt you've taken good care of her..."

"I'm her mother! Say it, Jack. You and your wife made her and she carried her but, as far as Lizzie is concerned, I'm her mother!"

"And I'm her father."

"If you cared so much about her, why are you doing this? Why are you tearing her life apart?"

"I want to be with her, Mar. I need to be."

"But why this way? I would have let you be with her," she cries. "We could have worked it out." The tears are streaming down Mar's face and she wipes at them angrily.

"We consulted a psychologist," Caroline starts.

"Oh, wonderful. Another really smart man who knows nothing about Lizzie. That was cute, impress the court with his degrees and his articles in famous journals. The man isn't even a parent. That's like asking a priest to give you pointers on having sex."

"He's the best in his field."

"He's never even met Lizzie. She's just a future article for him."

"Mrs. Delgado, look, I'm sure this hurts. Losing is never fun, but if you have anything else to say to my client, please do it through your attorney."

"Dammit, Caroline, I asked you to stay out of this."

"Jack, this is wrong! She's just trying to upset you."

"I'm trying to get through to him."

"He's her father! Don't you think he knows what's best for her? By dragging this whole thing out, you're the one hurting her! You're the one keeping her from her family."

Mar's blood turns to ice. "Listen, lady, I'm sure you're a real nice person when you're not being such a bitch. And I'm sure you're a helluva lawyer. But don't you dare try telling me what's best for my daughter. Not now, not ever."

"Are you threatening me?"

"You bet your New York ass I am."

"Lovely. I'm sure the judge will just love to hear about this."

"Goddammit, Caroline! Enough!"

"No, Jack, it's fine. This just goes to show you what kind of a person you're saving your daughter from."

Without thinking, Mar launches herself at Caroline, all the months of hurt and fury focused in that one instant.

Jack reaches out and catches her, pins her, holds her tightly as she struggles to get free, to get to Caroline. Caroline, her eyes alight with hatred, stands there, gloating.

"Dammit, Mar, stop it. Caroline, get out of here."

"I'm not leaving."

"Mar? Shit. Caroline? Get the fuck out of here. Now!"

Caroline turns on her heel and strides to the interconnecting door, slams it shut behind her.

"Mar?" Jack pulls her more tightly to him. "Mar? Stop. Shhhhh. Stop."

Mar is crying. She doesn't know why. She wants nothing more than to get to Caroline and tear her fucking eyes out. But, she is crying. The fury leaves her suddenly and she is crying, big, heaving tears. And goddamned Jack is holding her. She struggles to push away from him, but he holds on.

"Mar, shhhhhh. Stop."

"Leave me alone," she mumbles into his chest.

"Are you going to hit me?"

She can feel the anger coming back. Anger at him, at his stupid attorney. Mostly, at herself. How could she have thought reasoning with him would make a difference? "Let. Me. Go."

Gingerly, Jack holds Mar away from him. "Mar..."

She looks up at him, her eyes aflame. "You suck, Jack Westfield. You really suck."

She makes sure to slam the door on her way out.

One-Hundred-One

Mar.

Mar reaches for the pearl earrings and considers them as they lay, weightless as memories, in the palm of her hand.

Under the microscope of the past three months, everything has taken on new layers of meaning. Her house, her clothes, her work. Her past. Her life has been picked apart, analyzed and judged. Now she wonders what the earrings, last worn on her wedding day, will imply about her. That she is competent? Trustworthy? She closes her eyes and takes a steadying breath. At this point, what does it matter? She drops the small studs back into the jewelry box that is open on her bathroom counter.

Mar drags her eyes from the box back to the mirror. It isn't fair. But then, she no longer believes in fair. She'd been married once. For all of ten days. She'd had a child, and he'd been murdered. She'd adopted a second child, had played by the rules, had been a good mother. And in less than three hours, that child, too, might be taken from her. No, she doesn't believe in fair.

Mar's eyes are bloodshot and puffy. No amount of makeup can hide the pain in them. And even though she's trowelled on concealer, foundation, powder and blush, her skin still looks gray. Her attorney had insisted on the makeup, the hair, the suit. She is supposed to look confident, composed.

Her eyes fill. A tear slips down her right cheek. Another down her left. Mar leans on the counter and watches as her carefully applied confidence washes down her face. She takes a ragged breath and reaches for a washcloth.

Mar goes to Lizzie's room. The little girl, exhausted, is finally asleep. Mar sits on the edge of the bed and reaches out to stroke Lizzie's back. It is not enough. She slips her shoes off and lies down next to her daughter, wrinkles be damned. As the waves of the water bed settle, Mar reaches for Lizzie, pulls herself to her and wraps herself around her. She begins to cry.

Later, she hears the sound of the front door slamming, as if someone rushed into the house. The overweight hamster pauses in his endless run. Within moments, the air inside the house settles and, *crick-crick-crick*, the hamster once again runs.

Her father parts the pearl cascade that guards Lizzie's door. "Mar, it's time to go."

Mar knows that, pending the judge's decision, this could be the last time she'll ever see her daughter sleep. She wishes she had taken Lizzie and run. Mar looks up at her father. Don Bloom's eyes are filled with tears. "Daddy, no."

Her father, looking older and more tired than she's ever seen him, reaches out a large hand to her. "I know, Sweet Pea, I know," he says, "but we can't keep the judge waiting."

One-Hundred-Two

Jack.

Across town, Jack cuts his face shaving. His eyes had been on the photograph that is wedged between the hotel bathroom mirror and its frame, and his thoughts had been miles away, lifetimes away. The slice of the razor startles him back to the present and he watches as crimson blood blooms through the white of his shaving cream. As the red spreads to pink, he remembers how it had all started and his stomach heaves. It had all begun with blood.

He wipes away the last of the shaving cream and examines the cut. It is wide, but not too deep, though the bleeding hasn't yet slowed. He presses a washcloth to his face and reaches for the photograph. She looks so young. She had been so young. It kills him to think that this is as old as she'll ever get and that he'll continue to age without her. Still, Jack had made her a promise to bring her child home. As she lay dying, he had promised her that, the only thing he'd had left to promise her. Today he'll find out if he can make that promise come true.

In the bedroom, Jack finds a suit, shirt and tie laid out on the bed. Caroline, still trying to be his girlfriend as well as his attorney. He bites off a curse. He can pick out his own damn clothes. Quiet confidence, Jack, is what she'd recommended the night before. And when we win? Stay calm. No one will like it if you rub it in her face.

Jack sits on the edge of the bed and drops his head into his hands. He doesn't feel confident. He wonders what Mar is feeling and then immediately shuts that thought down. What she is thinking or feeling doesn't matter. Can't matter.

Still, true to her word, and much to Caroline's surprise, Mar hasn't mentioned a thing about DeJon to either the press or the judge. She'd been there for DeJon when he himself hadn't been. She'd even gotten through to him when he himself hadn't been able to. It shames Jack.

He is right. He knows in his heart of hearts that Lizzie belongs to him. He knows the law is on his side, can foresee the judge's verdict. Unfortunately, though, he also knows Stan had been right. Sometimes being right is much different than doing right.

Jack thinks back to his younger years, to his parents always helping out. The banks could foreclose, it was their legal right to do so, on farm loans, and they did. So many families totally wiped out. Still, his father did everything he could, usually free of charge, to keep the banks at bay, to work out a payment plan, to find a way around the law. Hell, that's where Jack had learned it, to defend the underdog. And, he had to admit, if he hadn't been personally involved in this one, he'd have been the first to line up to defend Mar's rights, to help her to find a way to keep Lizzie.

Is he wrong wanting Lizzie with him? No. But then, he isn't right, either.

Later, Jack exits the elevator. It feels strange not to be carrying a briefcase, though the weight of the photo in his pocket is heavy enough. He strides across the hotel lobby to where Caroline waits for him. She is dressed in a gray tailored suit and there is no mistaking the confidence in her bearing. As he approaches, he watches her appraising him. When her eyes hit his tie, one slim eyebrow reaches toward the heavens. He is wearing the suit she'd laid out for him, but not the tie. Today, he is wearing a tie Lindsey had given him. It is decorated with flying pigs. Jack smiles grimly and waves at the door. "Shall we?" he says.

One-Hundred-Three

Mar.

Mar waits until the last possible moment to enter the packed courtroom. She doesn't want to sit there, to feel the weight of so many eyes on her back. As she enters, she nods gratefully to her many friends who have come to support her, and tries to ignore the din and press of reporters. On the drive to the courthouse, she'd vowed not to look at Jack, but as she nears the gate, her eyes flick to him regardless. His back is turned to her, yet, from the way he is sitting, he appears relaxed and confident. Mar feels her fear spike. And then his barracuda of an attorney looks up at her with those icy green eyes and smiles. Mar's steps falter and it is only Don Bloom's tightening grip on her elbow that keeps her moving forward. She passes through the gate and sits heavily in the chair her attorney holds out for her.

For the next several minutes, Mar sits frozen in her seat. She keeps her eyes closed, as if not seeing the courtroom can mean she isn't there. Below the table, her fingers shred the soggy handkerchief Diane had slipped her. When her attorney leans in to ask a question, Mar ignores her. *Please, please, please*, the litany drums through her head. She takes a deep breath and digs her nails into the palms of her sweating hands.

There is a rustle of activity at the front of the court and Mar begins to panic. She bites back on the moan that is building in her throat and forces her eyes open just as Judge McClaine comes swinging through the doors to the bench.

"All rise," the bailiff calls.

One-Hundred-Four

Mar.

After the preliminaries, Judge McClaine looks out at the assembled group. His eyes pause on Mar and she feels herself shrink. Stacey nudges her under the table and Mar sits up straight before the judge's eyes move on.

"This case, this one before me, is absolutely the worst I've ever seen," Judge McClaine begins. "In most cases, the issues are black and white, and I'm not talking about skin color, though that was the case that taught me that there is right, and there is right," he says, making a reference to Max. "I mean, what is right is usually pretty clear, and we have laws written to support that. Here, though, now," he shakes his head, "there is no right. A mighty injustice has been done to you, Mr. Westfield, and to your family. But not by Ms. Delgado. She had no part in that, and I'm happy to see that you finally agree and have withdrawn all your motions to that effect." He looks over his glasses at Caroline, who chooses that moment to examine her pen.

The judge sighs and continues. "As I said, not by Ms. Delgado. By all accounts, she is every bit a victim in this as you. While you might say that she's had the benefit of being with your daughter all these years, of watching her grow, while you haven't, well, you'd have a point. But, again, it's not because of anything she did that you've been denied that. I say she's a victim just as you are because she's now in my courtroom threatened with losing the daughter she loves. The child she had every right to believe would be hers forever. The child whose adoption papers I, myself, signed.

"Ms. Delgado, you, on the other hand, have to recognize that a terrible injustice has been perpetrated against Mr. Westfield. I know you do. And I know you understand that he has every right to want his daughter with him. And, of course, that brings us to the crux of this case."

He shakes his head and sighs again. "You know, sitting up here, making decisions about people's lives, it's the worst job there is and, Mr. Westfield, I certainly wish you'd taken Ms. Delgado's offer of mediation instead of putting this burden on my shoulders. There's no justice in this case and, attorneys, don't get your pants in a dither, I'm sure if there's an appeal, one of you is going to use that statement against the other, but it's a fact. There's no justice that is fair to all. We can't split this child down the middle, and the parties here have made it obvious they can't, or won't, come to any workable understanding between themselves. So, it's an all or nothing thing.

"Before I tell you my decision, I want you all to know that I've done my job on this one. Thoroughly. I've spoken with Ms. McGowan there. Ms. Carruthers, please don't give me that look. I certainly know you've been able to have her opinions voided as you claim collusion with Ms. Delgado in mishandling the adoption. However, as I've said, that has been dropped, and I've spoken to Ms. McGowan, whose opinions on child welfare I trust completely, and whose ability to separate the well-being of a child from her own personal interests has always been above reproach," and he gives Caroline that look again. "Ms. McGowan believes wholeheartedly that it is in the child's best interests, emotionally, to stay with her adoptive mother. She's shared her files, and they support that the child was unresponsive and withdrawn before being placed with Ms. Delgado. But, as I know attorneys do, they'll look for anything to jump on in order to fight for their clients, as I concede they should. I know Mr. Westfield's attorneys would jump all over my verdict if I only took Ms. McGowan's opinions into consideration. So, I've had other social workers, three, in fact, due to the complexity of this case, and child psychologists, you've all received copies of their reports, meet with Lizzie Delgado, a.k.a. Mia Westfield, to make their own determinations about her mental, physical and emotional health. I've also received reports from a court-appointed social worker in New York who assessed Mr. Westfield's living conditions and his ability to support his daughter's well-being should she move with him. And, of course, the same can be said for Ms. Delgado on this end. In all, you've all been poked and prodded and every single rock that could be overturned, has been, in an attempt to help determine what is best for the child.

"I have to say, that by all accounts, it appears that Ms. Delgado has done a fine job of raising her daughter and, listening to all the learned people who have studied the issue, she should be allowed to continue to do so."

Mar gasps. They believe she should have Lizzie! She squeezes her hands so hard, she doesn't feel her nails biting into her palms. Jack, across the aisle, also has his hands clenched, and is staring intently at the judge.

Judge McClaine finishes wiping his forehead with his handkerchief and replaces his glasses. "Before I go any further, and certainly, as parents, you will be allowed to make changes, do what you will with this decision, maybe offer visitation, etc., but it will not be at that point court-appointed visitation, it would only be a parent deciding what to do with his or her child. What I'm saying, is that the experts were very clear that it's not in the child's best interests to be pulled back and forth. She needs to be settled in her home, to be sure of her surroundings, sure of her parentage. That being said, I've decided against joint custody."

Mar turns to her father and grins. She's not only won, but

she had the sure, firm support of the courts behind her. She begins to beam. If it weren't for the anchoring weight of her Stacey's hand on her arm, she'd jump up and whoop for joy!

The judge looks down at her, realizing, belatedly, his mistake. "I'm sorry, Ms. Delgado, you seem to have misunderstood me. While the caseworkers were very clear that you are doing a splendid job with the child, they can find nothing that would suggest that Mr. Westfield would not do an equally fine job raising his daughter. And the courts have already made clear that he lost his child not through any actions of his own, but as a result of a crime perpetrated against him. That, taken into account along with the precedence of such cases as the notorious Baby M case, among others, leaves me no choice but to return full, legal custody to the child's father, Mr. Westfield. I'm truly very, very sorry, Ms. Delgado."

Both Mar and Jack jump out of their chairs and shout, "No!" Mar, however, immediately sinks back down, all ability to stand gone. It is another twenty minutes before she is recovered enough to sit at the table, to hold back her tears, during which Jack and Caroline hold a heated, though quiet, argument on their side of the room.

The judge, having returned to chambers during the drama, returns to the bench. He leans forward and glares at Jack.

"There seems to be a bit of a disagreement with my decision," he begins, "and, while it is no longer debatable, unless the parties involved choose to appeal, I am very curious because it seems that both sides are unhappy. Mr. Westfield?"

Caroline jumps up. "Your Honor, no, that was a misunderstanding. My client is very happy with the verdict. Thank you, Your Honor."

"Actually, I'm not," Jack says.

"Jack," Caroline hisses, "shut up!"

"Ms. Carruthers, please, I'd like to hear what Mr. Westfield has to say for himself."

"I, um, I think Mar, Ms. Delgado, is a fine mother, has been a wonderful mother. I think my daughter should continue to be raised by her. Though I, of course, want full access to her."

"Mr. Westfield, are you saying you've just wasted this court's valuable time?"

"No. I mean, yes. Maybe. It's just very confusing. I've been confused."

"Mr. Westfield, as a father, I can tell you, it is very confusing. I'm confused all the time with my own children. However, this is a serious matter. I've never heard of the prevailing party immediately asking for an appeal because they want to be the losing party."

"I'm sorry, Your Honor, it's all been a terrible mistake."

"Your Honor, please, my client's been under a great deal of stress. Please disregard him," Marion Jenson, Jack's local attorney, begs.

"Yes, I believe he has," the judge acknowledges. "I believe everyone has. However, that's not going to change my decision. Again, I'm sorry, Ms. Delgado. Mr. Westfield, you've asked for this court's decision and you've received it. If you're not happy with it, I'm sorry, but now you're going to have to live with it. The thing that worries me greatly, though, is that you've now forced not only your daughter, but Ms. Delgado to live with it, too. I suggest you do some serious soul searching and find it in yourself to be as good a parent to that child as has been Ms. Delgado. Court adjourned."

One-Hundred-Five

Mar.

The days pass too quickly. Mar has been given one week to prepare Lizzie for the dramatic turn her life is taking. One week during which she will live with Mar, but spend time with Jack and DeJon each day. Lizzie, for her part, becomes extremely clingy and withdrawn. She doesn't know what is going on, but she senses it isn't good.

Mar refuses any additional medication to calm her because she doesn't want to be too zoned out to miss any of her last moments with her daughter. Hence, she feels the horror in every minute of every day. The two hours Lizzie is away each afternoon are but a small glimpse of the awful eternity that awaits her. During one of those times, Mar asks Shirley and Dylan to come over to meet with her.

"Oh, baby, I am so, so sorry, honey," Shirley hugs Mar and holds her while they both cry. Dylan does what he does and rubs her back, finally gives in and envelopes both women in his long-armed embrace.

Later, settled in the family room, Mar tells them what is on her mind, "I know I'm putting an awful burden on you guys, and I'm sorry, but you're the two smartest people I know, and I trust your opinions. The thing is, I need to know what you think, but I don't want you telling me what you think I want to hear. I want you telling me what you really, really think is best for Lizzie, without thinking about my feelings."

"Oh, baby, what's best is for her to stay with you. We know that, everyone knows that, even Jack knows that."

"That's not what I mean, Shirl. I mean, Jack has offered me visitation, said I can come out any time I want, to see her. What I want to know, is if that's a good thing for Lizzie?" Mar starts crying again, "I know that's what I want. I want to see her all the time. I'm even willing to move to New York, if it means I can see her. But I need to know if that would only confuse her more. She's going to freak when he takes her away. Should I just let her have a clean break and start her new life there, or should I try to be a part of it every now and then?"

"Oh, Mar. Oh, man." Shirley shakes her head, not wanting this.

Dylan takes off his ever-present bandana and shakes out his long curls, begins rubbing his head as if it hurts.

Shirley finally speaks, "Before we go there, Mar, tell us. Have you decided to appeal?"

Mar looks down at the wad of torn Kleenex in her hands, finds a corner and begins to shred anew. "No," she shakes her head, "I'm not. The adoption rights people are saying I have no balls, that I should force it, but that's because they want me to be their poster child. I can't. I mean, I know what Jack said in court, but give him one week with her, and he's not going to be able to give her up. He won't, and it's like McClaine said, he has every legal right to her. His rights precede mine. So, what? She gets all settled in with him and then I turn around, make a huge fuss? Drag her through this again? And what if I win the second time, which would take a visitation from God, or at least Jesus and the entire Bible cast to accomplish, but what if I do win and then she's settled and I rip her back here? It'd be back and forth and back and forth...No, I don't think that's good for her."

"Divorced people do it all the time, sugar."

"I know, but that's not what this is. Divorce kids know

this is the way it is. This week you're with Mommy, next with Daddy, whatever. They have their rooms in two different places, have a schedule, stability, consistency within that schedule. We'd be like telling her you're here and then, boom, she wouldn't be anymore. Then, she'd be there and, boom again, she's not there anymore. There's not, like, any schedule or meaning that she can follow. I need to know what's best for her and I trust you guys to tell me the truth."

Shirley looks at her husband, her eyes begging him to be the bad guy.

"Mar, I'm sorry," Dylan says. "You know, psychology is a very imperfect science."

"I know, Dylan. Just tell me. Please."

"Well, studies have shown, and this information comes from a lot of studies. Divorce, cases when kids have had to face the long-term illness of a parent, foster kids that are moved around from home to home, things like that. Well, it seems that dragging it out puts a helluva lot of stress on the child. Kids are resilient. They can deal with just about anything. I'm not saying that Lizzie's not going to miss you. This is going to hurt like hell. Eventually, though, most kids, if they were put into Lizzie's position, would come to terms with it, find some emotional ground again on which to stand. It would be, and forgive me for putting it this way, as if you'd suddenly died. She'd find her way again and, hopefully, stability. On the other hand, kids that are moved around a lot, who are never able to develop a sense of trust in their surroundings, in their lives, well, they don't seem to do as well socially, emotionally, or even academically."

Mar nods. "That's what I thought. I guess that's why the judge gave Jack full custody rather than having us share her."

"I know it seems harsh, but he really was trying to look out for Lizzie's best interests. Considering."

"But, Mar, you have to understand that I'm not fully comfortable making that assessment with Lizzie. Personally, I believe that her first abandonment, if you want to call it that, when that woman who had kidnapped her died, well, I believe that she remembers that on some level. She only learned to trust life again with you. She's an extremely sensitive child, and I'm afraid that her feeling of being twice abandoned, this time by someone she fully trusts, won't be very good for her. I don't see her easily settling down into a different life."

"But, Dylan, you're saying two different things! On the one hand, I should stay out of her life, on the other, I should stay in it. What am I supposed to do?"

"Mar, honey, you're going to have to make up your own mind on that. Baby, I'm sorry," Shirley says.

"No, please, tell me what to do! Please!"

Dylan speaks up. "Mar, she's going to be angry at you. At her age, she'll be very, very angry. She'll feel that you left her and won't understand that it wasn't voluntary. If you don't see her, most likely she'll be able to come to some closure, just as when a parent dies. If you continue to see her, she'll probably begin to act out, first against you, and then against the world. She won't understand why you keep leaving her over and over."

"You're saying I should just let her go."

"I'm sorry, Mar, but that's what I believe is best for her. Shirley doesn't fully agree," he shrugs, "but, there it is."

"Contrary to what McClaine said, I can't separate what I think is best for her from my feelings for her," Shirley explains. "Even though my experience says otherwise, I can't think of not having her around. Of her not being with you."

One-Hundred-Six

Mar.

The day of separation comes too quickly. Way too quickly. If possible, Mar has lost even more weight in the past week. While she'd been unable to eat or sleep, she had made a valiant effort to be cheerful for Lizzie, aware that she was creating the last memories her daughter would have of her. For all her efforts, she must not have carried it off overly well as Lizzie has been fussy all morning and has, herself, refused to eat.

"But why can't you come on the trip, Mommy?" Lizzie asks for the umpteenth time that week.

"Because, baby, it's a special trip, just for you."

"But I don't wanna go on a trip! I wanna stay with you." Lizzie is truly upset and has been working herself into a mighty tantrum all the way to the airport. Not only has she sensed the somber mood in the house that morning, but the mob of reporters camped out on the front lawn had terrified her. Reporters had banged on the windows to get her attention and flash bulbs had blinded her.

"I know you do, honey. I want you to stay with me. Don't forget that, OK? Don't ever forget that Mommy loves you more than anything, more than life itself, OK? You're my most important important." Mar bends toward Lizzie, whispering urgently into her ear, smelling her special smell for the last few minutes and dying inside. She isn't going to be able to hold on much longer.

"We're here, Mar," her father says, as he pulls up to the gatehouse of the private landing strip. For security's sake, and to protect Lizzie from over-exposure to the press, Jack has hired a private jet to take them back to New York. That morning, Stan and Amanda had taken Lizzie's belongings with them, and these are now stowed safely on board. All that is missing is Lizzie.

Mar begins to cry. She can't help it. No matter that she'd promised herself she wouldn't, for Lizzie's sake, she can't help it. "Oh, god, no. Please, Daddy, turn around. Please," she cries.

"I know, sweetheart, I know. I can't."

"Please, Daddy, please. I can't do this. Just turn around."

Don Bloom clenches the steering wheel, his knuckles white. "I'm sorry, baby." He pulls up to the waiting jet and turns off the ignition.

They sit there like that, with the engine off, while Mar cries in the back seat and Don cries in the front. Lizzie, terrified, begins to wail and that finally gives the adults the impetus to try to bring their own emotions under control.

Amanda is waiting at the bottom of the stairs, Stan beside her, his arm supporting her. Strangely, while Lizzie will continue in their own lives, they are so very sad at the way things have turned out. Amanda wipes her eyes and smiles bravely at Lizzie, who refuses to come out of hiding in her mother's neck. "Hi, there, sweetheart," she says, rubbing Lizzie's back. "Do you see the big plane we got for you? Have you ever been on a plane? Well, this one's especially for you."

Lizzie just digs in deeper.

"Lizzie, honey, it's OK," Mar urges her, lies to her for the first and last time. "It's going to be OK, baby. Now, say bye-bye to Grampo. Come on, baby, say bye-bye."

"Don't want to, don't want to, don't want to!" Lizzie screams and begins hitting Mar, kicking her, not understanding why her mother is making her go away. "I don't want to, Mommy,

I don't want to. I wanna stay with you!"

"I know, baby, but you can't. You've got to go on this beautiful plane that Daddy got for you. See? You'll have so much fun on it, it'll be just for you and you can order whatever food or drinks you want and I think they even have a TV on it and you'll be able to see a movie. And DeJon's up there waiting to play with you. Now, baby, give Mommy a hug. Come on, sugar, give me a big, fat, big girl hug and go to Mandy. She's going to take you up to the plane so you can meet the Captain. I think he's even got wings for you."

"Only angels got wings."

"OK, but he's got some special ones for you that you can pin on your shirt. Very special ones because this is your first plane trip. Now, give me a hug, our special hug and go to Mandy, honey. She's waiting."

Soothed by her mother's assurances, Lizzie allows herself to be transferred to Amanda.

"There now, honey, let's go up." Amanda gives Mar one last, long look.

"Go, please," Mar whispers to her, not sure she can hang on any longer to the fake smile plastered on her face.

Stan pats her shoulder, shakes hands with Don and smiles sadly at Mar before he follows his wife up the stairs.

At the bottom of the stairs, Mar begins to shake but she stands there bravely, not sure if Lizzie is looking out the window at her. Then, suddenly, just as the attendant begins to close the door, Jack bursts out of it and hurries down the stairs. He comes up to her. "Mar," he begins.

Mar reaches back and with all the strength in her body, she smacks him. "You bastard!" she hisses. "You got what you wanted. There, now you've got my daughter."

Jack has his hand to his face. "Mar, god, I'm sorry. It's not what I wanted."

"Listen, you fucked up piece of shit, get the hell out of my face. Do you hear me? Go take care of my daughter, but let me tell you one thing. If I ever hear that she's not happy, if you ever do even one small thing to make that little girl unhappy, I swear I'll hunt you down. Now, get the hell out of here."

"Mar," he tries again.

"Jack," Don speaks up as he cradles his weeping daughter in his arms, "I'm not one for violence, son, but I'm telling you, if you don't get the hell away from my daughter, I'm going to have to kick the living shit out of you myself."

Jack looks helplessly at Mar, then turns and returns slowly to the plane.

Almost before she can think, the plane is a speck in the sky. Eight, Mar begins counting the minutes away from Lizzie. Nine.

One-Hundred-Seven

Mar.

For the first two days, Mar glides. Just sits in Lizzie's room and glides among the abandoned furniture, clutching the one teddy bear she's kept for herself. Tries desperately to smell her daughter on it. As she glides, she watches the sharks. Her mind has become convinced the dolphins painted on the wall are sharks. Mar glides and watches them. If she thinks anything at all, it is, *bring it on*.

Sometime around the three-thousand-twenty-fifth minute without Lizzie, Mar decides to move to the little girl's bed, to try to fall asleep forever. She lies down, exhausted beyond reason, not caring that The Dream will start up if she allows herself to do anything but doze fitfully.

Mar melts into the bed, stretches out, eyes closed, thinks if she only tries hard enough, she can will Lizzie to be back here, to be in her arms. Unable to fight it anymore, she begins to sink into sleep and, in doing so, curls her hand beneath the pillow. It isn't a conscious thought that wakes her, more like a hazy urging that winds itself through her tired mind. But, suddenly, there it is, and, grasping under the pillow, Mar comes fully awake. In her hand, she holds Boosie. Lizzie has not slept without her blanket in almost five years. Mar is out the door in a flash.

***

Somewhere over the Midwest, it occurs to Mar that she should have left a note for her father. She knows he'll be terrified when he returns from his walk with Picasso and finds her gone. He's been so worried that she'll do something drastic that he's practically set up vigil outside of Lizzie's room. Mar digs out her credit card and uses the telephone in the back of the seat in front of her to call him.

As the plane banks over New York Harbor, Mar looks down into the deep, gray waters. Startled, she realizes it is the first time in years she has left Boulder, has moved in any direction where there is a large body of water. Strangely, it doesn't terrify her anymore. Rather, it looks like home. She presses her face to the window and watches it, so peaceful from up here. How silly to have been so scared for so long. There, right there, she could jump in and float, just float until even that is too much trouble, then sink, slowly sink below the waves, watch her last bubbles slowly rise to the surface, the surface without Lizzie. But there, just there, Joaquin would be waiting for her, so nice to be loved again, to be held again, to be whole. Looking out the window, Mar mentally apologizes to the other passengers and then begins praying the plane will crash.

The nervous urgency of finding Boosie, coupled with a desperate case of the heebie-jeebies, cause Mar to move quickly, unthinkingly. Her desperate need to get to her daughter, who she knows must be suffering for the lack of her beloved blanket, leaves her with no need more urgent than to get to her, to give her the blanket so that she can sleep. She is out of the cab almost before it comes to a full stop in front of Jack's building. Shoving four twenties into the change slot, she jumps from the car and heads toward the door.

***

Jack had answered the urgent call from Don Bloom and

knows that Mar is on her way. He'd called down earlier and asked Robert to just let her through. He is waiting for her when the elevator arrives at the private landing.

"Mar."

Mar looks desperately past him, hoping for, dreading, a glimpse of Lizzie. "How is she?" she asks. "How's she doing?"

"Not so good. She'll hardly eat and she won't speak. She can barely sleep."

"She needs this, she needs Boosie." Mar holds the blanket out to him. "She's never slept without it."

"Thank you."

They stand there, uncertain what to do, what to say.

"Would you like to see her?" Jack finally offers.

Mar looks up at him, her eyes begging. "May I?" she asks.

Just then, the apartment door is flung open and Caroline lounges in the doorway. "Well, look who's here. I believe the court order was for no visitation, or did I misunderstand?"

"Caroline, shut up."

"Oh, yes, of course, don't upset precious Mar. Fine. Whatever. In any case, Jack, will you come in here, please, and do something about your daughter? She's throwing a fit and won't eat the apple I cut up for her."

"She doesn't like apples. I wrote it on the list I gave you. Didn't you read the list?" Mar desperately questions Jack.

"She'll have to learn. They're good for her." Caroline smiles. "Jack?"

"Give her hot dogs. She loves hot dogs. You just cut one up and give it to her with ketchup. No matter what, she'll always eat hotdogs."

"Mommy?" Lizzie screams from somewhere inside the apartment.

"Just what we need," Caroline moves to head her off.

Panicked, Mar hits the elevator call button. It opens right away and she jumps inside. As the doors slide silently shut, Jack can see she is crying again. He raises the soft blanket to his face and breathes in the sweet scent of Mar intermingled with Lizzie.

One-Hundred-Eight

Mar.

Mar has thought of suicide, of course she has. She won't allow her thoughts to move too far in that direction, however, as she knows what that would do to her father. She also holds out hope that one day, perhaps when she is a teenager or even an adult, Lizzie will somehow reach out to her and, more than anything, Mar wants to assure Lizzie that she was a very much wanted and greatly loved daughter.

And so she has lived, done the necessary to ensure that she'll continue to breathe. Her father clearly doesn't trust her, though, as she awoke one morning to find the knife set gone. She guesses her father had seen her staring at it a little too long. No, she isn't going to kill herself, though she thinks about it often enough.

Diane has moved the gallery downtown and things are going well there. All the publicity the case had brought has caused a dramatic jump in the price of her paintings. The other artists whose work the gallery sells have also benefited. Mar, however, barely makes it there. She'd lost interest in just about everything when her daughter had been taken from her. Every now and then, she'll pick up a brush, try halfheartedly to paint something, anything. But she doesn't have much of an attention span, can't work up much interest.

Mostly, she sleeps. After her turnaround trip to New York, The Dream hasn't returned. She is so dry inside, the sharks must have gone on to a more tasty, a more meaty meal. So, she sleeps the sleep of the dead and wanders through the days trying to get through.

Eventually, she put the house on the market, even though her father urged her not to. He'd urged her to give herself time before making such a big decision. She'd gone ahead and done it anyway. There is too much of Lizzie everywhere she turns, and now that she isn't using the studio much and the gallery is gone, she can't see much use in holding onto it.

Well, not completely. The gallery is not completely gone. The day after she'd returned from New York, a package had arrived. Not surprisingly, it had been from Jack. *Mother & Child* is back in its place on the gallery wall, one small pin light focused on it.

Diane had been outraged when Jack sent it back. She thought it was a screw-you to Mar and had wondered if it hadn't really been Caroline who had sent it. Mar doesn't think so. She'd looked into Jack's eyes as the doors to the elevator slid closed and all she could see was regret. She takes the return of the painting as an 'I'm sorry.'

Mar now sits before the painting in the glider she'd brought down from Lizzie's old room. She likes to sit there, in the empty gallery, and look at it. It is amazing how it had foretold the sorrow she would come to know. How the mother looks so desperately afraid she'll lose her child. How the child is too damn trusting.

On this afternoon, Don Bloom is upstairs, watching TV probably. Diane is off in the kitchen, probably cooking a meal she hopes Mar will eat. Loyal Picasso is at her feet, sleeping, snoring peacefully. While she glides, Mar worries about the latest news from Amanda, who calls faithfully and brings Don up-to-date on Lizzie's activities. Amanda knows Don will give the news to Mar, but she feels too guilty about her own ability to see Lizzie to speak with Mar herself. Mar doesn't mind. She really doesn't feel like talking to anyone anyway.

Apparently, Lizzie is still acting out. She spends a lot of time with DeJon, who is the only one who can make her smile. He and Jack are getting along, which Mar supposes is a good thing.

The doorbell rings. Picasso wakes up and looks at Mar, almost asking out loud if she'll have to get up to see who is there. "Yes, fatso, it's the door," Mar tells her.

Affronted, Picasso huffs and struggles to her feet. She shakes off her sleep and pads lazily to the door where she barks once and turns to Mar. *There, are you happy?* Mar rolls her eyes and gets to her feet. Damn dog is useless.

Without looking through the peephole, Mar flings the door open. And her heart falls to her feet. "MOMMY!" Lizzie lunges from Jack's arms to hers. "MOMMY!" she repeats.

"Baby?" Mar whispers. "Lizzie?"

"Surprise!" the little girl happily tells her and wraps her arms and legs more firmly around her mother. Picasso begins to bark crazily, jumping up to get to Lizzie.

"Jack?" It grates past the lump in her throat.

"Hello, Mar."

"What? What are you doing here? Down, Picasso. Be quiet!"

He shrugs. He, too, has lost weight, she notices, and looks like he's lost a lot of sleep as well. There is more gray in his hair than there'd been four months ago. He shakes his head. "She needed you. She needs you."

"But, the judge..."

"Was wrong," he finishes. "It was all wrong. As much as everyone tried to make it right, it was wrong. Lizzie needs to be with you."

"You're leaving her?"

He shakes his head. "No, we're staying."

"Here? You're staying here?" It isn't making any sense.

"No, not here. We're staying in Boulder." He indicates the rental car, where DeJon is hanging out a window and waving at her madly.

"But, your job?"

"I quit."

"You quit? What are you going to do?"

"Right now? Right now, my only priority is to learn to be a good father. I've made a lot of mistakes and that's the one thing I need to get right."

"What about Caroline?"

"She's mean, Mommy," Lizzie whispers loudly into her mother's neck.

"I know, honey."

"She said she wants to be my mommy."

"I'm your mommy, Lizzie."

"She doesn't even paint," Lizzie says, her voice tinged with disgust.

"I know, baby." Mar is still looking at Jack.

"As you can see, they got along great."

"But what about her? Where is she? I thought you two were an item? Picasso, down!"

"She's home. Back in New York. That wasn't going to work out."

"Because of Lizzie?"

Jack looks off into the distance. "No. Because of me." He sighs heavily. "I'll tell you about it sometime."

"And now you're here. Just like it's OK, and you think you're moving to Boulder?"

"Yes."

"So what's your great plan for Lizzie?"

"I thought, if it's alright with you, she can live with you."

Mar's heart is beating so fast, she can't keep up with what he is saying. "You thought what?"

"That she should live with you."

"With me?"

Jack shakes his head. "Look, Mar, I know this is sudden, but she needs you. She likes me, yes, and I hope she even loves me. But, she needs you."

"Really?" Mar feels the first fluttering of hope coming back to life. It scares her. "How do I know you won't just wake up some day and decide to take her away again?"

"I won't."

"But how do I know?"

"I'll give you joint custody. Legal joint custody. We'll stipulate you have physical custody."

Mar realizes she is shaking. She buries her face in Lizzie's neck, inhales her fresh, clean, Lizzie scent and begins to cry quietly. This is her baby, her daughter. She is holding her daughter. She looks up at him, tears running down her cheeks. "You better not be bullshitting me," she whispers.

Tentatively, he reaches out and brushes a tear away, looks down at the dew on his fingertip. "I'm not, Mar, I swear to you, I'm not. She needs you." He looks away, and then back at her. "I need you," he admits.

It is surprising how quickly her wonder turns to anger. Her head snaps up, "You...Cover your ears, Lizzie. Good girl. You lying prick! How dare you say that! You used me."

"I didn't, Mar. I didn't use you. I was confused."

"Confused? Do you know how many lives you hurt because you were confused? Jesus Christ on a broomstick, Jack, you almost killed me with your confusion. And what about Sy? Do you realize how much you hurt Sy? Do you?"

"I know. We talked some. I know he's here visiting Diane. I'll go see him later today and apologize in person. I didn't know about that, though, Mar. I swear."

"And what about Shirley? Get down, Picasso! Jesus! Stupid dog!"

"She's not stupid, Mommy."

"You're supposed to have your ears covered, Lizzie."

"I do, but you're screaming."

"Oh. Sorry." She turns back to Jack, but forgets to lower her voice as her indignation rises. "What about Shirley and Dylan? That weapon of mass destruction you called your lawyer almost cost them their jobs! And don't forget about my father!"

"Mommy! You're yelling in my ear!"

"I'm sorry, sugar!" She kisses Lizzie's ear. "My father,"

she continues, almost without pause, "taking Lizzie broke his heart! He didn't need that shit! And then, my dad's so freaked about me, he hid all the kitchen knives! Do you know what it's like to cut a tomato with a plastic knife! Do you?"

"I'm sorry, Mar."

"Sorry! You're damn right you're sorry, Jack Westfield. You're a sorry sack of shit! I'm sorry, Lizzie. You're supposed to have you're ears covered. OK, honey, forget your ears, cover your eyes. No, better, close your eyes and cover your ears. There. Good girl. I'm going to tell you something, buster, and you'd better listen and listen good. This little girl is mine. We can have joint custody, but she's mine, and you'd better make sure I have the papers to prove it by tomorrow, latest, or I'll sue your sorry ass. And you'd better live up to your promise. You'd better settle down here, or risk losing seeing her, because from now on, she's home, get it? She lives here and so, if you want to see her, it's here. Do you understand?"

Jack bites his lip, a smile playing at their corners.

"Are you laughing at me? Are you? Lizzie, are your eyes still closed? Good girl!" And then, for only the second time in her life, with a forty pound cling-on clutching tightly to her, Mar winds up as best she can and smacks him right across the face. "That's for everything you've put us through!"

And then she bursts into tears. Just like that. A ranting, raving lunatic one second, a crying, hysterical mess the next. She sinks down on the door step, Lizzie buried in her lap. Picasso tries to push herself between Mar and Lizzie, to share Mar's lap. "Oh, baby, oh Lizzie, sweetheart, you're home. Baby, it's so good to see you home," Mar is crying again.

"Mar?" Diane calls from inside the house. "What is it? What's going on?"

"Diane! Ohmygod! I have to tell them. Come on, Lizzie. Get up, honey, we have to go tell Dee and Grampo you're home."

"Dee?" Lizzie calls.

"Lizzie? Oh, sweet Jesus alive! Is that you?" Diane's voice comes closer.

Lizzie scrambles to her feet. She pushes the door open

and runs to Dee, throws her arms around her. “Dee Dee! I’m home!” she shouts.

“Ohmygod! Don, Don! Get down here! She’s home, Lizzie’s home!”

“Mar?” Jack asks quietly. “Are you OK?”

She looks up at him, her eyes red and puffy. “I hate you,” she says.

He sighs. “I know. It’s OK.”

“No, it’s not. I hate you. I really do. But I’m so goddamned grateful. I don’t want to be grateful to you. I want to hate you.”

“You’ve got a lot of time to do both. I’m not going anywhere.”

She gets to her feet. Smiles at the sound of her father’s whoop of joy. She digs her hands deep in her pockets and looks at the ground between his feet. “Can you go away now, please?” she whispers. “For awhile? Can you please just let us get used to this? Please.”

He nods. “Of course. How about if I stop by tomorrow?”

“You’re going to bring the papers, right?”

“I think we can probably get the judge to sign them right away. They’ll have to be filed to be real, but I’m sure he’ll sign them right away.”

“And she lives with me?”

“Yes.”

“OK, you can come by tomorrow, but you have to bring the papers. Even if they’re not filed yet.”

He nods again. “I can do that.”

“OK. Good.”

***

Jack stands there another moment, looking at her. She has her eyes closed and is rocking back and forth on her bare feet.

“Jack,” she breaks into his thoughts.

“What?”

“Go. Now. Please,” she adds.

“Yeah, OK. Tomorrow, then.”

She nods. “Tomorrow.”

After Mar has gone back in and closed the door, he hears her scream of delight. He grins. It hurts his face. The woman may be small, but she sure packs a mean punch. He'll have to remember that in the future. On the way back to the rental car, he finds himself admiring the soaring strength of the Front Range. It is a beautiful sight, one he feels pretty damn good about. He remembers Boosie. He'd forgotten to leave the blanket with Lizzie. He shrugs. Somehow, he doesn't think she'll need its comfort tonight.

Damn. Life is good. Jack thinks he just might go buy himself a pair of boots.

ACKNOWLEDGEMENTS:

Writing a book is a very solitary endeavor. The day eventually comes, though, when you have to let it go, to release it to the world. That's scary.

Happily, I am blessed to have a group of funny, warm and talented friends (and writers) who generously offered me a "soft" release. That is, they were my beta readers. They pointed out my mistakes and, occasionally, questioned my judgement. Because of them, this novel is so much better.

First, I would like to thank Diane Breton. Diane is not only a writer, but she is also a professional editor. No matter how careful I am, Diane cleans up after me, which saves me a lot of embarrassment. Thank you, Diane, for your skill, your guidance and your good sense.

Along with Diane, Heather Maurice-Stirnweis, KD Pryor, Karen Stivali and Trudy Gendron acted as my sounding board as I worked my way through this story. It was their continuous encouragement, in fact, that convinced me to finally release this book. Thank you, ladies. The next round of coffee at A&E is on me!

Heartfelt thanks and gratitude, as well, to Margarita Barresi - your kindness and generosity of spirit are inspiring. And to Ande Mariaca, Holly Johnson, Audrey Tyler Cook, Nicole Austin, Liz Mariaca,and Maryann Brennan, thank you, thank you, thank you.

And, finally, to the incomparable Mia Mariaca who lent her name to this book and whose image graces its cover - thank you!

AN OFFER TO READERS:

As you may know, in today's publishing world reviews matter a great deal. Because I want to encourage readers to review this book and to thank them for doing so, I am offering a free copy of my upcoming eBook, **The Stages from Grace - a Novel** (to be released on November 15, 2013), to any reader who leaves a review on Amazon and/or Goodreads and who sends me an email via MadaketLanePublishers@comcast.net to let me know once it is posted.

Thank you!

Sincerely,

Katherine

A NOTE FROM THE PUBLISHER:

If you have enjoyed **Water from Stone** by Katherine Mariaca-Sullivan, please take a moment to leave a review of the book on Amazon.com. As you may know, reader reviews are one of the best ways to encourage other readers to discover new authors.

If you would like to be a beta reader or a book reviewer for other books published by **Madaket Lane Publishers**, please send an email to us at MadaketLanePublishers@comcast.net with "Reviewer" as the subject. We'll send you information about this program.

Thank you,

Madaket Lane Publishers
www.MadaketLanePublishers.com

THE STAGES OF GRACE - a Novel:

Coming November 15, 2013

A coming of age comedy that would be a tragedy if it wasn't so funny...

DENIAL

After fifteen years of marriage, cartoonist Gracie Carpenter discovers her husband is a serial cheater. Not only that, but she is struggling to resuscitate her career, to care for her widowed father who has Alzheimer's, to find a way to re-connect with her teenage son, and to help her best friend through her latest crisis. And just when things reach a breaking point, she meets the ghost of the daughter she never had.

NEGOTIATION

Gracie wants nothing more than for her life to return to the way it was. Even with everything that is going on, she thinks her daughter's sudden appearance is a sign that she and her husband should try again.

DEPRESSION

As her life falls apart, Gracie discovers that the root of so much pain may lie in a terrible mistake she made as a young girl-a mistake that left a boy dead.

ANGER

To save herself, her son and her life, Gracie must confront her husband. And her past.

ACCEPTANCE

Can Gracie find the strength to overcome her past? Can she start over and forge a new life-one built on strength and love and acceptance? Can she, in fact, find grace?

www.ingramcontent.com/pod-product-compliance
Lightning Source LLC
Chambersburg PA
CBHW051546250626
47157CB00001B/207